PRAISE FOR THE NOVELS OF
Lynn Abbey

Behind Time

"Another compact and literate fantasy novel from Abbey . . . Thanks to superior characterization, perspicuously detailed settings, a carefully and intelligently worked out system of good and evil magic, and brisk pacing . . . even seasoned fantasy readers won't find it easy to put the book down until the last page is turned."   —*Booklist*

"A haunting, multifaceted story powered by strong characterization."   —*Bookwatch*

"An exciting fantasy thriller that takes readers on quite a ride."   —*BookBrowser*

Out of Time

"In many ways, this smart modern fantasy reads like a suspense novel . . . *Out of Time* is an enjoyable novel with a good number of surprise twists that will leave readers eager to follow Emma as she continues her walks through time."
                                    —*South Florida Sun-Sentinel*

"Lynn Abbey juxtaposes elements of the fantastic with the mundane routines of everyday life . . . compelling."
                                —*The Youngstown (OH) Vindicator*

Taking
Time

Lynn Abbey

ACE BOOKS, NEW YORK

TAKING TIME

An Ace Book / published by arrangement with
the author

PRINTING HISTORY
Ace edition / April 2004

ISBN: 0-441-01153-5

ACE®
Ace Books are published by The Berkley Publishing Group,
a division of Penguin Group (USA) Inc.,
375 Hudson Street, New York, New York 10014.
ACE and the "A" design
are trademarks belonging to Penguin Group (USA) Inc.

PRINTED IN THE UNITED STATES OF AMERICA

10 9 8 7 6 5 4 3 2 1

One

"**H**ave you heard from your mother?"

Emma Merrigan pretended not to have heard her companion's question. She kept her eyes on the horizon where a seething magenta sky met a landscape that was dark, barren, and deceptively flat. A moment earlier, she'd seen a wisp of bluish light rise from cracks in parched mud. It had vanished a moment later, but if it rose again—

"There!" She pointed at the pale-blue fingerling, which was much closer to her than the horizon. "This one's mine. I've got it!"

With a painfully practiced flick of her wrist, Emma grasped the laser pen she wore on a jogger's coiled plastic bracelet. She pointed the brass tube at the fingerling and, with her thumb and index finger, gave the barrel a clockwise twist. A ruby-red beam of light shot out of her hand and froze the fingerling where it grew.

"One . . ." she whispered while the laser did its work, "two . . . three . . . four . . . and, five . . ."

Five seconds of a synchronized light ought to be enough to moot—that was the word experienced curse-hunters used to describe the process—any curse seeping into the wasteland, but Emma took no chances. She painted the fingerling for a full ten-count. It was gone, completely and utterly, when she twisted the barrel to its "off" position.

"Good! Well done."

Her companion draped his arm around her shoulder. He gave her a gentle, oblique hug, then guided her toward the place where the fingerling had risen. Em welcomed the praise, even knowing that there was a critique or correction lurking in Blaise Raponde's next breath. If there weren't, she'd be suspicious. Blaise was, among other things, Emma's mentor in this odd land, and he took his responsibilities seriously.

He didn't disappoint. "Your confidence is getting stronger, but you hold back at the beginning, then overdo at the end. That's a surefire way to attract the wrong kind of attention."

They'd come to the fingerling's breech—a patch of dirt only a bit darker than its surroundings, centered around a hole less than a half inch in diameter. Blaise scuffed the dirt with the toe of his black leather boot.

"It's a bit like clamming," Emma observed when the hole and the stain were both gone.

"Clamming?"

"Digging up clams at low tide . . . seafood in shells. When I was little, my father took me to New England for summer vacation. When the tide was out, we'd walk across the mud flats—a lot like this, except wet—with three-prong rakes. We'd watch for spits of water—that meant there was a clam in the mud below—then we'd rake like crazy to dig it up. The fingerlings, they remind me of the clams."

"Ah. Is life still hard in the New England, all mud and scrounging for your next meal?"

"Only if you want homemade clam chowder. I'll bring some with me next time—not homemade; I don't live by the ocean. I can't get fresh clams, but I can get scrod—the freshest fish in Michigan, hundreds of miles from the nearest salt water. I'll fix you some mesquite-broiled, cajun-spice scrod."

"Scrod?" He gave her an amused glance. "I do not believe there is a fish named scrod, Madame Mouse."

Madame Mouse was the nickname Blaise had bestowed upon Emma at their first meeting. He rarely used it anymore, except as a warning that his patience had worn thin.

The wonder was that Emma Merrigan and Blaise Raponde could communicate at all. She was a university librarian living comfortably in Bower, Michigan, with two cats and an off-campus townhouse. He was a Parisian gentleman who'd died in 1685, murdered, he said, by a disgruntled lover as he slept off the effects of too much wine.

Well, perhaps not quite a gentleman. But never a rogue.

Rogue had a special meaning under the wasteland's magenta sky. As acorns might become mighty oaks, so a fingerling could, with luck and malice, mature into a rogue: a curse disguised as a human being. It was Emma's *wyrd*, her birthright and obligation, to transport herself out of the day-and-night real world into the wasteland's stormy twilight and moot curses, preferably in their less potent fingerling form. Fortunately for Emma, Blaise Raponde shared this destiny.

Emma had tangled with a rogue during the previous winter. She wouldn't have survived to threaten anyone with trendy seafood if Blaise hadn't taken her under his proverbial wing.

"Sorry," she apologized. "You're right, there is no fish called scrod—that's just market-talk. Assuming you want the freshest fish in the market, and not a specific type of fish, you ask for scrod. And it tastes best broiled with just a squeeze of lemon to bring out the taste. You'll like it. I'll bring wine, too."

Blaise said nothing. After three-plus centuries in the wasteland, subsisting only on memories, he confessed that he'd forgotten what food was supposed to taste like. He welcomed any meal Emma could spirit across the inexplicable divide. By the same token, whether it was a plain, meat-and-potatoes stew or the latest in Mexican-Thai cuisine, there was a quiet moment during every meal, a silence when they both remembered that Blaise, unlike Emma, could never leave the wasteland.

He didn't even see the landscape the way Em saw it—which, considering that the wasteland was a subjective, not empirical, reality, wasn't completely unexpected. Still, she'd been astonished when Blaise had explained that what he called "*au-delà*" wasn't an endless, rolling plain beneath a magenta sky. For starters, his sky was *purple*, not magenta. For a vintage 1685 Parisian, Magenta was just another city near Venice. Venice, he'd informed her, was a republic of considerable economic and political importance, while Italy was simply a peninsula.

And although Blaise did describe the ground as dark, barren, and laced with cracks like a long-dried mud flat, his horizon was a massive fog bank "as high as heaven, as long as life, and as dark as Lucifer's soul." When Blaise and Emma stalked fingerling curses along the invisible line that corresponded to the real world's absolute present, his bleak horizon was never more or less than a few paces away. From Blaise's perspective, Emma disappeared into the fog—which she didn't perceive in any way—each time she returned home to what she considered her real body and real life.

Not that the wasteland wasn't a real place, at least where danger and damage were concerned. Fall down on the rock-hard dirt and she'd have a big, painful bruise when she got out of bed. Misjudge a curse's power and she'd be brought down as surely as any gazelle on the Serengeti Plain.

It would have been easier—not to mention safer—to have stayed home in Bower. It wasn't, after all, as though Emma had been mooting curses all her life. She'd come into her curse-hunter inheritance only a year ago, and at an age when her real-world contemporaries were worrying about retirement and reading glasses.

Besides, what was a curse, anyway? No one, including Blaise Raponde, had been able to answer *that* question to Em's satisfaction. And what good did lasering a dozen or so fingerlings each night accomplish? If the curse-hunters' goal was a reduction in human misery, despair, cruelty, or outright evil, then they were attacking the ocean with a thimble and falling further behind with every tide.

But since she'd mastered the art of transferring herself from *here* to *there* and back again, Emma Merrigan hadn't missed many nights of mooting curses. She told herself it was simply the right thing to do: The ability to vanquish a curse became the obligation to vanquish as many as she could point her brass pen at, regardless of how many curses five billion human beings might spawn each and every day. She told herself, as well, that the look on Raponde's face each time she left—a nightly interplay of loss and hope, anxiety and fatalism—had nothing to do with responsibility.

Of course, it *was* a handsome face; and it wasn't as if there was a husband or lover curled up around her in Bower. . . .

Em caught herself staring and looked away.

"You didn't answer my question. Have you heard from Eleanor?"

"No. Not since April."

"And Harry?"

Harry Graves was Eleanor's husband, Emma's stepfather. Em had made heroic efforts to hate her stepfather. In addition to the usual reasons, Harry was pompous and inscrutable. He delighted in self-importance, and he was a master of half-told truths. But a half truth from Harry Graves was more information than Emma could get from anyone else—including Blaise, whose understanding of curse-hunting, though broad and deep, was entirely practical, not at all theoretical.

"Harry says he's not worried, not yet. It's not like this is the first time Eleanor's run out on him—or on me. She did that when I was a baby. Just up and walked out of our lives without a word of warning one day before I turned two—"

That wasn't entirely true. Eleanor had written Emma a letter. Unfortunately, it reached Emma nearly forty years too late. "Look, Blaise, technically, Eleanor is my mother, but that's the end of it. I got along without her before, and I can get along without her now."

"She suffered."

"I'm not denying that," Emma replied too quickly. Eleanor Merrigan *had* suffered unimaginable torment starting the same night she'd waltzed back into her daughter's life. She'd been overtaken by curses and rogues—never mind the role her own stubbornness and prejudice had played in her misfortune. As Blaise had said at the time, no hunter *deserved* to be overtaken by curses or rogues.

Rogues had the wherewithal to break any hunter. Surrender and submission were only a matter of time. A lesser spirit than Eleanor's would have given up in days, perhaps hours. Eleanor was no lesser spirit. She had held out for nearly two months—her body abandoned and comatose while her consciousness endured in the wasteland.

It had taken Emma, Blaise, and Harry working together to even *find* where the rogues had hidden Eleanor. They'd attempted a rescue, but all Eleanor required was a diversion. Once she wasn't the focus of the rogues' attention, Emma's mother had found the strength and courage to free herself without anyone's direct help. Afterward, Emma made herself look for the admirable qualities of the woman who'd abandoned her. For two months, while Eleanor underwent physical therapy to rebuild her withered muscles, mother and daughter had cautiously explored the idea of friendship.

"Even Harry thought Eleanor had changed." Emma confessed a bit of history she hadn't shared before. "He'd started doing whatever it is that he does to set up a new identity for her so she could live in Bower again. He assumed—and I assumed, too—that she'd get over her fears and be able to hop between there and here. . . ."

Em left her thought unfinished as her memory played through the events of the previous spring.

Curse-hunters needed new identities every few decades because they didn't age the way other people did. Correction: Curse-hunters who haunted the wasteland regularly didn't age the way other people did. Emma had aged the normal way up until her mother's reappearance. She'd taken a certain satisfaction with the way she'd shown her age until she met her stepfather who, on a bad day, looked fifty and was at least as old as Blaise Raponde—as old as Blaise would have been if he hadn't been murdered.

Given Emma's age and the information on her parents' wedding license, Eleanor couldn't be a day less than seventy-five. Before she took off in April, she could have passed for Em's daughter, or as a sister for Em's stepdaughter, Lori, since, despite two marriages, Emma hadn't had any children of her own. But there was no telling how long that unnatural youthfulness would linger since Eleanor had awakened from the coma with what could best be described as a wasteland phobia. Although Eleanor put up a fight, her fears grew rather than shrank with each passage between the two realities. Em believed there was connection, not coincidence, between her mother's second disappearance and her utterly bungled attempt to heave herself into the wasteland the previous evening.

"I think she woke up one morning, saw wrinkles, and ran. Unless it was worse than wrinkles. Harry won't say anything more than that he's convinced she's still alive and well—"

"Harry can be wrong," Blaise said after a moment's silence.

To the best of her knowledge, Harry and Blaise didn't know each other. They both insisted a meeting was impossible without her cooperation: Blaise couldn't visit twenty-first-century New York, and not even Harry Graves owned a landmark map of the wasteland. Still, Emma sometimes suspected that her mentor and her stepfather had found a way to compare notes.

She could have dug deeper for the truth, but one of the many lessons Em had learned during her second and far-more-traumatic divorce was: Never ask a question unless you're prepared to deal with the answer.

"You must look for Eleanor," Blaise continued, "at least until you find her and know that she does not need you."

Em cringed—a small movement, not intentional, but enough that she came free of Blaise's arm.

She couldn't know how much spending three centuries alone in the wasteland had changed Blaise Raponde— Well, she *could*, but Harry and Eleanor had both advised her against poking her nose into his past. Never mind that rearranging tiny bits of history was one way curse-hunters mooted the curses they didn't catch at the fingerling stage, probing one's own past or the past of a significant other was a *bad idea*.

If the advice had come from just Harry or just Eleanor, Emma would have ignored it, but she had firsthand experience with the consequences. Thanks to one rogue's meddling during their attempts to rescue Eleanor, Emma's real-world career had been upended. After years of strategic evasion, she'd been saddled with an assistant and all the headaches that went with personnel management.

So, Emma had taken a dose of advice, and she knew less about her mentor than she did about the aforementioned assistant. She could only guess that isolation had drained the wildness out of Blaise Raponde, leaving him with a sense of duty that seemed more desperation than compassion.

"I'm running short tonight." Em put a stop to the discussion. "Only three curses mooted, and it feels like I'm halfway to morning already. Better get back to work, if I want to sleep the sleep of the innocent and the just all the way home."

Emma started walking, taking the lead, as she rarely did when they were together. Navigating the border between the past and future was harder for her. All Blaise had to do was follow his fog bank's serpentine contours, while Em wasted most of her time looking over her shoulder at a small black boulder. The boulder, which was as invisible to Blaise as his fog was to her, marked her personal boundary between the tenses and her gateway back to the real and physical world. It magically—there was no better word for the boulder's behavior—followed her, never more than a sprint away, wherever she wandered through the wasteland.

Em called the boulder the "way-back stone," and in the subjective reality that was *her* wasteland, it marked the absolute present. In the past year, she'd mastered a half dozen different methods to transfer her consciousness between realities, but the most reliable—the one that would work even in a blind panic—was to kneel before the unnaturally cool stone, place her hands on its polished surface, and let it guide her back to her body's safety.

There was another way to track the border between past and future. The future was cold and windy. The distant future, she'd been told by Harry who, naturally, swore he'd tried to explore it, was lethally frigid and hiding under a dome of high-pressure air that generated an outflow blast of icy wind. If Em concentrated, she could feel a very faint, cool breeze and, like a sailboat, go forward along the present by tacking across the wind.

Emma concentrated on the breeze, walked forward more slowly than before, and tried not to dwell on the silence behind her. That proved at least one too many mental divisions for a novice curse-hunter to handle. She missed the warning signs and yelped with surprise as a fingerling erupted not fifty feet in front of her. The fingerling immediately began drifting sideways over the cracked dirt like a miniature whirlwind.

She fumbled her first attempts to get the laser pen focused, and muttering a few choice curses of her own, Emma raced after it. The chase's outcome wasn't seriously in doubt. Em had improved; she knew how to take care of herself and wispy, little curses. Some nights she even hunted alone as Blaise combed the deeper past for rogues, especially the one who'd murdered him.

Her heart rate had scarcely risen when Em nailed the writhing malignancy with ruby light. Mindful of Raponde's criticism, but not yet ready to heed it, Em painted the fingerling until it was gone and a few seconds more.

In a perfect subjective reality, Blaise would have been standing there when Em turned around, arms folded solemnly across his chest, while the peacock feathers trailing from his hat shook with a mixture of amusement and dismay. But nothing was perfect. One hunter's subjective reality impinged on another's, and sometimes the hunters became the hunted.

When the ground beneath her suddenly began to quake, Em knew what the trembling meant: a firestorm curse many, many times the size and potency of a fingerling on its way. Harry had described the phenomenon in the curse-hunter's manual he'd given her months earlier. Em imagined his voice assuring her that there was no need for panic—

The bigger they are, the slower they breach. Take a deep breath, then look for a shadow on the ground and hie yourself away from it—

Harry's subjective wasteland must be considerably brighter than hers.

"This place is nothing *but* shadows!" she shouted.

The ground made a sudden lurch to starboard. Emma fell to one knee. Logic screamed *lie flat!* She could break an ankle on the shifting ground—really break it, no matter that her body was snug beneath the covers in Bower. And there was no reason to run, not when her chance of running away from danger was no better than her chance of running toward it. Then her eyes snagged on the way-back stone.

The boulder couldn't be more than fifty or sixty feet away. How difficult could it be?

Damnably difficult. Emma fell twice in the first twenty feet, but she picked herself up and staggered on.

Then Em saw it—not anything she'd describe as a *shadow*, more of a toxic slick welling up through the patchwork cracks and already cutting her off from the stone. A handful of fingerling-sized wisps rose from the slick. More blossomed as the quaking ground seemed to move in two directions at once.

Emma fell a third time, landing badly on her right side. By the time she'd levered herself upright again, the wisps were merging into a fiery column. Em slid her right foot back, then her left. The quaking subsided; the ground was secure again. She could have bolted, but some silent, subconscious part of her made the decision to stand firm, so stand she did.

It wasn't the first time Em had faced a firestorm pillar. On her very first journey to the wasteland, she'd dueled one to a stalemate with nothing more than raw anger and outrage for weapons. Of course, that was before she'd understood that the flaming spire was a curse and what a full-sized curse could do to a hapless hunter, before she'd understood that the wasteland was more than a dream.

Knowledge was power in a subjective reality . . . usually . . . unless it nurtured the seeds of self-doubt.

She grasped the laser pen firmly and trained it at the base of a burning column as yet only a few feet taller than herself. The ruby beam disappeared in the flames. Emma feared it had been absorbed, feared it was *feeding* the flames rather than destroying them—which was a very dangerous thought to have loose in her mind.

Not long ago, Em wouldn't have known how to get a thought out of her mind, and in a heartbeat she'd have become her own worst enemy. But Blaise was a good tutor; Emma squelched her doubts swiftly. She made the laser—which was, after all, only a figment of her own imagination—hotter, brighter than it had ever been and aimed it at the curse's heart.

Flames howled and surged toward the magenta sky—twenty feet, thirty . . . more than she could estimate. Then the curse sprouted blazing arms that reached for Emma and threatened to wrap her in fire. Though scared to the bone, she kept her poise. She drew swirls of laser light and deftly snared the fiery arms, one by one, until so much of the curse was caught up in her light web that its whole substance leaned toward her like reeds in a gale. With its power so tightly bound, the great curse became no different than a fingerling, and, by all she'd learned from books and lectures, it was only a matter of time until she had it mooted.

Or, rather, time, concentration, and stamina. Emma wasn't concerned about her concentration, but the curse *pushed* against the ruby light and the little brass tube grew heavier, harder to hold on target, with every passing moment. She braced her right hand with her left, even dropped down to one knee to plant her elbows on her thigh, because, though the curse had stopped growing, it refused to shrink.

Time was always hard to measure in the wasteland. Em would have guessed she'd been locked in her sniper crouch for about ten minutes when the metal in her hand started to warm up. She spared a thought to cool it down; and the curse immediately sprouted a half dozen fresh tendrils of fire. Emma got those bound up with the rest, but the pen was warm again when she finished.

The good news was that the curse was starting to dwindle. Em clenched her teeth and assured herself she'd have it mooted before the brass got too hot to hold. She'd sapped the fire down to man height before she knew her assurances were lies. It didn't take much imagination to feel her palm blistering around the metal, but she didn't dare retreat or falter. Curses were like bacteria: If she didn't wipe this one completely, it would likely spring back, more potent than before. And quickly—though Em wasn't sure how quickly.

There were some lessons she didn't want to learn. She'd scream in agony, if she had to—and she had to—but she'd hold on to the laser pen until the curse was mooted, even if it burnt her hand to the bone.

Em was numb to everything but pain and the ever-so-slowly shrinking curse. She blinked when the lightning-bright bolt shot across her shoulder, thick as a brawler's wrist, but her mind didn't register its meaning until the curse imploded. Even then, Emma was mostly aware of her fingers.

She could neither feel nor move them. Like the legs of a dying insect, they twitched by themselves. The brass pen, heat-twisted and glowing, fell to the ground. The pain had vanished with the curse, *displaced* to the bottom of a deep well. She saw it when she turned her hand over and knew it was headed her way, but for the moment, staring at the blackened crater where her palm had been, Emma felt nothing.

"Madame—*Emma*—?"

A sword with an amber pommel bounced on the dirt beside Emma. A masculine hand with strong, callused fingers wrapped around her wrist, steadying her ravaged hand, which had, she realized blankly, begun to tremble violently.

"Hush. Hush, now. It's mooted. You're safe."

Hush? Em wondered, then heard the strangled scream spilling from her mouth. She made the sound stop and immediately felt faint. Blaise was there to catch her against his shoulder.

"My hand," she gasped. "My hand."

"Yes. Did I not warn you that your chosen weapon was too small? That it must be great enough to sustain an attack without reserve?"

Emma nodded. He'd wanted her to carry a sword; she'd refused. The pain returned. She greeted it with a whole-body shudder.

"*Pardieu*, we will talk of such things later. Can you stand?"

With Blaise's help, she could. "There was a little one— a fingerling. I mooted it. No problems. Then, before I knew it, the ground shook and there was another one, a fire-storm pillar. I thought they were too big to move that fast—"

"They are, but they are curses, too, and curses do not obey rules. They are the essence of deception, and they hunt us as surely as we hunt them. This is not the first time I have seen a fiery curse stalk the border or dangle a piece of itself as bait to lure a hunter in close. I tell you Madame Mouse, you must always be prepared for the worst. Sometimes these curses, they surprise even me."

Blaise released Em's hand. Driven by morbid curiosity, she strained to get a better look at the damage at the end of her arm.

"No, madame. That will not help."

He regrasped Emma's forearm in such a way that she could not see her palm, then, with his free hand, he unwound the cloth he wore around his neck. For months, Em had considered the four-foot-plus swath of linen and lace as one more demonstration of how civilization—not to mention fashion—had progressed since the seventeenth century, but as Blaise expertly wound it around her damaged hand, she saw the advantage that a rough-living man might gain by wearing his bandages.

After knotting the cloth, Blaise released Em's arm. She pivoted away from him, looking for the way-back stone.

"I've got to go home," she told him when she'd spotted it close by.

Blaise captured her arm yet again, holding it gently, but very firmly. "That will not help, either."

There were moments—this was one of them—when a hardness fell over Raponde's eyes and he became as alien as any rogue or curse.

"You will take the wound with you," he continued. "Better to stay *au-delà*."

Or, not an alien, but simply a man of the seventeenth century, when all the physicians of Paris put together wouldn't be able to keep that hole in her hand from killing her.

"Better to go to an emergency room," Emma countered and knew by the narrowing of his eyes that her phrase had made no sense to her companion.

"It's different now. Doctors can help, in my *now*."

But Blaise refused to release her arm.

"In God's world, your hand will hurt for many days before it heals. It will scar and stiffen. A month will pass before you can make a fist without wincing . . . *if* you can make a fist again—"

That was precisely the reason Emma was determined to leave. She tugged futilely against Blaise's grasp.

"Stay a while *au-delà*, and your hand will be whole when you awaken in your own bed."

"I don't—"

"I will show you."

Emma had inherited her talent for walking the wasteland from her mother, but she'd inherited something equally useful—equally cursed—from her father: the engineering gene otherwise defined as a ravenous curiosity about how things worked. A lesson in subjective healing? How could she walk away from that? With a sigh, Em let Blaise lead her away.

The bolthole toward which they walked was Blaise's home: the place where he tucked himself out of the wasteland's danger, but it was Emma's creation, borne of proverbial necessity after one of Blaise's attempts to rescue Eleanor had gone dramatically wrong. He'd lost his previous bolthole to a rogue and had calmly expected to die, in consciousness as well as body, if Em couldn't whip up a new bolthole out of her imagination.

His wounds then had been worse than hers were now.

Guilt combined with curiosity had been all the inspiration Emma had needed—well, almost all the inspiration. In the end, she'd engineered a copy of a picture hanging in the back bedroom of her townhouse, itself a copy of *Marianne*, a pre-Raphaelite painting by John Millais. In a very real sense, Emma had left her creation before its bones had hardened or its paint had dried. By the time Em returned, the bolthole's decor was more seventeenth-century French than Victorian Gothic, with a multifunction hearth, massively uncomfortable furniture, and a leaded-glass window overlooking a garden that was usually in autumnal disarray but could be subjectively persuaded to reveal the past.

When Emma had first imagined it, the door had risen in two-dimensional absurdity from the wasteland dirt, visible only from the front. Blaise had moved the iron-strapped wood (or perhaps it had moved itself; Em hadn't asked) to a merely improbable location at the back of a steep hollow shaped like an orange section.

The way-back stone rose a few feet from the door. Usually, Emma's engineering gene compelled her to try to catch the stone as it relocated itself. She never had, but this time—with her hand throbbing within a bandage that had grown too tight—she didn't even try.

The bolthole was pitch black and freezing cold. A glance toward the garden window revealed the darkness of real-world moonlight and the frosty crescents of wind-blown snow against the leading. Emma had no idea which one of them was responsible for the wintry details, but it was Blaise's job to rouse a fire in the hearth. She stayed by the door, cradling her hand, while he tended the bolthole's primary source of light and heat.

A glazed jug and two glass goblets waited on the table.

Without asking, Blaise filled a goblet with red liquid and held it out, waiting silently until she took it with her un-bandaged hand.

"The first lesson of making yourself whole: Ignore what isn't."

"Easy for you to say," Em groused before she sipped the hearty wine. "You're not the one who nearly melted her hand."

"Try, madame."

Blaise removed his feathery hat and coat, then unbuckled his sword belt—

Emma remembered him dropping the sword, but didn't remember him picking it up again. She closed her eyes. On second thought, she clearly remembered that he hadn't picked it up. Subjective reality: Stones moved, swords moved, smoke rose up a chimney that vented who-knew-where, and her hand hurt like hell.

"Aren't you going to tell me that it's my own damn fault and none of this would have happened if I lugged around a sword?"

"No, Emma, if you have not learned that for yourself, then there is nothing more I can say tonight or tomorrow. Try to put it out of your mind. It happened; it's over; now you must make yourself whole again. Tell me about the glass of wine you remember above all others."

She opened her eyes and glowered. "I can't begin to re-member a glass of wine. . . . This isn't working. If you can't tell me how to fix my hand, I'm going home—"

Blaise Raponde sprawled in a claw-foot armchair with lion's head armrests, way too much fringe, and striped up-holstery in shades of maroon and green that, Emma assumed, were the height of 1680s interior design. He scowled before saying:

"*Pardieu*, madame, I am telling you: Ignore it and an-swer my question!" He made his point with the goblet, thrusting it as though it were his sword. The wine swirled, but stayed away from the rim. "Of all the wine you've drunk, which glass was the best—for taste, for company, for the smell of spring in the air? Which is so sharp in your mind that you can hold it again in your *hand*?"

There was a second armchair in the room, a smaller version of the one beneath Blaise. Emma kicked off her shoes and sank into it, tucking her feet beneath her, searching for the comfortable spot she would eventually find. She wasn't a fool, and, unlike Harry, she wasn't contrary for contrariness's sake. Blaise was right: Belief—expectation or assumption—was the key to everything in the wasteland.

"I don't know where to start—" *Maybe I can't remember my best glass of wine,* Emma thought, *but the worst pain of my life is down at the end of my right arm.*

"Choose one. Pluck it out of the air; make it real. Or pluck out something else entirely, but something vibrant."

"It was a dinner with Jeff—" Em decided, sticking with the wine and a moment when she was falling in love for the second time. "Before we were married. When we were young . . . a long time ago—"

"Was the wine from Anjou? The wines of Anjou are the taste of love itself. Do you know the wines of Anjou?"

"Yes," Emma assured Blaise, "I like them best with sugared strawberries, but that night Jeff and I were having dinner at our favorite restaurant, Veneta—it burned down years ago—and we were drinking Chianti—Italian wine from a straw-covered bottle."

Blaise's dark eyebrows signaled dismay—Emma suspected a classic case of French oenological prejudice—but he said nothing, so she plunged into her memories of a meal remarkable only because she and Jeff had been so much in love that night, so convinced that they knew exactly how the future would unfold before them.

Hunkered down in an antique chair, sipping Raponde's potent wine, Emma heard Jeff's voice more clearly than she had heard it in years. She reeled in her wayward thought and concentrated on a single dinner. The salad had been plentiful, but mostly iceberg lettuce; she was remembering the seventies, after all, years before arugula, endive, or crisp romaine. The entrée had been veal, before she'd lost the ability to eat baby cows, with (exotic for Michigan in the seventies) pasta al pesto on the side. The dessert—

"They called it a chocolate mousse, but it wasn't like any mousse I'd had before or since. It was thick—more like a soft fudge than anything else—and so rich that the waiter warned us to order just one with two spoons—"

Em had mastered the trick of bringing food to the wasteland, provided she had the appropriate taste lingering in her mouth. Could she conjure up Veneta's long-lost chocolate mousse the way Blaise conjured up their wine? Should she try? The pressed-glass bowl was *there* in her mind's eye, the creamy texture, the bittersweet taste. . . . If she concentrated hard enough—If she *expected* with all her heart and, especially, her stomach—

"Didn't you tell me that sharing a plate was no longer done in your time? That some great thinker had declared sharing to be unhealthy?"

Emma blinked and lost the image. She didn't remember saying anything of the sort, but it was the little things— side comments, idioms, and manners in general—that kept them just a bit alien, one to the other.

"I must have meant germ theory. Germs: Think of little bugs, too small to see; bugs that get on your food. You swallow while you're eating and then you get sick. If I'm sick, then I've got my disease bugs in my mouth. They get on my fork and then, if my fork touches *your* food, touches *your* fork, touches *your* mouth, you'll get sick, too."

"But you were lovers, yes? Surely, you were closer than *forks*?"

One of the first things Emma had learned when she became a stepmother was: Never discuss hygiene with a ten-year-old. That rule went doubly with Blaise Raponde. He asked the questions ten-year-olds could only dream about. Em hid a blush behind her hand . . . her *right* hand.

The throbbing was gone. Her hand was quiet: not numb,

but normal. She stared at the bandage, wiggling her fingers, one by one.

"It—it worked." She brought her thumb and forefinger together. It was difficult—because of the bandage, not pain.

"Ah?" Blaise swung himself around in the armchair. He seized her hand and attacked the linen knot. "*Pardieu*, that *is* quick. Madame Mouse, have I not told you that you learn quickly—when you agree to learn?"

"I was thinking about chocolate and Chianti and my ex-husband. I'm not sure what I learned. . . ."

"To become what you were. To restore yourself according to your memories."

The engineering gene did somersaults. Blaise had just explained the wasteland's fountain of youth, a challenge Emma had put to Harry more than once without success. Eleanor had faced the real world with a twenty-five-year-old's face, because that was the face she remembered best. Harry Graves could pass for an aging rock star, because the years didn't matter, only the mileage.

"Maybe there's hope for me after all."

Blaise quickly unwound the bandage. Emma beheld her palm: smooth and pink except for a narrow, dark streak paralleling her lifeline. She made a fist and opened it again. All the while the back of her hand rested in Blaise's palm.

There was a sensual attraction between them; there had been from the beginning, though how much—on either side—was genuine and how much sheer opportunism, Emma refused to guess. They were intermittent lovers, which Em suspected was more her doing than his. The glimpses he'd provided of his past hinted at a man for whom *l'amour* was as necessary, and as casual, as a goblet of wine. He would not likely have stood on ceremony, but she struggled with the engineering gene: What happened back in her Bower bedroom when she lay in Blaise's arms?

What was self-image after you'd discovered that you had two selves?

Some nights the paradoxes weighed so heavily that Emma abandoned the bolthole before the first, chaste kiss could be exchanged—but not this night.

Subjective hours later, when the hearth had gone to embers and Blaise was a warm comfort against her shoulder, Emma started thinking again. She'd nearly gotten herself killed. She'd healed herself. She had a meeting in the morning with the other library directors to thrash out the latest budget crisis, and she couldn't remember if she'd printed out her revised allocations or if they were still on the computer.

If she were smart, she'd head for the way-back stone and double check. . . .

Blaise sensed the change. He murmured, "*Dormes*,"— or something equally incomprehensible, equally French— and kissed Emma lightly on the cheek.

If she were smart, she wouldn't be sleeping with a ghost, but she was, and the way-back stone wasn't the only way back to Bower.

Emma rolled over and returned Blaise's kiss with an embrace.

Considerably later, Em opened her eyes to her alarm clock's glowing aqua display—3:37AM—about an hour later than usual, but nothing to worry about. She pulled the covers up over her ears. The library's budget could wait another few hours.

T*wo*

T*he board meeting* could have gone better, but Emma and her fellow directors had managed to shrink the Horace Johnson Library's budget by the desired seven percent without laying anyone off or leaving blood on Director in Chief Gene Shaunekker's prized mahogany table. Each of Emma's proposals for acquisitions, her little fief within the library's kingdom, had passed without exception, or even discussion, although her assistant, as one of the newer hires, could easily have faced the "last in, first out" axe.

She'd acquired that assistant as the result of a rogue's meddling and, until the subject emerged around the mahogany table, Em would have sworn she would leap at the slightest excuse to shed the woman. But for years, Emma had been badgering Gene and his predecessors to upgrade the library's Arabic Studies collection. When the towers fell in New York, she'd seemed prescient and when Rahima Maali came along, a single mother who'd lived in every Islamic country worth mentioning and was fluent in classical Arabic as well, Emma would have been a fool not to recommend hiring her merely because a rogue had meddled.

Rahima was a puzzle Emma hadn't come close to solving. The thirty-something woman was grateful enough for the job. She'd been widowed when her husband's car was demolished by a drunk driver, and despite her best efforts, she'd been losing the struggle to raise her two children alone. At least that's what her brother-in-law, a professor over in chemistry, had said when he started pulling the strings that led to her hiring.

They got along well, and Em had no complaints whatsoever about Rahima's diligence, but there was something in the woman's dark, haunted eyes that forbade questions, however casual or friendly. The gulf separating the common run of American citizens from many of its immigrants was wider than the Red Sea and harder to cross. Trying to respect those differences—fearing that even one bumbling, thoughtless mistake on her part might prove irrecoverable—kept Em mentally rehearsing her encounters with her assistant and second-guessing them for days afterward.

She ran through several possibilities as the elevator brought her down from the board meeting and discarded them all when she spotted Rahima in her tiny office, hunched over a keyboard and hiding her face behind her hands.

Should she ask *What's wrong?*

Heaven knew, there'd been many moments in the past year or so when Emma been overwhelmed by accumulated chaos and desperate for conversation. But what could she say to a woman whose husband was dead, not divorced, and whose brother-in-law benefactor was under scrutiny not only from the U.S. government, but the tenure committee as well? Perhaps it would be better to simply slip past the open door and into her own office without comment.

Rahima put an end to Emma's indecision, lifting her head, gazing out the door. Their eyes met, and Em forced a smile she hoped didn't look nervous or insincere.

"I'm back." She announced the obvious. "Pending approval, we've all survived the budget crunch: no layoffs."

Rahima said something that Emma didn't catch. As offices went, the library's were fairly quiet. No one had ever had to shout to be heard, except Rahima. It wasn't that Rahima couldn't speak above a whisper—Em had overheard her shouting at her oldest daughter—but when it came to the rest of the world, a combination of culture and personality had put a governor on Rahima's vocal cords. She couldn't make a sound that traveled beyond an arm's length.

Em had tried talking to Rahima about the problem, but that only made it worse, so she entered her assistant's office. "Sorry, I didn't hear . . .?"

"There was a call for you. From someone named Eleanor? She is a cousin?" Rahima's English was near perfect, but oddly inflected and burdened with formalities.

Emma got that long-legged, weak-kneed feeling that usually came with the unpleasantly unexpected. "Did she say where she was?" Em's voice was suddenly as powerless as Rahima's. She knew only one Eleanor and, except within a very select circle of confidants, Em referred to her uncannily youthful mother as a cousin.

"That she did not say. I asked for a call-back number, because you were not here, and she said she did not have one. She said she would be at a luncheon named Ivy at noon and that you could meet her there. I said I would tell you, but there was no saying where you would be at noon, because this meeting you were at was to be difficult and there was no ending decided. She said that did not matter. She had to eat, no matter. I am sorry, Miss Emma—" The university had policies about titles and surnames: Those who taught, got them; those who didn't, didn't. At the Horace Johnson Library, it was first names from Gene on down, except between Em and her assistant. "I did not know what else to do."

"It's all right. No one in the family knows what to do with Eleanor either," Em replied, compressing a world of irony and omission into a statement that was not quite a lie.

She glanced at a nearby clock: 11:25. Enough time, if Eleanor was waiting in a campus eatery. "Where did you say she'd be waiting?"

"I did not say, exactly. I did not hear ... understand." Rahima shrank with shame. "Miss Eleanor said the word *ivy*, of that much I am certain. Is there such a luncheon with ivy?"

Emma shrugged. The university was covered with a proper blanket of ivy. It was fossilized onto the exposed brick wall uniting her office with Rahima's. But an Ivy-something restaurant? "If there is, it's got to be new."

She retreated to her office and attacked the Internet, coming up with a newspaper feature about the opening of the Ivy Bower, a traditional tearoom in the downtown, as opposed to the campus, area. Em calculated the distance from her office to the staff garage, factored in the probable difficulty of finding a downtown parking space, and concluded that her best chance of reaching the Ivy Bower by noon was on foot.

Emma was two blocks out of the library before she asked herself if it wouldn't have been smarter—easier, at least—to have the sandwich she'd brought from home at her desk the way she did most other days. The simple answer was curiosity, the irresistible curiosity she'd inherited from her father. She wanted to see how the past several months had treated Eleanor and hear her excuses. A more complete answer would have touched upon guilt and responsibility but curiosity was sufficient to keep her moving.

She was annoyed that she couldn't summon up a memory of the Ivy Bower. Restaurants were a vital, ever-changing part of Bower's culture. Officially, there were more than three hundred, or three for every hundred residents and, as a lifelong resident, Emma took pride in tracking the myriad openings, closings, and renovations. From the address she'd found on the Internet, she knew she drove past the Ivy Bower two or three times a week, but had somehow overlooked it. Her annoyance doubled when she'd walked close enough to see every storefront on the designated block and none were hanging a shingle for the Ivy Bower.

Before blaming Eleanor for the sort of practical joke she detested, Em poked into a more established sandwich shop and asked about the competition.

"Upstairs," the cashier explained. "Over the jewelry shop. The little door to the left—it's got a sign with ivy painted on it."

Emma retreated. It wasn't right—it shouldn't be possible—for Eleanor, whose most notable skill was leaving Bower without warning, to have chosen the one downtown eatery that Emma couldn't find without directions for their reunion.

Don't go up there, warned a voice that came to Em from the back of her mind.

Emma had been hearing, and often heeding, that voice since childhood. Whereas other little girls conjured up imaginary playmates, Emma Merrigan had given herself a "mother-voice." If she'd ever discussed the matter with them, psych-types might say she'd personified her super-ego—probably not a healthy thing—but the mother-voice had dispensed the comforting wisdom Emma had imagined real mothers gave their daughters, more often than it scolded, at least until Em's real mother had reappeared.

She's just going to make you crazy. That's what she does best.

Emma didn't disagree, but for the moment, the engineering gene's curiosity trumped the mother-voice's wisdom. She closed her hand around a green-painted doorknob and braved an ivy-muraled stairway.

The murals continued into the restaurant, which contrived to resemble a springtime courtyard with blossoming fruit trees, wisteria, and—of course—ivy covering the walls. In the tiny dining room there were silk-flower vases atop lacy, white tablecloths of the sort she'd found in the attic of her father's house on Teagarden Street and donated to the University Hospital thrift shop.

Of the dozen or so tables, three were occupied, but not by Eleanor Merrigan.

With apprehension building in her gut, Emma let the fresh-faced hostess—probably a moonlighting student—guide her to a table with a view of the street below.

"Tea?" the hostess asked, handing Em a half-sheet menu.

Em nodded absently, then had to choose among the varieties the young woman rattled off at impressive speed.

"Gunpowder," she decided, because she genuinely liked the taste and not because it so perfectly captured her mood. "With lemon, not milk."

Disaster! the mother-voice warned when Emma was alone with the menu.

The Ivy Bower did not have a kitchen, at least not one with an oven. Steaming tea was the closest they came to hot food; the rest of the menu consisted of salads, sweet breads, sweeter desserts, and exotic sandwiches, most of them made with mayonaised seafood and cucumber spread between crustless slices of bread, "whole wheat or pumpernickel by request."

Anglican sushi!

There definitely was something about island kingdoms, their gardens, and their cuisine.

Emma's stomach snarled in anticipation. She didn't need or want a super-sized grease-burger, but a chicken breast—even a cold chicken breast—would have been a welcome sight.

The tea arrived in pieces—cup, saucer, pot, leaf-packed ball, and a tiny dish just for the lemon wedge. Em kept herself busy dunking, swirling, squeezing, and waiting. In the end, she recognized Eleanor only because she was expecting her; otherwise they could have bumped into each other on the sidewalk without Emma being the wiser.

When she'd first returned to her daughter's life, Eleanor

Merrigan had been a living image drawn from the wedding portrait Emma had brought home from Teagarden Street, right down to the Andrews-Sisters hairdo and dark, parenthesis eyebrows. Then Eleanor had fallen victim to fiery curses, and, while her consciousness had suffered in the wasteland, coma had mercilessly transformed her body. Her unused muscles atrophied and her tendons shrank, slowly contorting her skeleton into grotesque angles. Her skin, deprived of sunlight and attention, had taken on a dusty, gray pallor. The day Eleanor was transferred from hospital to nursing home, the staff had sheared her increasingly wild and tangled shoulder-length hair down to a more easily managed cap length.

When Eleanor had awakened from the coma, she'd found herself exchanging wasteland torment for a wasted body that moved awkwardly and painfully when it moved at all. She endured weeks of physical therapy as grueling as the curses' tortures, relearning the basics: walking, sitting, standing, holding a spoon, getting it safely to her mouth.

Emma, who scarcely knew Eleanor, thought her daily progress was remarkable, but Eleanor saw the days differently, very differently. The face Eleanor saw in the therapy room mirrors wasn't the face she knew, the walk wasn't hers, and none of the gestures. Even her voice, she swore, had been transformed. Before her second disappearance, Eleanor had been grimly plucking her brows and growing out her hair in a desperate campaign to recreate the face—the self—she knew.

Something had happened to that grim resolve to recapture the past. The Eleanor who walked into the Ivy Bower tearoom was a loose-limbed coed, casually dressed in knits and denim, toting an impossibly tiny purse. Her tousled hair was scarcely a finger's length and dyed a dark, rusty orange with maroon—or maybe purple—tips. Emma recognized her mother by the way her eyes raked the room, suspicious and commanding at the same time.

Snatching the menu from the hostess's hand, Eleanor wove across the room and made herself comfortable in the other chair at Emma's table.

"You're looking good," she said in lieu of any other greeting.

"And you—" Em couldn't find a satisfactory word. "You've—You're—"

"Different," Eleanor declared. "It was *time*. I'd never understood that before. Resisted it, tooth and nail. I didn't want to walk away. I wanted to carry every moment with me, you know, never letting one drop. Then I woke up one morning in April, looked in the mirror, and I knew what Harry had been talking about. It was *time*, and there was no reason to put it off any longer."

Emma watched her teacup, not Eleanor. There were no leaves drifting in the amber liquid; they offered neither hints nor clues to her mother's transformation. Oddly, Em understood perfectly what her mother was saying. After divorcing Jeff, friends and colleagues had urged her change her style, dye her hair, do *something* different. She'd resisted their good advice for months. No, not months, but years. She'd made more changes to herself since she'd started walking the wasteland than she'd made in the previous decade.

Like mother, like daughter—God help them both—resisting tooth and nail was an accurate description.

"We worried. . . ." Emma paused and corrected herself: "*I* worried. At least you could have sent a postcard."

Eleanor frowned and gave her order to the waitress who'd appeared beside the table, while Em hastily changed her preference from Waldorf salad to a sampler plate of stripped-down sandwiches, easier to nibble or ignore.

"And then what? I needed a clean break. If I'd stayed in touch, I'd have stayed Eleanor Merrigan." Eleanor lowered her voice. "By the way, it's Graves now. Eleanor Graves." She wrinkled her nose, as if a faintly sour odor had wafted between them. "That was always Harry's plan, and there wasn't time to change it." With that confidence shared, Eleanor sat back in her chair, a smug smile on her face. "I've become a brand-new person!"

Em kept her mouth shut, as a flood of snide and bitter comments filled her mind. She censored the worst, but there were too many and one got through. "If you're so all-fired brand new, why come back to Bower?"

Eleanor's eyes widened. She looked very young, which did nothing to improve Emma's mood. "Because you're here. My daughter. Why else? I want us to get to know each other . . . be friends."

The sandwiches arrived—precise polygons of dense bread separated by bright layers of substances unknown. Em selected a triangle, the filling of which nearly matched both colors of her mother's hair.

"And first you needed to disappear for five months?"

"Yes—because I was still the woman who'd left you the first time. . . . Trying to get back to being that woman. You were right, Emma: What I was doing was so wrong. So, I left. I'm not the woman I was, and I've stopped trying to re-become her. I'm different now—new. We can start fresh. No baggage."

Emma chewed slowly, buying time. The sandwich was surprisingly flavorful—sweet pumpernickel bread layered around subtle curried shrimp with the merest hint of cinnamon.

"It's not that simple," she replied after swallowing. "I'd have to change, too. I'd have to forget decades of not having you around; and, frankly, you haven't given me a good reason to."

Eleanor didn't blink. "I'm going to get a job at the university. Something that will get me qualified for resident tuition. I never went to college. What do you think I should major in?"

Another slow bite and swallow. She could answer the

question thoughtfully, honestly . . . *maturely*, like the experienced adult she both appeared to be and usually was.

It's not completely her fault. She's weak—

Emma recalled Eleanor surrounded by curses and, mere days later, struggling to lift a plastic-coated dumbbell in physical therapy. She took a deep breath and advised—

"You shouldn't think about majors until you've been taking classes for a semester or two—until you can find something you like *and* something you do well." That was the same advice Emma had given her stepchildren, Jay-Jay and Lori, before they'd taken the university plunge. "Everybody changes their major. I started out in physics and wound up in European history."

"No wonder you get along with Harry."

Despite herself, Em laughed. "I hadn't thought of it that way, but I suppose you're right." She relaxed and asked, "So where have you been since May?" with genuine curiosity.

"Empty places. Open places. Places I'd never been. I rented a car and drove around the places where nobody was: Nebraska, the Dakotas, a bit of Wyoming. Not a post-card in sight."

"Mount Rushmore."

"Didn't go there."

"Yellowstone?"

"Didn't go there either."

"How could you do Wyoming and *not* visit Yellowstone National Park?"

"It was the height of summer. I would have needed a reservation just to sign up for a reservation . . . and I wanted to be alone. There's no alone in Yellowstone in July and August."

"You'll have to go back," Emma told Eleanor with all the fervor of a tourist on a quest. "Old Faithful is one of those must-see things. Mount Rushmore, too."

"There's plenty of time," Eleanor replied, and those few words changed the mood at the table.

Emma nibbled at an octagonal sandwich. Bland tuna spread with too much celery, not her favorite.

"And you?" Eleanor asked into the silence. "What have you been doing? You *do* look good, Emma. Something must be agreeing with you. Something or some*one*."

"For heaven's sake, Eleanor, don't be coy. It doesn't become you. If the question is about Blaise, then the answer is, yes we are."

Eleanor had the decency to look abashed. She'd come to Bower last year for the express purpose of freeing Emma from Blaise Raponde's influence. Someone— maybe Harry or someone else in the Atlantis Curia, that mysterious organization to which all American curse-hunters save Emma apparently belonged—had marked Blaise for a rogue and given Eleanor the task of destroying him.

Needless to say, their initial meeting had not gone well. Eleanor had been blasting Blaise with a ridiculous berib-boned wand when a pack of fiery curses swirled over the wasteland horizon. If Eleanor had listened to Blaise's warning, if she'd been willing to believe that a dead man could be an ally, she might not have gotten herself captured, tortured.

Emma wasn't the only one in the family afflicted with irrational stubbornness. If Eleanor was prepared to say something pleasant about Blaise Raponde, then Nebraska and the Dakotas truly had transformed her.

"Do you see him regularly?"

Em shrugged. "Pretty. I've worked out a routine for myself: Get up, go to work, come home, relax and go to bed—" Em lowered her voice, suddenly aware of everyone else in the tearoom, none of whom were party to the secrets of the wasteland, curses, or curse-hunters—"go to work again. I've come a long way in that department. Good teachers."

"Teachers, plural? Are you including Harry?" Eleanor asked, arching her eyebrows and becoming the harder, world-weary woman Em had known for a few hours last November.

"Including Harry," Em agreed and realized that, in the absence of proper nouns, they might not have been talking about Blaise at all.

She hadn't gotten a handle on Harry and Eleanor's marriage. Eleanor spoke of it as an arranged marriage, a penance imposed by the Curia when Eleanor had returned to the curse-hunting fold after her fling with the American Dream and Emma's father, Archibald Merrigan. But in a three-page biography Emma had found in her mother's suitcase the day after her collapse, Eleanor had spun a tale of Harry Graves as the family friend who'd rescued her from childhood catastrophe: the 1983 deaths of her missionary parents in darkest Africa. According to the biography, Harry had raised Eleanor, overseen her education, and—maybe—married her in a scenario straight out of a nineteenth-century governess novel.

When Harry showed up at the hospital, determined to get his wife transferred to a hospital closer to his New York home, he'd spouted the biography script. Emma knew for a fact that Eleanor had not been orphaned in Africa, at least not in the 1980s. She could only guess how much of the rest was also fiction.

For his part, Harry was one of those unfortunate souls who couldn't open his mouth without tripping over his best intentions. Armed with Eleanor's statements and her own first impressions, Emma had misread him completely. Harry *was* pompous, and he could be a ruthless bastard, but he was genuinely devoted to Eleanor—though his affection seemed less that of a husband than of the guardian of an immensely talented, immensely troubled orphan.

And maybe that's what Harry thought he was, or maybe, at his age, there wasn't much difference between being a husband and a guardian. Harry was coy about his past, but he'd admitted to having a front-row seat for the American Revolution (on the winning side, thank you).

Harry looked old enough to be Emma's own husband, while Eleanor looked younger than Em's stepdaughter. So, Harry could be a few decades younger than Blaise Raponde or centuries older, but exposed to the real world, not sealed in the wasteland. That meant he had at least three centuries worth of day-to-day living stowed in his memory. On the surface, Harry Graves was a chameleon adapting seamlessly to the changes around him, but underneath, where experience and personality simmered together, he might just as well be a bug-eyed alien.

All the curse-hunters were aliens, and if Emma kept up her schedule of visiting the wasteland nearly every night, she would eventually become one herself, unless she got unlucky in one reality or the other—

"—needed a place to stay."

Emma's attention snapped to the tearoom and Eleanor, who was waiting for a response.

"Everyone needs a place to stay," Em improvised, unwilling to admit that she hadn't been listening.

"I was sure you'd feel that way." Eleanor grinned with relief. "Funny, isn't it? That I'd wind up coming back here? If you'd asked me, even a year ago, Would *I* return to Bower, I'd have laughed and told you that you were crazy. I had all the best intentions when I came the first time, with Arch."

Emma tensed. Dr. Archibald Merrigan was the man she called "Dad," the man who'd raised her, who'd never been far away until he'd died, mere months before Eleanor's reappearance. He hadn't been a saint, and they hadn't always gotten along, but he was *Dad* and, though the odds were that she'd have been uncomfortable listening to the intimate confessions of any eighty-year-old woman, listening to Eleanor Merrigan, now Graves, talk about her father was excruciating.

Arch Merrigan had run his life according to sound, proven engineering principles. Life in the big house on

Teagarden Street had been good—so long as Emma had stayed in step.

Staying in step hadn't been difficult—most of the time. By nature and habit, Emma was her father's daughter. There'd been times, though, when the walls of Teagarden Street had loomed both tall and thick. Emma never won arguments with Dad; over the years, she'd simply learned how to avoid them. Eleanor hadn't had years, and Emma didn't have to know Eleanor any better than she did, to know that her mother wouldn't have learned the art of obedience without compliance. That was the strategy of a chameleon, of herself and a man like Harry Graves.

And because Em *could* empathize, she refused to listen.

"That's past history, Eleanor. Take a look at yourself— you're not the person you were when you met—" Emma caught herself before she said *Dad*. Eleanor's eyebrows flickered, and they shared a moment's silent caution that Emma would rather have skipped entirely. "When you met *Arch*."

The name seemed enough to shove Eleanor against the back of her chair where she sat, wide-eyed and open-mouthed, until a delighted grin burst onto her face. "You're right," she whispered, then repeated the words with enthusiasm. She leaned across the table. "You're *absolutely* right! And I knew you would be. You're grounded, Emma. Your feet are always planted on the ground. Your eyes see what's really there. You're like Arch, but different, too." The grin became a laugh. "This is going to be so good."

Em forced herself to be calm, to return her mother's smile while her gut shifted toward panic. "What's going to be good?"

"Why, living near you, of course."

The panic shift completed itself.

Eleanor didn't notice. "I looked at apartments closer to the college. Some of them were all right, but expensive, and even the best were crowded together. I couldn't have made myself at home—there are limits, you know. And Harry would have been aghast; he thinks leases are a waste of time. No, worse than that—" She cleared her throat and squared her shoulders before saying, in an approximation of Harry's voice: " 'A lease is a nightmare with a paper trail that grows longer every month!' I scarcely bothered looking at apartments that weren't close to the college— they weren't much better, anyway. That left me looking at *houses*—huge houses, with huge *yards*, multiple-car *garages*, and a million things to go wrong that I wouldn't know where to start to fix. Then it came to me in the middle of the night—*Emma* doesn't live in a rented apartment. And you don't live in a monstrosity of a house either. First thing the next morning, I started calling around. I called a half-dozen real-estate offices before I found one that had a listing for the Maisonettes. I met the woman at noon. She led me right past your front door, Emma—right past it and four doors more—"

"The Naughton townhouse!" Emma shouted—but softly, because she'd forgotten to breathe.

"The layout's different: three bedrooms upstairs—way more than I need. And the kitchen's smaller, not that that matters: I'm not much of a cook. It's going to need some refreshing; I guess it's been empty for quite a while. She said houses wear more when they're empty than they do with a family inside. The basement's a bit strange . . . an awful lot of wiring and overhead lighting. They must have spent a lot of time down there—"

"Empty for a while!" Em sputtered. "Three years, Eleanor. That place has been empty for three years!"·

Every community had its white elephant, its black sheep. At the Maisonettes—and for considerably more than three years—the Naughton townhouse had been both. As the veteran secretary of the Maisonettes' owners' association, Em had logged all the details from the complaints—which predated her own arrival in the community—and the lien war, which finally forced the troublesome family to take their animals, their offspring, their abundant, but rarely functioning, vehicles, and, last but not least, their hydroponic marijuana business elsewhere.

"Refreshing won't come close to fixing that house's problems. The Naughtons' house went through some very hard times. It was front-page news. The whole town heard about the holes in the walls, holes in the floors, the plumbing, the furnace. They had over a thousand marijuana plants in there! They were sleeping under the leaves. If you ask me, it hasn't sold because there's no broker in Bower who's sleazy enough to show it—" Emma caught herself. "Good God, Eleanor . . . you didn't make an offer for the Naughton place?"

Eleanor squirmed. "It was very reasonably priced, and I came in below the asking price—Harry said. Even if I have to put in a new furnace—the woman warned me that it and most of the appliances were running on borrowed time—it will still be reasonably priced, at least compared to what I'm used to in New York."

"The bank. The bank." Em clung to hope, while in the back of her mind her mother-voice succumbed to hysteria and wailed, *Eleanor. Four doors away. The Naughton place*, in heavy rotation. "No bank in Bower is going to give anyone a mortgage for the Naughton townhouse. They'll do an appraisal, and then they'll back out. It's happened before."

"No mortgage."

"No mortgage?"

"A mortgage is really just a long-term lease, with the bank as landlord and a paper trail that's a mile wide and *glowing*." Eleanor once again quoted from the Wisdom of Harry Graves, which made sense, considering a curse-hunter's unique situation, but was a formula for catastrophe with the Naughton townhouse.

"I want my own home," Eleanor continued. "I don't want to share it with some bank."

"You're telling me that you offered cash up front?" Emma whispered.

Eleanor shrugged. "I said I had a trust fund from my parents who'd died in an accident. It happens—insurance settlements, things like that." She shrugged again. "They checked with the bank—Harry's pet bank. Everything was on the up-and-up. Harry's good, Em, very good. Everything cleared this morning. I called you from the real-estate office. The closing took a little longer than I thought—there were so many other papers to sign— including waivers on the furnace, the wiring, and the plumbing. I didn't buy it *blind*. I know it's not perfect, but it's mine and it's close to you."

"Eleanor—" Em began, then closed her eyes behind her hand and rubbed her forehead. At the same time she was reeling from the notion of having Eleanor for a neighbor, she was outraged that her own mother had been conned into buying the Naughton place—and she'd done nothing to prevent it. "I wish you'd spoken to me first."

"I thought about it and about what you'd say. Don't deny it—you'd have tried to talk me out of buying it."

"Of course—"

"And I didn't want to be talked out of anything. I don't care about your Naughtons or what crimes went on in their house. It's mine now. I'm going to fix it up and fix me up at the same time. I want to be close to you, too. Not next door, but close. You're all I've got, Emma. I'm not quitting until we're . . . we're not enemies."

"We've never been enemies," Em protested. "We're—"

"Family?" Eleanor suggested when Emma found herself unable—unwilling—to say the word.

"Strangers. No, not strangers, either. Strangers get to start with a blank slate. We're strangers with baggage . . . *history*. I am, anyway. A lifetime of baggage, and I'm sorry, I truly am, Eleanor, because it's clear to me that you're not carrying the same baggage. You're not my—" Em balked. She'd kept her voice down, trying not to draw

attention, but they weren't alone. Self-censorship, because
it was *self*-censorship, took the fire out of her anger.
"You're who you are," Emma concluded wearily, "and I'm
the one who's having a hard time with that."

"But you're trying, right? We could be friends . . .
someday, right?"

"Someday."

"And it will be easier, now that we're neighbors."

"Easier," Em agreed, because she didn't have the stomach for an argument and because Eleanor was probably
right. Her appetite was gone. She pushed her unfinished
sandwiches aside and sipped her lukewarm gunpowder tea.

"I thought I'd be finished, once I got a place to live—
but that's just the beginning. Utilities, phone—I've got to
set up an account in person, you know. Everything's so
much more complicated now that we don't trust *anyone*.
And I've got to go to the post office to tell them to start de-
livering mail. And furniture! I need everything, starting
with a bed. I'm going to get myself a king-sized bed!"

"Better measure first," Em warned. "I'm not sure you
can get a king-sized box spring up to the bedrooms; I know
I couldn't in my place. The landing at the top of the stairs
is too narrow."

"Oh." Eleanor deflated. "I hadn't thought of that. What
should I measure? I've never done this before—started at
the beginning with a house. The houses where I've lived
were always there before I was. Is there anything else I
should know about buying furniture?"

Em took a deep breath. It was her self-image at stake
now—the person she had to face every morning in the mirror—and she couldn't afford anything less than honesty.
"I'd say your kitchen comes first, then the bathroom. You
can sleep on the floor, if you have to, but you can't eat off
it or wash on it. Coffeemaker, a cup, and a shower curtain
and a sleeping bag I'd borrowed from Nancy—that's all I
had my first week at the Maisonettes. Tell you the truth,

the only thing I couldn't have lived without was the coffeemaker."

"Oh." A further deflation.

In so many ways, Eleanor was the Gen-Y student she
appeared to be. Even Em's stepchildren seemed older. Or
at least they'd gotten their disillusionment taken care of
during their parents' divorces. Em took another deep
breath; she couldn't take the easy way, the callous way.
She had to be fair, even generous, if she wanted to face
herself in the morning.

"You can borrow from me—for now. I'll put together a
care package when I get home and bring it over. You can
show me around. I've learned a thing or two about what's
possible with a Maisonette."

"Before that—could I borrow your car? Just for today?
This afternoon?"

"What's wrong with yours?" Em countered, as she
would have with her stepchildren, especially her stepson.

Flustered, Eleanor shrugged and grinned and admitted,
"I don't have one."

"You were wandering America for five months!"

"Rental. I told you. Harry howled, but I ignored him—
that's easier to do when you're in North Dakota and he
doesn't have your cell phone number. I turned it in when I
got here. You're the one who says Bower's a walker's
town. I've been staying at the University Centre Inn. The
buses really are pretty good, but not when you've got a lot
to carry."

Emma hated when she had to argue with herself.

Eleanor caught Em's reluctance and made a new suggestion. "I could arrange for another rental. They'll deliver
a car to the hotel, I think. I've got to go back there anyway,
to check out. I've already got a couple of suitcases worth
of stuff. None of the things you mentioned. Nothing useful
at all—pictures for the walls and a lamp for the bedroom
that I just fell in love with."

"No." Em conceded defeat. "No reason to spend good

money on a rented car." She sounded like her mother-voice—her original mother-voice, which had counseled wisdom and responsibility throughout her childhood, not the newer one that was sulking loudly. "You can borrow mine . . . for the afternoon."

"Super!"

For a moment, Emma couldn't escape the suspicion that Eleanor's primary reason for arranging to eat lunch with her daughter had been to borrow the car. The moment passed; there was no sense in getting upset over things she couldn't control, like her mother.

She said, "We can walk over to the garage—" while Eleanor probed the corners of her small, but bulging purse.

"Don't worry, I remember where you usually park it." Eleanor pulled out a crumpled ten-dollar bill and dropped it on the table. "If you'll just give me the keys, I'll be on my way. Ten dollars should cover my share?"

Suspicion became certainty. Emma swallowed a sigh and produced a key ring from which she detached her car key.

"You can pick me up at five-thirty, around the back of the library in the half-hour lot, okay?"

"Five-thirty, you're on." Clutching the key, Eleanor looked at her watch. "That gives me four hours to find a coffeemaker!"

Emma watched her youthful mother weave and dash for the door. *I can't believe I did that*, the mother-voice complained. *I can't believe I'm not going to regret this. But what choice was there? At least this way, I'm standing on the high ground—Good God, I forgot to tell her it's manual transmission! No—she's got to be able to drive a stick; she was driving when I was born. . . .*

Em squelched the mother-voice and signaled for the check. The waitress had prepared two; Emma paid them both and left a generous tip. Walking back to the library, she thought she saw her car running a red light, but all black Japanese coupes tended to look alike.

Rahima was on the phone when Em approached her office. Assuming that body language was universal, the conversation was personal and not going well. Emma gestured nonspecifically, to indicate that she was back from lunch, and hurried into her own office.

The wall between director and assistant was largely glass. By what Em could see after Rahima hung up the phone, her assistant was upset about something, too upset to be productive. Of course, the reason Em was watching the back of Rahima's head was a similar distress, a similar lack of productivity of her own.

A better manager—one with more experience and skills—might have known how to turn their separate malaise into a "bonding experience," but Emma had avoided every management course the library had tried to slip into her schedule. She had enough trouble being responsible for Emma Merrigan; she'd never wanted to be responsible for anyone else, not Rahima Maali nor Eleanor Merrigan, now Eleanor Graves.

The two women stewed in their respective miseries until four-thirty, when Rahima slipped silently into Emma's office and, after promising to make up the time doubled, asked if she could leave a half-hour early. Em sent her on her way and wasted the last hour of her own day in a spiraling debate. Should she let Harry know that Eleanor had returned, thereby giving him an opportunity to admit what he already knew? Or, should she keep quiet and let him worry about her reaction to his wife's reappearance?

The phone was untouched when the clock ran down to 5:25. Were she the one borrowing the car—were she the sort of person who'd borrow a car from an acquaintance—Emma would have had that car tucked in the half-hour lot, close to the library's back door, by 5:15. But Emma wasn't Eleanor, and Eleanor wasn't waiting when Emma pushed open the fire-door exit to the short-term parking lot.

The meter maid was dutifully writing the day's last citation for a van that had already collected more than its share. They acknowledged each other, the meter maid looking a bit grim, as though she expected an argument over the white rectangle she wedged under an already crowded windshield wiper. Em shook her head and leaned back against an empty-space meter.

She had a good view of the Victorian-gothic clock set in the tower of one of the U's oldest halls. Legend said the clock ran five minutes fast—giving students a last chance to reach their classes on time. Legend was generous. The clock was closer to ten minutes fast, and Emma watched it creep toward six. She kept an eye on the western horizon behind the clock. A bank of heavy clouds had rolled in and was hiding the sunset. The sky was darkening fast, and precipitation could occur at almost any moment.

Em's umbrella was in her car . . . with Eleanor.

The meter maid was long gone, and the van's owner hadn't appeared. Another few minutes—when the clock showed six—and Em's anger had transformed into a peculiar, toxic sort of guilt: Eleanor might not be missing because she was out joyriding; she might be dead or injured at the bottom of a ditch. Or she might never have made it to the car—

The bell tower carillon—a more accurate keeper of time—chimed six times.

Emma considered her next move: Check out the garage? Return to her office? Phone for a cab? Start walking home and hope she didn't get caught by rain? She chose her office and its phone book, then had a better idea. Instead of going up four flights she headed downstairs. A dark-haired man of average height and build stood midway along the basement corridor, locking the several locks on his door.

"Matt!" Em called. "Matt, wait up!"

He recognized her and met her halfway. "What's up? You look worried."

"Worried, angry," she quibbled. "I think I need a ride home."

"You think?"

"My mother reappeared this morning—" Matt Barto was part of the select circle who knew who Eleanor Merrigan really was. "—We met for lunch. She told me she'd bought in at the Maisonettes, then asked to borrow my car so she could go shopping for furniture, and I, complete idiot that I am, said yes. I've been outside waiting for her the last half hour, but she hasn't shown."

Matt nodded. He was bright and sharp, the way computer gurus were usually bright and sharp, and he'd been party to Emma's secret life pretty much from the beginning. "No shit," he said after a thoughtful moment. "Did she say where she's been since she left?"

"Around—out west, mostly, I guess. Transforming herself. You might not recognize her; I nearly didn't. She's shed her skin like a snake. She's calling herself Eleanor *Graves* now. She could pass for a freshman."

"You think she's in some kind of trouble?"

Emma snarled expressively. "Eleanor *is* trouble. Tell me your car's working?"

Matt's ancient Escort had seen better days, but the young man who kept the library's computers in tune with the rest of the university and in step with network technology refused to replace it or take it in for the engine work it so desperately needed.

"Every day's an adventure," he admitted, "but the rust bucket got me here this morning, and it'll get you home tonight."

Matt did an about-face and led the way to the garage.

"Do you think she set you up?" he asked as they approached the Escort.

"I don't know. She's got to know it's a bad idea to drive off with my car. Look, would you mind circling up a level—so I can assure myself that my car's truly gone?"

Matt circled all the way up to the roof, in case Emma was wrong about where she'd left it, and back down again.

"What do you want to do next?" he asked when they were on the streets and pointed toward the Maisonettes.

"Grab her by the shoulders and drop kick her into the middle of next week."

"You can do that?"

Emma gulped. She'd been indulging a little football-season humor, but Matt's question was completely serious. If curse-hunting were a teachable skill rather than an in-born talent—a *wyrd*, Eleanor had called it—Matt Barto would have signed up for the immersion course. As it was, he wore his envy wistfully, and Em trusted him with her secrets.

"I don't think so . . . not really. Might be interesting to try, though," she mused, and followed up with more details about their tearoom lunch.

"She wouldn't set you up like that—" Matt insisted.

He and Eleanor had struck up a friendship during Eleanor's post-coma convalescence. Emma had judged it too odd for words until Nancy Amstel, her confidant since elementary school, pointed out that Matt and Eleanor had one thing in common: They both wanted to sink their roots deeper into Emma's life.

"—She could get lost, or forget what time she said she'd pick you up, but she wouldn't *leave*. Maybe she had car trouble," he concluded, as the Escort coughed and stalled at a stop sign.

My car does not misbehave, the mother-voice sniffed, while Matt coaxed his car back to life. Her black coupe was almost as old as the Escort, but it had been a better car to begin with, and Em kept it scrupulously maintained. She expected to put another 50,000 miles on it, maybe 75,000, before she even started thinking about replacing it. It had acquired a few quirks over the years. The clutch was worn to her preferences, and the engine needed a little extra gas when it idled cold. Nothing a good driver wouldn't adjust to in a few minutes . . . if Eleanor was a good driver. Emma had never ridden with her mother, at least not that she remembered.

The Escort chugged onward.

"Damn," Matt muttered when they reached Em's street. "No sign of it—I had a hunch maybe she'd just forgotten to pick you up."

Emma hadn't considered that possibility. Parking was at a premium around the Maisonettes. Just because she didn't see her car, didn't mean it wasn't on the next block, though there were two empty spots in sight. More significantly, there weren't any lights on at the Naughton—now Graves—townhouse.

"I wish she wouldn't push so hard," Em muttered.

"What?"

She hadn't meant to speak aloud, but chose not to make excuses. "If it wasn't a crisis every time Eleanor crossed my path, maybe I could get used to the idea of her as family. But it always is a crisis, one way or the other, and I always wind up feeling guilty. I can't stand that. She wanted me to go shopping with her. I could see that across the table; and I didn't want to go, so I gave in and let her borrow my car. See? If I'd gone with her, she wouldn't be missing right now. My car wouldn't be missing. Right under the surface, I think it's my fault."

"I could stay with you. My car would be here if it turns out that you've got to get her from someplace. . . ."

Emma rejected the offer without a second thought. "Just drop me off here."

Matt stopped between two cars.

"The prodigal will return," Em decided, willing it to be true. "With a big smile on her face and not a care in the world." She opened the door.

"I'm home tonight, if you need me."

"Thanks—I'm probably making more of this than I need to."

"Right," Matt agreed.

Emma closed the door and waved as the Escort chugged to the next stop sign. She picked up her paper and the mail and called to her cats, Spin and Charm, as she opened the door. Spin came bounding, yowling for dinner. Em dumped her burdens on the hall table then squatted down to scratch between his ears. She glanced into the dark living room where a red light was blinking.

There were five messages on the answering machine—about four more than usual. Without turning on a light, Emma pressed the playback button.

Three

The first message was a reminder for a noon dentist appointment the next day, which Emma would have forgotten otherwise. The second two were busy signals generated when someone else's machine hung up on hers. The fourth was a man who'd called just after noon.

"Merle?" the baritone inquired.

He got Emma's complete attention in a heartbeat. Merle was the name on her birth certificate, the name her mother had given her, the one that should have eased her transition into the curse-hunting life several decades ago, the one she'd never used. Courtesy of a pair of divorces, Em had convinced even the government that her name was Emma Merrigan. Before her life got exciting, Em hadn't given her birth-certificate name two thoughts in any given year. That had changed, of course, but there still weren't more than a half-dozen living souls who knew the name she'd been born with; and none of them matched the voice on the answering machine.

"Merle Merrigan? I certainly hope so."

The caller had a speech-maker's voice—a politician's voice: articulate and just enough of an accent to mark him as a Southern man, but several vowels short of a full drawl. He was definitely no one Emma knew.

She draped her jacket over the closet doorknob and led the cats back to the phone.

"This is Longley, Red Longley. We have . . . *friends* in common, Merle: Harry Graves, up in New York, and your lovely mother, Eleanor—"

Em sank into her favorite chair. A light switch was in easy reach, but she left it untouched. If there was one lesson she should have learned in the past year, it was that nothing involving her mother was ever coincidental.

"I have what you might call a business proposition. I believe we can work together to our mutual advantage. And we should work together, Merle. You need to get out of all that cold you're living in. Call me. I mean it. Doors are opening near you. Give me a call when you get this message. I'll be right here waiting."

He recited his phone number, slowly and clearly, so it would have been easy to write down, if Emma were in a writing mood, which she wasn't. There was no risk of losing it; the machine stored messages until it had accumulated five minutes' worth or Em deliberately deleted them. She sat, almost in shock, as the answering machine announced its last message, time-stamped less than five minutes earlier. Em wouldn't have been surprised to hear Eleanor's voice, but it was her friend Nancy.

"Missed you at the office. Listen, I've got to cancel Friday's lunch. There's been another mix-up with Alyx's roommate. I know we haven't gotten the whole story, but John and I didn't like what we did hear. Alyx insists she can handle this problem and it's nothing we need to worry about, but she'd say the same if her hand were stuck in the car door, so we've decided to look into it ourselves. . . . This is the third time since school started that she's had to abandon her dorm room because of what her roommate's up to! I'm driving down tomorrow—A bit of mother-daughter time first while we try to get this resolved. John will come down on Friday—moral support and a strong back, in case we decide to move out of the dorm on the spot. Anyway, give me a call, and I'll fill you in on the gory details."

There was no mistaking the concern in Nancy's voice, or the fierce determination that no other mother's child was going to disrupt her daughter's education.

By all John and Nancy had been able to glean (and share with Emma) from Alyx's cryptic e-mail and over-the-phone comments, the girl's roommate had a serious drug problem and abusive boyfriends. On the proverbial one-to-ten scale, protecting your kids from drugs never ranked lower than nine. Confident that Nance wouldn't have called if she hadn't had the time for a substantial conversation, Emma pressed auto-dial for the Amstel residence.

Nancy was calm—Nancy was almost always calm; reasonableness was both her strength and weakness—but welcomed the chance to hash out her concerns. Em listened, as lifelong friends were meant to listen to each other. She never mentioned her missing mother or car, even when she heard herself agree to visit Nancy's mother, Katherine, at Meadow View Manor, the assisted living facility cum nursing home where she lived and where Eleanor had been during the weeks of her coma.

There wouldn't be a problem fulfilling her promise, Emma insisted silently, still listening to Nancy. There would be no problem, because there was no possibility that Eleanor would not return with her car. Eleanor might have already returned, might even be trying to call. Over the summer, Em had upgraded her telephone to a cordless model, but she hadn't signed up for call-waiting or caller-ID. Instead, she wandered to a street-side window, where there was no sign of her car among the dozen or so she could see lining the curbs. Given the neighborhood's chronic parking problems, even that didn't mean her prodigal mother hadn't returned.

Emma couldn't see Eleanor's front door from her living room. She had to stand on the sidewalk first, which she did once she and Nance had finished talking. The townhouse her mother claimed to own was as dark and deserted as it had been for years. In a fit of frustration and futility, Emma hammered on the front door. After a few unsatisfying thumps, she walked away, resigned to waiting for her mother's next move.

A breeze had sprung up as evening deepened. The sunset clouds had cleared, and stars overhead were brighter, sharper than they'd been since spring. Wise Michiganders knew that when the stars shone like that, Indian summer was history. Chafing her arms for warmth, Emma hurried toward home. The chrysanthemums bracketing her front door would hold their color through Thanksgiving, but the coleus and salvia were doomed, possibly by midnight. She paused in the porch light to imprint them and the summer they'd brightened in her memory.

Spin and Charm closed in before Em had the door locked, weaving around her ankles and between her legs. Maybe they sensed the changing weather or the worry building at the back of their human's head. More likely, they were simply offended that she'd ignored them the first time she'd come through the front door. Her cats were generous creatures at heart, always willing to give her the chance to correct egregious mistakes. Emma got down on one knee, like a Victorian suitor. Doling out affection with both hands, she asked them questions about mothers and daughters that no feline would deign to answer.

Little, gray Charm walked away quickly; a few moments of attention were all reassurance she required. Her departure allowed mostly black Spin to throw himself against Em's leg with his purr-motor revved up to its red line. He followed her into the kitchen, hoping for a pre-dinner treat that he wouldn't have to share with his greedy sister. Such miracles sometimes happened, but not this night. An afternoon of worrying had burnt through the Ivy Bower's crustless sandwiches. Em devoured the wilted salad and sandwich she'd hauled home from work, while her dinner—the last portion of last weekend's stew—spun in the microwave.

In sufficient quantities, food vanquished worry as well as hunger for cats and people alike. Em washed her few dishes with her confidence restored: Her car and her mother were certain to return, both safely and soon. Not even Eleanor would dare disappear from her daughter's life for the *third* time and not with one of life's most necessary possessions!

Besides, Emma had other things to worry about. She was living a double life these days: journeyman curse-hunter by night and university librarian by day. The dual duty was manageable because she did her curse-hunting while she slept, and, somehow, that worked. Walking the wasteland toned her muscles without exhausting them, and, although she never remembered her dreams anymore, she hadn't succumbed to the craziness of sleep deprivation. Em assumed her body still dreamt while her mind was in the wasteland. The U's own sleep-research lab had proclaimed that brains needed dreams to keep themselves healthy, but minds, apparently, got along fine without them.

Lately, Emma's serendipitous arrangement had fallen into jeopardy. The university's academics weren't the only caste expected to contribute to its prestige; nonteaching senior staff had to carry the burden, too. This year, Emma's scheduled contribution to the U's reputation was a hefty paper for the annual November meeting of one of the larger national library associations. She'd finished the hard part—data collection and research—during the summer. All that remained was wrapping the data in words. Writing academic prose hadn't been a problem for Em in the past—the reason she'd "volunteered" for the assignment—but the words were coming slowly this time, possibly because she didn't lie awake nights composing her sentences and paragraphs.

Emma carried a pot of fragrant herbal tea upstairs to the

spare bedroom, where the computer shared space with her hobbies. After successfully resisting the temptation to check her e-mail, Em got down to work. She stuck with it, writing and rewriting the same four paragraphs, until her eyes were burning. Though she managed to keep thoughts of Eleanor Merrigan, now Graves, at bay, Emma couldn't purge Red Longley's voice from her mind.

The man had to be from the Curia—the Atlantis Curia, the inner council of curse-hunters, which Eleanor had frequently described as an unholy mating of the mafia with a global corporation. The Curia was the only place where someone might know Em's birth-certificate name and her mother's, too. By her own admission, Eleanor had a conflicted relationship with the curse-hunters' umbrella organization, but once awakened from her coma, Eleanor had been determined to get Emma accepted into its ranks. And Harry was a Curia member of some importance.

There was, of course, a simple, direct way to sate her curiosity: Replay the message and call the number it contained. Em replayed the message and got as far as writing the number in the notebook she kept by the phone, but she didn't tap it in.

All her life, Emma hadn't liked surprises. She read the last page of a novel long before she reached the middle of the story; she wouldn't own an oven without a window in the door; and she wasn't going to call Red Longley until she'd learned a little more about him. Harry Graves's phone numbers—office, home, and cell—weren't on Em's speed dialer, but they were lined up inside the notebook.

Considering the time, Emma focused on the home number and tapped it in. The line rang six times; Harry's answering machine normally cut in after four. Em was about to hang up, when the circuit clicked and an unfamiliar masculine voice said, "James here."

"I'm sorry," Em replied, "I've dialed the wrong number."

She'd started to cradle the receiver, when James asked, "You want to speak to Harry?"

"Harry Graves?" Em stammered and, hearing a sigh for a response, quickly added, "Yes, if he's there, please."

"He's upstairs. Hold on, I'll get him. Whom shall I say is calling?"

"Emma Merrigan." Another poorly stifled sigh. "He knows me. We're almost family."

The line was quiet long enough for Emma to wonder who James was—another curse-hunter, or a houseguest who happened to answer Harry's phone.

"Emma, what a pleasant surprise! I've got it now, James; you can hang up." The line clicked and strengthened. "How's the weather out in Michigan? Snowing yet?"

"No, it never snows before Halloween. Well, almost never. Not this year, anyway."

"Well, that's good to hear. What can I do for you, Emma?"

She sank into her chair. "I got a phone call this afternoon—my answering machine did. It was from a man calling himself Red Longley. He mentioned your name and Eleanor's and said he had a business proposition for me."

"Longley, eh?" In her mind's eye, Em watched Harry's eyes narrow and his lips pull into a calculating half-grin. "Did my esteemed colleague say what sort of business he had in mind?"

"Nope, only that he knew my mother . . . and you . . . and that he believed we could work together for our mutual advantage, his exact words."

"Oh, does he think that now?" Harry mused artificially. "I wondered how much time would pass before Longley decided to pounce. Have you returned his call?"

"No, I decided to call you first. He's Curia, isn't he?"

"We're *all* Curia, Emma dear, goes with the territory. It's not a country club you have to join; you're born into it. *You've* been de facto Curia since the day you were born. You're official now, if Redmond Taylor Longleigh's proposing to do business with you. Never trust a man with three last names, Emma. It's a clear sign of inbreeding."

With the expansion from Red to Redmond, a light went on in Emma's memory: Eleanor, not Harry, had dropped Redmond Longleigh—English spelling, Southern pronunciation—into a conversation. It had been a warning reference, but Emma couldn't summon the full context from her memory. Not that it mattered; she knew from experience that Harry was warming up for one of his patented lectures.

"Should I make an appointment to get my locks changed?" The words were in New York before Em recalled that new locks were no guarantee against another curse-hunter.

"Not necessary. Longleigh's a gentleman—a Southern gentleman of the *old* school, if you catch my drift. He could have told that Mitchell-woman a thing or two about Atlanta."

"A real Rhett Butler type?" Em asked, and asked herself if the label wouldn't fit Harry equally well.

"That scalawag? Heaven forfend! Longleigh doesn't bend so close to the ground. No need for bribes or collusion to make his fortune, my dear. He threaded *his* ships through the blockade with just enough scratches to keep suspicion down on all sides."

Harry paused long enough for a witty riposte, which Emma couldn't deliver. A year wasn't long enough to get used to casual conversations that spanned wars and centuries. "You've known him a while, then," she said lamely.

"Long enough."

"And he's with the Curia?"

"Longleigh is the Curia, Emma," Harry countered in a more serious tone. "Or, better, the Curia belongs to Longleigh. He built it, built it right out of the same network that got his ships to port. All that we are today, we owe to Redmond Taylor Longleigh." By its tone, Harry's conclusion fell short of an openhanded compliment.

"So, what is he? The *capo di tutti capi?* Has he made me an offer I can't refuse? Should I be real suspicious of horsehead-shaped lumps under the blankets?"

"No more than usual. Forgive me—the Curia is not an unrelenting bad thing, and Longleigh is not the villain of this piece. If the journey is a thousand miles, he and I can march together at least nine hundred before we draw swords on each other. But, it's that last hundred which matter most, isn't it? No, if Longleigh's made you a proposal, Emma, by all means, listen to it; embrace it, if you can; and confer with me whenever you choose. James said you told him that we're almost family."

Emma switched ears and massaged the bridge of her nose. No matter the subject, a conversation with Harry Graves was wading through a swamp, dodging quicksand, and catching innuendoes she couldn't decrypt. Eleanor had lived with the man—been married to him—for fifty years, give or take. If Harry was typical of the Curia, Em could almost understand her mother's brittle, impulsive behavior.

"If we're all Curia, Harry, what's my role, my rank? My mother's? Yours?"

"Your mother's the black sheep, my dear, and you're the black sheep's mysterious daughter. The question in Longleigh's mind, I suspect, is are you also a black sheep?"

"There's doubt about that?" Em scoffed.

"Black sheep are as rare as they are troublesome, Emma, and certain to be cherished. Much is expected of them. Too much for your mother; too much and much too soon. But you? Oh, no doubt that you're troublesome, Merle Acalia Merrigan, but are you *rare*? Are you to be cherished? That's what Longleigh wants to know."

"Wonderful. It's not like I know the answer to that question or, for that matter, that I particularly want to know the answer."

Harry laughed. "No need to worry about that, Emma. I

can give you your answer in a single word: Yes. You're quite rare. Not one hunter in a hundred has your ability to plunge into another consciousness . . . and get out again. Every hunter is different, Emma—you've realized that, haven't you?"

She hadn't, at least not until Harry asked the question.

"We have the Netherlands in common—if anything so subjective can be held in common. You have to think it started ages ago as a paradise, the garden of Eden. But beyond the Netherlands, we're all human, all different. Walking can be taken for granted; running a four-minute mile, now that remains exceptional no matter where you are. Plunging into another consciousness, that's a mile in, say, three-fifty-five . . . three-fifty-three . . . and raw, without training. Oh, you made a big noise, Emma Merrigan, when you reappeared last November."

"Reappeared?" Em asked. Any satisfaction she might have taken from her rarity was tempered with caution.

"Eleanor never hid the fact that she'd left an infant daughter behind; she couldn't, had she wanted to. All infants have ways of making their desires known. We could have found you—Merrigan is not the most common name, and we knew she'd gotten it from a professor—but Eleanor maintained there wasn't any need. She said she'd left you a map. She *expected* you to reappear, *expected* you to carry the weight she couldn't bear. Her bargaining chip, if you will. Her way back into good graces."

"Must have slipped her mind while she was here. She never mentioned anything like that to me."

"No need. You *didn't* reappear on schedule. You were decades late, and when you arrived no one knew how to take your measure, least of all Redmond Longleigh."

"Which is where you come in?" Em interrupted.

"I was already there, Emma," Harry corrected. "The old man. Redmond Longleigh's prime exhibit of what his precious Curia would *not* become. The original damned Yankee . . . kept around to scare the children." Bitter fire edged Harry's words. He paused—Em could imagine him taking a deep breath, restoring his façade of diffidence—and continued: "It was the sixties—about the time your mother was expecting you to appear. We weren't immune to the times. There was a coup brewing in the ranks, the uppermost ranks—very civil, of course, subtle and quiet. Longleigh came to me, because I was already handling the long-term affairs for many of his friends and all his enemies. He offered me half of everything; I refused—but I voted for him—we may not be democratic, but we take our voting very seriously. As elder member, I vote first. When I favored Longleigh, the writing was on the wall and the coup evaporated. Redmond Longleigh's dream survived."

"Thanks to you."

"Officially, no. Remember—I'd refused his offer; I'd voted my conscience. We're not nearly nine hundred miles into our journey. My guess is, we'll never be, not against the curses and rogues."

"Ah," Em said. "So, Red Longleigh wants to see what I can do?"

"You're a plunger," said Harry. "Longleigh wants to know how deep you can go, how fast, how thorough. Wouldn't surprise me to learn he's had the bunker on alert for months, looking for a curse that's tangled, but not too dangerous."

The bunker was the Curia's headquarters in the wasteland. A veritable anthill of boltholes or their equivalent, the bunker was the size of a respectable village—or so Emma had heard. Like everything else in the wasteland, the bunker's location was subjective and could only be found by those who knew where to look.

Eleanor had wanted to take Emma there, but she'd been so traumatized by her ordeal with the rogues that, once her mind had been reunited with her body, it refused to disassociate. Without Emma's help, Eleanor hadn't been able to transfer herself to the wasteland. Their subjective travels had been limited to the places Emma knew, the places

Blaise knew. And, when it came to the Curias (by implication, there were several; Emma didn't know their names or locations. It was all very subversive and revolutionary), Blaise Raponde was adamant; his knowledge was limited to avoiding them.

Beyond doubt, Harry could have led Em to the bunker, but she'd been wise to the dangers of debt long before he'd come into her life.

"Well, then, as long as it's not dangerous, I guess I can give ol' Longleigh a call and listen to his proposition," Em said, lapsing into a deliberately clumsy imitation of the answering-machine drawl as her way of signaling Harry that their conversation was nearly over.

"Never any harm in listening," Harry agreed. "Keep track of your fingers when you shake his hand and you'll do fine, Emma."

"I figured as much. I just wanted to make certain. Thanks for listening. " Em was scrupulous with her thank-yous. Her father had taught her that. A university faculty had a lot in common with the Curia, ditto a university library, for that matter.

"I'm always here for you, Emma. And, if you'll tell me the real reason you called, maybe I can help."

Em sputtered, "What real reason? The Curia's lord-high-muckety-muck leaves a message on my answering machine. That's not real enough?"

"All right, we'll quibble: Longleigh's a real reason, perhaps the reason you're most comfortable with, but I'm sure he's not the only reason."

Whenever Em was on the verge of calling Harry Graves a friend, he found a new way to irritate her. "You've misplaced your confidence again, Harry. I told you why I called, I appreciate your advice, and now—"

"I rarely misplace my confidence. I wouldn't be here today, if I did. There is a tension in your voice, Emma, for which our conversation cannot account; ergo, something else is bothering you."

Harry wouldn't have been nearly as irritating, if he were wrong more often. "All right. You win. I had lunch with Eleanor this afternoon."

"Your mother?"

"Of course, my mother. Don't sound surprised. You know she's here; she said as much. She whirled back into my life, suggested lunch, announced that she'd bought a townhouse a few doors down from me. Then she asked to borrow my car to help her get set up, and, like a fool, I gave it to her. I wound up stranded at work. There's no sign of her or my car around here, either." The mother-voice shot a searing thought through Em's mind. She shot it at Harry: "Is *any* of this even remotely surprising to you, Harry, or were you expecting my call? Were you planning to call me? Where is she, Harry? What's she up to?"

"It's quite surprising," Harry replied without a moment's pause. "I assure you, I have no idea where Eleanor is."

"You expect me to believe that you weren't keeping an eye on her bank accounts? That you didn't notice a teeny-weeny five-digit transaction? Good God, Harry, I'd swear she said she'd talked to you about the house and the money, and, foolish me, I didn't pick up on the implications right away. You know where she is, Harry. You know, and you're sitting on it."

"I'm not giving you a choice about what to believe, Emma."

Harry's voice had gone cold and sharp, a tone Emma had mastered when Jay-Jay and Lori were in middle school and used less effectively with their father during the divorce. She had managed to learn her own lessons about when to let a conversation die.

Though she chose not to believe her stepfather, when he asked a defusing question—"How did she look?"—she took the easy way out.

"Young. Not old enough to order her own drinks. And she said she's Eleanor Graves now, not Eleanor Merrigan.

She said she'd been traveling—" Emma's neck cracked as she shifted in the chair. The twinge was more loud than painful, but a reminder, either way, of the tension she was carrying. "We were in a restaurant, Harry. It wasn't crowded, but it wasn't empty, either. We were talking in code, you know, the way people talk in public about something private. I probably sounded like a mother trying to give her daughter advice. She's kept her hair short, dyed it a dark, coppery color, except for the ends which looked purple—"

"Watch yourself, Emma: To the untrained ear, that did sound very maternal."

"You asked what she looked like; I'm telling you. If I'm upset, it's not because my mother's got two-toned hair. She's disappeared . . . *again*. With my car. Gone. Vanished. Left me stranded at the library. I don't know what to think. Should I call the police? File a missing persons report—?"

"I'd rather you didn't, except as an absolute last resort," Harry interjected.

"So—*did* she talk to you after she took off with my car?" Em snarled. "Should I be worried, or is this all part of an elaborate practical joke. I hate practical jokes, Harry."

"And in that respect, you and Eleanor are alike."

"Worry or don't worry?"

Harry hesitated. "Worry. I have not heard from Eleanor since yesterday. I'll concede I knew she'd returned to Bower. Last week. She plunged directly into house-hunting. I told her to call you, but she refused. She wanted to wait until her affairs were settled. You intimidate your mother, Emma."

"Me!?"

"You live your own life, have a career, make your own decisions. Eleanor's in awe of the woman her daughter's become."

"And she expresses this how? By stealing my car?"

"I can't imagine that Eleanor's stolen your car. No, I think it's more likely that something's gone awry. The car's broken down, or she's lost, or had an accident—"

"I'm calling the police—"

"Have you been to your Netherlands bolthole?"

Had she been a dog, Emma would have growled; instead she said, "This isn't about curses—" in her sternest voice, then caught herself. A year wasn't long enough to integrate the wasteland into every thought. She and Blaise left messages for each other on the bolthole table, but it simply hadn't occurred to Emma that her mother, who had been to the bolthole and could, therefore, find it again on her own, might have done the same thing.

"No, I haven't been to the bolthole," she admitted in a calmer, wearier tone. "I don't think it would matter, anyway."

"It would to Eleanor. She's been to your bolthole. I know; she told me so before she took off. Your mother's a hunter. She'd sooner remember the way across the Netherlands than a seven-digit phone number. If she needed to tell you something, a message in the bolthole would be her first thought."

"Maybe, but, Harry, after she woke up in the hospital, while she was in rehab, Eleanor couldn't will herself into the wasteland. She'd freeze up—too many bad memories. It was like a bad phobia. The harder she tried, the worse it got. Those times I took her to the bolthole, I pulled her through; and that wasn't pleasant for me. Or her, I think. Eleanor wouldn't talk about it, so I don't know, except that I'm sure it bothered her a lot."

"Doubtless," Harry agreed, sounding sympathetic. "She didn't mention it to me, either. If she had, I wouldn't have been so surprised when she took off. Eleanor runs away from failure. Might I suggest, then, that her reappearance signals that she found a solution?"

"Maybe," Em agreed without enthusiasm. "Or, maybe, a solution found Eleanor," she worried aloud.

The line between them fell silent for several moments, until Harry said, "Unlikely. A watcher would have noticed the change."

Emma didn't know any of the watchers, didn't know how they performed their particular magic, but they did it from the Curia's bunker complex. And, suddenly, with Eleanor freshly vanished, the head of the Curia had a business proposal for her to consider. How convenient. An hour earlier, Em had been worried about her car and her mother, in that order. Now, her list of worries started with rogues and fire and went on endlessly from there.

"Em? Emma? Are you there?"

"I'm here," she conceded after another lengthy silence.

"It needn't take but a moment. Pop in, pop out. If Eleanor's there, or if she's left a message, the mystery's solved. If she's not, well, then, we'll think about the police."

Emma had nothing to say in response.

"If you'd rather not investigate by yourself, we could go together."

Truth to tell, the offer was tempting. Em didn't know how Harry Graves faced down a curse, but, dollars to doughnuts, it wasn't with an overheated laser pen. There was, however, one insurmountable problem.

"You've never been there. You don't know where it is . . . *when*, or anything else. Don't you have to have a guide the first time around and start from the same real-world location?"

"Oh, that's the easiest way, all right. But you can be drawn, or I, the same way you're drawn to the root of a curse. Stand outside your bolthole and call my name."

"I'd draw you and what else? Turning myself into a broadcast antenna doesn't sound like the smartest idea under the sun."

"There's always risk, no denying that, but it's hardly more dangerous than scouting along the absolute present. We can do it by the numbers. Fifteen minutes, I go through. Twenty minutes, you go through and call my name—once. When I hear it—feel it, actually—I'll follow my instincts and join you. It's been done before—many, many times before and everyone's lived to tell the tale afterwards. Or, we could do it the other way, if you'd be more comfortable. I don't maintain anything like a bolthole, but I could call you to my portico."

Em weighed her options, staring at the thin, dark line across her palm as she did. Were everything equal, she would have gone alone, but the memory of disaster was fresh in her mind. "Twenty minutes is more time than I need. I could be there in ten—"

"I need fifteen, and I need to be Netherward before you call. Twenty minutes—and, Emma, I'm sure there's nothing seriously wrong. Life with Eleanor is one little catastrophe after another. There's always turmoil, much ado about nothing."

Not the last time, Em corrected, in concert with the mother-voice, as she and Harry concluded their telephone conversation. Twenty minutes gave her time to brush her teeth and change into a comfortable flannel nightshirt as well as check the locks, lights, and cats. She was in bed, propped up comfortably on the pillows, with Spin purring beside her and a stainless-steel table knife (effective on cooked meat, but unlikely to cause trouble if her body rolled over it) clutched in her hand when the digital clock redrew its face for the twentieth time.

Emma scratched between Spin's ears and whispered, "Here goes nothing."

After months of practice, Em's transfer ritual was both familiar and reliable. She touched the parched ground in a balanced, three-point crouch. The kitchen knife had vanished, replaced by a fresh copy of the laser-pen—habits, it seemed, were hard to break in a subjective reality. The way-back stone was a few paces to her right, rising by its lonesome from the dried-blood dirt. Without standing, Emma spun around on her toes. No sign of the bolthole . . .

or a curse. She had a sense of the bolthole, though. It lay within easy walking distance and behind the way-back stone. She stood and scanned the horizon, but it remained hidden.

"Harry? Harry Graves?" Em called in her normal speaking voice.

Perhaps she should have shouted, or kept the words locked inside her skull? But he'd said call once, and once only. There was nothing to do but wait. Marking time in the wasteland was problematic at best. The magenta clouds cast no shadows and seethed too fast for measure. Once, Emma had managed to bring an old wristwatch through; its hands had spun erratically, forward and back.

The one reliable measure was a human pulse. She guessed hers was about seventy beats per minute, and started counting. After three minutes, Em gave that up. The wasteland wasn't as flat as it looked. The land *rolled* like the great American prairies. The hilltops might be a mile apart and the valleys only twenty feet deep, but you could hide a lot in a twenty-foot valley and see a lot from a twenty-foot hill. Emma set out for the hilltop between herself and the bolthole.

The land was empty from the hilltop, meaning, she supposed, that Harry hadn't felt her call and wasn't coming. She could have sunk into the way-back stone but chose to visit the bolthole first.

"Blaise!" Em called as she started down the slope to the door, in case he was inside, though she didn't have the sense that he was, and she usually did. "Eleanor!"

"Emma!" came the reply—not from Eleanor, but from Harry Graves, who appeared on the bluff above the bolthole door, as sudden and unexpected as the way-back stone's relocations. He carried a black cane beneath his arm.

She waited for her stepfather to make his way around the crescent, not once relying on the cane for support. Harry was breathing hard when he joined her, as though he'd come running, or walked several times farther than

˙she had. What Em had taken for a cane was, instead, an elegant walking stick made from dark, highly polished wood, tipped in steel or iron and capped by a brass Venetian lion. It was almost certainly Harry's version of Blaise's sword, though he also had a ring, a black onyx ring, that could serve the same purpose.

"I'd about given up on you."

"And I on you, my dear." Harry wiped his forehead with an immaculate handkerchief and tidied his clothes (black turtleneck and slacks, gray tweed jacket, all tailored to a perfect fit). "One peep, then nothing. May I assume that you stayed put awhile . . . and some distance from here, say about a half-mile, as the crow flies?"

"That would be fair enough."

"Fascinating, Emma, fascinating. We must talk. Growing up *outside* has left you with unusual instincts."

Em shook her head and finished her descent to the bolthole door. The interior was dark; she found matches in a never-empty drawer and lit a pair of oil lamps that were never empty, either. In contrast to the barren plains, which were always on the verge of stuffy-warm, the bolthole was chilly. They kept fresh wood piled beside the hearth. Emma left the wood untouched; fire-making and hearth-tending were Blaise's responsibility, and he wasn't around.

Neither was Eleanor. That had been obvious from the moment the lights came up. The only curiosity in sight was a pot of red and yellow tulips on the table, with a scrap of paper tucked between two leaves. Emma plucked the paper out and puzzled over the scrawl. Her spoken French was getting better; Blaise's handwriting, not to mention his spelling, remained a challenge.

"We've missed Blaise," Em explained when she'd decrypted the significant nouns and verbs. "He's off on the track of his favorite rogue, the woman who murdered him."

Harry nodded, his attention more fully absorbed by the window. Night reigned on the other side of the glass—

night broken by flickering red, green, and bright lights. It had never done that before. With a calm that was only skin deep, Em checked the wrought-iron bolt—it was thrown and latched—then closed the curtains.

"Where does *that* go?" Harry asked when she'd finished.

"I really don't know, but my guess—for tonight—is a motel parking lot. Sure as anything around here, that light's coming from a neon sign."

"Another first: not merely a bolthole to call your own, but one with a window. Have you ever . . . ventured through?"

Emma grimaced. "It is exactly what you're thinking it is, Harry—a portal to history. Blaise calls it his window on the world, *fenetre du monde*, if I'm not mistaken. We've played tourist, visiting the great cities of Europe—in his lifetime. He thinks, if he goes beyond those years, it'll be the end of him."

"Who knows about it?"

"You're the second—aside from Blaise and I. Eleanor's the first. That takes care of all the hunters I know—not counting Red Longleigh, of course. Should I tell him?"

"Only if you want him living here." He picked up a ceramic bottle from the sideboard, swirled it, then held it up to his nose. "Fascinating. Claret?"

"Beats me. That'll be from Blaise's imagination. Any wine I manage to get through arrives in a bottle with a screw-on cap. Go ahead, have a sip. I'm sure he won't mind. The jug's always full."

Blaise might indeed mind a visitor—paranoia came naturally to a murdered man—but he was too much the generous host to begrudge a taste of his wine.

Harry poured, swirled again, and sipped. "Claret, plain, simple, and a bit rough. A good cottage wine. You've done well for yourself, Emma. Does Blaise Raponde often leave you gifts of wine and flowers?"

"He tends the fire, too, and bakes bread—well, not exactly *bakes* bread, but it's hot and smells fresh. He's a regular SNAG—sensitive, new-age, kind of guy," Em said with a dose of irony. "I bring the chocolate and Jell-O. He's a regular nut for Jell-O." She wasn't ashamed of Blaise, their affair, or the hideaway they'd built, but except for Eleanor's few visits, everything they shared had been private. "Look, Harry, my mother's not here, and I don't think she's been here either. If you know where she is, you'd better tell me now, or I'm going home and calling the police, the hospitals, and anyone else I can think of."

"I only know what you've told me: Eleanor borrowed your car and did not return with it at the appointed time. She could be any number of places, in any number of conditions, but I know no more about which place, what condition than you. We are both concerned, and I *will* check after her, but my ways are indirect and, not to put too fine a point on the matter, if her situation is acute, I might be too late. If you must contact the regular authorities, I won't gainsay you, but I suggest you report a missing *car*, rather than a missing person. In the short run, the effects will be much the same, and down the line, if necessary, you can always say you thought you had to wait twenty-four hours to report a missing person."

Emma shivered from the chill and the realization that she agreed with Harry.

"Have a sip," Harry suggested, offering his glass.

Em accepted. "It still surprises me," she confessed. "It's one thing to say that something's changed your life forever; another to come up against the change, again and again. It's like waiting for a centipede to drop the other shoe. Or someone dying." She closed her eyes as her mind filled with thoughts of her father. What she wouldn't give to be talking to him rather than Harry Graves.

Emma finished the wine and refilled the glass.

Harry took her arm instead of the glass. "You're doing fine, Emma," he said, tightening his fingers. "Better than fine. I could name a dozen hunters—decades older than you—who've always known what they were, and they still come a cropper whenever the wind changes. Take advantage of the differences for a change: a minute here is not a minute there. Catch your breath before you head back."

Em kept the glass. She settled into Blaise's massive chair, knowing that wine wasn't the answer to a sudden attack of the mournful weepies—the first in at least a month. She was getting beyond, if not over, her dad's death. Time *was* healing the wounds, and, for the moment, that only deepened Emma's misery.

Harry didn't help. He parked himself in her usual chair, while Em wanted to be alone. She had nothing to say. He changed topics with every sentence: music, art, food, the price of tea in China. His intentions were good, and his strategy wasn't all that different from those Blaise had employed after Em had wrecked her hand. But his scattershot diffidence contrasted poorly with Blaise's intensity.

"I can't stay here," Emma decided, as Harry warmed up for a discourse on the decline of the West. "I've got to get back home. Stay as long as you like, but I've got a life to get back to."

Em knew good hosts never abandoned their guests and didn't care. She knew Harry would be at the window the moment her back was turned and didn't care about that, either. Leaving her half-empty wineglass on the table (where it wouldn't be when she returned) she said her good-byes and escaped. She was headed up the longer slope of the orange wedge when she heard crunching noises on the other side. There wasn't time to quibble about weapons. Emma shouted Harry's name and dropped to one knee; the fallible laser pen was in her hand and pointed toward the noise.

"*Pardieu*," a familiar voice called. "What were you expecting?"

"Not you," Em stammered.

For a heartbeat it seemed as if Blaise might leap down from the bluff, but he thought better of it and followed the crescent around until the drop was less perilous. By then,

Harry had come to Emma's defense. About ten yards separated the men when they caught sight of each other. Blaise's hand fell to the hilt of his sword.

"This is Harry—" Em began.

"*Henry* Graves," the man himself corrected. He strode up the slope with his right hand extended and his left clasped at the feet of his walking stick's leonine finial. "*À votre service, Monsieur Raponde.*"

Blaise replied with a phrase that wasn't English and wasn't in any of the French textbooks Emma had studied, either. Harry laughed, and a moment later they were grasping hands, not weapons. They came Em's way, relaxed and smiling. She allowed herself to be caught between them and swept into the bolthole.

Three truly was a crowd, especially when the other two each had a couple centuries on Emma and were chattering away in French—which was doubly irritating, because the wasteland was a subjective reality. Expectation mattered beneath the swirled magenta sky. *Desire* mattered. If Emma couldn't understand the men's conversation it wasn't that they were excluding her, more that, in her own heart and mind, she didn't want to participate.

Stop sulking! the mother-voice chided.

The men in the room weren't the source of her problem. Em had soured her own mood by foolishly mourning not the father she'd lost, but the changes that followed his death. She could wallow, or she could straighten herself up.

Take advantage of the differences, Harry had said.

The men in the room weren't the solution to Emma's problem, either. She could leave them. Ah, that notion touched a raw nerve in Em's psyche: When you introduced your friends, your acquaintances, or associates to each other, you risked that they would find you unnecessary. She cared about that, but not enough to stay.

"I'm leaving," she announced from the doorway.

In silence, both men turned to stare. Blaise seemed surprised; Harry didn't. Emma pulled the door shut behind her. She knelt beside the way-back stone, placed her palms against its smooth surface, and, after a moment that was neither falling nor awakening, found herself curled up around her pillow with tears creeping across her cheeks.

F*our*

E*mma blotted her* face with the sheet. She opened her eyes. According to her bedside clock, she'd lost all of ten minutes. There was time to return Longleigh's call, to check the nearby streets for her missing car, to slog through another paragraph of her paper, to give her teeth an extra brushing in preparation for tomorrow's appointment, or just stay where she was, under a cloud of private gloom. Though staying put was the easiest, even the most attractive, option, Em hauled herself out of the bed. She retrieved her tea from beside the turned-off computer, set it in the microwave to reheat, and tapped Redmond Longleigh's number into her phone.

The line rang long enough to leave Em doubting that she'd tapped it in correctly. Then, just before she lowered the phone from her ear, a baritone drawl invited her to leave a message.

"This is Emma Merrigan returning your call. I'd like to learn more about your proposal—" She paused a moment, in case Longleigh screened his calls. He didn't, or he wasn't going to pick up hers. "Well, I hope to hear from you again."

Spin was napping in the chair. Emma scooped him into her arms after hanging the phone up. "There are laws," she explained, nose to nose with the blinking feline. "Watched pots never boil, and there's nobody home when you finally make a dreaded call."

The cat expressed his sympathy with a sharp-toothed yawn and a blast of tuna-tainted breath. Em didn't complain when he squirmed free, his rear claws pricking through her sleeve and skin in the process. Spin had done his job for the evening—the job all pets were contracted to do. He'd distracted her, amused her, lightened her mood.

Em carried her still-steaming tea out to the sidewalk where the same cars were still parked against the curbs and there were no signs of life at Eleanor's would-be home. With an ear for the phone, which didn't ring, Em scrubbed her teeth and took a long, hot bath. She watched CNN's *Headline News* until it began repeating itself, and caught a cycle of the weather channel, too. Both stations featured the same story: an Atlantic hurricane that might veer toward Florida but wasn't coming close to Michigan. Confident that the morning would be clear and crisp, Emma laid out her clothes for work—not something she ordinarily did, but she had to factor the time it would take to walk across town to the library into her morning routine. Selecting her clothes in advance would save five minutes. Making tomorrow's brown-bag sandwich tonight would save at least another five, meaning Em could get away with moving the alarm back thirty minutes instead of forty.

Not that it mattered. •

She couldn't sleep. Spin did his best, curled between her knees and purring up a storm. Even Charm snuggled in close—a sure sign that the seasons were changing. Emma thrashed them both off the bed. Maybe it was resetting the alarm clock, or her decision not to return to the wasteland. Let Blaise and Harry hunt her share of curses for one night! Maybe it was the prospect of remembering her dreams. Whichever, Em couldn't find a comfortable position in the bed or a quiet place in her mind. If she looked at the clock once, she looked at it a hundred times, and that was just between midnight and one AM.

Lie quiet, rest, you'll get some sleep, more than you think, the mother-voice said, and Emma obeyed.

There was a *thunk* against the front door. Em recognized the sound: the paperboy—paperwoman, actually—lobbing the Detroit paper through the passenger window of her car. She sat up in the bed, rubbing her eyes. The clock read 5:37. The last time she remembered looking, it had read 4:03. The alarm was set for 6:10. Another half-hour's worth of the sort of sleep she was getting—assuming she did fall back to sleep—wouldn't make any difference. She might as well get up and brew an extra cup of coffee; she was going to need it.

Frost had formed overnight. Everything from cars to flowers sparkled beneath the streetlights. A neighbor who was scraping his windshield spotted Emma picking up her newspaper and stopped to wave. Em scanned the street for signs of a familiar car or life in the Naughton place. No luck, and her bare feet were freezing on the brick steps.

Scampering inside and standing on warm carpet, Em unfolded the newspaper. The headlines revealed nothing she hadn't seen or heard on television the night before; the good stuff—the tidbits that made a paper more interesting than its corresponding Web site—would be on the interior pages, which she usually read at lunch. She tucked the main section into the tote bag she'd haul to the library and carried the rest of the paper into the kitchen. While her coffee burbled fragrantly, Emma spread the state and local news section across the counter.

The lead story featured a fatal multicar crash near Detroit Metro Airport the previous evening. The picture was an unintelligible tangle. The odds were against Eleanor going to the airport, but Emma's breath caught in her throat anyway. Her eyes scoured the article, looking for details of the three vehicles involved; one was an SUV—

Em's missing car was a sedan—the second was a pickup truck, and the third was a white, late-model sedan.

White?

Em read the sentence twice before exhaling. Her car was *black* and ten years old. Whatever tragedy had occurred on I-94, it hadn't involved Eleanor. Em poured coffee. The moment of cold panic faded only to be replaced by the kind of anger she hadn't felt since Lori or Jay-Jay stayed out past curfew.

She sipped scalding liquid and forced herself to find another article: a house fire in Union, a tiny town several hours northwest of Detroit, the sort of town that had been in slow decline for the better part of a century. Emma only knew its location because during her student days back in the sixties, a single Union family had put three brothers on the offensive line of what remained the only undefeated team the U had fielded in her lifetime. Things like that stuck in a Boweran's memory, but a Union house fire, with or without the storied Kennison brothers, seemed unlikely fodder for the front page of any section of a Detroit daily.

She read further, learning that the blaze had been the second suspicious fire in less than a week, the third suspicious house fire since August. The Union authorities—such as they might have been—recognized they had a firebug loose in their community and had turned to their county for assistance. The county had turned to the state, and the sovereign state of Michigan was consulting with the acknowledged experts: the Detroit arson squad.

Emma thought it should have taken more than a handful of suspicious house fires to lure a team of arson specialists out of the Motor City. There had to be more to the Union story than the paper was printing . . . a drug connection, most likely. For years, the news had tracked a growing methamphetamine trade between depressed urban neighborhoods and equally depressed rural towns. The Naughtons and their eight-foot marijuana plants seemed almost quaint by comparison.

Em understood pot. She didn't indulge, preferring a glass of wine to anything that had to be lit and inhaled; but Bower had effectively decriminalized small amounts of it years ago. The local authorities, though, drew a line at crystal meth. The easily concocted drug was a curse. . . . A curse. The police, of course, were speaking metaphorically, but Emma's engineering gene wondered if there might be truth behind the metaphor. What was a curse, after all, but an essence of despair more potent than death? Maybe, instead of hunting fingerlings, she should be looking for backyard drug labs.

She was dreaming up ways to enlist the wasteland in the war against drugs when Charm jumped up on the kitchen table. The gray cat muttered a feline oath, as Emma shooed her off the forbidden surface. She joined her brother by their empty bowls.

"All right. I wasn't going to leave without feeding you. It's still early—"

But it wasn't. Between the newspaper and daydreams, good and bad, Em had squandered precious minutes. She raced through her morning chores and left the house, certain that she'd forgotten something important. There were still no signs of her car or life in the old Naughton place as she walked past it, hitting her stride and asking herself how long it had been since the last time she'd walked to work.

After her father had died, a friend in Emma's embroidery guild, speaking from a widow's experience, had told her to walk. "Walk because it's good for you and because walking will take you past the pain." Em had taken the advice to heart. She'd walked her way through all the flavors of Bower's spring and summer. Her sorrow had grown manageable, and by the time the days had grown short, Em had returned to commuting by car more often than not.

Then Eleanor showed up and, with a mental jolt, Emma realized it had been almost exactly a year since she'd walked from the Maisonettes to the Horace Johnson Library. She did her walking in the wasteland now. Pursuing curses across the parched dirt kept Emma in shape, but there were no trees in the wasteland swaying gently in a sunrise breeze.

She'd have to remember to thank her widowed friend—a half hour on the sidewalks of Bower and Emma saw the world—the *real* world—with more peace, more resolution, than she'd felt in weeks. Her optimism had been restored. The whole episode with her reappearing mother and her missing car would resolve itself by noon, because, by then, either Eleanor would have returned—with or without an explanation; it didn't matter so long as she returned the car—or Em would have called the police.

So much for Harry and his secrets. So much, too, for Redmond Longleigh. Em resolved that she'd pick up the phone if he returned her call, but she wouldn't play telephone tag with him.

Staff usually entered their behind-the-scenes part of the library through a walkway attached to their garage, but, if she didn't mind threading her way through the library like a rat in a psych-department maze there was no reason Emma couldn't walk through the front door, past the bronze bust of Horace Johnson himself. She was a finger's length from the elevator buttons when a uniformed guard challenged her from across the atrium.

"Stop it right there, lady. You can't take that elevator!"

Em swore silently and dug into her purse, seeking her wallet. The U had been issuing ID cards since her student days back in the sixties—fairly turbulent times themselves—but hiring guards to actually *check* them was a twenty-first-century phenomenon.

She raised her wallet-filled hand and nailed the guard with the stare which had earned her the elementary-school nickname, "Snake-eyes." The young man had the wits to look embarrassed as he glanced down. The two-inch portrait wasn't flattering, but it was undeniably Emma Merrigan and the lime green plastic—the rarest color in the university's rainbow—surrounding it proclaimed her status as de facto faculty, entitled to wander the campus at will.

"Uh, okay. You can take the elevator. Sorry."

"Thank you."

Em smiled and tapped the up arrow. She was still smiling when she got off the elevator.

"She's not coming in. Personal time," Betty, the secretary Em shared with four other staffers, announced in lieu of a more traditional greeting.

Emma's smile faded. There was no need to clarify the pronoun; only Rahima left Betty's voice dripping that much acid. "Did Rahima say why?"

"Her daughter. The older one. The terrorist."

Emma had seen Rahima's eldest daughter just once—or rather she'd seen a pillar of black cloth sweep into her assistant's office. Whatever qualms Rahima's nameless daughter had about being *seen* didn't extend to being *heard*, though Emma hadn't understood a single shouted word. Her instinct was to support Rahima—at the very least to protect her from the consequences of too many absences.

"I'll call Human Resources—" Emma began, mentally choosing the words for a conversation she might not have: Attendance reports weren't due until *next* Friday; if Rahima made up the time before then—

"Don't bother. I already did."

Never mind that Betty and Emma's relationship had never been better than prickly or that she was completely unqualified to become the assistant to the director of Acquisitions, Betty had applied for the position when it was first posted last winter. When Em hadn't leapt at the chance to hire her, Betty had filed a discrimination complaint with Human Resources. In an astonishingly blunt act for that oh-so-sensitive department, H-R had dismissed the complaint without a hearing. Betty had been willing to direct her outrage in their direction, until Emma had approved Rahima: an immigrant, a Muslim, and—in Betty's mind, at least, a clear and present threat to all things American—for the job.

Wait it out, Em's boss, Gene Shaunekker, had advised, when Emma had reluctantly brought the siege to his attention. *These grudges fade with time.* Easy for him to say from his wood-paneled office. The mother-voice had had a better idea: *Kill the bitch with kindness.*

Em flashed a saccharin smile. "I don't know what I'd do without you keeping track of us all."

Betty wasn't fooled, but she was nonplussed and immediately thought of something that needed to be done, something that didn't involve eye contact with Emma.

No car, no mother, an encounter with the lobby guard and another with her putative secretary—Em's day hadn't gotten off to a good start, yet her mood was rising as she settled in at her desk. She churned decisively through a stream of e-mail and was warming up her coffee prior to attacking a stack of old-fashioned paper mail when Matt Barto showed up for a mid-morning chat.

"How'd everything turn out?"

Emma shrugged and led him to her office.

"You didn't call for a ride, so it must have turned out okay, right?"

"I walked," Em corrected as she shuffled paper from the seat of her side chair back onto her desk.

"No car?"

She nodded.

"Did she *call*? Have you been able to learn anything?"

"Not a word from Eleanor, but I talked to Harry. He knew she was back in town—Did I mention that she bought a townhouse just up the block from me?"

"Yeah. Did Harry know about that, too? You called him, right? Or did he call you?"

"I called. Of course he knew. He's the Curia's money-man. At lunch, Eleanor as much as admitted that he shuffled the money around for her."

She'd slipped there, adding the Curia into a conversation that didn't need to expand beyond her mother and stepfather. Matt was a confidant, but she hadn't consciously decided to tell him about Redmond Longleigh's call. Fortunately, he didn't seem to notice her slip.

"That Harry's a cold bastard when he wants to be. Do you think he knows where Eleanor really is?"

"Hard to say: Harry's a good actor, too, goes with being a cold bastard."

"Damn—about your car still being missing. If you need a ride after work . . .? Or one tomorrow morning. But—" Matt twisted with discomfort. "I'm leaving for Indiana right after lunch. A bunch of us got tickets for Saturday's game and a hotel room for Friday night. We're driving down together—" He brightened. "Hey—I could just leave my keys with you. You could drive the rust bucket. Save me the trouble of picking it up from the lot Sunday afternoon."

Emma considered her options. At their worst, they didn't include driving Matt's rusted-out Escort. She'd rent a car before she'd drive a car with an extra airway around its gas pedal. "Don't worry. I appreciate the thought, but Eleanor's bringing my car back."

"You got a premonition or something?"

"No, I'm trying to think positive. It's a choice: I can assume the worst, or I can assume Eleanor will walk in here with my keys before eleven-thirty. Of course, if she doesn't, then I'll call the police at eleven-thirty-one and still make my noon dentist appointment.

Em grinned, Matt grinned in reply, and they started talking computers, specifically the library's archaic, semi-independent network, over which Matt ruled and which had been the foundation of their friendship. Matt flattered Emma when he asked for her advice—and there were still a few dusty system secrets she hadn't needed to share—but mostly she served as his audience, the only person in the Horace Johnson Library who could appreciate the elegance with which he'd thwarted the latest hack-attack.

Emma was tempted to keep Matt talking in the side chair until Eleanor's eleven-thirty deadline, but that would have been the sort of privilege abuse she reserved for true emergencies. He lingered in the doorway a few moments then left for his basement domain, whistling the team fight song as he went. After recreating her chair-seat files, Em tackled her inbox without notable success. A little before eleven-thirty she picked up the phone and dialed her own number and the code to trigger her answering machine's remote playback.

There was one message, recorded a few minutes before ten. It began with a blast of static and touch-tone screeching, then a woman asked:

"Is this recording—?"

Em needed a heartbeat to recognize her mother's voice.

"I didn't hear a beep. I don't think your machine's working right, Emma. I'm calling because there's been a little accident—not my fault, I swear. I was under the speed limit, minding my own business. First a dog ran out in front of me; I swerved not to hit it. Then this little boy ran out after the dog, and I swerved harder . . . with my foot on the brake—"

Em took a deep breath and held it.

"I didn't hit the kid, but I banged into something else and lost control. There was a tree, a big old tree. That damn air bag exploded. Supposed to save lives! All it did was knock me silly. I don't remember a thing until after the ambulance showed up. They got me out and took me to the local hospital. Everyone said it wasn't my fault and how it was a miracle I hadn't hit the kid. But, I tell you, I was out of it. They pack those damn bags in *powder*. It got in my eyes, my nose, and—wouldn't you know?—turns out I'm *allergic* to the stuff. There wasn't anything wrong with me that the damn air bag didn't cause. I could have walked out of that emergency room, if I could've seen the door! They admitted me because of my eyes. They were burning bad, and I couldn't call anyone."

"You could have called me!" Em complained as Eleanor continued.

"This morning they told me to wear sunglasses for a few days and let me go. The police told me which garage had your car. Oh, Emma, I'm so sorry."

Em flattened against the back of her chair, braced for the inevitable.

"That tree scrunched the passenger side of your car like a cardboard box. The insurance people had already looked at it. I spoke to them a little while ago, and they're calling it 'salvage,' which I thought meant everything would be okay, but when a claims adjuster says 'salvage,' she doesn't mean *salvage*. The garage people had a box of stuff they'd taken out of the glove compartment and trunk. I said I wanted to look under the seats and places like that, but they said the car wasn't mine—*yours*—anymore and they couldn't let me look for anything else. I was speechless, but the fact is: Your car's total toast, Emma. Total."

All the air in Em's lungs escaped with a sigh. She'd loved that car, could clearly remember sitting down at the dealership, picking her options, not worrying about cost because this was the car she was going to keep for a long time. And she'd had it for ten years, well over a hundred thousand miles. Just last month her mechanic had said the engine was wearing nicely and should be good for another hundred thousand miles.

It was hard enough to mourn people without trying to mourn things, especially when Eleanor's narration never missed a beat.

"I didn't know what I was going to do, then I looked across the street and—can you believe it?—right there was a car dealership! So, I crossed the street and asked them what kind of cars they had available. A man showed me this cute little purple—"

The playback ended abruptly with another time stamp. Emma kept her answering machine on a diet. It cut off after fifty seconds because Em had blithely assumed that any message longer than that was a sales pitch, and she wasn't interested in anything sold over the phone.

Em hung up her phone. She steepled her forearms over her keyboard and covered her face with her hands. Her fingers, massaging her forehead and temples, brought no relief. Em raised her head and caught sight of Betty watching her through the glass partitions. She knew her next move: a long-distance call to one Harry Graves in New York, but she wouldn't make it with Betty spying on her.

Make that her second move. Emma's first move was the dentist's office and she'd wasted enough time fretting about her mother that she was going to have to hustle to make the appointment. After shutting down her computer and checking that her cell phone was in her purse, Em strode past Betty's desk.

"Dentist appointment, then lunch," she announced. "I'll be back by two."

She threaded her way across the quad and down a maze of side streets to her dentist's office. The dentist was a relative newcomer to the Bower medical scene, but the office was the same one she'd been coming to since junior high. Teagarden Street was within easy walking distance, and until last year, dental appointments had been excuses to have lunch with her father.

If you had decent teeth, brushed morning and night, and flossed regularly, a dentist's chair wasn't a bad place to rehearse the terser parts of the conversation you hoped to have with your stepfather. Forty-five minutes after she arrived, Emma left the dentist's with shiny teeth and a battle plan. She hiked quickly back to the campus area where she found an empty concrete bench—Class of '33—behind the building where her dad's office had been. Em took out her cell phone and dug a worn business card out of her wallet. Next she tapped in the number that would connect her to Harry's New York City office.

"I'd like to speak with Mr. Graves," she told the man who answered on the second ring.

"Whom shall I say is calling?"

"Emma Merrigan," she replied, and waited a handful of seconds for Harry's voice.

"Emma! What may I do for you?" he asked cheerfully.

"For starters, you can stop lying."

"Emma, my dear," he said, sobering quickly. "I haven't lied to you."

"The hell you haven't. All that nonsense last night—what else was bothering me? Don't try to tell me you didn't know Eleanor had wrecked my car and was in a hospital."

"All right, I won't—but I haven't lied. I don't have time for lies, Emma, too much effort and maintenance."

She was in no mood for fine distinctions. "You knew she'd been in an accident, didn't you? You knew my car had been totaled. Call the police; don't call the police. You led me on, Harry. You let me worry myself silly. Why should I ever trust you?"

"So many questions, Emma. Yes, to the first, apparently I've still got the nod in the 'next-of-kin' department. No, to the second, not when we talked last. And for the third, because I would no more break your confidences than I'd break Eleanor's. She does *not* want me coming between her and you. I can disagree with her, argue with her, call her a goddamned fool, but I can*not* break her confidence."

"There are exceptions to every rule."

"Not to this one. I don't break confidences, Emma, and I don't make exceptions. Now, may I assume that Eleanor has, at last, spoken with you?"

"No, you may not. She called me at home this morning, when she knew perfectly well I'd be at work. She left a message on my answering machine, which cuts off messages after fifty seconds. I'll concede she probably didn't know that. The last I heard, she'd just spotted something cute and purple at a car dealership. I know there was an accident—not her fault. That she spent the night in the hospital because the air bag's packing powder did a number on her eyes and that my auto insurance company's claimed my car for salvage."

"The whole frame's bent, Emma. That's hardly worth fixing on a brand-new vehicle."

"So, you know?"

"I spoke with a claims adjuster briefly yesterday and again at eight-thirty this morning."

"Who are you to be releasing my car for salvage! Maybe I want to get it fixed anyway!"

"It wasn't a matter of releasing it, Emma. Your insurance company doesn't need your permission to decide that one of their vehicles is beyond repair. So cute and purple, is it? I might have guessed. She omitted those details when she asked me to transfer the money to her account."

"We're not talking about Eleanor here. We're talking about you turning my car into scrap metal without my permission!"

"Very well, I apologize for acting rationally. I apologize for assuming that you were a rational woman. Let me make it clearer for you, Emma. The adjuster faxed me a photo of the front end of your car. It's not a dented fender or a minuscule hitch in the alignment. The passenger side front is crunched like an accordion. The tire's cockeyed and a half-foot higher than the rest. The warp's so bad, the driver's side door popped open and will never close again. Eleanor can complain all she wants about the bloody air bag, it saved her life. Your car's totaled, Emma. No bodyshop—no reputable one—would even try to fix it; no insurance company would take the risk if it did. If you'd bought that car new last week, it would still be a total loss."

Emma gasped. "Eleanor said she hit a tree because she'd swerved to avoid a little boy chasing a dog. She made it sound minor. She said she wasn't at fault?" Never mind that she'd just accused Harry of lying, Em waited for him to confirm her mother's story.

"So she says, and so say the police. From all I've been

able to learn, Eleanor was doing about twenty miles per hour when the kid ran in front of her. She swerved, hit something lying on the side of the road, and when she hit whatever it was, she lost control, and when she lost control, she wound up with her foot on the gas, not the brake. Who's to say what would have happened if the tree hadn't been there to stop her? She might have gotten the car under control; she might have wound up in a lake. I gather she was driving around a lake."

It could have been worse. Anything could have been worse; that was an axiom of the human condition. Emma stared at the clouds a moment. "I'm glad it wasn't more serious. I'm even glad that Eleanor's found a cute, purple car—"

"In Union, Michigan—of all places. Where exactly *is* Union, Michigan, Emma?"

"Union?" Em whispered. In her mind's eye, she saw the morning's newspaper.

"As opposed to Confederacy," Harry quibbled. "I'm supposed to set up a funds transfer to the First Federated Bank of Union this afternoon. I might as well be sending twelve thousand dollars to Borneo for all I can learn about it."

"It's a little town a couple of hours northwest of here," Emma answered softly. "We hear about it maybe once a year, during deer-hunting season or for a snowmobile accident." Or two arsons in a single week. And what were the chances that there'd been a third? Before or after Eleanor's accident? It couldn't be a coincidence; there were no coincidences in a curse-hunter's world.

"Emma?" Harry's voice turned sharp with concern.

"I'm here."

"Eleanor's a survivor, Em, and she's survived much worse than a little car crash. You know that. I'll transfer that money, and she'll have her car. She'll be out of Union before you can catch your breath."

"Did Eleanor say what she was doing there?"

Harry replied, "She said she got lost," and, by his tone, he didn't believe Eleanor's explanation any more than Emma did.

Em said nothing, but Union wasn't on the Interstate. Union wasn't a town you just happened to pass through. It wasn't on the way to anywhere else.

Harry hadn't expected an answer. He sighed like a door closing and changed the subject. "What about you, Emma? You're in need of a new car; unexpectedly, I assume. You've got insurance money coming, but after your deductible it's not going to cover a reliable replacement. That's the problem with keeping a vehicle so long."

"Thanks for the advice," Em snapped. "I'll manage."

"I'd prefer you did better than manage. The accident might not have been Eleanor's fault, technically, but she drove off in a car she can't return. I'm not sure whether I'm supposed to be her husband or her father anymore. Either way, it's a gentleman's responsibility to make good his family's blunders."

"That's not necessary. If I want a new car, Harry, I can afford it without outside help." In no way could Emma swing the sort of expenses Eleanor had racked up in the last week without dipping into the money she'd inherited from her father.

Em meant that to be her final word on the subject, but Harry was unphased by sarcasm.

"Good! But a *new* car, Emma? Do you need a *new* car? New is all well and good for Eleanor; *new* is all that matters to her these days. Telling her that her car's going to lose one-third of its value before the day's over goes in one ear and out the other. You, on the other hand, I take you for a someone who's buying a car, not a smell."

Harry paused, waiting for a response Emma didn't provide. In the silence, she heard the sounds of keyboard tapping. Odds were that he was mining the Internet.

"I prefer the Saabs. There's simply no better vehicle for cold weather, which, you'd have to admit, is a major consideration out there where you live. Solid, reliable engineering—you ought to respect that, but, admittedly, when it comes to design, they're listening to an eccentric drummer. The Saab's an independent's car. I haven't been without one since they first arrived here in 1956. Before that, it was Packards. Do you remember the Packard?"

Despite herself, Em answered politely, "No, not personally," and wondered whether Harry had once preferred Morgans or hackneys, or if he'd favored some more obscure horse breed.

She could still hear Harry tapping away on his computer. Her dad had been into electronics all his life. Em had always admired the way he adapted and adopted new technologies. Dad had been the one urging her to study programming back when computers were the size of small houses and the well-dressed engineering student never went anywhere without his slide rule and a long, cardboard box of punch-cards under his arm. Dad had foreseen computers invading bedrooms and living rooms.

"Ah! Here it is!"

Em heard the triumphant *click.*

"Acura. Integra. 'S'-series. Last of its kind. Loaded, but manual transmission—you'll appreciate that. Black—naturally; you're buying a car, not a crayon. I seem to remember, your old car was black. The mileage is a bit high; on the other hand, it's a one-owner trade-in at the originating dealership, so you'll have access to all the records, and the warranty's transferrable."

"I can find my own car," Emma cautioned, never mind that she never had before. Dad had always been there, offering suggestions, much the same as Harry, and backing her up on the car lots.

Harry replied with a price that he considered ideal and that left Emma gagging, though she suspected that she'd gag more than once before she found a replacement vehicle.

"And," Harry continued, "it's sitting on a lot less than

thirty-five miles from Bower. I'll venture that this afternoon it's the only used 'S'-series for sale between Chicago and Detroit."

It dawned on Emma that, short of disconnecting herself, she wasn't getting out of this conversation without a promise to take Harry's advice. "I'll look at it," she said with the enthusiasm usually reserved by teenagers talking to their parents.

That satisfied her stepfather. "Good—I'll e-mail the details."

"Wonderful. Look, I've got to get back to work."

Harry didn't offer any objections. Em signed off with a sigh. She ate her sandwich without tasting it, while weaving together a string of questions that, when put to her insurance agent, would confirm the most important part of the morning's events: the fate of her car. With the questions honed and memorized, Emma stood in line for an ice-cream cone in the basement food court at the student union before returning to the library.

Betty was off at lunch herself and hadn't left any pink message slips clinging to Emma's door or computer. Her message light wasn't blinking, and a call home informed her that no new messages had arrived there either. She spoke to a clerk at her insurance agent's office, asking her memorized questions and learning that her car was, indeed, dead. The clerk cautiously raised the question of who had been driving the car when it struck the tree. With equal caution, Em said, "a cousin. I'd loaned her the car for the day."

The clerk didn't have a problem with a related, occasional driver demolishing Emma's sole means of transportation. He assured Em that her salvage claim had already been turned in, the check would be sent directly to her home address, and reminded her to call for binder coverage the moment she found a replacement vehicle.

Emma stared into space after hanging up the phone. The reality that her car was gone—she'd never see it again—

settled through her mind. She shut her eyes, squelching tears, because she wouldn't grieve for a *thing* while she was still mourning her father. The tremors in her tear ducts subsided. Her car was gone, simple as that; she'd get another; even simpler. The situations of her life were as stable as they got anymore, and no barrier to doing the job she was paid to do.

Around mid-afternoon, when the patches of sky visible from her desk had turned from bright blue to pale gray and she was ready for her afternoon cup of tea, Emma wandered down to Matt's basement office.

"Eleanor got out of the hospital this morning," she said from the doorway.

Matt's eyes widened, but not enough to interfere with reassembling the PC disarrayed across his desk. "Whoa! No shit? What happened?"

Emma quickly summarized Eleanor's message and her conversation with Harry. She left out the color of her mother's new car and anything about Union, but included the Integra.

" 'S'-series?" Matt laid down his screwdriver. "Cool. You going to get it?"

Never one to admit that she didn't get a joke when everyone else was laughing, Em shrugged awkwardly. "I'll consider it. I don't want to rush into anything."

"Hey, don't turn it down just because Harry found it."

That was, perhaps, the least-welcome piece of advice Emma could have heard. She affected an interest in Matt's disassembled hardware, then beat a retreat to her office. And just as well—the mail cart had rolled past Em's office while she was gone, leaving a pile of envelopes on the seat of her chair. The pile contained not one, but three mangled international requisitions.

It was a dark eight o'clock by the time Emma had straightened out the paperwork. In an ideal world, she'd have hopped in her car, picked up a marginally healthy supper at the grocery store, and been at home eating it by quarter of nine. The world was less than ideal. She weighed her options.

Hokkaido, her favorite Asian restaurant—a quick, safe walk from the library—served sushi on Thursdays and Fridays. Em was in the mood for wasabi. She indulged until her eyes had watered, then called a cab, which got her home shortly before nine-thirty.

There were no lights burning in Eleanor's windows nor any sign of a cute, purple car along the curbs. Emma collected her mail and let herself inside. The cats greeted her according to their personalities: Spin circling her ankles, convinced that he was to blame for any disruption and needing reassurance otherwise, while Charm remained on the back of the sofa, bunched up and glowering. With Spin cradled in one arm, Emma scratched behind the gray cat's ears until she consented to purr softly.

Every piece of mail went directly into the wastebasket—there wasn't even a bill to demand Em's attention. She made another cup of tea, collected the classified section of the morning paper, and went upstairs to do some car searching on the Internet. Harry's e-mail with its underlined link was waiting for her. The mother-voice suggested the delete key, but she clicked the link instead.

"Way too much," she told the cats who were keeping her under watch from the guest bed.

But a half hour and uncounted Web sites later, Emma hadn't found a better price on a better car.

Truth was, Emma could easily afford the used Integra. She could have afforded a new car, had she wanted one. She'd been living small since her divorce, substantially below her income. Her father had lived small, too, making smart investments right up to the end. Between her own savings and his estate, Emma could have bought a Maisonettes townhouse and a new car both in the same week.

But when did making your own choices devolve into stubbornness—*foolish* stubbornness? Maybe she'd have an answer after a night's sleep or a night without sleep. Em reasoned she was entitled to a night spent tossing and turning rather than walking the wasteland. Hunting curses was a personal obligation, not a contractual one, and choosing a car, choosing whether or not to take Harry's advice, wasn't a decision she needed to share with Blaise Raponde.

F*ive*

E*mma surprised herself* by falling asleep quickly, sleeping soundly, and awaking refreshed a few minutes before the alarm went off. Her radio came to life with the words "twenty-nine degrees right now." If Em had been thinking before she'd turned out the lights, she would have prepped the thermostat for a shot of early-morning warmth. Instead, she hit the snooze button, wrapped an arm around Spin, and stole another ten minutes under the covers.

She hadn't dreamt up a solution to her auto dilemma, nor had any other dream that she could remember, but, curled around her cat, Em could imagine herself in a sleek, black car without hearing Harry recommend it.

I'll ask Nancy—she thought.

Nancy's in Ohio with Alyx, her mother-voice chided. *John's going, too. Joining her for the weekend.*

I'll ask Matt—

He's leaving for the game at noon. You're on your own, child.

Em eased out of bed, leaving Spin in undisturbed, undisputed possession of the warm spot.

They'll both be back by Monday. If it's there, it's there. If it's gone, I'll find something else. I'm not going to worry

*about it. A weekend without a car wouldn't be so bad. I can
finish that damn conference paper. Maybe dig up my frost-
bitten annuals, and pack up my summer clothes. That'd
keep me busy. I don't need to go anyplace I can't walk to.
There's plenty of food in the house. . . .*

Emma had a mental schedule arranged before she
thought of Eleanor. At the very least, Eleanor owed her a
ride to any car dealership in southeast lower Michigan, but
Em knew as soon as the idea had floated through her consciousness that she wasn't going to ask her mother for anything.

The Merrigans had always had a stubborn streak. It
wasn't something to be proud of. Her father hadn't become
chairman of his department because of his. Most times,
when Emma became aware that sheer stubbornness was
controlling her life, she made an effort to break free. Not
this time. This time intransigence locked itself around her
like the world on Atlas's shoulders and stayed there the
whole walk to the library.

The same young man who'd challenged Emma the previous day was on duty in the library lobby. Their eyes
snagged the moment she walked through the doors, then
Em smiled and flashed her ID. He waved her toward the
elevator without comment. Betty was in, likewise Rahima.
After giving Betty a smile that was less sincere than the
one she'd given the lobby guard, Emma paused in her assistant's doorway.

She cleared her throat and said hello before asking,
"Everything back under control?"

Rahima's fingers froze over her keyboard, and the face
she turned toward Emma was unreadable. "Indeed. My
brother-in-law has taken my daughter into his family. It is
for the best."

No matter the syntax or accent, Emma recognized a
bald-faced lie when she heard one and didn't need a clearer
warning not to meddle in affairs she could neither understand nor improve. The best an outsider could do was offer

Rahima the chance to make up her missing hours, a chance Rahima eagerly embraced.

Betty's face, when Emma turned away from Rahima, was the essence of sour grapes. It was no surprise that Betty followed Em to her office.

"You shouldn't do that," Betty scolded, not bothering to lower her voice. "She hasn't been here six months yet. She's still provisional—no personal time, no makeup time."

"We both know that's baloney. Personal time's always discretionary . . . *my* assistant, *my* discretion."

Em met the other woman's stare and held it calmly. Betty changed her tone and tactics in a heartbeat.

"Then *do* something! You heard what she said about her brother-in-law and her daughter. The daughter's what—fourteen? You know there's got to be something wrong with that. He's probably going to make her his next wife. Don't they do that—marry their dead brother's wives and daughters?"

"Not in this country," Emma retorted, then realized she was being drawn into a dangerous conversation. "Look, I'm not the culture police around here; and neither are you."

"Then who is?" Betty demanded. "Somebody's got to be." She returned to her desk and promptly picked up the phone.

Em turned on her computer with frustrated vigor. She mowed through the overnight accumulation of voice and e-mail messages and was almost grateful for the three back-to-back committee meetings that kept her away from her desk until mid-afternoon.

Two pink rectangles sprouted from her monitor. One was from Matt, headed out for a weekend of alumni boosterism and wishing her luck in finding a new car. The other was from some functionary in Human Resources asking her to return their call; Betty's initials were etched across the bottom of the paper. Em glanced at the monitor, not to watch the screen-saver graphics but to confirm—because she could follow the other woman's reflection on the glass—that Betty was watching her every move.

Don't be childish, the mother-voice warned.

But Emma had already decided that Human Resources could wait until Monday. With great care and drama, she folded the two messages together before tucking them under her keyboard. She wasn't surprised to see Betty promptly pick up the phone—though she would have been surprised had her own phone rung immediately after Betty hung up. Human Resources might be the terror of the campus, but their minions were no more interested in a Friday afternoon skirmish than she was.

Em called home a few minutes later and listened to the messages accumulated on the answering machine. Of marginal interest, the president of the Maisonettes owners' association had left a message—because Emma was the secretary and kept track of such things—that the Naughton place had finally sold to a woman named Eleanor Graves, who'd purchased it for cash.

"I hope we're not in for another round of trouble. Without a mortgage, there's not much information, but the realtor says she's about twenty-five and seems quiet. What twenty-five-year-old has that kind of money, eh?"

There was another question Em knew she'd never answer. The other three messages were of no interest whatsoever.

Finishing the week's work took Emma hours longer than she'd expected. Hiring an assistant was supposed to have lightened her workload, and it did . . . sometimes, but not when Rahima took a vendor's invoice at face value and logged an entire shipment into the system at the wrong prices.

It was an honest mistake. Em faulted herself: She'd passed the invoice along without warning Rahima to check the conversion of every euro. The staff side of the library was deserted and the windows were black by the time she shut her computer down.

She called her answering machine, hoping—futilely— that not only had Eleanor returned to Bower in her new car, but that she'd considerately left Emma with a way to get in touch with her. But there were no new messages and, worse, Bower's only cab company wasn't answering its phones. Feeling sorry for herself, Em took the long way home, sticking to the best-lit streets and stopping at a notoriously overpriced deli for a seafood salad that almost certainly looked better than it would taste.

Like it or not, replacing her car had become a priority.

Emma's mind was deep in personal budgets and options as she passed between the decorative brick pillars that separated the Maisonettes from its neighbors. She'd just about decided that she'd swallow her stubbornness and track down Harry's black Integra—if it were still available— when she caught sight of a car so factory bright, so intensely purple, and so terminally cute that it could only be her mother's.

She'd come abreast of the Naughton townhouse— Eleanor Graves' townhouse—without realizing it.

Less car than cartoon, Em wouldn't have been surprised if the little hatchback had winked; or if Eleanor had come running down the sidewalk to greet her. The porch light was shining, and there was a rectangle glow around each front-facing window. Someone was definitely in residence and didn't know how much Detroit Edison charged for each precious kilowatt, or, just possibly, someone was afraid of the dark.

A dutiful daughter would have knocked on the door. Emma weighed her guilt and, finding it lighter than expected, resisted duty's call. She collected her mail and slipped inside her home with an end-of-the-week sigh. The cats demanded food and attention, in that order. Em filled their bowl before shedding her jacket or sorting through the mail.

After examining the day's quota of bills and consigning them to the decorative basket she kept for that purpose, Emma poured herself a glass of wine from the refrigerated box of "Chillable Red." She'd doused her salad with guaranteed organic dressing and had barely settled in at the dining room table when the door knocker clanged loudly. Convinced that Eleanor awaited her, Emma savored a gulp of wine before abandoning her dinner.

Viewed through a fish-eye peephole incorporated in the knocker, her visitor was a youngish woman, but not Eleanor, not anyone recognizable. For security's sake, Emma planted herself behind the door and cracked it open.

"Emma?" the stranger asked, with the bold friendliness of an experienced saleswoman.

She was an inch or two taller than Emma, a decade or so younger, with striking, shoulder-length blond hair that might have been natural but more likely came out of a bottle. She wore a dark leather jacket of considerable quality, roughened and softened by hard wear. Beneath the jacket Em glimpsed an equally dark turtleneck sweater. Southwestern jewelry—large chunks of quality turquoise and malachite embedded in smooth, shining silver—embellished her fingers and wrists and circled her neck like armor.

"You are Emma Merrigan, aren't you?" There was an odd inflection to the stranger's vowels, not at all Southwestern, possibly the remains of a deep-south drawl or something altogether foreign.

Emma didn't answer. She didn't welcome solicitors in the middle of the afternoon, much less by moonlight.

"I'm Sylvianne—Sylvianne Skellings."

The name meant nothing to Emma. She pressed her knee against the door and nudged it forward.

"Wait!" Sylvianne raised her hand, as if to stop Emma from shutting the door, then, wisely, lowered her arm. "Didn't you—?" Her composure faltered. "Aren't you expecting me?"

"No."

"Red called . . . didn't he?"

"Red who?" Em asked, though the name Redmond Longleigh had rocketed out of recent memory.

"Why, Red Longleigh, of course," Sylvianne replied with a Scarlett O'Hara smile. "May I come in?"

Curse-hunters weren't witches, and they certainly weren't vampires, nonetheless, Emma couldn't suppress a nervous twinge whenever her peers appeared to charm their way into her home. She backed up, letting the door swing wider and giving Sylvianne a better view of her, but didn't get out of the way.

"Longleigh and I have been playing telephone tag the last few days," she conceded to her visitor. "Right now, he's still 'it'."

Sylvianne gave her blond mane an artfully casual shake. "Men! He swore before I left that he'd talk to you—get a message to you at the bare minimum. He knows how I *hate* surprises. And you do, too; I see that by your face. You did leave a message for him? Saying you were interested in our proposal? He didn't make that up?"

Emma conceded, "No, I returned his call yesterday morning. You've come all the way from Atlanta just to talk to me about a business proposal?"

"Jumped at the chance, Emma. I couldn't wait to meet you. May I come in?"

This time Emma stepped out of the way. She collected her guest's leather jacket and hung it in the closet. Sylvianne had squatted down in the living room, holding still while the cats sniffed her fingers. Her black jeans fit like a proverbial glove. Her boots fit the same way. The overall impression was of someone who lived an active, outdoors life without, for even one moment, needing to.

"Can I get you something to eat or drink? I haven't eaten myself—" Em gestured toward the table. "I only just got home."

"Don't I already know. Since six, I've been alternately

walking around the block and sitting on the only park bench I could find. It's been cold, dark, and deserted around here all evening."

Emma resisted the tug of guilt strings. If apologies were owing, they weren't hers. It wasn't her fault Sylvianne had traveled seven hundred miles unannounced, uninvited. Still, hospitality was among the oldest virtues of civilization. "You must be starved, and cold. Let me at least heat something up for you. Soup? Chili? It's canned, but decent. I can add sour cream and cheese shreds."

Sylvianne nodded and looked pointedly at Em's nearly full wineglass. "Any more of that?"

Moments later, Sylvianne leaned in the kitchen doorway, wine in hand, while Emma prepped chili for the microwave.

"If Red didn't call, then I best start at the beginning. The watchers traced a curse to somewhere maybe sixty, seventy miles northwest of here, then they lost it."

"Watchers?" Though Harry and Eleanor both used the word, Em wanted to hear Sylvianne's definition.

"Red calls it our 'Distant Early Warning' network. About twenty of them. They meditate in the Netherlands to sense the big ones—the rogues and older curses—shifting back and forth. They hang at the bunker, away from the background noise along the absolute present.

"You know, Emma, we don't pretend we can moot every curse humanity hatches. Misery may be common as fleas on a dog, but, thank goodness, it's also unique. It's a damned rare curse that manages to perpetuate itself. Most of the background noises never find a second-generation host. They wither whether we moot them or not. The watchers sense the ones that have gone the cycle a couple of times and are starting to *evolve*."

That explanation squared with everything Emma already knew. She tapped the final numbers on the microwave's keypad and gestured Sylvianne toward the table. "I don't know how much help I can be if you're talk-

ing about a curse that's been around the block a few times.
I'm still a novice in the curse-hunting business. I think it's
fair to say that I spend my time mooting your background
noises, but I'm willing to try something more challenging;
and that's pretty much what I told Longleigh."

Em speared a shrimp from her deli salad. It was, as
she'd expected, about as tasty as the clear plastic container
that held it.

"Good, that's just what we're looking for. The watcher
who sensed this curse says he's sensed it before—twice
before, since the fifties. The last time, he thought it had
weakened, but this time, when it crossed his bow, he said
it made him stand up and take notice."

"After a half century, how does he—or any watcher—
know it's the same curse? There have got to be thousands
of curses cycling through humanity. Hundreds of thousands." As soon as she'd asked the question, Emma could
think of one answer to it, but she waited for Sylvianne's.

"Thousands, yes, but not hundreds of thousands. Like I
said, most of them wither. You go out hunting every night,
and that's good—good practice—but, lucky for us, nearly
all of those tiddlers are too unique to find another host. You
could say a tiddler that grows into an inferno is less unique
than the rest." Sylvianne's chin bobbed; she was pleased
with her analysis.

While Emma chewed, Sylvianne continued. "When
Red got the word, he sent a team of trackers out, but the
curse gave them the slip. That's when he sounded the
alarm. The trackers are good, really good, at what they
do."

Em raised her eyebrows. "So, is this about pride and
saving face?"

Sylvianne sipped wine. "Saving the downtrodden
masses. It takes time for a curse to find a new host, time
and luck. Usually, they're popping in and out for months,
getting weaker every pass. A big, old inferno may take a
couple of years or more to find a mind bent enough to sus-

tain it—we think some of them give up parasitism altogether and survive by hunting other curses, same as us. Anyway, if watchers spot one of them popping in and out of the here and now, the trackers go out to narrow the search to specific places both here and in the Netherlands, then the hunters set up an ambush to finish the job.

"But this curse of Pietro's, it popped in, popped out, and that was that. Best guess is: It caught a host on its first try. So, not only is this curse a fast-cycler, burning through hosts like so many charcoal briquettes under the grill, it's flattening out, adapting itself to a wider range of personalities."

"And increasing the likelihood that it'll find someone it can turn into a rogue?"

Sylvianne sat back in her chair, a calculating, puzzled expression across her face, but the microwave buzzer sounded before she or Emma had anything more to say. Em garnished the chili with a dollop of sour cream and a sprinkling of shredded cheese, both staples in her refrigerator. Truth to tell, the steaming bowl looked more appetizing than her salad. She was still picking at her greens when Sylvianne had spooned up the last of the chili.

She asked, "Do you get along well with Harry Graves?" as she put down the spoon.

The question took Emma by surprise. "Well enough," she stammered.

"Well enough to believe his wild theories? The man's a wizard—a positive wizard—when it comes to financial planning. And there's nobody who knows where more bodies are buried. But, Emma, those ideas he gets about curses turning ordinary human beings into rogues. And all that business about genetics!" Sylvianne shook her head in mock sorrow. "He's a pit bull, and once he's had an idea, he doesn't quit just because no one agrees with him. Before genetics, he was on electricity; and before electricity, it was magnetism. He's looking for God in all the wrong places."

Few things appealed more to Emma's engineering gene than a new perspective on an old problem. Wondering if Sylvianne personally recalled a time before genetics and electricity, Em abandoned her salad.

"If I believe him and my mother," she said carefully, "Harry's been searching a long time."

"Nobody but Harry knows how long. There are other adrêsteia who might—"

"Say what?" Emma interrupted. After a half-century of living in a university town and nearly half of that time working for its library, Em didn't hear too many words she hadn't heard before, but Sylvianne had just shot one across the dining room table.

"Adrêsteia. It's what we are, you and I, Red Longleigh, Harry Graves, and your mother. We're adrêsteia."

"Ay-drey-stee-ah?" Em wrapped her tongue around a word that almost certainly wasn't in any English dictionary. "I thought we called ourselves curse-hunters."

Sylvianne wrinkled her nose. "That's what we do. What we are is adrêsteia: inevitable and inescapable."

"In whose language?"

"Greek," Sylvianne admitted. "Red coined the name when he founded the Curia."

"A little Latin, a little Greek: How very ecumenical." Em didn't trouble to hide her disdain. Harry Graves might be a blowhard, but he did his blowing in the queen's English.

Sylvianne shrank a bit and lowered her voice. "Red does get carried away sometimes," she said, conspiratorially. "It hasn't been that long since a hunter couldn't always tell the difference between a rogue and another hunter. Red's only trying to give us a sense of family."

Blaise had said much the same thing—about the similarities between hunters and rogues, at least. "Nothing like four or five syllables strung together to give a sense that we're *us* and they're *them*—which I imagine puts me somewhere between a black sheep and prodigal daughter."

"If you say so." A shadow of contempt tightened Sylvianne's expression. She shed it with a deliberate smile. "It's not as if full-grown adrêsteia pop out of the woodwork every other day. Harry said, 'go easy,' and that's what we've done, but you're welcome—more than welcome. No prodigals here. Not with your *wyrd*. We've been waiting for someone like you."

"A librarian?"

"A plunger."

Emma blinked hard and sat back against the chair. Off the top of her head, plunger had two meanings: an amateur plumber's best friend or a rash Briton. She didn't aspire to either. Her distaste must have been obvious, as the blond woman shook her head slowly and donned a put-upon expression.

"My apologies. It's hard to remember that there's so much you've missed. Red says it's like the old days, when we didn't know one another and had an abnormally high incidence of orphans and adoptions. It's better now, with the Curia. When I was growing up, we had summer camp. But, you didn't, and now you've got to play catch-up. Among adrêsteia, we have hunters, trackers, delvers, lurkers, watchers, priests, *and* plungers."

Emma grimaced. "And I'm a plunger. Sounds like the adrêsteia come in flavors like quarks." Librarians were notorious for their odd bits of knowledge; Emma had named her cats after quarks.

Sylvianne ignored the gibe. "That's what we hear, what the watchers heard last November. First try out of the box, you not only delved a curse back to its root, you mooted it by getting inside the root's head. Now, *that's* a *wyrd*."

"Not common, eh?" Em mused, recalling her inaugural curse-hunting misadventure in the depths of the eleventh-century English—make that Norman Conquest—countryside. She didn't think about the people—the long dead, but presumably once living people—she'd encountered there. But they were people, not *roots*. Emma's mental armor quickened; she smiled through her growing displeasure. "My mother said I did it well, but I'd had so much trouble with everything else, I took it as a backhanded compliment."

"That's Eleanor for you. Jealous or bitter, probably both."

Never mind the number of times Emma had wanted to drop-kick her mother into the middle of next week, family was family, and she bristled at the relative insult. "I don't think so. My mother's got her faults, but long-term grudges don't seem to be among them. If anything, she's the one who plunges into things left and right."

"That's not for me to say," Sylvianne said, making her opinions clear all the same. "Eleanor could have been a plunger . . . should have been. *Her* mother and aunts were prime delvers. You *do* know that you inherited from your mother, not your father. The *wyrd* is gender-linked. Mothers to daughters, fathers to sons . . . most of the time."

Em nodded, though she was curious about the "most of the time" caveat; she hadn't heard that one before. For the moment, though, she was more curious about where Sylvianne was headed than filling in the gaps in her curse-hunting—make that *adrêsteing*—education.

"Plunging, if you must know, is the rarest *wyrd*. A good plunger can moot a rogue without confronting it—even a rogue has to be careful crossing its path. But first the plunger has to *find* the root. So we start with a good delver. They're just trackers across time: not common, but findable enough. Then we see if our delver can plunge. Truth is, plunging's not just *wyrd*, it's temperament: You've either got it, or you don't. If you don't, you're Eleanor."

"I see," Emma nodded, trying to remain polite.

She had the stomach for getting inside someone's head, the same as she had the stomach for riding the monster roller coasters at Cedar Point. And for much the same reason: No matter how hard her body lurched, no matter how much her senses screamed, her mind rejected the notion that she was in any real danger. Though the subject of roller coasters had never come up with Eleanor, Em was confident that her mother steered clear of them. Eleanor wasn't bitter, she was brittle; and roller coasters, whether wooden, steel, or woven from the thoughts in a stranger's mind, were no place for a brittle woman.

"Red's a prime delver, best in Atlantis. He plunges, too, when that's the only choice. It's a temperament thing. The whole idea of plunging is a subtle nudge to keep the root from creating a curse. Red's got too strong a hand on the tiller for that plunging. What we need—what we've been waiting for from the beginning, is someone who can be both reckless and subtle. Red thought it would be Eleanor . . . or one of her sisters or first cousins."

You have family, the mother-voice whispered. *Quite a bit of family, from the sounds of it.*

Any other evening, that would have been grounds for a celebration, but not this evening. A larger picture of Eleanor Graves, once Merrigan, was coming into focus, and it wasn't pretty.

"But they all turned out to be brittle?" Em asked before a full moment had passed.

"*Brittle*? Not the word I would choose. Red thought he could work with them—master and apprentice." Sylvianne looked past Emma's shoulder, recalling something that made her shake her head just once, but decisively. "He learned the hard way: Plunging's strictly a solo performance."

That didn't surprise Emma. She hadn't even met Redmond Longleigh, and she knew she wouldn't want to be his apprentice, or anyone else's. "Which leads to you, and not Longleigh himself, coming to Bower to tell me about this curse you want plunged out?"

"In a sense, you could say that. Yes. According to Pietro, we're not looking for a rogue. He says the curse is a fast-cycler, but it's not roguish. You'll be able to handle it, even if you wind up confronting it by mistake."

"That's a comforting thought. If you don't mind me asking, what flavor are you? Hunter? Watcher? Lurker? Or are you what you called a priest?"

"Hunter, my dear. None of that fancy stuff, just point-and-shoot, that's me." She seemed quite proud of her limitations, if limitations they were. "Keeps things simple. Tell you the God's honest truth: I don't envy you, if you are the plunger Red's been looking for."

"Why?"

"It's not me, that's all," Sylvianne insisted, and the lie detector in Emma's mind spiked wildly.

She took note, as she'd taken a dozen notes since Sylvianne knocked on the door, then let the falsehood pass. No sense asking questions and risking information overload before Sylvianne told her more about Pietro's (not Peter?) curse. Besides, the wrong question would reveal more about her own ignorance than it could possibly reap.

Em summoned her best soothing, diplomatic tones, "But it is me, apparently, and, well, if I can help rid humanity of fast-cycling curses, I figure that's what I should be doing—for the good of humanity and all. Every mooted curse has got to be worth more than acquiring, oh, forty copies of the latest edition of "Gargantua and Pantagruel" for Gordon's second-semester comp. lit. reading list. So, tell me, where do I need to plunge? Or should that be when?" She grinned and invited Sylvianne to share a laugh.

Sylvianne didn't laugh, but she did relax. "I told Red you'd seize a challenge. I don't mind telling you, I've been pushing him to open the door. He wasn't sure . . . wasn't sure it would be worthwhile. The Skellings have to stick together."

The Skellings. Taken at face value, the phrase meant nothing more than, in Redmond Longleigh's Curia, blood's thicker than water; and Emma had already figured that out. But there was something about the inflection, the way Sylvianne's eyes locked on to Emma's and held them, that left Em with the impression that blood flowed thickly across her dining room table. That was a question for another time . . . a question for Eleanor, or even Harry.

Until then, Emma contented herself with specifics. "I don't suppose this Pietro drew a map?"

That brought a smile to Sylvianne's face. "I'd have thought he'd have told you! It's all Harry's work, you know: the ring of platforms—he called them towers, but they're just circles—around the bunker and the grids. Translating a map—any map, flat or a globe—accurately into the Netherlands would be prohibitively hard, so Harry came up with his grids: columns upon columns, rows upon rows scratched into the ground. Sometimes that man is a positive genius: Who else but Harry Graves would have guessed that arithmetic translates *perfectly*?

"Anyway, when a watcher senses a curse, all he has to do is drop a few pebbles onto the grid and, an hour later—after all the watchers compare their grids—we stick a pin in a map. Of course, usually a curse hangs around for a while and the watchers will build up a pretty good pinpoint location—*pinpoint!*" Sylvianne celebrated her quip with a broader smile. "This one's a fast-cycler, and Pietro had only one sense of it, but, fortunately, two other watchers caught a sense of it at the same time, weaker, of course—"

Sylvianne made eye contact, and Emma nodded without understanding why.

"Pietro took the three sets of numbers and came up with a footprint that's—maybe—ten miles across. In the absolute present, that is. The old-timers talk about how curses used to stay put for seven generations, but that hasn't been true since the Rebellion—the Civil War—when Red got the idea for the Curia. Nowadays, there's just no telling where a curse is going to surface, because there's no telling how far its host is going to wander. It's like they've all become rogues, in a way. When you do your delving, there's no telling where you'll wind up. . . .

"Oh, Red said to tell you: If you can't delve it, to let him know. He'd be willing to delve it for you but, after the way it went with Eleanor, he doesn't want to crowd your first effort."

"Much appreciated," Emma agreed with a stiff smile. "Don't suppose you brought the grids with you?"

"No." Sylvianne shook her head—not to emphasize her statement, but wearily. "The grids don't translate, just the numbers. Pietro brought them out and Red fed them into the computer. It used to take *days*; now the Mac flashes the coordinates almost before Red's done. The computer even prints out the maps for us. It uses the Internet to get the maps, right down to the nearest street, and puts an "X" where the curse is hovering. Most of the time. Like I said, Pietro only had the one sensing, plus what the other two watchers could give him. Ten miles across is a pretty broad area. There's a chance—a good chance—you won't be able to find it. It's a long shot at best, but Red thought it was worth a try."

Sixteen years of classroom schooling, a slew of post-grad courses, and Emma had never clutched during a test. She warmed to the challenge. "Let me see what you've got. Ten miles centered on downtown Detroit is a whole lot different than ten miles in the Upper Peninsula."

Sylvianne retreated to the hall and the shapeless satchel she'd left there. Em shuttled the dishes to the sink and turned on the ceiling light over the dining table. Two of the bulbs popped and died; the rest cast their light through a dust-crusted spiderweb. Emma would have died of embarrassment, had that been an option, though Sylvianne seemed not to notice.

She dealt paper across the table and hunkered over the sheets. Em observed from the opposite side. The maps were in color, with red "X"s on the larger scaled sheets and circles of varying sizes on the others. Most of the maps were road-type maps, a couple were topographic, and one—the largest and definitely not generated by a Macintosh—was a hybrid of roads and contours and unfamiliar symbols.

"Here's the best one—" Sylvianne rotated a letter-sized sheet and nudged it toward Em. "Bower's off the edge to the southeast, about sixty miles. "Do you recognize any of the towns?"

"I've lived in Michigan all my life," Em replied, buying time while she absorbed what she saw: There were *no* coincidences in a curse-hunters world. "We spent the whole of seventh-grade social studies learning the state's history and geography."

Ten miles across was indeed a sizeable chunk of real estate. But there was only one name that mattered inside the red circle someone had drawn on the map; and it was dead in the center of the circle: the sleepy, smokey town named Union.

Don't let on! the mother-voice hissed, because the mother-voice tended toward both greed and paranoia. *Keep this one for yourself,* it continued, while from another corner of memory Em could hear Harry counseling her to keep the Curia in her debt and never let the balance swing the other way.

"Red knows it's a lot of territory," Sylvianne explained, unaware of the chatter within Em's mind. "A lot of places for a curse to hide; and we're not looking at a major curse, not yet. We like to get rid of fast-cyclers whenever we spot them. They're sure to become rogues. But there'll be another chance; that's the way with fast-cyclers. The question is, do you want to try delving it—and mooting it—at this stage?"

"I'm game," Emma reassured her guest. "You can leave the maps with me?" She began gathering them into an irregular pile.

Sylvianne interceded, pulling the large, unfamiliar one to her side of the table before Em laid a hand on it. As her turquoise-ringed fingers folded it, Em caught a brief glimpse of the reverse side. One word stood out: *Aviation*.

"Longleigh flies a plane?" Emma guessed.

"No, I do," Sylvianne corrected, and Emma made quick revisions to her mental portrait of Sylvianne Skellings. The scuffed leathers made more sense now: This was a woman who flew solo. "Red hates the idea. He's come around since 9-11—along with half the corporate world—but he still doesn't like the idea. He'd rather do everything at the bunker, as if there weren't limits on what you can do there."

Em could have asked about limits; she chose to ask about relationships instead. "You and Longleigh—?"

"Are friends . . . good friends, like you and Harry—"

That was hardly a reassuring answer.

"I keep a place for myself outside Athens, but it seems like I spend all my time in Atlantis—"

Emma blinked; she couldn't help herself, not when she heard Athens and Atlantis in the same sentence.

"Athens, *Georgia*," Sylvianne drawled, removing any doubt about her native state. "I tell you, I don't know how Harry does it—staying up in New York, that is. It would be easier if we were all together. The good lord knows Atlantis is big enough even for egos the size of Red's and Harry's. But I guess the two of them together would draw too much attention. That's what they say. Red keeps Atlantis just the way it's always been, charges admission on weekends, rents it out for weddings, and passes himself off as the caretaker, living in a little cottage out back. You've got to come visit, Emma. You're practically family, and anyway, you can't truly call yourself adrêsteia until you've seen Atlantis."

The question Emma couldn't answer was, did she want to call herself adrêsteia?

"Maybe the next time I'm looking for some place for a vacation—"

"Oh, just come on down for a weekend."

"Atlanta's too long a drive for a weekend."

"What *drive? Fly!* Give a call, tell us when you're free.

I won't mind coming to get you. You've got yourselves a nice little airport here."

Emma hesitated. Small planes didn't bother her, though it had been years—decades—since she'd flown in anything smaller than a commercial jet. Sylvianne's sudden hospitality, though, had the feeling of a spider's invitation to the fly. Em hadn't grown up in a football town without learning that the best defense was a good offense. She led Sylvianne to the more comfortable chairs of her living room and invited her guest to spend the night.

Sylvianne rejected the offer. "Thanks, but no thanks. No rest for the wicked—I've got to be in Atlanta at noon tomorrow. If you'll just drive me out to the airport—"

Em froze.

"Unless you've got more questions about Pietro's curse. I've told you pretty much everything I know about it; but if you feel I've left something out—?"

"No. No, it's not that. I—I'm car-less right now," Em stammered. She didn't want to go into details.

"Oh." Sylvianne affected surprise that seemed genuine and might even be genuine, if Harry actually played his cards as close to his vest as he claimed. She looked at her watch. "Can I call a taxi?"

The company that hadn't answered its phone when Emma needed them at the library was back on the job and offered to send a car in a half hour. Sylvianne accepted the offer.

"If you don't mind my asking, what happened to your car?"

"It's a long story," Em replied with a groan meant to forestall further questions. She'd lie, if she had to, but she'd rather not.

Sylvianne took the hint and tried a different line of casual conversation. "So, you're a librarian. I don't recall meeting a librarian before. What do you do—besides put the books back on the shelves?"

Patiently—because she'd answered the question countless times—Em explained that the library hired students to do the scut work; her job was director of acquisitions. That was more information than many people needed, but she and Sylvianne had a half hour to kill, and by mutual, unspoken agreement, Emma's job was a safe subject for discussion. Sylvianne did a good job of seeming interested, particularly when Em slipped and described how the library's resources had come in handy the few times she'd found herself data-mining the past for curses and rogues.

"You've used *old maps* to delve a curse?"

"Desperation is the mother of invention," Em laughed and wrenched the conversation around with a question about airplanes and flying.

Sylvianne answered Em's question and was polite enough—canny enough—not to ask additional questions about Emma's curse-hunting techniques. Despite everything, Emma found herself warming toward this woman who might be a cousin. Minutes before the cab finally showed up—five minutes late, which, for the Bower Cab Company, was almost early—Em asked for Sylvianne's phone number.

"Don't bother. I'm almost never home. Just call Red; he'll add your message to the rest. You know, I'm not sure I can *remember* my phone number. Four-one-four—is that the Atlanta area code?"

Em didn't believe anyone who had a pilot's license could be ignorant of their area code, but she let the matter slide. Once Sylvianne was gone, she leaned against the front door, sifting her memory like tea leaves and trying to recall everything the other woman had said.

Emma's first conclusion, one that came out of the blue and seemingly disconnected to anything Sylvianne had said, was that she had to get a new car. Her second conclusion, which probably had something to do with envy, was that she'd pay the premium for the Integra, if it were still available and even if she had to beg a ride from Eleanor to complete the transaction.

Sighing, Emma pushed away from the door, locked it, and headed for the computer. She wasn't halfway up the stairs when the phone rang. There were perfectly good phones beside her bed and the computer, but Em had turned their ringers off years ago to keep vagrant calls from disturbing her sleep. The only phone that *rang* was in the living room. She turned on a dime and skipped down the stairs to answer it.

Sylvianne must have forgotten something, Emma thought as she lifted the receiver.

She couldn't have been more wrong.

"What did *that* woman want?" Eleanor demanded, her voice sharp with an anger Emma hadn't heard before. "I saw her come, and I saw her go, so don't pretend she wasn't here. What did she want?"

Six

Emma could have shouted any of the dozen or more retorts that hovered in reach of her tongue, but she held silent a moment, waiting for better words to cross her mind. Fortunately—or maybe not—Eleanor was willing to wait, too.

"I've had a little visit from that Curia you've told me about—the ones that are half Mafia, half Engulf and Devour Inc," Em said calmly. "They sent someone up to talk business with me."

Eleanor began her reply with a snarl. "Not someone. *That* woman. Sylvianne Skellings: a snake in the grass in a skirt if ever one slithered out of the swamp."

Emma sat down in her chair. She might have guessed that there'd be bad blood between her mother and Sylvianne. In a heartbeat, Em resigned to more complications in an already complicated life. "I don't know about that. She seemed pleasant enough . . . *rational* enough—" Em could deliver an insult herself, when she needed to. "A bit on the intimidating side, but I'm getting used to that when I'm dealing with the Family."

"She told you!" Eleanor erupted. "*Damn* that woman. Damn her to death everlasting! I'm coming over."

Belatedly, Emma recalled Sylvianne's *"The Skellings"*

remark and wondered if it had been as innocent as Emma had thought. Once again, though, the moment wasn't ripe for questions.

"It's late," Em informed her mother. "Too late for a lecture. We can talk about the Curia tomor—"

"No. I'm coming over."

"You're not."

"Emma, that woman's dangerous, more dangerous than you can imagine! What did she tell you about me, about yourself?"

She was curious, curious as hell, but Em needed to know her own mind before her curiosity was sated. "Not now, Eleanor—"

The line went dead with a click. Emma knew with cold certainty that her mother was on the way over. In an instant she was as angry as Eleanor had been and determined that *this* confrontation wouldn't explode in her living room. Grabbing her keys and the map of Michigan that Sylvianne Skellings had left behind and giving the spring-bolt lock a twist on the way out, Em hit the Maisonettes sidewalk.

A glance ahead revealed Eleanor's silhouette headed her way. It revealed the little, purple car, too, and that only thickened Emma's already dark mood. They met at the car's front bumper.

"Emma, I was—"

"You're the one who wanted to be neighbors. We can argue in your living room as easily as we can in mine."

"But I—"

Emma paid no attention to Eleanor's protests. The sidewalk was too wide for one woman to block. She sidestepped her mother and kept going. It was a safe tactic: Her own front door was locked and, courtesy of her position in Maisonettes Owners' Association, she had a key to the Naughton place on her key ring. Em was willing to bet that her mother hadn't changed the lock.

She didn't have to test her judgment. Eleanor raced

ahead and opened the door before Emma set foot on the red-brick steps.

"You're welcome," Eleanor said, as her daughter surged around her.

If there was any magic associated with a curse-hunter's threshold, Emma couldn't feel it. Instead she noticed the barrenness of Eleanor's new home. The flat white paint the association had slapped on the walls sucked the light out of the halogen floor lamp shining in the center of the living room, leaving only harsh shadows behind. A folding chair, spattered with white paint and dating back to the Naughton era, stood beside the lamp. Otherwise, except for a half-finished bottle of soda and a pizza delivery box peeking out from under an open newspaper, the room was empty. Dead empty. Even the sound of breathing seemed to echo off the walls.

Her choice! the mother-voice hissed. *If she's here in an empty house, eating off her lap, and sleeping on the floor, it's her choice. There were a million other ways, but she chose this one.*

"I'd say sit down and make yourself comfortable, but entertaining visitors is awkward with just one chair," Eleanor said from the doorway behind Emma. Her tone was equal parts defensive and defiant. "I've ordered furniture, but it won't get here until Monday, maybe Tuesday. I can offer you wine—white zin—or soda—diet cola. They're both cold; the refrigerator's working."

Emma wondered if Eleanor planned to sleep on the floor; that, too, would be her choice. She turned around, a snide comment at the ready, but swallowed her words and some of her anger when she got a look at Eleanor's face.

The air bag had done its job; at least Emma supposed the safety device was responsible for the bruise on the left side of Eleanor's face, from hairline to chin. Eleanor's left hand was swollen and discolored, too, as if she'd tried to ward off the explosion of polyester and powder. Fate didn't award points for kicking cripples. For the first time, Emma

entertained the possibilities that the accident that destroyed
her car had truly been an accident, that Eleanor hadn't been
at fault, and that it could have been much worse.

"I'll have a glass of soda."

Eleanor led the way into a kitchen as starkly white as
the living room.

"You'll need to paint," Em said while Eleanor opened a
cabinet door. Brand-new glasses and plates—prepackaged
service for four by the look of them—sat in neatly
arranged piles. "When we had this place cleaned up after
we finally got the Naughton's out, we didn't exactly pay
premium prices for the paint. If you scrub it, you'll be
down to the color these walls used to be, and, trust me, you
don't want to see that."

Eleanor hesitated, one hand holding two pristine
glasses, and the other on the refrigerator door. She was
pouring from a two-liter bottle before she said, "I don't
care what was here before. I don't care how run-down or
scandalous it was. It's my home now, the first home that's
really been mine; and I'm going to be happy here."

Emma took a glass in silence. She'd felt the same fierce
pride when she'd taken possession of her own home, four
doors down, after her divorce from Jeff; but what about the
house on Teagarden Street? Dad had gone to his grave so
firmly convinced that his wife had loved the big home
they'd shared for a few, brief years, that he would neither
move to smaller, easier-to-maintain quarters nor replace
anything that wasn't beyond repair. Em wasn't angry because she objected to Eleanor's pride, but because it hurt
to think of her father as a man who'd clung to foolish
dreams for fifty years.

"What's that?" Eleanor asked, indicating the map
Emma held in her other hand.

"A map that Sylvianne flew all the way up here to give
me—the business proposition. You know, I actually
wanted to talk to you about it. You or Harry. Maybe both
of you."

Em looked around for a surface large enough to support the open map. There wasn't any, except the floor.

"You can't trust her," Eleanor insisted.

"I know that, *Mother*," Em retorted. "When it comes to hunting curses, or at least when it comes to curse-hunters, I can't completely trust any of you."

"When have I ever lied to you?"

Emma gave a heartbeat's thought and shook her head. "All right, it's not lies," she conceded. "It's the omissions, the half-truths. You and Harry are good at telling me how dangerous my life has gotten without giving up the necessary details. I'm telling you, the wasteland's the easy part."

Eleanor let that overly provocative remark slip by. "I've got a lifetime of experience—a long lifetime. I don't know where to start with you, but, I'll try. I'll seriously try. Tell me what happened with that woman. Ask your questions."

"When were you born?" Emma asked without a moment's hesitation or thought.

"Does it matter?"

"There you go! You say you'll answer my questions. How simple does a question have to be? When were you born? What year? What country?"

"Nineteen-fourteen. Near Boston, I think. I don't remember, and you can be sure that there's no birth certificate lying about somewhere. Harry's good about that. Harry's good about most things.

"My mother died in nineteen-eighteen, influenza, I think, the timing was right; but maybe during childbirth, I'm not sure. I was what, four years old? I remember quiet and crying and being told that I had an infant sister, period. I tell you the God's honest truth: I don't ever remember seeing the child. What Harry's best at is keeping secrets. He knows—he's got to know if there was a younger sister—but he won't tell; and he doesn't keep records, not where I could find them; and, believe me, I've looked.

"My father died right after, maybe influenza, too. He must have been an outsider, because I was sent to live with his family—his parents and a maiden aunt who wasn't quite right—and there wasn't a hunter among them. Just me, not my sister, my *older* sister. Her name—the name I remember her having—was Jeanette, and she went to my mother's people—*our* people—and I managed to forget all about her. I grew up not knowing until I was fourteen and everything came down on me like a November rain. We were all in Paris, right before the Crash, believe it or not; and once I'd woken up, the ones who tracked me were Europeans.

"They claimed me for their own; I've got a talent, a special *wyrd*. You've got it, too. We can follow a curse back to its root and moot it there, inside the mind that makes it, where there's never any mistakes. You know the problem with having a talent you don't understand? Everybody's nice to you. Everybody *wants* you, and you can't trust any of them. That's your problem, too, Emma—and it breaks my heart that I can't help you through it.

"I ran away from my father's people when I shouldn't have, and I ran away from the people I ran to later than I should have. I laid low. I was laying very low when I met Arch, your father.

"He thought of me as a child, I think—a waif of war—though I wasn't, of course. He said he'd take me back to America. I thought I'd be safer in America; I thought no one would remember. I was wrong about that. They found me quick enough and marked me—I swear to God, they marked me, your Redmond Longleigh, *he* marked me. Told me to take my time because he'd married my sister Isabel—the sister I'd known and forgotten as Jeanette—"

Eleanor paused for a bark of bitter laughter. When she spoke again it was in a calmer voice on a tangent to her earlier words: "Have you been to Paris, Emma?"

She nodded, stretching the truth a bit: She'd flown into Orly airport once, on a guided tour the university had sponsored: "The Footsteps of William the Conqueror." At the time, William hadn't bothered to conquer Paris; he wasn't interested in unimproved real estate. She'd seen the Eiffel Tower and the rooftops of Montmartre from the window of a bus.

"Bower it's not. I tried, Emma, I swear I tried, but I wasn't cut out to be a professor's wife. Arch knew it, I think, from the moment we got here. But Arch—Arch didn't make mistakes. No, that should be Arch didn't make mistakes he couldn't fix . . . or live with, come hell or high water. We didn't fight; that wasn't his way. His way was to find another way around the problem, not *solve* it, just find a way to get around it. A way to ignore it . . . me.

"I don't know where we were headed, but it wouldn't have been pretty, Emma. You weren't deprived of some smiling, happy *Father Knows Best* family. It would have been one of those quiet, walking-on-eggshells families—if we'd gotten that far. If they hadn't marked me.

"There were *incidents*. You told me that your rogue gave you an assistant you can't get rid of. Well, that was one clumsy, careless rogue. The usual rogue punches teensy little holes in your life, just enough to start an argument or make you wonder if you're going mad, until you *are* mad and the last thing you're thinking about is some damn rogue. That's when you see him face-to-face for the first time . . . standing beside your daughter's crib . . . and you think, just maybe, he's the man you've loved all along—

"I left you with your father, where you'd be safe, the way you wouldn't have been safe with me. And you were; so safe that Harry said he couldn't find you when we thought the time had come." Eleanor paused, shaking her head in private disbelief. "*Harry* couldn't find you! Call me a fool because I believed him. I wanted to believe him. *That* I apologize for, for wanting to believe the lies that Harry told me. For all the rest, I make no apologies."

Eleanor looked very young standing silently, defiantly, with the harsh, halogen light glaring off her two-toned hair. And maybe she was. Maybe bodies weren't the only thing that moving back and forth between the wasteland and the real world kept young. Maybe Eleanor was locked in an interminable adolescence. Maybe it was Never-Never Land and not the Netherlands.

"Any more questions? Do you want to know what I did during the war? How I kept myself alive?"

Emma shook her head. Not that she didn't have more questions, but she'd have to think about the story she'd just heard before she asked any of them.

"All right. I've answered yours, now you answer mine: What did that woman want?"

Em had a good memory for conversation, and she repeated the one she'd had with Sylvianne—the important parts, at least—word for word, right up to *adrêsteia*, at which point Eleanor began laughing.

"Oh, he's quite the scholar, that Redmond Longleigh. Wouldn't want anyone to know he started out a red-dirt farmer."

There was too much pot-calling-the-kettle-black in Eleanor's tone for Emma to resist. "Is he so much worse than the rest of us? As near as I can tell, Harry got his start as a war profiteer—Revolutionary War, that is, and Blaise was some sort of seventeenth-century confidence man and numbers runner before he got himself murdered."

Eleanor grimaced. "It's the company we keep, the job we do. Hang around with rogues and curses long enough and it can get hard to tell us apart. Hard, but not impossible. What else did *that* woman tell you?"

"She called me a plunger and said you could have been one, should have been one—"

That curled Eleanor's lips into a snarl, "Oh, she's a fine one to talk! Still looking for a talent that doesn't require a man or a machine."

"Really, Eleanor, Sylvianne just didn't seem that bad to me and definitely not someone who needed a man in her life. She's a pilot, for heaven's sake. Flew her own plane up here to give me the map personally—and had a few choice comments about Longleigh because he hadn't let me know she was coming. If anything, Sylvianne gave me the impression that if it weren't for her, the Curia would grind to a halt."

Faced with a choice between admitting Longleigh or Sylvianne's competence, Eleanor bit her lower lip and did neither.

"There was one other thing," Emma said quickly. "Before she showed me the map, she said something: 'The Skellings have to stick together.' Is there a family connection between us and her?"

"I believe I mentioned Red had married my sister—"

"Sylvianne!?"

"Is her daughter."

"My cousin?"

Eleanor nodded, "And an out-cross, like you, like me, like most of us. Something you should know, Emma: All that coming and going, it messes with your organs, makes it hard to get pregnant. You want a baby, you've got to stop crossing over and stay stopped until it's born. And sometimes even that's not enough. As any good dog-breeder would say: The blood's a bit thin.

"The doubles—the ones with *wyrd* on both sides of their family tree—they think they're better than the rest of us, but the truth is, all a daughter needs is a mother, all a son needs is a father. My sister thought Longleigh wouldn't notice so long as he was raising a daughter. No telling whether she made her own luck on that score. Truth was, Isabel and I might have been sisters, but I didn't know her. Only saw her, maybe, a dozen times, and she sure as hell didn't share her secrets with me. Her secrets were safe from everyone . . . until she died. Auto accident. Head-on at seventy-plus on one of those dark roads in the hills outside of Atlanta. No fixing that with a few pills or a quick slip to the Netherlands.

"She wasn't in the ground before the grieving husband found a diary in her bed table. Strange, don't you think, that Isabel would have left it in an unlocked drawer, where anyone could find it, after having kept her secrets so close for so many years? If you ask me, she never kept a diary at all. My sister was not one of those Southern literary ladies. Don't think there was a book in Atlantis that hadn't been printed before I was born. A bit hard to believe that she wrote one all by her lonesome." Eleanor aped a drawl.

"There was a scandal, as you may imagine, all very hush-hush. Sylvianne—she was about eighteen, between high school and college—found herself shipped out of Atlantis in the middle of the night. She stayed gone for a good ten years. Nobody dared mention her name, not where Red Longleigh could overhear. The man was mortified to think he'd been taken for a fool. And then, suddenly, she was back, calling herself Sylvianne Skellings and living at Atlantis. Neither she nor Red Longleigh tried denying what all had happened; they just ignored it. Sylvianne's a decent tracker, not that trackers aren't a dime a dozen. More important, she *is* her mother's daughter, and the Skellings line *is* known for its *wyrds*. Since they're not father and daughter, there's no reason not to try again for another Skellings-Longleigh cross.

"Rumor has it—and I believe the rumor—that Red offered a marriage contract and rumor has it, too, that she's holding out for more than he's been willing to offer, so far. And why not? There was no accident out on those Georgia hills; dear, sweet Sylvianne set the whole thing up. She uncovered Isabel's secrets—it's not hard, if you're willing to take the risks—and then she killed Isabel. She's had Red to herself, founder of the Atlantis Curia and the most powerful man in it. Her game works because she's had no rivals—until you showed up.

"You're a threat to her, Emma, and we've seen what Sylvianne does when she feels threatened. Last thing Sylvianne Skellings wants is for you to go into business with Red Longleigh. What she's asked you to do, what she really wants to know is how much of the Skellings *wyrd* did you get? God help you, Emma, but you've got it all, plus something from your father. Something that can't be measured in the Netherlands. God help you twice when you catch Redmond Longleigh's eye. You're the one he's been waiting for: a new breed."

The mother-voice whispered *Paranoia strikes deep* through the back of her mind, and Emma was inclined to agree. She aimed to put a stop to it—to the recitation of it—with a not so gentle reminder: "I'm no threat to anyone's dynastic ambitions. In case you hadn't noticed—and I imagine Sylvianne did; she struck me as the observant type—I can pass for Harry's wife a whole lot easier than I can pass for your daughter—no matter what age you happen to be passing for. I missed out on the fountain of youth, and my biological clock hasn't ticked for years—"

"You can change that—not overnight, but gradually—"

"Good grief, *Mother*, I haven't decided if I want to be fifty forever, but I sure as hell don't have any desire to turn myself into a brood mare! If my new-found cousin wants Redmond Longleigh's children—and from what I saw of her, that wouldn't be a foregone conclusion—then she can have him. And I'm perfectly willing to tell her that—"

"You can't be serious!"

"Watch me. I'm a child of the sixties, Eleanor. I don't believe in keeping secrets—which brings me to another question: What were you doing in Union *before* you totaled my car?"

Eleanor's mouth opened and shut before she said, "I had no idea I was in Union until it was too late. I was just taking a ride, looking at the leaves."

A lie, Em judged without any help from the mother-voice. The fall colors in Michigan weren't bad, but, by everything she'd ever heard, they didn't compare to the sugar-maple explosion of New England and the Hudson Valley where Eleanor had lived in her previous incarnation. She opened Sylvianne's map with a shake and let it drift to the carpet between her and her mother.

"See that circle? That's what Sylvianne came up here about. That's Longleigh's business proposal. Seems one of their watchers—someone named Pietro—spotted a curse zooming between here and the wasteland. Sylvianne called it a 'fast-cycler' and said that because it was fast, Pietro hadn't gotten a good fix on it, and rather than send in the Marines, Longleigh decided—since the circle's practically in my backyard—to ask me to check it out. You want to read the name of the towns inside that circle, the name of the one closest to the center of it?"

"Union," Eleanor said bleakly, without looking down.

"So, you knew?"

"I smelled smoke. I was out at the mall, looking at blankets and sheets and, suddenly, I smelled smoke, so I followed it."

Emma recalled the arson reports in the morning paper, but Union was an hour's drive away, closer to two hours. She shook her head, silently demanding a better explanation.

"All right, I smelled *Netherlands* smoke, Emma. After three months in those flames it's not a smell I'm likely to forget, now, is it?"

Emma conceded the point with a glum nod. "You can smell a curse from that far away? That's news to me. I didn't know we could *smell* curses."

"Not curses. Smoke. I'd never smelled it before—here, I mean. Or *before*. I didn't know what it meant myself, only that having smelled it once, I knew I had to find out where it was coming from, so I went back out to the car—your car—and started tracking it, pretty much the same as I would have tracked it in the Netherlands, only not as easy. I couldn't go straight at it; a car has to stay on the road."

"I guess you changed your mind about that once you got to Union." Em loosed the snide remark before she had the wit to censor herself.

"I was coming into the town. The smoke smell had gotten very strong . . . very thick, and, maybe, I was paying too much attention to it and not enough to the road—but I wasn't speeding. I'd passed the reduced speed signs and slowed down; I wasn't taking chances getting a ticket, not in your car and my identity suspended between Merrigan and Graves. Then I came around a curve and there was this dog in the middle of the road, standing there, staring straight at me, like he owned it. I couldn't find the damn horn, and there wasn't enough time to stop. I didn't want to hit it, so I hit the brakes, instead, and swerved onto the shoulder."

"What about the little boy?"

Eleanor grimaced. "There was only a dog—but, Emma, I swear, I was on the shoulder, getting past it, and there it was in front of me again. That's when I panicked, just plain panicked. If I'd been thinking, I should have pulled back onto the road, right? But I swerved to the right, into a *rock*, and woke up in a damn emergency room, covered in dust, hurting everywhere, and counting backward from ten. They told me I would've gone into a lake if I hadn't hit the rock! Thank God, I got my wits about me. A cop was right there, asking questions. They'd gone through my purse *and* the glove compartment. They had my name as Eleanor Merrigan—from my New York driver's license. The picture's so bad, they never questioned *that*, but they wanted to know why I was driving Emma Merrigan's car. I said we were cousins and that I'd borrowed your car to go antiquing—there's always an antique store in those little country towns. I didn't seem to be winning them over, so I made up the story about the little boy. I couldn't very well tell them that a *dog* had frightened me."

"I suppose not," Em agreed slowly. "Do you think the dog had something to do with the curse—maybe a warning?"

"A warning? Not to my knowledge. Curses aren't like that. It wasn't like the dog stank of Netherlands smoke. It was just a dog. Just a coincidence. For that matter, I didn't know I was tracking a curse—I mean, I didn't know where I was going or what I was going to find when I got there. An open door, I guess. Some kid with a *wyrd* he or she didn't know she had—like you would have been. Almost. I gave you a name; I would have heard you, if you'd kept it. Every few years someone comes along, out of nowhere. They leave a door open where it shouldn't be, and we have to get to them before the rogues do."

Emma nodded. She had a book at home—several handwritten copies of it, all bound in black leather—that purported to be the sum of curse-hunting lore. According to the book, there was only one way to make a rogue: A big, fiery curse got the better of its hunter and, for lack of a better word, *possessed* the curse-hunter's mind and real-world life. In practice, listening to Eleanor, Blaise, and even Harry Graves, there were so many other likely ways, so many questions they weren't asking about their *wyrd*. Redmond Longleigh's Curia had too many dilettantes, not nearly enough engineers.

"Sylvianne didn't say anything about left-open doors or kids with nightmares," Em mused, looking for a way to end the conversation and go home. She had the answers she'd come for and then some. "It could all be coincidence—" Emma didn't believe in coincidences, but maybe Eleanor did.

"There's only one way to find out."

"I know you've got a brand-new car and you're probably eager to drive it, but it's way too late to go hauling up to Union."

"Not drive, walk—you and me, together, through the Netherlands. That's the best way, whatever we're looking for. I—I didn't want to go it alone . . . in the Netherlands. That's why I took your car up there in the first place."

"You're—You're over the problems you were having?" Emma remembered her mother's last failed attempt to shift between realities. Eleanor had wound up in a fetal position on her daughter's living-room carpet whimpering like a whipped dog.

Eleanor dismissed Em's concerns with a sidelong glance. "For the two of us, together, it's a piece of cake, Emma. If I could smell that smoke here, it's bound to be stinking up the Netherlands. Union's close physically, not like chasing down something that got here from another continent; and we're only going back a few days—"

Whenever Emma heard that phrase, *piece of cake*, she always thought of Marie Antoinette and guillotines. Without enthusiasm, she asked, "What about crossing your path, your lifeline? That's the great no-no—"

"We won't be crossing paths. I never *got* to Union remember? All we have to do is be careful where—when—we come out of the Netherlands. You can slip out first and make sure we're not lined up on the edge of a road outside the town—look for ruts in the dirt, a honking-huge rock and white powder from that damned airbag. We'll see what's making that smell, and if it's Pietro's fast-cycler, so much the better!"

Emma met her mother's eyes and measured the reckless enthusiasm she found there. "No," she decided instantly, then grasped for a reason. "You're the one who's saying I can't trust Sylvianne. If you're right, there's no way it can be a good idea to go chasing after her curse. It could be a trap."

"She'd never expect you to move this quickly. And she doesn't know you have help. You didn't tell her about me? About me setting up housekeeping here in Bower?"

"No," Emma admitted, then repeated herself in a harder tone. "No, period. It's not a good idea. I'm not ready. I need to think about this."

"Fine!" Eleanor dropped precipitously to her knees and planted her hands on the map on either side of the circle. "I'll go myself. I need the practice."

"*Practice* is plinking the little stuff on the border between now, then, and forever after."

Their eyes locked, and as hard as Em tried to tell herself that she didn't care, as much as she believed Eleanor was old enough—more than old enough despite her appearance—to make her own mistakes, she couldn't let go.

"You can be my anchor," she offered, changing tack in a heartbeat.

The leather-bound book warned against rummaging through history without a trusted companion keeping watch over one's physical self.

"We'll go together!" Eleanor countered. "You don't need an anchor—"

Emma tried to object, but Eleanor cut her off.

"Only *beginners* need anchors, Emma. It's like anything else that comes with instructions—cell phones, bicycles, *pillows*—once you know what you're doing, the training wheels come off. Do you think everyone uses the buddy system like they hadn't left nursery school? Do you think Sylvianne Skellings waits for an anchor?"

The fact was that less than a year after her introduction to the curse-hunting life, Emma did treat many of the rules written in her leather-bound guides as training wheels to be stripped off and ignored. And hadn't Sylvianne implied that the Curia thought she could handle their business on her own? The blond pilot certainly hadn't offered herself as an anchor for Em's reconnaissance.

Em didn't need to say anything. Eleanor read capitulation from her daughter's eyes.

"Be right back," she promised and bounded for the stairs, ascending them two at a time, the way Emma had when she still lived on Teagarden Street, and hadn't in the decades since. She returned, breathless and beaming, with a teardrop-shaped vial in one hand and a virgin bottle of Scotch beneath the other arm. "All set!"

"You said you weren't going to do that anymore," Emma demurred.

She didn't want any part of her mother's curse-hunting methods. Eleanor used drugs to transport herself into the

Netherlands: alcohol, ideally in the form of a single-malt Scotch, and opiates she procured from who knew where or how. Emma's favorite way—visualizing a spinning coin and calling it in the air—took more concentration, more discipline, and that was the way she intended to keep it.

"You've certainly turned into one holier-than-thou purist. I do what works," Eleanor replied, draining her diet soda before pouring a few fingers of Scotch into the glass and topping them off with a half-dozen or so drops of dark liquid from the vial.

"You're the one who said that stuff made you hallucinate, gave you flashbacks to when the rogues had you."

"I got over it. Are you coming, or are you going to sit here on your thumbs? It's not like you've got to come down off your high horse; I'm not offering to share anything with you. Just swallow your pride and follow your mother."

And because her curiosity had gotten the better of her, Emma sat down on the north side of the map, opposite Eleanor, who sat to the south.

"Give me your hands."

Eleanor held hers out, and Em complied, noting as she did that her mother's were ice cold.

"You're sure about this?"

"I'm sure. On three. One . . ."

Emma envisioned her spinning coin.

"Two . . ."

It began to fall. She imagined reaching for it, imagined that it would be heads, and made good her prediction just as Eleanor said—

"Three."

Em hadn't traveled in tandem for months and not as a follower since Eleanor first reappeared. She didn't know what to expect when she closed her eyes, or, rather, she expected to feel disoriented and uncomfortable. Several moments passed before she grasped that the queasy feeling in her gut wasn't the result of her mother's leadership, but the complete lack of it. They hadn't come to roost in the wasteland but were drifting free in pearl gray nothingness. With a growl worthy of a very large dog, Emma tightened her grip on Eleanor's icy fingers and took command.

She envisioned the magenta sky and brought it into being, then did the same with the crescent-shaped slope beside the bolthole. A proper sense of gravity settled Emma's stomach but did nothing to calm her mother. Eleanor's thrashing nearly defeated Em's control. They landed hard, Emma on her knees and Eleanor on her rump. The way-back stone was close at hand, but the bolthole was nowhere in sight.

"What was the meaning of that, getting ahead of me?" Eleanor demanded once she'd sat up. "If I hadn't let go, we could have landed on our heads, gotten knocked unconscious or even *killed*."

Emma wouldn't buy that with a plugged nickel, but she bit her tongue and apologized anyway, then asked, "Smell anything?" She'd gotten a sense of the bolthole; it wasn't far off. Union could have been in any direction; that was to be expected in the wasteland. But there wasn't a hint of smoke wafting into her nostrils.

Eleanor insisted that the odor was strong and easily followed. Em suspected another round of bravado and deceit. She changed her mind after they'd walked about a quarter mile.

"You're right," she admitted between strides. "I can definitely smell smoke now. Sour smoke, like whatever's burning was rotten before it caught fire."

"Dead," Eleanor corrected. She stopped to scan the horizon. "It's death that's burning."

"Death?" Em asked, but Eleanor wasn't in an answering mood.

Without warning, Eleanor started walking again. Em broke into a sprint to catch up with her. They trudged along in silence for what felt like a couple miles.

Subjective reality be hanged, Emma was sure they'd

walked far beyond Union. The burnt odor had gotten stronger, but it remained a small part of each breath they took, and there was no sign of fire or smoke on any horizon. Stamina-wise, Emma was breathing easily. Her nightly sojourns with Blaise had walked her into the best shape of her adult life and, irregular as her wasteland arrival had been, she hadn't forgotten to imagine herself a pair of comfortably sturdy walking shoes and double-layered socks. Old habits died hard: Emma had outfitted herself with the brass laser pen, too. It was fully restored, but it had failed her once and she'd lost faith in it, which would make it a poor weapon in the wasteland's subjective reality.

Her mother, in contrast, was dressed exactly as she'd been in her living room, complete with a pair of thick-soled sandals never meant for long-distance walking. Eleanor's face was lock-jaw grim and growing tighter with every plodding step.

"We could slow down," Em suggested. "It's not a race, is it?"

"I don't understand," Eleanor admitted. "The wind's to my left, the glow's to my right, and we're walking straight along the absolute present. We should have been there an hour ago. That stupid town is less than a hundred miles from where we started. We could be in Rome, ancient or modern, by now."

"We haven't been walking for an hour—"

"Speak for yourself," Eleanor snarled. "*I've* been walking for hours. Three at least. My feet are so tired I can hardly lift them. I feel like I'm on a damned treadmill. We should have arrived by now. I should *know* that we've arrived."

Emma didn't argue; there was no point in arguing the details of subjective realities. They agreed on the important part: They'd walked far enough. They should have come to the place where the wasteland and Union converged.

"We're missing something," she decided. "Or our visions of Union are incongruous, not unified."

"That shouldn't make any difference." Eleanor sank to her knees. "Unless you've been challenging me as we go."

"No," Emma answered quickly, then added, "Not consciously."

Em didn't have any more faith in her mother's abilities than she did in the brass tube dangling from her wrist. When push came to shove, Emma Merrigan didn't have faith in much of anything outside of herself. In subjective realities, she made for a difficult traveling companion.

Emma glanced at the way-back stone and took her bearings from it, like a hiker who'd swallowed her compass. If Em had faith in her gut—and she did—the bolthole was to her right, not to her left where she'd expected to sense it.

"This is strange," she told her mother. "I've got a sense of the bolthole, but I feel like we've wandered onto the wrong side of the present."

"You shouldn't be getting a sense of anything. I said I'd take the lead. Stop challenging me! Let me lead the way. I know where we've got to go."

"Sorry." Emma could will herself to believe in Eleanor's abilities. All she had to do was close her eyes and imagine herself with her arms bound behind her back and a blindfold over her eyes. The way-back stone was gone when she reopened her eyes. "Lead on," she said, trying not to sound too grim.

Em wished she'd been looking somewhere else as Eleanor climbed to her feet, wished she'd seen something akin to confidence in her mother's expression. Despite misgivings, she followed, playing the part of a dutiful daughter.

The wasteland wasn't as flat as it looked. The parched ground rose and fell in waves that were many times wider than they were high. Gentle hillsides meandered from one horizon to another. Emma wondered—because she hadn't put a stranglehold on the engineering gene—if there could be a pattern to them, some giant message or cosmic joke, intelligible only from above. She wondered, too, if she could subjectively teach herself to fly. Mostly, though, she wondered why time did indeed seem to pass more slowly with Eleanor in the lead.

Perhaps it was related to the sense that they'd been climbing a steep hill for an eternity.

The uphill sense was all in Em's feet. To her eyes, the wasteland topography hadn't changed. Somehow Eleanor had created the subjective equivalent of an optical illusion—one of those tourist-trap "magnetic hills," where the road seemed to fall away in front of your car, but if you were to put the car in neutral and ease off the gas, the wheels began to roll the other way and you had the sense that you were rolling uphill. Emma and her father had spent a memorable afternoon exploring just such a magnetic hill in the Canadian Maritimes when she'd been about nine.

Illusion or not, Emma would have welcomed a parking brake for her ankles. "Hold up," she shouted at Eleanor's back. "I've had it. We're not getting anywhere, and my legs feel like Jell-O. It's time to head back to the barn."

"I don't—"

Eleanor was turning, but she lost her footing and the rest of her objection midway around. Emma watched in confusion as her mother's arms flailed and her body arched desperately uphill as though gravity could change its rules in the space of fifteen feet—and gravity, according to Harry Graves, was supposed to be one of those rare wasteland phenomena that *wasn't* subjective.

Then Eleanor's feet dislodged a fist-sized clod of dirt that tumbled toward Emma. It bounced cleanly between her legs and kept going.

Don't look back! Em thought in concert with her mother-voice. She didn't understand what was happening—didn't want to understand it, lest she become trapped in the illusion.

Eleanor shrieked, "Fire!" as her knees hit the ground. She grabbed dirt, but it didn't hold. The horrified expression on Eleanor's face said everything: She believed utterly that she was sliding feet-first into a flaming cauldron.

For a heartbeat, Em was sucked into her mother's perceptions, her mother's reality. The ground dropped beneath her feet like the trapdoor on a gallows. She began to slide.

No!

Emma refused to believe what Eleanor believed. Closing her eyes, she cast off her self-imposed restraints: The ground was *flat* and *solid*. There was no *fire*. And when she opened her eyes, the way-back stone would be within easy reach of her right hand.

Her imagination imposed itself on the wasteland's subjective reality for one and a half counts out of three. On the minus side, something very warm was sweating up her back, and the ground, though solid, was still a long way from level. But the way-back stone was exactly where she'd imagined it. Emma fell forward, wrapping her body around the rock. She reached for her mother, who was stretched out on her stomach, clinging to the dirt while slipping slowly, inexorably, toward doom.

"Grab on," she shouted and tried not to imagine the consequences of failure.

"I can't!"

"You can."

"I'll drag us both down."

"I'm holding on to the way-back stone. Grab my hand, Eleanor!"

Eleanor was beyond panic. She couldn't make herself move, even to save her life. Emma snaked around the way-back stone, clamping her knees inelegantly around it before extending herself in Eleanor's direction and wrapping her fingers around her mother's wrist.

"I've got you!" Em shouted, which was a bit of an exaggeration.

Once their flesh touched, the power of Eleanor's subjective reality was overwhelming, and that reality was of a bug being sucked down a drain. A heavy bug. Emma's arm was strained to its limit. She hadn't a prayer of contracting her shoulder or elbow.

"You've got to help, Mother. I can't lift you. You're going to have to haul yourself up my arm."

Eleanor's eyes widened, and her scream became a thin, terrified wail. Em felt her own strength ebbing. She didn't know how much longer she could hang on, then, without warning, Eleanor heaved herself against gravity and caught Emma's forearm with her free hand. With her eyes squeezed shut and every muscle screaming from strain, Emma relaxed her own grip on Eleanor's wrist and prayed for strength as Eleanor pulled herself toward the way-back stone.

"What now?" Eleanor demanded with one hand fastened to Em's shoulder and the other wound in her hair.

"Nothing. Just hold on."

Emma gave herself to the magic of imagination, and, though they tumbled wildly for several endless moments, she brought them safely home to Eleanor's living room. Em curled onto her side, gasping for air and waiting for feeling to return to her right side. Behind her, Eleanor sobbed uncontrollably.

Emma opened her eyes. Her arm was a swirl of bruises that threatened a long, aching recuperation. Her watch showed a few minutes after eleven. There was still time to catch the late news and weather.

Seven

"**I** *thought it* would be different this time," Eleanor whispered.

She'd accepted Emma's invitation and left her unfurnished home for her daughter's more comfortable one. Curled up in the corner of Em's sofa, she'd welcomed the soft warmth of a hand-pieced, hand-quilted quilt. Except for her hands and face, the shades of blue and lavender covered her completely. Her hands were exposed because they clutched a mug whose steam she inhaled deeply.

"Well, was it?" Em countered from her favorite chair. She'd changed into a sweatshirt and leggings, her not-for-work uniform three seasons out of four.

Eleanor sipped from the mug and immediately fell into a coughing spree. No wonder. The mug contained a double hot toddy—an inauspicious concoction of sugar, lemon juice, a splash of water, cloves, and two shots of Scotch, heated to perfection in the microwave and served with a cinnamon stick. Emma had mixed it up under protest. In her experience, which was undoubtedly more limited than Eleanor's, alcohol, especially steaming alcohol, never improved anything.

It was worth noting that whatever else had happened, Eleanor had reduced her swollen bruises to shadows.

"Yes and no," Eleanor croaked after mopping her eyes with a quilt corner. "I'd been practicing—I swear to you I had. I'd gotten so I could force myself across to the Netherlands and hold myself there for hours at a time. Walking was hard, but not too hard. If I kept my mind clear, I could do it. The smoke-stink should have made it easier to stay focused. When my thoughts wander, I attract curses."

Emma shook her head. "You didn't attract anything, Eleanor. It attracted you."

That remark brought another flow of tears down Eleanor's cheeks. It was disconcerting to watch her mother sob, an offense against the natural order of the universe, not to mention that tears stirred Em's latent guilt and threatened to become contagious.

"I don't know. It's not as if I were marching into some rogues' stronghold. I was just tracking the smell, keeping my head down and following my nose. If I can't do that much—? I don't know. I don't want to become one of the hunters who can't hunt."

More tears fell. Emma lowered the footrest of her reclining rocker. She knelt on the floor at her mother's side and took the toddy from her trembling hands—more to protect her quilt than from any excess of compassion.

"There's nothing more to do tonight. Why don't you head upstairs? I've cleared off the bed in the back bedroom. You said you slept well there. Tomorrow's Saturday. I don't have to go to work. We can talk some more and, maybe, get some more stuff for your house. That should be something pleasant to think about while you're trying to get to sleep."

Emma felt as though she were talking to a child rather than an adult . . . or talking the way Nancy talked to her mother, which reminded Em that her Saturday wasn't free and clear. She'd promised Nance that she'd visit Katherine at Meadow View. The way things looked, that was going to require a ride in Eleanor's purple car.

Eleanor jolted Emma out of her thoughts with a question: "Did you close the door?"

"You did, don't you remember? Closed it and locked it. I watched you."

"Not that door. The other door, the door to the Netherlands. Did you close it? We can't leave it open, Emma. You don't know what could come through."

As a matter of fact, Em did. Back in those turbulent days when she'd been uncertain of the difference between the wasteland and insanity, she had indeed left the undefinable door between her subjective and objective realities wide open. An armed knight of the tenth century had appeared in her living room, not far from the sofa. He'd threatened her with a sword that had been more massive than the one Blaise carried. She'd slain him—mooted him—on instinct alone; and since that time Emma didn't leave the wasteland without closing the door behind her.

"Don't worry. It's shut. Word of honor."

"But I opened it—"

"And I shut it. There's nothing to worry about. Nothing's coming through to hurt you."

They were less than an arm's length apart, close enough for Em to watch her mother's pupils widen with surprise, then contract.

"You've become quite the hunter while I've been gone," she said in a tone that was more astonished than argumentative. "Harry must be quite proud."

"Harry, Blaise, and you, too. I've learned from all of you, and sometimes I pick things up on my own. You can go to sleep knowing that we're not going to be invaded by ghosts or curses. I promise."

Eleanor managed a wan smile. "I knew from the moment you were born that you were going to be someone special."

"Not now, Eleanor. Just go to bed."

Eleanor reached for the mug, and Emma handed it to her. They said goodnight with neither hugs nor kisses. Em folded the quilt and busied herself in the kitchen until the upstairs plumbing was quiet and the light in the back bedroom had been turned off. Her bruised right arm was growing stiff and warm to the touch. She doubled her usual dose of ibuprofen and, with the cats following slowly behind, climbed the stairs for bed.

Except for her arm, which she propped up on a spare pillow, Em had no complaints as she turned out the lights. The day had thrown her several curves, and she'd handled them as best she could, better than she would have predicted had she known they were coming. She'd even saved her mother's life.

That bothered Emma more than her arm. Not the saving part; she could comfortably feel both smug and altruistic about that. What bothered her was not knowing how they had gotten into trouble and what, if any, connection bound the arsons in Union, the Atlantis Curia, and Eleanor's topsy-turvy gravity together.

A light, snoring sound from the end of the hall assured Em that Eleanor was sleeping. Had the clock not read 1:17AM, she might have sneaked downstairs to call Harry. He was always telling her to call whenever the need struck and, for all the secrets he kept, Harry deserved an early-hours awakening, but getting out of bed, now that she'd finally found a comfortable resting place for her arm, was too much effort.

Besides, it was time to find out if she could learn from her mother's example and do a little accelerated healing on her bruises.

The wasteland transition was effortless and uneventful. Emma found herself in a crouch on familiar dirt with her weight evenly distributed over her toes and fingertips, comfortably dressed, sensibly shod. The only discordant note came from the brass laser pen, once again dangling from her wrist.

One glance, even by eerie magenta light, assured her that her arm was restored to a uniform color. She balanced on the lip of the bolthole's crescent-shaped depression. The way-back stone was in its customary place. The door—the only door that mattered just then—opened to her touch, but no one was home.

From the doorway, Emma cast a thought at the table lamp, and a small flame leapt into being on the wick. Light fell on a sheet of thick paper folded into a tent on the table. Em recognized Blaise's bold handwriting from across the room and guessed that he was off chasing rogues until further notice.

For more than three centuries Blaise Raponde had kept himself busy and sane by mooting rogues; Emma couldn't expect, nor ask, him to give it up. Blaise's quest was actually a bit more complicated than an endless search-and-destroy-all-rogues mission. He lived—if that could be the right word for his existence—to moot one particular rogue, the blond seductress who'd murdered him. She'd turned up among the rogues and curses who'd held Eleanor prisoner, and it was the distraction of the duel between the two long-time enemies that had set Eleanor free.

But rogues were wily critters with more lives than a cat. The duel had ended in a draw, and Blaise still had his quest.

Reading Blaise's handwriting was a challenge. Unlike their conversations, which reached Em's brain as English, Blaise's letters were invariably in French, but not the tidy, follow-the-rules French she'd encountered in high school and college. Her lover took pride in the artistry of his script and the originality of his spelling. In his time, only priests and spinsters had worried about stringing letters together in a consistent fashion. When she'd complained of the difficulties, he'd replied that his letters were meant to be read aloud, and if she would simply read them as they were intended, she'd hear his thoughts as if they'd come from his own tongue.

So, read aloud Emma did and slowly decrypted the note. She learned that Blaise had indeed come across a rogue's handiwork and was determined to put a stop to its malignance. He begged Em not to worry; it was not a bold rogue, not the rogue who'd murdered him; and he expected no difficulty mooting it, once he'd found its equivalent of their bolthole. Blaise predicted he'd be back in a day or two—a subjective day or two, which might work out to be hours or weeks from Em's perspective.

Until his return, Blaise advised his beloved to be careful, to stay close to the present and to her way-back stone if she couldn't resist the urge to moot a curse or two. The eruption that had seared her hand had proved to be a harbinger of increased activity in the bolthole's vicinity. Blaise hadn't detected any rogues, but he'd encountered packs of fiery curses (he spelled them, variously, as *tours, tourres,* and *toureze*) vying against one another several times since their last meeting. Though the curses had seemed intent on cannibalism and had paid scant attention to his wanderings, Blaise warned Emma against getting near them because,

You have not yet chosen your new weapon, much less practiced with it.

Emma refolded the paper and stared at her wrist. Even a journeyman like herself knew better than to go curse-hunting with a weapon she no longer trusted. That meant no walking across the wasteland in search of a Union congruence or the curses her mother had found instead of Union, but it didn't mean Em couldn't poke around Union itself. The garden window could take her anywhere, anywhen, if she put her mind to it.

She scribbled in the wide margins of Blaise's note, wishing him success in his hunt and warning him that packs of fiery curses weren't the only problem in the neighborhood. Then she flipped the paper over and asked him to stay close to the bolthole when he returned. They needed to talk—she, at least, needed to talk to him, because the Atlantis Curia had come calling.

When the ink had dried, Emma blew out the lamp. She

went to the window where the view outside was as dark and featureless as her own reflection. She pressed the palms of her hands against the glass, but lowered them quickly after the laser pen, swinging freely from her wrist, chattered against the glass.

In theory, walking the past was less dangerous than walking the wasteland. Curse-hunters were like ghosts when they walked the past, and although Em had a talent for invading the minds of the people she encountered, she hadn't developed the skills necessary to interact with the past in a more tangible way. Although she felt real and substantial enough to herself when she went strolling through the centuries, she couldn't open a door or book or move any other object. On the plus side, while she was playing the part of ghostly tourist, nothing from raindrops to runaway horses could, theoretically, harm her. Even a curse, locked inside the psyche of its unwitting host, was unable to perceive her presence and was powerless against her.

The theory worked only so long as Emma encountered neither rogues nor fellow curse-hunters. The rogue exception was understandable; rogues were everything that curse-hunters were, only more so. They opposed one another with an intensity that only siblings—twin siblings—could rival. Emma had been surprised, though, when both Blaise and Harry warned her that when walking the past it was more dangerous to cross paths with a noncontemporary curse-hunter than it was to cross her own.

The camaraderie—not to mention the authority—of the Atlantis Curia was a new wrinkle in the fabric of time. Until the latter decades of the nineteenth century, curse-hunters had hunted one another as readily as they'd hunted rogues or curses; and alliances between hunters had been as fleeting as they were fragile.

Blaise Raponde, it turned out, didn't carry a sword to moot wasteland curses. The egg-sized lump of amber in the sword's pommel performed that job. He carried a sword wherever he walked, because he never knew which rival or relative he might encounter on the streets of Paris.

Emma couldn't quite wrap her mind around the paradox, but when she moved through the past, generations of curse-hunters, along with the usual assortment of lunatics, children, and small animals, could notice her passage. Worse, they could come after her, and she had only the vaguest notions—and a failed laser pen—with which to defend herself.

Em reached for the wrought-iron window latch but could not bring herself to grasp it. When it came to walking through time, an anchoring partner—or, at least, a well-armed partner—was a prudent necessity.

You're not looking for a rogue; you're looking for a curse, a plain-and-simple curse. And looking is all you're doing. Once you find it—if you find it—you're finished for tonight. The curse can't hurt you, and as close to the here-and-now as you're going to be walking, the odds of bumping into another curse-hunter or rogue are pretty slim. It's not as if Blaise's bloodthirsty relatives can walk forward from their time—

Call Nancy tomorrow; she'll be more than happy to play the part of anchor—

Nancy! Like a loose tooth, Emma's ill-conceived promise to visit Nancy's mother crept into her consciousness. She came within a heartbeat of retreating to the way-back stone, then shoved all her worries aside and opened the window.

A gentle breeze entered the bolthole, carrying with it a tang of charcoal and burnt plastic. In Emma's subjective realities, scents and sounds were often muted. It was a good sign that she smelled what Eleanor had smelled.

She stuck her head out the window. The charred odors strengthened, and, as her eyes adjusted to the faint, ambient light, she realized that her chin was only about eight inches above a burnt and sodden carpet. While Emma puzzled out the angles, drops of cold water fell on and through her head. The sensation, muted though it was, confirmed her suspicion: The bolthole's window had aligned itself with a closet where a fire had recently been extinguished.

Climbing and crawling, Em made her way into a burnt-out bedroom. A girl's bedroom, she thought, or a girl on the cusp of adolescence. By moonlight she saw among the black-scarred walls, tattered curtains, broken windows, and ruined furniture. The ceiling had collapsed, and the attic above had also burnt—Em could see a half moon through the rafters. A smaller hole opened between the closet and the foot of the bed. Emma skirted it carefully.

She'd thought of Union and the curse the Curia wanted her to moot; and the magic window had brought her to this place, this moment. By the cause-and-effect calculus of subjective realities, Emma assumed there had to be a good reason. She recalled the double arsons of the newspaper article. Was she standing in the middle of a crime scene or an accident? Had someone deliberately burnt a child and her family out of their home? Someone under a curse's influence? Or had an outright rogue drawn a bead on an innocent family?

Emma resisted the conclusions forming in her mind. The only thing she could be sure of was that she'd inserted herself into the aftermath of a fire, but even that didn't necessarily mean she'd inserted herself into Union, Michigan, much less tucked into one of the town's two arsons.

She eased around the hole again and looked out a window. The bolthole window hadn't transported Emma back to Bower. Bower had ordinances against keeping chickens inside the city limits, and she could hear a rooster crowing mistakenly at the moon. Judging by the uniformly dark color of the leaves and condition of a good-sized vegetable garden, she'd propelled herself back to the height of summer, maybe two months past, or fourteen months, or a decade of months. She took another look at the water-logged posters. The faces of pop idolatry were as good as tree rings when it came to establishing chronologies.

Em didn't recognize the pouty youth with the narrow, dimpled chin, but his dark hair was fairly short and worn in gelled spikes with bleached ends. Definitely not the eighties.

Emma had another reason to study the room. The way-back stone didn't follow her through history the way it followed her across the wasteland. Without someone like Nancy watching out for her, Em needed to take careful note of the exact place where she'd emerged from the window. There were other ways home, of course—curse-hunting was a bit like operating a personal computer: Anything that could be done, could be done in a variety of ways. If worse came to worst, Em could knock her time-traveling self unconscious and hope for the best—but her first choice would be a cautious return to the dripping closet.

Having learned all she could from the bedroom and imprinted the closet threshold into memory, Emma was ready to explore the rest of the house. One step into the hallway and it was apparent that, among the upstairs rooms, the girl's bedroom had taken the bulk of the damage. There was smoke damage and water damage in the master bedroom, but actual fire damage was limited to scorch marks on the wall that adjoined the girl's room. The other two bedrooms—a boy's room and a younger girl's room, if Em's Holmesian instincts were on target—weren't even wet, though they were smoke-stained and reeking.

The stairway was a mess. Firemen had better things to do than wipe their feet. At least Em assumed that the dark splotches on the light carpet were mud. She didn't want to consider any other possibilities, and the firemen had been in a hurry. The front door was off its hinges, lying on its side with a great hole battered through its middle.

Someone had made amends by tacking a sheet of heavy plastic over the open doorway. Emma touched it. She couldn't feel anything, and it didn't move. Blaise had the knack—the *wyrd*—for manipulating objects in the past. He made it sound as simple as sneezing. Em closed her eyes and tried again to follow his advice. She thought about meeting the edge of the plastic sheet with her fingers. The effort failed. She felt as though she'd thrust her hands into something soft, sticky, and warm; and, fearing that she would do herself real harm if she persisted, she backed away completely.

"Damn!" Em muttered and began looking for other ways out of the house.

She found them, too, in the form of broken windows. Each pane was framed with jagged shards, and try as she might, Emma couldn't pound them loose. Symmetry didn't exist in a curse-hunter's world. An inability to affect the glass didn't mean a shard couldn't disembowel a clumsy curse-hunter. At least Emma didn't believe the glass couldn't slice her skin, and belief trumped just about everything else when a curse-hunter wandered the timeline.

Em wandered the downstairs, hoping to find a less traumatic way out and learning more about the displaced family in the process. They kept their unpaid bills in a straw basket on a kitchen counter. Their last name was Pierson, first name, William, and they lived at 1412 Union Street in Union, Michigan. The Piersons took the local paper, but didn't appear to read it very thoroughly. A stack of perfectly folded papers grew beside the fireplace. They treated the magazines they got from their church more familiarly. There wasn't a chair in sight that didn't have a creased, dog-eared tract in easy reach.

The Piersons were a Christian family then, one that took its church-going seriously. They took their beer seriously, too. Between the empties piled beside the sink and the unopened cartons stacked beside the refrigerator, Emma counted thirty cans—and that, of course, was without opening the refrigerator door. The family had gotten their kitchen calendar from a snowmobile dealer and their coffee cups from Michigan State University.

Although there were those in Bower who'd say that all Michigan State fans were indeed cursed, at least during the football season, the truth was that as Emma had wandered through the house, she'd found nothing to indicate that any of its regular occupants harbored a curse.

The fire was suspicious, but it took more than simple bad luck or despair to create a curse. The usual ingredients included despair, futility, and simmering outrage, none of which were palpable in the burnt-out home.

Unless she died. Curses were freed when people died. If the girl in the upstairs bedroom had died in the fire, if her death had been particularly unpleasant, particularly pointless—and it was hard to imagine a child's death that wasn't pointless and unpleasant—then her dying thoughts could have become a curse. Newly released curses emerged into the wasteland as the easily mooted fingerlings. Emma's rare *wyrd* was tracking mature curses back through time and meddling just enough to thwart their creation.

Emma imagined a strategy: work her way along the time-stream a few hours, to a moment just before the fire started, and find a way to get the little girl out of the room. No death, no curse, it was as simple as that.

There were two problems with that strategy. Although her *wyrd* was supposed to give her the ability to consciously navigate up and down the time-stream, she had absolutely no experience doing it. The other, just as substantial, was that Sylvianne had called the Union curse a fast-cycler, implying that it had grown substantially beyond the fingerling stage.

The girl who'd slept in the burnt bedroom could have harbored such a curse. Emma's leather-bound books abounded in tales of mighty curses squeezing themselves into the psyches of innocent children, but the timing was off. She was looking for a curse that had taken possession of a mortal host, not one in the process of freeing itself and returning to the wasteland. If the girl who slept in the burnt-out bedroom was involved, then she was also alive.

Moreover, if the girl had been a long-term host, Emma

thought she should have sensed something malignant in the bedroom, and she hadn't.

There was still so much Em didn't know about curses. She had questions her leather-bound books didn't come close to answering. Only Harry seemed to care about her questions. Eleanor certainly hadn't last spring, and Blaise saw everything in theological terms. Even if Harry had had all the answers, he hadn't had time to share that knowledge with his stepdaughter.

Emma sat down in a kitchen chair—she could *sit*; she just couldn't *feel* the vinyl. She rethought everything she'd done, as if curse-hunting were a thorny math problem that would yield to pure persistence. Slowly she convinced herself she'd made her mistake at the very beginning, in the bolthole when she'd stood in front of the window. Sure, she'd thought about Union and the Curia, but she'd also been thinking about Eleanor's smoke and the newspaper's arson article.

Em became convinced that she'd jinxed the window. She was ready to return to the closet to write the whole misadventure off, when there was a commotion on the back porch that included several failed attempts to insert a key into the door lock.

Never mind that she was, in all probability, completely invisible and intangible, Emma wasn't one for taking chances. She hied herself into the room's deepest shadows beside the refrigerator and waited there, watching and listening. By their voices, Em concluded that there were two intruders, a boy and a girl, young, but not children. They were whispering, trying, Em supposed, not to attract attention, and failing as they punctuated their conversation with loud, nervous laughter.

The lock clicked, the door swung open, and a single, moonlight shadow on the spatter-pattern tiles preceded the pair into the kitchen. Rather than close the door, they wrapped themselves in a passionate embrace. Em asked herself if the pair were high and decided that while a can or two of beer might be involved, the primary culprit was hormones. They couldn't keep their hands off each other, and had she been as visible as Santa Claus on Christmas Eve, Emma could have walked past them without getting their attention.

A sixth sense, or maybe a seventh, had her thinking that the girl belonged to the house, maybe to the fire-scarred bedroom. When they unwound enough to walk, she followed them up the stairway. It didn't take a genius to guess where they were headed—there was only one double bed in the entire house—or what they intended to do when they got there.

Emma's memory of her own late adolescence was too strong to pretend outrage or even surprise. When she first went to work at the library there'd been a couch in the students' lounge that she couldn't pass without blushing. She'd been immensely relieved when the lounge furniture was replaced.

The pair disappeared into the master bedroom. Emma stopped short with one hand resting on the door frame of the girl's room.

Not another step, the mother-voice chided, and Em agreed. Curses or no curses, she wasn't a voyeur.

Her timing had indeed been off from the beginning. She'd learned a valuable lesson: If the bolthole window didn't line up properly with the past, there wasn't any point to climbing over the sill. She didn't intend to dwell on why the window had brought her to *this* moment out of the gazillions of moments of human history. The answer to that question would undoubtedly say more about her own conflicts and loneliness than Emma wanted to know.

Em turned right, into the girl's room, and made her way to the closet. The whole door frame shimmered in the moonlight. She approached it cautiously, piercing the plane with the tip of one of the less-useful fingers on her left hand. Where her eyes saw painted wood, her fingertip felt the bolthole's stone and mortar. She stepped across the closet threshold and lowered herself into the bolthole.

The bolthole was dark and quiet. Em made a light and checked the table in case Blaise had passed through. Her note was exactly as she'd left it. Convinced that she'd pretty much wasted the night, Emma knelt beside the way-back stone and opened her eyes again in Bower.

While Emma had been off chasing wild geese, her body had thrown the blankets and sheets aside. The oversized T-shirt she'd worn to bed was damp with sweat. She turned on the light. Both cats were hunched up on the cedar chest, broadcasting displeasure through narrowed eyes.

"Sorry, guys. It's not exactly a picnic for me, either."

Of all the times to come into her curse-hunting inheritance, menopause had to be the worst. The thought of spending years—decades—in the throes of hot flashes and night sweats was intolerable. One of these nights she'd take the plunge and reset her biological clock. Until then, she needed a glass of ice water and another T-shirt. The cats followed Em downstairs, hoping for a midnight—make that three AM—snack.

One swallow of ice water and Emma was shivering. She'd left a sweater hanging on the backdoor knob. Pulling it on, she noticed that her arm's restoration wasn't pure cosmetics. She'd gotten rid of the swelling, too.

How much more difficult could backtracking five years be?

"Plenty difficult," Em said aloud.

The best scientists in the world didn't understand how a woman aged, or why. Look at the raging debate on hormone replacement. Em had been on and off the little pills twice already. But clearly Eleanor had bathed herself in the fountain of youth, and Eleanor was no scientist.

Three AM was no time to make life-changing decisions. It was no time to be making any decisions at all. Emma turned out the lights and headed back upstairs. A noise—a groan, almost a cry of pain—from Eleanor's room snagged her attention. She tapped lightly on the door.

"Eleanor? Eleanor are you all right?"

No response. Emma waited, ear to the door, for another sound. She had her hand on the knob, ready to open the door, when a stray image of her father flitted through her mind. Nine times out of ten she could weather such stray memories without tears; this was the tenth time. Em turned her back on Eleanor, scooped up Spin, who was weaving around her ankles, and put herself to bed.

E*ight*

T*he next thing* Emma noticed was the aroma of coffee seducing her nose. She opened her eyes. The cats were gone, the sun was up—which at this time of year, a few weeks before the end of daylight saving time, meant she'd slept hours later than usual—and, no doubt about it, there was fresh-brewed coffee down in the kitchen.

When Em thrust her foot out from the bedclothes, she found that her room was frigid. The temperature must have dropped like a stone before dawn, and she'd forgotten to goose the thermostat on her way to bed. With an armful of fleecy, knock-around clothes, Emma dashed for the bathroom, where an electric heater kept her warm while she got ready to face the day and her mother.

Eleanor was sitting in Em's recliner, the quilt wrapped around her and both cats contributing their furry warmth to her comfort. She was reading through a stapled sheaf of white paper that Emma immediately recognized as her unfinished library-conference report. Em cleared her throat at the foot of the stairs.

"Morning."

"Morning," Eleanor agreed, brandishing the paper. "I found this beside the computer. Is this what you do every day?"

"Computers are the libraries of the future," Em recited on her way to the kitchen. "That's as true today as it was twenty-five years ago when we first started saying it. I firmly believe that nothing's going to replace the feel of a book in your hands, but a database of searchable information—not just titles, but the data itself—is our equivalent of the Holy Grail."

"Really? I thought your job was all about signing out books with date-stamps and putting them back on the shelves."

"Not hardly," Em replied, shelving all the other comments that came to mind. Eleanor must not have been paying attention to anything beyond her own rehab during the spring.

"But librarians do that, don't they?"

Emma poured herself a steaming mug of dark liquid. "Not if we can help it." She laughed then turned around to see the disappointed look on Eleanor's face. "I can go a week, easy, without laying hands on an actual, cataloged *book*." Her job was acquisitions, and she got to handle the books before they were cataloged.

Eleanor's expression grew darker. "I'm still trying to decide what I'm going to do. I thought working at a library might be nice. I like to put things back where they belong."

Em contained her surprise. Eleanor was the least-likely librarian she'd met. And as for putting things where they belonged, not only were the coffee and the white-paper filters still sitting on the kitchen counter, so were the measuring spoons and a loaf of bread.

"If that's what you want, you can almost always get a part-time job shelving. We go through a ton of undergrads each year trying to keep the books shelved."

"But would a part-time job be a good way to start becoming a librarian?"

Emma shrugged. "No better than herding burgers for McDonald's is for a would-be chef. Let's face it, the days of working up from the bottom are over. There's no escalator out of the mail room or off the shelving cart." Never mind that she'd started out shelving books. Libraries, like everything else, had changed dramatically since the sixties. "If you're really interested, the U's put together something it calls a library-science degree, but there're better programs around. I recommend the one at Wisconsin."

"What's the pay scale like? Does it pay well?"

Eleanor had transformed more than her appearance. She'd done a remarkable job of capturing the economic pragmatism of the current crop of undergraduates.

"Well enough. You won't get rich, if that's what you're planning on. No cash payments for houses or cars." Emma retreated into the kitchen. "By the way, thanks for making the coffee. Did you find yourself something for breakfast?"

The answer was obvious, but Em was determined to overlook that. She opened the refrigerator for inspection. Eleanor hadn't answered, so she pulled out a single English muffin and slid it into the toaster oven.

"I've been thinking," Eleanor announced from the kitchen doorway.

Emma startled backwards. It was a good thing her hands were empty. "I didn't know you were there."

Eleanor ignored her daughter's embarrassment. "I've been thinking about your car situation. You need one, and it's my fault you don't have one. And you need a decent car. Not that your old one wasn't decent; you'd taken very good care of it, but, when I bought mine, I asked the salesman what the trade-in would be on your car, and, even if it had been driveable, you wouldn't have gotten very much. In fact, they politely suggested that you donate it to a charity and take the tax write-off."

"I knew that, Eleanor. I've been saying for years that I was going to drive that car into the ground. It turned out a little more literal than I'd planned, but—"

"But here you are, needing a car when you hadn't expected to be. Out of the blue you're looking at a choice between paying cash for a clunker like Matt drives or putting yourself in debt. I feel badly about that. Very badly. I want you to have a reliable car—a new car, and I'd like to give you the money for it. It's what mothers do for their children, when they can. I don't know what you had planned for the day, but let's go out looking."

Em's emotional needle got stuck between astonishment and outrage. "I—I can take care of myself, Eleanor. I'm not poor." She'd managed her finances reasonably well. "If I really wanted a new car," she said defensively, "I could go out and buy it, cash on the barrelhead. But I don't want a new car. A used car will do me just fine."

"Then we'll look at used cars."

The toaster popped. Emma fumbled the steaming hot muffin onto a plate for buttering. "I'll get a car when I'm ready!" she snapped.

"I'm only trying to help!"

"I know. I know." She reined in her irritation at Eleanor and the hot, crumbling muffin. "It's a big decision. I've got to do some research first."

"There's another Integra—"

Emma swore as a chunk of the muffin broke off and melted butter stung her fingertips. "You've been talking to Harry!"

Eleanor writhed a bit. "He left a message last night. I got it this morning when I turned my cell on. He said the car he'd told you about was gone, but another had popped up in its place. It's the same year but with lower mileage, and right here in Bower. Think of it as a gift, Emma. A gift of fate, and from me—"

"I don't want, or need, a gift from you."

"Fine!" Eleanor shouted. "But you still need a car. At least let me drive you around to the local dealerships." It was hard to be persuasive at the top of your voice, and Eleanor wasn't. "Your car's dead, Emma. Totaled. I killed it. Please, let me help you replace it."

Em chewed her muffin with great determination, swallowed, and said, "Come Monday, I'll have studied the papers and maybe the Internet; Nancy and Matt will both be back in town; and one of them will help me make the rounds."

"It's me, then. Because you blame me for everything. I'm trying to start over, but please, Emma, please, meet me halfway."

"There's no starting over. You can't go from being a kid one minute who's asking me about college majors to being my mother and buying me expensive presents. Hell, Eleanor, you couldn't buy me a car if we'd been face-to-face every day of my life. Dad couldn't. I've been taking care of myself for quite a while now, thank you. I'll go car shopping on Monday. In the meantime, I've got plenty of food in the house. I don't need—"

But Em did need a car. The promise she'd made to Nancy popped out of her mind's shadows. She didn't want to visit Katherine; that's why Emma could forget the promise as soon as she'd remembered it again. Nance would understand. Nancy had infinite understanding, which was all the more reason Em would have to get out to Meadow View.

"What's wrong?" Eleanor demanded.

"Nothing."

"Don't 'nothing' me. I know that look. Something struck you. Something's bothering you. What? Was there something you were supposed to be doing today? Let me help!"

Em's coffee hadn't percolated to her brain, and she was still operating at midnight speed. She didn't have the energy for, or an interest in, arguing with her mother. "All right, you win. Yes, there's something I need to do. Nancy and John are in Ohio visiting Alyx, and I promised Nancy that I'd visit Katherine while she's gone. I need a ride out to Meadow View."

Her tone hadn't exactly been gentle, but it wasn't nearly nasty enough to account for Eleanor's sudden pallor. She sipped from her own coffee mug with an expression that said she wished it were something stronger. Lowering the mug, Eleanor said, "All right. I'll drive you out there, but I won't set foot in that place. I'll wait in the car. Fair enough?"

Emma swallowed another bite of buttered muffin. "Fair enough."

An hour of showering and dressing passed before the two women met at the bright purple car. Eleanor pushed a button or two on her new key-ring controller. Locks clunked, lights flashed, and the car emitted a cartoon-ish beep. Em lifted the door latch and got in, with Harry's description of a crayon-colored kids' car, echoing in her head.

Eleanor didn't know the way to the nursing home. No great surprise, she hadn't been conscious either when she arrived or when she left. Em provided the navigation, first to Kroger's for an assortment of fresh-baked cookies (never visit a nursing home without gifts for the staff: That had been Emma's policy while Eleanor languished on the sixth floor, and she saw no reason to change it merely because Katherine Neeley dwelt in more freedom on the third), then on to Meadow View Manor. During the journey, Eleanor mistook the windshield wiper lever for the turn signal just once.

The Meadow View parking lot was nearly empty—Sunday, not Saturday, was the big visiting day. Eleanor pulled into a parking space that left the car pointed away from the building.

"I won't be long—a half hour at the most. The mall's right down the road. If you'll be more comfortable, why don't you do a little window shopping and pick me up in, say, forty-five minutes?"

"You trust me to come back?"

Emma couldn't tell if the remark was Eleanor's attempt at humor. If it was, it failed. She shrugged and said, seriously, "I trust you to do what you want. I hope that means you'll be waiting for me when I come out again."

With Eleanor's stunned expression burnt onto her retinas, Emma closed the car door. She trudged into the Meadow View lobby, weighed down by anger that she directed at herself. Gaining a mother had turned her into a sulky teenager in a way that two divorces never had. Her timing was off, and her instincts. Whatever Eleanor did, Em did or said something to make it worse.

Since 9-11, security had tightened even at assisted-living facilities. It seemed ludicrous, yet, short of a nursery, what other terrorist target would strike the American heart so deeply? Emma obediently signed a guest book and walked through a metal detector on her way to the elevators.

Katherine lived on one of the mid-level floors where the residents were free to wander, so long as they didn't leave the building. On the advice of the staff, who said, in so many words, that Katherine regularly reduced her roommates to tears, Nancy paid a supplement so her mother could have one of the private rooms at the ends of the corridors. Em would have been very surprised to find Katherine anywhere other than the chair between her bed and the window.

Emma raised her hand to knock on the open door, but there was no need. Whatever was wrong with Katherine, it was subtler than Alzheimer's. She recognized Emma and invited her in cordially. It was only when they began talking, when Katherine began a tale of the abuse she suffered at the hands of her daughter, the other residents, the staff, and the world at large, that the deterioration in the woman Em knew best as "Mrs. Neeley" became uncomfortably apparent. Em couldn't vouch for the staff or the world at large, but she knew Nancy had only done the best she could for the woman who had become as much a stranger to her as Eleanor was to Emma.

After twenty minutes Em thought she'd stayed long

enough, listened long enough, but Katherine wasn't ready
to let her visitor escape. She led Emma to a closet, where
her clothes were hung haphazardly on crochet-covered
hangers and piled to ankle depth on the floor. Seizing a
robe of deep burgundy fleece, prominently labeled with
another resident's name, Katherine jabbed the hanger into
Emma's ribs, hard enough to hurt.

"See this?" Katherine jabbed again; Emma forced herself not to flinch. "Jimmy gave it to me for my birthday."
Jimmy was Katherine's husband, dead these last twenty
years. "You keep it for me, Emma," she insisted. "If that
so-called daughter of mine sees it, she'll just take it away.
Just take it away same as she takes everything that's mine.
You keep it, and I'll tell you when to bring it back. Jimmy
and I are going to run away, you know. He's got a car, and
a house with servants, and a pool."

Helplessly, Emma took the robe and made the hollow
promises. She returned the hanger to the closet pole. As far
back as Em could remember, Katherine had crocheted covers for her hangers, even the cheap wire ones she got from
the dry cleaner.

Eleanor will never come to this, Em thought as she retreated toward the door. *I don't ever have to come to this. I
have the power. I'd be a fool not to use it—whatever the
cost.* She made her good-byes and stopped at the staff station, which, on this residential floor, was tricked out like a
concierge's desk. "I found this in Mrs. Neeley—I mean in
Katherine's room." Everyone except the doctors was on a
first-name basis at Meadow View; it was just another layer
of indignity disguised as community. Emma draped the
robe across the desk. "I don't think it's hers."

The young woman held it up by the shoulder seams,
read the label, and shook her head. "That little devil—"

Em doubted that Katherine had ever been called a "little devil," even in the wildest moments of her childhood.

"We try to keep an eye on her, but she's quick, like a kid
in a candy shop." The staffer folded the robe and laid it

atop a pile of other, presumably misallocated, garments. "She's not the only one. They all take from each other. As much as Katherine's got in her closet, I can think of three other ladies who've rummaged through hers. The poor dears, they get so confused. I tell the families, don't leave valuables here, and, when you're buying clothes, best get one-size-fits-all."

Emma gritted her teeth and smiled. *I will never come to this.*

Eleanor was waiting when Emma escaped into sunshine. By the looks of things, she'd remained in the parking lot the whole time.

"How is she?" Eleanor asked before Em fastened her seat belt.

"Failing, but she doesn't know it. She thinks her dead husband's going to take her away from here . . . in a silver carriage, no doubt."

"That bad?"

When Emma didn't bother answering, Eleanor asked another question. "Do you see any floor mats in here?"

Em glanced down at her feet. "No—should I?"

"I've been reading my owner's manual, and it says I should have driver's side and passenger floor mats. I've looked in the trunk and under the seats, and I couldn't find them. I called the local dealership and asked if they had them, and they said, unless I'd bought the car from them, floor mats cost thirty-five dollars *each*! Do you believe that? So, I've got to go all the way back to Union to get the floor mats they should have given me when I bought the car."

"Floor mats," Em mused. True enough, floor mats were usually standard with a new car, and she didn't remember seeing one when she'd first sat down, but did Eleanor truly believe Em would buy the idea that floor mats were the reason she wanted to go back to Union?

"What else is on your docket?" Eleanor continued undaunted. "If you've got a couple hours to kill, the trip up to Union is an almost-pretty ride. The trees are turning colors, not like New York, but still pretty; and I promise I won't hit any dogs or kids along the way."

Emma had a car search to conduct, a refrigerator to clean, frost-stricken annuals to dig out of her garden, and a library association paper to finish. Any one of those projects could swallow the rest of the day, but the fact was that her own substantial curiosity had been roused and she wanted to see the town named Union.

"I'll hold you to your promise," she said, with what she hoped came across as good humor.

Eleanor positively radiated good humor from the driver's seat. "Great! There's so much we have to talk about."

Em couldn't stop a cringe, however faint, from freezing her body. "Let's steer clear of the big stuff, all right? No family secrets, great revelations, or soul searching; or, especially, anything about last night, including any *other* reason to drive up to Union—all that's off limits, okay? Let's focus on the ordinary stuff, like, what's your all-time favorite movie? I know you like Cary Grant."

They'd watched *Bringing up Baby* several times during Eleanor's rehabilitation months, once Eleanor realized Emma had it on tape.

Without missing a beat, Eleanor replied, "*Titanic,*" and gunned the purple car out of the parking lot.

"*Titanic*!?"

"That scene on the ship when she's standing in the bow and the wind's blowing around her and the voice-over says that the sun never saw the ship again. And near the end, when she lets Leonardo go, and he sinks to the bottom of the ocean. I cried for her, I really did. I never cried for Scarlett O'Hara. What's your favorite? Nothing romantic, I'll bet."

Emma stared out the window. There were, she realized bleakly, no *small* revelations. She couldn't stop herself from thinking that Eleanor would have seen *Gone with the*

Wind in its first-run release and that *Titanic* was an utterly appropriate choice for someone in her early twenties.

"No fair picking and choosing. What really comes to your mind?"

"Richard Lester's version of the *Three* and *Four Musketeers,*" Em admitted.

"Well, that explains Blaise Raponde, doesn't it?"

Em couldn't think of a suitably witty or evasive response to that.

"Sorry," Eleanor said after a moment's silence. "I didn't think that was a family secret, or a great revelation." She turned on the radio, perhaps for the first time, as static filled the speakers. "Find us a station."

There was disaster potential in that request, too. Emma tapped the seek-scan button and stopped the search when classic sixties rock filled the car. She'd read someplace that sixties rock had become the new generic sound in offices and construction sites alike. Apparently the Beatles and Stones were acceptable across genres and generations.

The choice seemed to work. Both women nodded along to the tunes, even sang a few choruses together. Then the reception faded, and Em went sound hunting again. Deep in the Michigan interior the best she could do was a scratchy Public Radio station that quickly switched from symphonies to talking heads.

"I wish I had my CDs," Eleanor announced without warning. "I always had about ten of them in the car with me. Lots of jazz and R-and-B. You'd like them, I think. I'll have to have Harry—oops, I shouldn't have said his name, should I?"

Grimly silent, Em tapped the seek-scan button again, this time settling for a call-in show focused on Big Ten football, but from an East Lansing, rather than a Bower perspective.

"Tight ends, lone ends, strong safeties, weak safeties, scatbacks, *wolfbacks!*" Eleanor muttered. "Either the game's changed, or I've forgotten everything Ar—everything I ever knew about college football. What are they talking about?"

Emma overlooked the near slip of Eleanor's tongue. It would have been difficult to live in Bower and not know how the game of football evolved from one season, one Saturday, to the next. From August to January, football was the subject of every other workplace conversation at the library.

Back in the sixties, when communication between father and daughter had been treacherous, football had been a rare and precious "safe" dinner-table topic. Archibald Merrigan had flown the school colors on game days and made certain that his offspring—and apparently his wife—learned how to follow the game. Em could go on for hours, if necessary, about the pluses and minuses of each Big Ten school, and most of the perennial top-twenty schools, too.

One hour, though, was enough. One hour brought them to the first signs of Union—a billboard for the purple car's auto dealership and a green, rectangular sign advising that the town was eight miles distant. Eleanor pulled off the road and lowered her window. She took a deep breath of pre-Union air.

"It's still here," she said with a hint of triumph. "Roll down your window. What do you smell?"

Though it broke the rules of engagement, Emma did as asked and reported, "Air, nice clean autumn air."

"No smoke?"

Em shook her head, but left the window down when Eleanor got the car moving again. The air was clean and fresh smelling, until they got closer to the town center. Even then, Emma wouldn't have said that she smelled smoke or any other burning smell, only that the freshness was gone. The air was flat, the way it got in underventilated rooms or in the wasteland. She said nothing, preferring to watch Eleanor make all the first moves.

They came to a fork in the road. Eleanor unhesitatingly chose the right branch over the left. Emma thought Eleanor was following her nose, but it was merely the route to the car dealership, which was closed and deserted. Apparently, rural dealerships had yet to embrace all-day Saturday hours.

"The nerve!" Eleanor complained. "We've come all this way for nothing!"

"We could have called ahead," Emma countered, though Eleanor wasn't the only woman in the car with a cell phone. Emma could have used hers and hadn't.

Eleanor steered her car back onto a two-lane road that was almost as empty as the dealership. "I'm starving," she announced as she turned the car toward downtown Union. "Let's find someplace to eat!"

"My treat, for my share of the gas," Em heard herself reply.

She doubted there would be a Union restaurant where the most expensive item would cost more than a half-tank of gas. They'd be lucky if they found a first-tier fast foodery. More likely they'd be choosing between Dairy Queen and the handful of other franchises that specialized in rural markets.

The obligatory Dairy Queen stood at one end of Union's main drag—three blocks of faded brick-fronts, hearkening back to the days before Interstates, and perhaps before gasoline engines. Eleanor had begun to turn into its moderately crowded parking lot, when she spotted an un-franchised eatery calling itself "The Mason Jar" on the other side of the street.

"Let's go there instead! Is that all right?"

Given a choice between char-grilled cardboard and a long shot, Emma agreed to the long shot. She passed on the house specialty—chicken-fried steak—opting for a traditional cheeseburger instead. Eleanor surprised both her and the waitress by ordering old-fashioned, homemade meatloaf and "smashed" potatoes ("Our lumps come from real potatoes, not powder") and coffee.

"Do you have any idea how difficult it is to find *good*

meatloaf," Eleanor explained when they were alone, sipping vaguely metallic water from Mason-jar glasses.

"Do you have any idea how few twenty-somethings *care*? Jay-Jay and Lori would eat meatloaf when I made it for them, but they're strictly burgers, fries, and soda when it comes to restaurant menus."

"Really?" Eleanor asked, and they discussed the habits of Emma's stepchildren until a silent, unhappy-looking youth brought the food to their table.

Em found her burger acceptable, despite its air-bread bun and the dollop of mayonnaise crowning the scarcely melted American cheese. Eleanor did little more than sample her meatloaf and creamy mounds of "smashed" potatoes.

"What's wrong?" Em asked.

From her side of the table, the items didn't look particularly appetizing, but meatloaf was a resilient entree. Em couldn't imagine one she couldn't eat, assuming that Eleanor was as hungry as she was. She'd already downed half her burger.

"How can you eat? Can't you smell it?"

Em set the burger down. "Smell what?"

"The smoke. It came on with that boy. He's *involved*. He's been somewhere, knows someone carrying the smell of smoke."

"I've got to tell you, Eleanor, I don't smell anything I shouldn't."

Eyes closed, Eleanor pressed herself against the booth's back cushion. "It's fresh," she whispered. "There's been another one. I'm sure of it."

Em did the same. She took a deep breath, then shook her head. "Sorry, there's nothing."

The waitress who'd taken their order, concerned, perhaps, by their yoga-esque antics, stopped over to check if everything was all right.

Emma Merrigan was not one for complaining in restaurants. "Yes, everything's fine. The food's great," she replied quickly. Most likely she'd have said the same thing if the food had been moving on her plate.

Eleanor, however, was eager to question the Union natives. "Has there been another fire?" she asked without preamble.

"You mean another arson fire like the ones they're investigating? No, but a barn burned down overnight, just outside of town. Don't really know whose barn it was. It was empty. Nobody got hurt, and they just let it burn down to the ground. I was talking to Ray a little while ago—he's with the sheriff's office—he didn't say anything about arson, but it's not like an old barn should just burn down, you know. If you ask me, it's someone who's got a grudge against the whole town."

That was more information than Emma truly wished to have, but Eleanor wouldn't rest until she'd convinced the waitress to find out where the burnt barn had stood. The waitress, who looked young enough to be in high school, disappeared into the kitchen.

"This isn't good," Emma hissed across the table. "You're attracting attention: two strangers, passing through, asking about arson. They've got Detroit cops out here investigating."

"Well, that hardly puts fear into my heart. From what I hear, half their city's burnt down. Besides, it'd be different if you were doing the asking. I'm *relating*."

Emma let her eyes roll. She stabbed a French fry with her fork and chewed it with unnecessary vigor. The girl returned.

"I'm still not positive, but probably it's out on the old mill road, you know where that is?"

When Eleanor admitted that she didn't, the waitress retrieved a much folded and stained map from beside the cash register. Apparently people got lost a lot in Union. Emma said nothing, while Eleanor and the waitress discussed routing. She asked for the check once they began folding the map. Two young faces gave her no-adults-allowed looks.

"I'm just along for the ride."

"I would have covered the check," Eleanor huffed on their way to the purple car.

"You're good, Eleanor. You've got the look and the style down cold, but twenty-somethings *always* let their parents pick up the check."

That earned Emma another sharp-edged look. Without warning, she turned and marched toward a gas station convenience store, the most modern building apparent in downtown Union. "I need one of those maps."

Armed with the map and a copy of the town's weekly newspaper, now three days old, they headed across the railroad tracks in search of Midland Road, which Eleanor insisted was known locally as the old mill road. They were about two miles north of town when Emma, not meaning to be helpful, spotted a dirt road with fresh, deep mud-ruts and a side-swiped sign that read: Mill Road.

The little purple car got its baptism of dirt while creeping down the road to an old gate and raw ruins beyond it.

"I can smell it now," Em conceded.

Eleanor scowled, turned the ignition off, and got out. She started through the open gate.

"I really don't think that's a good idea," Em called after her, pointing at the light green "POSTED" signs tacked to the gate and every post leading up to it.

"We're not hunting," Eleanor replied with a word that had hidden meanings. "We're just curious."

"We're curious about a crime scene."

When she'd been twenty-two, when it had been the sixties and she'd been fresh out of college, Emma could have taken the lead along the grass-striped road leading to the barn. With thirty years of respectable adulthood under her belt, Em veered instinctively toward caution. She stayed by the car, at least until Eleanor walked through the burnt-out doors and didn't immediately reappear, then she jogged up the muddy tracks.

Eleanor stood in the midst of the char, surrounded by crashed lumber and unidentified objects. Her head was bowed, as if in prayer.

"Eleanor!"

"Help me—"

Em ran and seized Eleanor by the wrists. She pulled toward the door. Eleanor resisted.

"Can you catch sight of them? I think I can, then they disappear. Help me—"

Before Em could shake her head, she became aware of distortion in the air around her, not unlike a double-exposure effect from a low-budget special-effects movie. There was one barn—the real-world barn—with its charred, but thoroughly dampened, timbers, and there was *another* barn—the special-effects barn—a little displaced, a little out of focus, with flames shooting up its walls like fireworks. The combination of the two left Emma light-headed and off balance. She clung to Eleanor more for support than to lead her out of the barn, though getting out was the topmost thought in her mind. She got one foot behind the other and pulled.

"Let's get out of here!"

Her voice seemed to be coming from someplace other than her mouth. Worse—far worse—the *other* barn, the burning barn—was coming into clearer focus. Although nothing remotely similar had ever happened to her, Emma leapt to the conclusion that she was slipping directly into the past—a conclusion that was strengthened not only by the heat she now felt, but by the silhouettes moving beyond the flames.

"Can you see them?" Eleanor asked. Her voice was where it should be, an arm's length from her daughter's ear, but her face was blurred at the edges.

"God, yes—" Not only could Emma see them, she was attracted to them like one magnet to another, and the only thing keeping her out of the flames was her hold on Eleanor's wrists. "We've got to get out of here! Quick— we'll be drawn into the fire!"

Emma pulled again, and this time her mother didn't resist. They moved in lockstep until they cleared the barn's threshold, then Em let go. She bent over, coughing mightily and expecting to see clouds of smoke emerging from her mouth.

Eleanor pounded Em's back. She meant well, but the pounding made it harder for Emma to breathe. She wrested away and staggered to one of the boulders lining the rutted tracks between the barn and the car. The harder she tried to catch her breath, the harder breathing became.

"Fire, Eleanor—" Em said between gasps. "Too close. I inhaled—"

Eleanor dropped to her knees. She took Emma's face between her hands. "Nonsense! You listen to me: That's *nonsense*. You were right here; you never left. There was no fire. Do you hear me? Look at me, Emma—" She got so close Em could see little besides her mother's green eyes. "There was no fire."

Eleanor's hands were like a vise against Em's cheeks. She didn't have the air to say no or the strength to shake her head. More to the point, Em wasn't an utter fool; she knew what her mother was trying to accomplish.

"Emma, whatever you saw—whatever you *thought* you saw, it was all in your imagination. Tell me that, Emma. Tell me you didn't inhale fire."

"No fire," Em agreed. "It wasn't real." Her throat was already relaxing. "And not a figment of my imagination, either." She pushed Eleanor's arms away. "I was falling into the past, Eleanor—the way we did in the wasteland, but there was no wasteland. How the hell can that happen?"

"You're stronger than me," Eleanor admitted, getting to her feet and backing away from her daughter. "I can see what I'm looking for, sometimes, if the time's short—a couple days or less. But that's it. I can't interact with them. I can't *plunge*, even if I wanted to."

"Even if?"

Eleanor wrung her hands together. "I never get away clean. I wind up dragging something of *them* along with me, and they're cursed, you know. They've got the pain inside that's going to make a curse. I don't *change* anything, not the way you can do; I just draw it into myself."

"That's what makes you run away," Em said thoughtfully.

Eleanor looked away, and Em stifled the remainder of her conclusion regarding how her mother had come to be the woman in front her.

"You're stronger than me," Eleanor repeated. "I shouldn't be surprised. I'm not, really. I thought I'd be in the lead, for once. But it's easier to follow. It's almost a relief."

The shadow of a cursed barn was no place for confessions. Em forced a grin and said, "You can lead wherever you want, so long as it's not back into that fire."

"We should drive through the town. I imagine that whoever set this fire is local."

Emma was amenable. Now that she'd escaped the dangers of her imagination, the engineering gene's curiosity once again had the upper hand in her mind.

"Tell me if you sense something," Eleanor said some fifteen minutes later when they'd begun their exploration of Union's streets. "Smell, taste, anything at all out of the ordinary. I'll trust your instincts."

But Em's instincts were dormant, or in hiding. She couldn't pick one street over another and had settled back, looking out the passenger's window when Eleanor hung a right.

"I can smell it again," she said. "Can't you?"

Emma shook her head, a gesture lost on Eleanor, who asked, as they neared what appeared to be the last intersection in this part of town, "Right or left?"

"Left," Em replied, because *left* was the word that had popped into her mind.

Left proved the correct direction. They hadn't gone a hundred feet beyond the "Dead End" sign when the short hairs on the back of Em's neck and everywhere else quivered. Her hand was on the door latch before she was aware that she'd moved it.

"What have you got?" Eleanor asked.

"I don't know, but go slow, there's something—"

"If I went any slower I'd have to put it into reverse."

"Familiar . . ."

And familiar it was. As they nosed past a thick lilac hedge, Emma beheld the house she'd visited from the wasteland barely twelve hours earlier. True, she hadn't seen the house from the outside, but there was a stained sheet of plywood nailed up where the front door should have been and plastic over all the windows. The soot-stained gables matched the bedrooms Em remembered. She had no doubt that one of the gables hid the roof hole through which she'd glimpsed the summer stars. She hoped someone had nailed plywood over that, too, or the whole house might erode before it could be repaired.

"I was here. Last night, I climbed through the window, and it brought me here. Here last summer, right after it burnt."

Em scarcely realized that she'd spoken aloud until Eleanor stopped the car.

"One of the other arsons?"

"The first . . . I think."

"Good. Let's get closer." Eleanor opened her door.

"No!"

"Why ever not?"

"We're being watched," Em replied quickly. It was a lie, a desperate attempt to keep Eleanor in the car. Who knew how much trouble they could get into by trespassing onto a crime scene? Then, suddenly, it wasn't a lie, and Emma knew for certain that they'd attracted attention, though she couldn't easily say how she knew, or where the observers were lurking.

"Nonsense. There's not a soul out on these streets. We can walk right up to what's left of the front door—"

"I said, *no!*"

Eleanor closed the door and restarted the car. "You don't have to yell. Us or them?"

"Pardon?" Em asked as she leaned closer to the windshield and tried to spot the spy.

"Are we being watched by someone we have to worry about or by someone ordinary?"

"I really couldn't say. I'm still doing things for the first time, but, I guess, because it *is* the first time I've been so sure that I'm on somebody else's radar, that it's got something to do with curse-hunting. Sylvianne was on the money: There's got to be a curse loose in this town."

Eleanor sniffed. "All the more reason to investigate that house. The better you know it in the here and now, the easier it will be to find on the other side."

"I know it well enough already."

Another sniff. "Walking didn't go too well? Unpleasant surprises along the way? A touch of interference from our dear Sylvianne?"

Truth or lie, there wasn't an answer to that question that wasn't going to cause trouble, so Em went with the truth: "The problem wasn't Sylvianne. I took what she said and what had happened to us when the wasteland went all lopsided and used that to crystallize a landscape beyond the bolthole window. And then I climbed through the window—"

Emma stopped in mid-explanation.

The side door of the house immediately to the left of the burnt-out one opened. A heavy-set, teenaged girl stepped onto the small, white-railed porch. Dressed for the height of summer instead of a brisk October afternoon, the girl wore skimpy shorts and a skimpier halter. The girl could have drawn Em's attention for that incongruity alone and for that reason, Em forced herself to look elsewhere for the spy.

Adults, after all, were expected to give children the benefit of the doubt. They certainly weren't supposed to cast judgment on them from a football field's distance. Yet when the girl threw something small into the rock garden along the foundation wall, Em would have sworn it was a cigarette and not a candy wrapper.

She wasn't alone in her judgment.

"There's trouble," Eleanor announced. "Is she the one?"

"Her? I don't know. Right now, at this very moment, that sense that we're being watched: I don't have it."

"Right now," Eleanor observed, "she's not looking at us."

That was remedied a moment later when the girl descended the three cement steps from the porch to the ground.

"Is she staring at us, or at the car?" Em asked.

"Both. Oh, dear—I wonder— The other day, when I bought the car, the salesman said something about why they had it on their lot. It was a special order, then the financing fell through. Something like that, anyway. Do you think—?"

"I think if someone had ordered a car like this—and, no insult intended—but this *is* a car meant to appeal to a young market—there's a good chance that half the high school knew, and knew that the deal had fallen through. You may own it, but you're driving a car that was meant for someone else."

While Eleanor explained that it had been love at first sight between her and the purple car, the Union girl walked slowly across the front yard of the burnt-out house and sat herself down on the porch steps.

"She's got trouble, all right," Eleanor interrupted herself. "It's all around her, like a dark cloud. Do you see it?"

Emma couldn't say that she saw anything to set the girl apart from other teenagers—sullenness was practically a badge of honor at that age and, heaven knew, she'd slunk out of the Teagarden house often enough. She wanted to give the girl the benefit of the doubt. There was always the chance that they were sitting inside the girl's purple dream. Em could have cooked up quite a scowl, if she were in the teenager's place.

And the sensation that they were being watched didn't return, even though there was no doubt, now, that the girl was watching them.

"I think we should just leave, before we make anything worse."

"No, look closely, Emma. Use your peripheral vision; sometimes that works when you can't see straight on. She might be our arsonist, or maybe not—either way, that girl's got a problem we can solve."

Reluctantly, Em took her mother's advice and looked at the girl through the corner of her right eye. There was a bit of glare, a bit of distortion, but nothing more than she'd expect from her contact lenses. "It's gone. I've lost that 'somebody's watching you' sense altogether and the girl herself—I admit, my instincts aren't generous, but—well, other rogues I've known didn't set off any alarms either. Maybe I just don't have the knack."

"Try. Tell yourself that girl's got a dark aura and will yourself to see it. It's like tying your shoes; you've just got to keep at it until you succeed. You know what they look like in the Netherlands; you've got to learn what they look like in the here and now when they've latched onto a human soul."

"It's not like tying my shoes; it's like wiggling my ears or raising one eyebrow at a time: My brain doesn't know which strings to pull."

But Emma made another attempt, as futile as the previous ones, until, in frustration, she closed her eyes.

"Great! Just great. Now I see it. There's a blur, like an afterimage from a camera flash, when I close my eyes. It's sort of a bilious green, and it's smaller than she is—maybe just her head down to her heart. It's a good thing she's alone. If that girl were in a crowd, I couldn't peg the blur to her or her neighbors."

"Anything, so long as it's different from what I suggested."

"No. I'm telling you what's happened. I didn't plan it," Em protested, though she feared her mother was right and feared, too, that she'd never look at a crowd or a stranger with an open mind, much less open eyes, again. "Let's just get out of here, please."

"Picture," Eleanor said, to Em's complete befuddlement. "Picture," she repeated. "We need a picture. With a picture, we'll know where to start when we moot that girl's curse. Open the glove compartment. There should be one of those disposable box cameras in there."

"You've got to be kidding," Em muttered, though she agreed they'd have to do something about the girl's curse.

"No, there's a disposable camera in there. I always travel with one. It was hard during the summer—it's so hot out there in the Dakotas and such. Fries the film. But I bought one when I got to Bower—to take pictures of all the houses I looked at. I didn't look at that many before I bought the townhouse. There must be half a roll left. Just get it out and snap a picture."

"Eleanor, I'm not going to take a picture of that girl while she's staring at us. For one thing it's rude, for another, if she really is cursed . . . It just can't be a good idea . . . sort of like tweaking a tiger's tail."

"You're such a pessimist, always imagining the worst. You've got to get over that, Emma. What you imagine makes a difference. A real difference. If you think bad things will happen, then bad things *will* happen. Don't you understand, you're putting ideas into that girl's head?"

"Fantastic," Em replied with morbid irony. "Now you're telling me that what I do can influence a curse. And *I'm* the pessimist. All the more reason to get gone!"

"Can you read the house number, at least, or see a street

sign? We need something to build an expectation matrix if we're going to moot that girl's curse."

Phrases like "expectation matrix" didn't come naturally to Eleanor. She had to be quoting Harry Graves. Emma had no desire for a proxy argument with her stepfather.

"Fourteen something. I think." Em said, unwilling to admit that she already knew the homeowners' name and their street address. "The last numbers are hard to make out. We're on Union, I think. I know we crossed Jefferson and Madison to get here. There's got to be a Washington and maybe a Lincoln somewhere in the neighborhood. That ought to be enough to bring up a map on the Internet." And if it wasn't—if Em was right about what Harry meant by an expectation matrix—she had all the specifics she needed already burnt into her memory.

"If not, we can always come back," Eleanor said as she spun the steering wheel.

"Right," Em agreed.

She closed her eyes. The greenish blur was still hovering in her mind's eye, a bit faded and drifting toward the back of her skull as they rode down Union Street.

She wouldn't have believed it possible, but they got lost leaving town and wound up fifteen miles east of Union when they should have been going southeast. Rather than turn around, Emma suggested they head due south. She'd recognized the numbers of the state roads they'd crossed. Sooner or later, all of them would intersect I-96. Once they were on the Interstate, Em could find her way home from anywhere in the country. She was right about the state roads, though she'd forgotten that the U wasn't the only football school in Michigan. They got caught in a heavy stream of cars flowing out of East Lansing.

By the way folks were driving, State had lost big. Eleanor stayed in the slow lane, her hands death-locked on the steering wheel. For her own safety, Emma abandoned all attempts at conversation. She fiddled with the radio, hunting for a station that might soothe her mother's nerves and settled for another classic rock station.

Things were beginning to look up. They were talking comfortably about the Beatles when traffic slowed to a crawl.

"Somebody zigged when he should have zagged," Eleanor said.

"We could get off at the next exit—if traffic isn't moving by then—and head down to I-94; it's bound to have less traffic than this."

But they were losing daylight fast by then, and as little as Eleanor liked heavy Interstate traffic, she apparently liked the prospect of a two-lane state road even less. They inched past the exit ramp.

Em stared out the side window. When an impatient driver decided his time was more valuable than everyone else's and made a third traffic lane out of the shoulder, she couldn't keep from closing her eyes. There was no ghostly glow behind her eyelids . . . but maybe that only worked when the person with the curse had already noticed her?

"I'm getting hungry," Eleanor announced. "Maybe we should stop for supper. This will all have cleared by the time we finish eating."

"We just passed an exit ramp."

"There'll be another one. What do you say?"

"Fine by me."

Traffic had eased by the time they reached the next exit, and Emma would have been just as happy to finish the day's journey without another interruption. She said nothing, though, when Eleanor left the road and drove into the parking lot of a restaurant known nationally for its huge steaks and deep-fried, whole onions.

"You can smell the onions from here," Eleanor said when they were out of the car. "I could eat one all by myself, but I'll split it with you, if you're interested."

Em accepted the offer. She'd regret that much onion, that much deep-fried breading come midnight, but the aroma was seductive, and the darned things were delicious.

A party of seven or eight hurried past them. Em caught herself scanning their faces and looked up instead. The last of the sunset was gone. The sky was nearly black, and the stars had begun their nightly show. The planets, too. Em spotted yellow Jupiter wandering in Aquarius. She'd learned the zodiac constellations and planets for a Girl Scout badge back in the fifties. The names and patterns had stuck with her all these years.

"The Pleiades are up." Emma pointed at the bright open cluster. If Eleanor were serious about building a friendship, she needed to know that her daughter paid attention to the stars. "Orion's on his way."

Eleanor rightly associated Orion with winter, but the Pleiades were new to her. Em got her mother looking in the right direction. "They're part of the constellation Taurus, the Bull—"

"I'm a Taurus," Eleanor said brightly. "Harry says I'll have to change the day I celebrate my birthday now, but not by too much, if I don't want to. I'm planning to stay a Taurus. It suits me, don't you think?"

Emma didn't answer. She tracked *stars*, not astrology columns or celebrities.

"And, of course, you're a Virgo. Taurus and Virgo— that's half our problem right there. Maybe I *should* change Eleanor Graves's birthday to something more compatible with Virgo."

"I don't think it works that way, Eleanor. If you believe in that stuff, then it was all determined by the stars at the moment of your birth. You can lie about that, but you can't change it. Either the stars are omniscient, or they're not anything at all."

"Oh, I don't believe all that much. I think maybe I'll switch to Pisces. What sign would you choose, if you could change your sign?"

"Good grief, Eleanor, what did I just say?" Em complained, but the engineering gene was susceptible to absurdity in addition to curiosity. "If we're going to play games, why should I limit myself to the zodiac? Why not say I was born under the sign of Orion, the Hunter? Nice bright stars. Easy to spot overhead."

Eleanor said nothing for a moment. Em thought that, once again, she'd put her foot in it. Then Eleanor said slowly, "We could all say that, couldn't we? That we're born under the sign of Orion, because we're all hunters."

No coincidences, no easy revelations. Em took a deep breath and agreed, "Yeah, I guess you could say that."

Nine

An hour later, one more cleverly cut and fried onion had disappeared into a memory of golden crumbs and driblets of ranch dressing on a plate midway between Emma and Eleanor. They'd each put a dent into their entrées, but neither had finished and both were waiting for plastic shells in which to ladle their leftovers. Eleanor had ordered dessert. Em just shook her head and settled for decaf coffee.

"This is delicious," Eleanor said after one taste of her key lime pie. "Sure you wouldn't like some?"

Em liked her key lime pie without a hint of green. Eleanor's dessert was ivory pale. She nicked off a crusty corner with her spoon.

"Have more," Eleanor urged. "There's plenty. I'll never finish it."

Em took another spoonful then held up her hands in defeat. A family in Bangladesh could have lived for a week on what they had eaten; their neighbors could have survived on what they hid inside plastic.

"I feel like I could go into a digestive stupor," Emma admitted as they settled into the purple car.

"Don't. I'm not sure I can find my way back to Bower."

Emma cracked her window for a breath of chilled October air and provided directions. Traffic was light.

They were twenty miles out of Bower and closing fast when Eleanor said, "You know, Emma, that curse we saw today, that can't have been the curse the Curia's got you working on."

"Why not?"

"You said they were looking after a fast-cycling curse and one that had passed through recently—"

"Sylvianne *implied* that it was recent; she didn't actually say that it was recent. Good grief, one glass of wine and I can't remember the watcher's name. I know she told me. Something vaguely Hispanic, or maybe Italian."

"That doesn't matter. What matters is the girl with the curse; the curse wasn't something new. She's been carrying it around for a while."

"How could you tell? What nuance of curse-hunting lore have I missed this time?"

"I could tell because she had a full aura. When someone's just copped a curse, the aura's fainter and limited, as though it hasn't penetrated everything. That girl shined from top to bottom. An aura doesn't say anything about the strength of a curse, mind you, and a rogue can usually hide its aura. But that girl's been carrying a curse around long enough for it to get down to her toenails."

"I'll have to look closer next time—or not look, since I don't seem to see anything until after I've closed my eyes. Damn, Eleanor, it would be so much easier if every curse-hunter didn't perceive curses differently."

"We don't. I mean, yes we're all different—different abilities, but not different perceptions. The sky is blue, the grass is green, curses have auras, rogues don't, and so on down the line. Everybody runs at a different speed, but we all run on our feet. It's like you run on your hands. I can't explain why everything is so different for you. Must be something to do with you being isolated and coming into your *wyrd* so much older. If I'd stayed with you or if you'd come into your inheritance when I expected, you might have been more impressionable, less inclined to do things your own way. The sky might be blue and the grass, green."

"I'm just trying to understand, not trying to be difficult or stubborn. It's like grabbing water most of the time; it just seeps through my fingers. When someone tells me something, I try to make sense of it. When Harry told me to imagine a coin flipping through air and to coordinate my transfers to the wasteland with it when I caught it and turned it, I got that immediately and haven't had any trouble since—"

"Harry," Eleanor muttered in a tone Emma knew well. "At least he doesn't care whether you take his advice."

Emma was about to agree when her mind's eye caught Harry from a different angle with an onyx ring on his right hand. "Damn! I'm not sure I should go curse-hunting—big-game curse-hunting—tonight."

"Why ever not?"

Em explained how the laser pen had melted in her hand. "It's probably good enough for stalking tiddlers or fingerlings along the absolute present, but I don't think I want to face anything stronger. I tried to switch to a knife the other night, but it didn't 'take' and I wound up with the pen in my hand again when I got to the wasteland even though I'd been holding on to the knife when I flipped my imaginary coin."

"I have just the thing for you. I'll get it once we're home. You can keep it."

"Keep what?"

"Let me bring it over first. I don't want to spoil the surprise."

"I can hardly wait," Em said and hoped she sounded more enthusiastic than she felt.

Emma hadn't given a lot of thought to her curse-mooting weapon, but Eleanor mooted curses with a sparkly, beribboned wand, and there was no way Em was going mano-a-mano against a fiery curse armed with something that could have fallen out of a little girl's toy chest.

The suspense wouldn't last very long. They were one Interstate exit from Bower.

Eleanor passed up a perfectly good parking space in front of Emma's townhouse. She claimed it was too short for the purple car. Em didn't argue, but to her eyes, the space could have held a full-sized pickup truck. They settled for a tight fit at the back end of a fire-plug gap on the next block.

"If you need help with parallel parking—" Emma offered.

"I'm fine with the parking. That other space was too small. People need to be more considerate."

Em shrugged. Parking was the chronic problem around the Maisonettes. She and the other board members heard complaints at every meeting. Eleanor's wasn't new. They hadn't heard a *new* complaint in years.

Eleanor made tracks for her townhouse. "I'll be right over. I know exactly where it is. Why don't you make something hot for us to drink? Cider or cocoa?"

The way life with her mother was setting up, Emma worried that she'd be gaining weight soon, undoing all the good her regular walks in the wasteland provided. She made herbal tea instead—one of the rich, fruity blends that were almost as good as potpourri when it came to filling a room with fragrance. When Eleanor arrived, she eyed the brew unenthusiastically, like a child confronted with a new vegetable, but took an experimental sip without comment before offering Emma a velvet-covered ring box.

Em flipped it open and beheld an old-fashioned ring with a brushed gold band and a dark oval cabochon stone. Removing it from the split pillow, she held it up to the nearest lamplight. The stone was dark red with six pale, radiating highlights, making it a star ruby. Two sets of ini-

tials were engraved inside the band, but Em couldn't make
them out, even with her reading glasses.

"Try it on," Eleanor urged.

The cool metal slipped comfortably onto the fourth finger of Emma's right hand. Harry used an onyx ring to
focus his will in the wasteland. He'd loaned it to Em before she'd gone off to do battle with the rogues holding
Eleanor prisoner in February. She'd worn Harry's ring on
her index finger. It had been easy to use, as simple as
pointing her finger. Em tried putting Eleanor's ring on her
index finger. It didn't fit, so she put it back on her ring finger and made a fist.

"Does it have a history?" she asked.

"It belonged to my grandmother."

Emma sat down in the nearest chair. "My great-grandmother."

The Merrigan family had been small: Em's father and
herself. Her father's parents had both died years before her
birth. An aunt and uncle, the only relatives to whom she
could put faces, were gone before she'd turned ten. Em's
husbands had had larger families, but she'd lost touch with
them, except, of course, for her stepchildren. When Emma
thought of family gatherings, she thought of Nancy and
John, who'd been kind enough to welcome her for the hol-
idays. She'd never given a serious thought to the in-
evitability of maternal grandparents.

"What was she like?" Em asked, automatically assuming the woman was dead.

Eleanor grimaced and shrugged. "Tall, dark-haired. She
had a sweet voice; I remember her singing as she went
around the house and singing in the evenings. She died before my mother did, before I'd turned four, Emma. I suppose I don't remember her much better than you remember
me."

Em could have argued that she had no memories, musi-
cal or otherwise. She said, "She left you the ring in her
will?" and tried not to sound bitter.

"No. Someone cut off a lock of her hair before they buried her. I had that for a while—until the war. I lost it sometime during the war." Eleanor shook her head and stared out the night-dark window. "I got the ring in the fifties, right after I married Harry. It came in the mail one day—no return address, just a note saying: Your mother would have wanted you to have this. Those are her initials inside the band, with her maiden name; the other set is J.E.B. for John Edward Baker, *Senior.* My father was John Edward Baker, Junior."

Eleanor Baker. Once upon a time, before Graves and before Merrigan, Eleanor had been Eleanor Baker.

"What was your mother's name?"

"Alice. Alice Margaret Baker, when she died. Alice Margaret Skellings before she got married."

Of course. Sylvianne had implied that Skellings was a family name.

"Was it—? Was the ring what she used to moot curses in the wasteland?" Em knew that daughters inherited from their mothers. She hunted because Eleanor hunted, and Eleanor had gotten the ability from Alice Margaret.

Eleanor shook her head. "Beats me, but it has the right feel, don't you think? I've worn it a few times—as jewelry, nothing more—but it's got the feel."

Emma twisted the ring a few times then made another fist. She could imagine something very similar to a laser beam jetting out of the stone. Weren't red lasers made from rubies? Small rubies. Tiny rubies. Nothing like the oval ruby in the ring, which was about a quarter inch across its narrow axis. A bigger ruby meant a bigger laser beam, a stronger laser. She unmade her fist.

"If you're sure you don't want to keep it for yourself—"

"No. I told you, it's not the talisman for me. I don't see myself as the precious-jewelry type anymore. If you think you can use it, I'm happy to give it to you. Happy for all sorts of reasons."

Em had never been the precious-jewelry type, either,

but she liked the look of the ruby ring on her hand and liked the thought of it as her weapon of choice in the wasteland. "Then, I'm happy to keep it."

"Good. That's settled. Now, I'll be your anchor."

Emma met her mother's eyes and opened her mouth to object. She was tired, a bit headachy, and more interested in introspection than mooting curses, but Eleanor barreled on.

"No, don't argue. I know it didn't go well last night, and it was my fault all the way. I'm going to beat my problems, I swear that I am, but not tonight. Tonight I'll stay here, ready to pull you out if anything starts to look hinky and you'll go after that girl's curse. Delve it down to its source, then plunge in and moot it, like I know you can."

Ordinarily Emma wasn't susceptible to false or inflated praise, but at that very moment the path of least resistance went through the wasteland. She changed into more comfortable clothes and settled into a modified lotus position on the living room carpet, Sylvianne's computer-generated, X-over-Union marked map between her toes. Emma stared at the map until it was burnt onto her retinas and starting to blur. A coin spun before her mind's eye. She caught it, turned it over with the thought, 'heads,' and felt herself shift effortlessly from the here-and-now reality to the wasteland.

The ruby ring was on her finger, the horizon was empty, and the way-back stone was some ten feet off Emma's right shoulder. The bolthole lay in front of her, not more than a football field distant and hidden in its orange-slice depression. Between the two, a straight line would take Em to that part of the wasteland that corresponded to Union, Michigan, in the here and now. She'd have to be careful—if there was one rule that everyone recited it was: Don't cross your own path while rearranging the past; and her path had wandered through Union very recently.

Truth to tell, Em wasn't quite sure how to avoid her own path. She had the raw ability to walk the past—to delve, as Eleanor and others described it—but not the practice to do it well or safely. The bolthole window was the easier way, the almost-familiar way. Using it, Em could find the girl an hour or so before she fell afoul of a curse and figure out a way to thwart it.

The window was on Emma's mind as she trekked to the bolthole. She forgot about the way-back stone; it had relocated itself before she remembered to check it out. The stars, Em decided, would be the best way to guide herself through the past. There were computer programs that would allow her to recreate heavenly patterns at any time, above any place. If she added stars to the vistas the bolthole window provided, she could improve her delving accuracy.

Emma opened the bolthole door.

Harry would be impressed. He and Blaise probably knew the stars. Nights had been darker when they'd been boys. Sixteenth- and seventeenth-century men, without maps, flashlights, or decent roads, relied on the stars to get them home.

"Madame!"

Blaise's voice took Emma by surprise, as her appearance had taken him. He'd sprung out of his chair, sword in hand, the amber hilt, rather than the steel point, was pointed at Emma's heart. For a heartbeat, they regarded each other as strangers. In Emma's case, for more than a heartbeat. Blaise had changed his appearance. He was still a Louis XIV-vintage Parisian, but his hair, formerly on the wild side of luxuriant, was more restrained and several inches shorter. Instead of the bleached and billowing shirt he normally wore beneath the layers of his coat and vest, Blaise had clad himself in a sleek, dark turtleneck virtually identical to the one Harry had worn Wednesday night. The combination might have been handsome, in an eighties sort of way, if Blaise had swapped his seventeenth-century pantaloons for a pair of dark slacks or jeans.

"I—I wasn't expecting to find you here," she stammered. "I'm early and, anyway, I figured you'd still be out chasing your rogues."

He shrugged. The gesture just wasn't the same without yards of cloth to magnify it. "Chasing? *Pardieu*, madame, I do more than *chase* rogues!" Blaise flashed a grin as he laid the sword across the table. "I mooted one in her lair, but, alas, it was not the lady I have sought all these years. Still, there is one less plague upon mankind. I was resting on my laurels until you arrived." He held up the note she'd left behind the previous night. "You asked me to wait for you. Something about danger?"

"I had a bad time—a bad scare with Eleanor last night—"

"*Pardieu*, your mother has safely returned to your life?"

"Yes."

A single word could answer Blaise's question, but a lot had happened since their last conversation. Eleanor had returned after totaling her car—not that totaling a car would have much meaning to Blaise. She'd met a cousin for the first time, a cousin who represented the Curia, and Blaise already had a low opinion of the Curia. She was delving after a curse of unknown strength—probably *not* the curse the Curia wanted her to moot—with a mooting weapon she'd never used before.

No, a single word wouldn't suffice.

Blaise caught her hesitation and leapt to his own conclusions. "What is the matter? Is it something with your mother? Did you find her? Has she become lost again? Is that why you wished me to wait for you?

"No, not exactly," Emma admitted. "We were looking for the Curia's curse. My cousin—I've acquired a cousin, my mother's niece—in the last three days. She's tight with the Curia and on Eleanor's short list of people I shouldn't trust inside the organization—"

"*Pardieu!*"

Blaise opened his arm toward the smaller chair, her

chair. He picked up the never-empty pitcher of wine, poured her a glass, and topped off his own.

"Start at the beginning, Emma. It's always better when you start at the beginning."

Emma closed her eyes. Sylvianne's map was still there, hovering like quicksilver in her mind's eye along with her memories of Union Street. They remained clear enough to impress on the subjective reality beyond the bolthole window, but Em couldn't count on them remaining detailed and strong enough if she got embroiled in conversation with her lover, however much he deserved an explanation, however much she could use his advice. She remained standing in the doorway.

"There's a curse—not the one the Curia wanted me to take care of, but one we found by accident. I'm going to track it down and moot it—practice for the real one. I really—I honestly didn't expect to find you here. I thought I'd slip in, use the window to get myself into the past, and slip out again. I didn't budget time for a debriefing."

By the change in Blaise's expression, the magic that allowed them to understand each other had stumbled over her last sentence. Em tried again.

"Wednesday, when Harry and I were here, Eleanor was missing because she'd had a purely real-world accident, which wasn't serious and from which she's completely recovered. Last night we went looking for that curse the Curia wants me to moot. We didn't find it. We found something else instead, something nasty—like a fiery curse living at the bottom of a deep hole—and that's why I left that note for you. Today, we decided to concentrate our efforts in the here and now, and we found a young girl carrying a curse, but probably not the curse the Curia had in mind. We thought, if I could moot the curse we'd found today—" Em paused. "Well, we thought it was something we *could* do, because we're not making headway on the Curia's curse, and there's something out there on the wasteland that's playing tricks with the landscape, so I didn't want to go walking anywhere.

"Eleanor's sitting guard for me even as we speak. She's so determined to be helpful it hurts, and I thought that going after the curse we saw today was the safest option."

"And you don't want to keep her waiting?"

Emma nodded.

"I understand. Let's go together and moot this little curse quickly, then you and I can sit together and you can tell about this 'nasty' curse in the ground. Perhaps it is something I have seen before."

Abandoning his wine glass, Blaise slid his sword into its scabbard. He pulled on his vest and coat with admirable speed. The visual effect against the dark turtleneck was better than Emma dared hope, far better than the turtleneck and pantaloons alone. Still, it was wasted effort. Em wasn't in the mood for a handsome distraction, and Blaise didn't brave the bolthole window when it revealed a time or place that had not existed during his natural lifetime.

"I'm guessing it's a modern curse," she explained. "At least I'm going to start tracking it pretty close to the absolute present; sorry."

Blaise settled his feather-covered hat on his head and surprised her with a grin. "Getting there might be difficult, but I have talked this out with Monsieur Harry, and I no longer think it will be dangerous. Where I once believed a circle existed and that I must remain within it to remain as I am, I now perceive a line and the freedom to walk beside it wherever it leads. It would be unwise—impossible—to attempt God's side of the here and now, but *certes*, what is not on God's side of the line is au-delà whether it is au-delà here where we meet, au-delà Paris, or au-delà any other time, any other place. I have nothing to fear au-delà, nothing but rogues, and I am prepared for them."

Emma would have better luck asking Monsieur Harry for a synopsis of whatever discussions he and Blaise had had after she left Wednesday night. It wasn't the translation magic that had failed. Blaise Raponde had a fundamentally different notion of how the wasteland—which he called *au-delà*—was put together. There was a lot of seventeenth-century theology in Blaise's worldview. Emma had spent more than a few lunch hours in the library stacks boning up on the French Counter-Reformation. What she'd managed to learn had convinced her not to pursue any conversations with Blaise that included the word *God*.

"You're sure?" she asked, trying not to sound too eager. The ruby ring had come through with her, but she would have preferred a few weeks of fingerling practice before wielding it against a parasitic curse.

"I am. I had thought my first venture would be to Paris, but—ah, our *fenetre du monde* will not reveal what has become of my city. Monsieur Harry, he says it is the impossibility to imagine the future that has kept me in the past. It seems I will need a companion. He offered to show me the New World, but I declined. You are the companion I would choose above all others for my first adventure beyond my own life."

Flattery came as naturally to Blaise Raponde as breathing. Away from the wasteland, Emma would have found the trait suspicious, even distasteful, but under magenta skies, she smiled and took his hand in front of the window. Early dawn, or perhaps deep twilight, held sway in the walled-in garden that was the window's default view. Emma inhaled and concentrated on the silhouettes of Union as she'd seen them that afternoon. In the usual way of the window—to the extent that there was anything *usual* about the window—a fog would seem to roll in from all quarters, blurring the outlines that had been visible, replacing them with the vista the two hunters desired.

After several moments with neither fog nor transformation, Emma let her breath out.

"Something's not right."

"You are, perhaps, distracted?" Blaise asked, releasing her hand.

He reached up to caress Emma's cheek. Em retreated, shaking her head; she truly wasn't in the mood for distraction. As soon as she'd put an arm's length between them, fog began to fill the garden.

"Well, I'll be—" she mused. "Harry's done it again."

"How?"

"I think the way it works is that we can hold hands and recreate the past together—*your* past—because I can imagine a seventeenth-century city, maybe not down to the cobblestones, but well enough that I don't interfere with how the window works. But when it comes to *my* past— the historical past that falls between 1685 and when I last saw my living room—I've got to do all the imaging and fine tuning myself, because I can imagine it and you—no offense—really can't."

Em squinted through the window's leaded glass. The garden was gone, replaced by the tired street-scapes of Union, Michigan. She unlatched the casement and filled her lungs with faintly smoky air.

"Okay—"

Without taking her eyes off Union, Michigan, Emma reached back to snare Blaise's hand again. The fog thickened immediately, but not so much that she lost sight of their destination. The casement wasn't wide enough for them to squeeze through together.

"Now, madame, which one of us goes first?"

"Me, I think. Do we risk letting go of each other, or should we hold on?"

"A gentleman should precede his lady into the unknown, but I will make an exception for an unknown which is more familiar to you. I will keep hold of your hand, though, and you will tell me if anything is amiss. Up you go."

Blaise easily lifted Emma up to the sill and steadied her as she made her second entrance into Union's past. The window had aligned itself with the street this time. There was a few-foot drop to the concrete sidewalk, and when Emma turned around to offer a hand to Blaise, she observed that for all intents and purposes they were climbing out of a maple tree in high-summer foliage. The burnt-out house was across the street. Em didn't breathe as Blaise took her hand lightly, and, one foot after the other, emerged from the tree trunk.

"How does it feel?" she asked.

"Warm, like a summer's night. Do you know where we are? When?"

"Summer, I think, in a little town about two hours' drive northwest of where I live." Emma covered her mouth, embarrassed by her useless answer. Two hours driving on the roads of seventeenth-century France probably equated to one exit on the Interstate. She rephrased her answer to, "About seventy-five miles," but even at that, she didn't know whether Paris miles were the same as Michigan miles. "I'm a little surprised; I expected autumn."

Blaise didn't seem to notice her frustration. He was preoccupied with the Union landscape. Emma watched in silence as he rotated slowly on his heels, taking in the cars and houses, roads and overhead wires, and everything else she took for granted. She could fairly hear the wheels of logic and analogy whirling overtime in his head and wondered if she had looked half as intelligent when she first set foot in seventeenth-century Paris.

"It is so quiet, so empty, so *bright*. How does that *shine* so?" He pointed at a streetlight. "Where is the flame?"

"No flame, electricity—lightning in a bottle. We run our world with electricity and petroleum. Remind me to take you to Niagara Falls sometime."

"Is it hot?" He asked, still gazing at the light.

"If you get close enough." She took his hand and gestured toward the burnt house. "We're going over there. There's got to be something special about that place. This is the second time the window's brought me here. I wound up inside it when I was trying to track down the Curia's curse. Then this afternoon, while my mother and I were looking for a curse she could sense, we wound up on this street, looking at this house. I would have sworn the girl we saw this afternoon had nothing to do with the one I saw when I came through the window, but here we are."

Blaise resisted Emma's effort to lead him onto the dark street. He pulled his hand away and knelt down to feel the asphalt before he'd set foot on it."

"What is this?"

"We call it asphalt, blacktop, or macadam," Emma replied and realized that for all her synonyms, she didn't really know what it was made of or how, exactly, it was made. "All our roads—almost all of them, anyway—are paved one way or another, if not with asphalt, then with concrete." They'd had concrete, or something very similar to concrete, in seventeenth-century Paris. Em remembered seeing it between the stones of the city's cathedrals and houses, but not underfoot.

"Where are the animals? There is so much empty space. Does everyone live in a palace so far apart from one another? Where are the cows, chickens, and pigs? The horses to pull your—"

Blaise didn't finish his question. His gaze had fallen on a full-sized pickup truck, polished and chromed to the gills and emblazoned with every decal Michigan State University had ever licensed. In the streetlight's slightly ruddy light, Emma couldn't be sure of its color, but she'd have bet her last penny that it was some shade of green. Color, though, was probably the last thing on Blaise's mind. He reached out gingerly to touch the deep, metallic finish.

Blaise had the talent—perhaps a *wyrd*—for feeling things, even manipulating them in the shadowy past of Paris. Em was about to ask if he'd brought his talent to Michigan when, in a coincidence she could never have planned, another pickup turned onto Union Street. It was full-sized, like the vehicle Blaise had been examining, but raised up on oversize tires and fitted out with an extra set of headlights in front of the radiator and a four-light batten above the cab. The truck was ready for the worst foggy nights Michigan could throw down in its path, or a herd of unsuspecting deer.

The truck's driver gunned his engine as he came down the street toward them. Blaise drew his sword as he turned to meet what had to be, for him, an awesome threat; and as much as Emma told herself that they were both safe, invisible and immaterial, she found her gut tightening with fear.

The pickup rolled past them. Emma caught sight of Blaise's eyes as he followed the truck with his sword. They weren't glowing, but they were far from friendly. He'd have taken a swing at the truck if it had come too close or if the driver had perceived them.

"We call them pickup trucks. They're a type of car—of automobile. They've pretty much replaced horses, except as a hobby. Horsepower hasn't died out. We still rate our cars in terms of how much a horse can pull. I'd guess that truck has the pulling power of about two hundred and fifty horses. The driver sits inside, behind a steering wheel—"

The truck stopped in front of the burnt house. Its doors opened. A beefy young man who carried as much fat as muscle on his bones lowered himself from the driver's seat. Out of sight on the passenger side, a girl's voice complained about a puddle.

"I've come back to the exact same moment as before, but from a different angle," Em mused aloud. "I was inside the house last time. The window had dropped me off in a bedroom closet. But it's the *exact* same night—" Emma looked overhead. "The moon's right, the stars, too. There they go up the walk."

From behind the girl was slender and light on her feet, not at all, in Emma's opinion, a match for the girl she and Eleanor had marked as cursed in the afternoon. She closed her eyes and looked again. There was a faint and ruddy horizon-to-horizon afterglow, the kind Emma sometimes got in the depths of a migraine headache, and, in the midst of it, a greenish blob of light where the girl had been. The blob was smaller and fainter than the aura Emma had seen around the afternoon's girl.

"I've gotten my wires crossed," she complained. The glow lingered after Emma opened her eyes. She'd managed to give herself a migraine.

Blaise gave Emma a crooked glance before asking, "Do you mean to follow them?"

The pair had climbed over the yellow police tape and onto the sorry-looking porch. They tore the plastic from the nails holding it around the missing front door.

The migraine had progressed quickly. A coil of pain circled Em's right eye and looped over her ear before grounding itself in her shoulder. All Emma wanted to do was go home. "I'm not sure, Blaise. I wanted to trace a girl I saw this afternoon, a girl carrying a curse back to the moment before she caught the curse. Instead, I'm standing here looking at a girl who already has a curse and isn't a physical match for the girl Eleanor and I were looking at."

"Can you make mistakes with the delving *wyrd*? If you can delve at all, don't you have to delve to the pivotal moment before a curse takes its host, and then you plunge to avert the taking?"

It sounded as though someone had been talking to Harry Graves.

"You're not talking to an expert. I make things up as I go—supposedly that's one of my strengths: no preconceived notions of what will or won't work. The problem here is that there seems to be two curses: one that the Curia wants me to investigate and the other that Eleanor and I stumbled across this afternoon. And I don't know which curse I'm tracking. I was thinking about the afternoon's curse, but I seem to have plunked myself down in front of the Curia's fast-cycling curse—

"That's if I'm tracking any curse at all and not just chasing shadows. There was a newspaper article about a series of three arsons here in Union. Do you know what I mean by arson—a fire deliberately set for the destruction of property?"

Blaise nodded patiently. "Arson is as old as wooden houses."

"Well, this is the second time I've drawn myself back to a few hours after the first arson. I can see that there's a curse tied to it—at least there's a cursed girl who's drawn to it. I really don't know what part the actual arson plays. It's hard to imagine two curses and three arsons in a town the size of Union, here, and them not having anything to do with one another. Then again, this isn't an auspicious time for curse mooting. The whole plunging thing, I've got to do it before the curse latches onto its host. I'm not an exorcist; I can't separate a curse and its victim."

"We are not priests, Madame Mouse. We cannot appeal to the sacraments. You have collected too many questions standing here while your answers have gone into that ruin. We should follow them."

Between the moon and the street lamp, Emma and Blaise could see each other clearly, though not quite naturally. To Em's eyes, Blaise had a faintly translucent quality, as if he'd been lightly painted on a living transparency, then lit from within by a single candle. In her own case, as she thought about where the young couple were headed, Emma feared the candle had turned crimson.

"It's the curse that's pushing you away," Blaise chided.

"It's not," she insisted, and tried to change the subject: "You agree the girl is harboring a curse?"

"From this distance, there is an aura, faint, but undeniable. From this distance, I would judge it a very minor curse, but I cannot be certain—nor can you—*from this distance*. We must get closer."

"It's wrong. The wrong time, the wrong curse, the wrong everything," Em complained as she led the way toward the ruined house.

The air was filled with light breezes, none of which Emma could feel against her not-quite-solid skin. A slightly more potent gust had shaken the nailed-up plastic and left it hanging over all but a few inches of the doorway. Em still couldn't pass through historical objects. A sheet of two-millimeter plastic was enough to stop her in her tracks.

"Allow me," Blaise offered, and, grasping a corner, lifted the plastic as if it had always been a part of his seventeenth-century world.

"Is that something I can learn to do?" Em asked before she stepped through the opening.

"Perhaps—if you have faith."

Emma groaned. Her faith, or the lack of it, was a tired subject. "Is it something you learned since—since you—" She groped for the right word, for any word that wasn't *died*.

"It is easier since then, but I could always move small objects—a lock of hair, a bit of lace."

Em would have preferred not to know that. "Why? It doesn't make a difference—Or does it? What would someone see if he or she came walking up the street right now?"

"It is not *now*, madame, it is *then*. We are *au-delà*, and what we do—what *I* do, changes nothing. You can get inside an ordinary person's thoughts and make a small change that changes everything, but even then, you are only a prick of conscience, you are not truly *in* the past; you are *au-delà*."

"So if someone comes down the street, they're seeing what they saw when this moment was the absolute present and not what we're doing now—not two oddly dressed people, one of them holding on to a sheet of plastic?"

"*Pardieu*, madame, exactly so—unless that someone is like ourselves or is a rogue, and if that were true, then our problems would be much greater than—what did you call it? A sheet of plastic? May I suggest that you step across the threshold, against the chance that I am wrong?"

Emma took the suggestion. The house was as she remembered it. She led Blaise confidently along the hall to the stairway and up the stairs. They were on the landing when the first sounds of passion erupting in the master bedroom reached their ears. She stopped cold.

"This is exactly where I was last night, and I've got to tell you, I'm no voyeur."

The American habit of adopting French euphemisms served Emma poorly. Blaise's next remarks were unintelligible. She raised her finger to his lips to end them.

"My mistake. What I meant to say is that those two kids are down the hall obeying the commandment to be fruitful, and I'm not interested in interrupting them. I'm going to have to dig up some other interception point to stop this girl from acquiring her curse. Or I'm going to have to figure out how to follow a curse through the past, instead of just intercepting it. Either way, I really don't think we're listening to the girl Eleanor and I spotted this afternoon."

"It is the curse itself pushing you away," Blaise insisted. "It is afflicting your thoughts. Mine, also, if the truth be told. I am averse to interrupting lovers without reason, and if, as you claim, you can do nothing about the curse, *pardieu*, there is no reason. Still, we are doing what the curse wants: *noli me tangere*."

Every so often translation failed on Blaise's side, not Emma's. She asked for clarification.

"It is the warning Our Lord Christ gave his Blessed Mother when He emerged from the tomb: Come no closer; touch me not. The curse is telling us the same thing."

Em would have argued that it didn't take a curse to keep her out of a stranger's bedroom, but by the sound of things, any further discussion was going to turn theological, and that would be worse than a curse. She headed down the stairs instead.

"Well, nothing's perfect," she said. "Once in a blue moon, even a curse can provide good advice. And I think that's all I'm going to get out of this evening's adventure."

Blaise slipped his arm around Em's waist. "I have seen a new world, a world beyond my imagining. The walls of my prison have crumbled." He kissed her lightly on the cheek. "I am most grateful and eager to celebrate my freedom."

Emma thought of Eleanor sitting watch in her living room. A truly dutiful daughter would hurry home; then, again, time flowed differently in the wasteland, usually faster. An hour in the bolthole was rarely more than ten minutes in Bower. . . .

She returned Blaise's kiss.

Ten

"**G**ood grief," *Emma* groaned.

The television was broadcasting a black-and-white movie she didn't recognize and the time display on her VCR glowed *4:15AM* and *Sun*. There was no guessing how long she'd lain asleep without moving on her living room carpet, but her left arm and leg were numb. With another groan Em levered herself into a seated position. Her arm regained its senses gracefully, but her left foot felt as though some invisible demon were stabbing countless hot pins into the sole. She massaged it gently and looked at the sofa where Eleanor slept peacefully, curled up in the blue and lavender quilt.

The sofa was comfortable enough—and Eleanor was young enough—that there was no need to awaken her. Em stood up carefully. The pins-and-needles sensation gave way to a more diffuse numbness, but from the ankle down, her foot belonged to someone else. She limped over to the television and touched a button to silence it.

"Wha—?" Eleanor asked, coming to a sort of wakefulness as soon as the room was quiet.

"It's late. Very late. Time to go to bed. Do you want to just stay on the sofa?"

Eleanor blinked and yawned. When she'd finished that

ritual her eyes and voice were clearer. "How did it go? What happened? Did you take care of that girl's curse?"

"No. Something went awry. I took myself back to the right place but the wrong curse and the wrong time."

"That can't be."

"It was. I put myself in the same exact time as I'd visited last night, except this time, instead of climbing out of a closet, I climbed out of a tree. We did, actually—Blaise and I. That's a whole 'nother story. The tree was right where you parked the car this afternoon. So I got to watch what I'd seen last night, only from a new angle. There was a girl and she was carrying a curse, but I can't believe it was the girl we saw—her whole body shape was different and the curse was dug in deep. It's hard to believe, but there must be at least two curses loose in the little town of Union, Michigan. The fast-cycling one that the Curia's watcher spotted and the one that we spotted today."

"If you delved yourself at the wrong moment, did you try to backtrack that fast-cycler to its origin? That can be hard work, but you're more than strong enough to tackle it."

Em yawned. Her foot was her own again, and she wanted nothing more than to climb the stairs to her bedroom. "I gotta admit, I didn't try." She was breaking one of her cardinal rules. Two failed marriages had taught Emma that discussing anything important after midnight was a recipe for disaster. "I made a strategic retreat to the bolthole with Blaise. He wanted to celebrate. Union's the first place he's seen that didn't exist in his lifetime. If we'd been planning, I would have suggested somewhere like New York, but Union it was. And then the bolthole."

Eleanor stared, disapproval written large on her face, but said nothing.

"Yes, Mother, I'm a necrophiliac—I sleep with dead people. The sex is good and very, very safe. Now, let's each tuck ourselves into our own little beds."

Em put one foot on the lowest stair step.

"Did you close the door?"

"Yes." She climbed another step.

"You have to be careful, really careful, if you're coming and going in your sleep, especially if you're ..." Eleanor left her warning unfinished.

"I've been coming and going, as you put it, since before you took off for the Dakotas. I've had lots of practice and, yes, I'm careful." She reached the landing. "The door is closed. Turn out the lights, okay?"

Emma paused in the bathroom. When she emerged, the downstairs was dark and the door to Eleanor's room was closed.

For the second day in a row, Emma slept well into the morning. The Sunday paper was scattered through the living room when she came downstairs in search of coffee. The cats were draped across the sofa, looking smug—as well they should; Eleanor had given them each a can of cat food rather than splitting a can between them. Eleanor, herself, had returned to her own home, leaving a note to that effect against the coffeepot.

Emma regretted almost everything she'd said at four-thirty AM. She put a mug of coffee in the microwave for reheating and picked up the phone.

"I'm sorry about my attitude and anything I said last night. I've always said I should be considered legally dead from midnight to six in the morning and not held responsible for anything I do or say."

Eleanor accepted her daughter's apology and offered to forage for deli sandwiches in lieu of breakfast. Emma, who had been staring into her refrigerator, waiting for inspiration to strike, accepted the offer and put in an order for Genoa salami and provolone cheese on a hard roll. When an hour had passed without hide nor hair of Eleanor, she toasted half an English muffin, slathered it with jelly, and took it upstairs to the computer.

After three visits to Union Street in Union, Michigan,

Emma could summon clear pictures of the street and its houses from her memory. Clear enough to recall the name and street numbers on the unpaid bills in the kitchen of the burnt house and on its mailbox. She typed the particulars into several of the proprietary search engines she could access with her librarian's credentials, and got back plat, lot, and tax information back to the early 1990s, but nothing useful for hunting a curse or two. Her best hit came from a public engine that offered a few tantalizing sentences from a newspaper article written in late August.

The Internet had turned the old maxim about yesterday's news having value only as birdcage lining and fish wrap on its ear. On-line, today's paper was free for the reading, but old papers went into a pay-per-view digital archive. If Emma wanted to read what had happened on Union Street in August, she was going to have to answer personal questions and fork over $2.95.

Muttering, "highway robbery," Emma spent ten minutes jumping through Internet hoops before the newspaper site accepted her credit card number and asked her to wait while it accessed the information she wanted.

The woman reporter had touched the necessary bases—date, time, number of fire trucks and men summoned to fight the fire, and a quote from the local fire chief that the fire was "suspicious"—but she'd found a compelling human interest story behind the fire story. That suited Emma just fine as the human interest turned out to be Kaylee Sharpe, a sixteen-year-old cousin to whom the Pierson family had opened their home only a few weeks earlier.

Kaylee, the reporter explained, had had a tough life, a tougher year.

Kaylee Sharpe's mother had died in an auto accident years earlier, leaving her daughter to be raised by her widower husband. A circumstance with which Emma could easily identify, except that her upbringing as the protected, even privileged, daughter of a university professor had little in common with a hardscrabble existence in that portion of Michigan's left-hand mitten known as the Thumb. According to the reporter, little Kaylee had been in and out of her father's custody several times as the elder Sharpe bounced from job to job, often with long stretches in the area's homeless shelters in between.

She'd escaped the July crash that claimed her father's life with minor cuts and bruises and the indelible images of a man trapped in a burning car. Andrew Sharpe's death, horrible as it was, could have been counted more of a gain than a loss for Kaylee. The man had died while eluding the Sanilac County police, who'd wanted to question him about a string of petty thefts. An autopsy pegged Sharpe's blood alcohol level at point twenty-eight, not enough to make him self-combustible, but getting close.

Casting aside the burden of objectivity, the reporter had written that Kaylee's life had taken its first turn for the better when the Piersons claimed custody of their niece. The Piersons were, as Em had suspected from her inspection of their ruined house, solid citizens of the tight-knit Union community. William Pierson was a foreman at a nearby auto parts factory and a deacon of his church. His wife's cooking and baking were welcome additions to any potluck dinner and renown beyond Union as well. Cindy Pierson had risen to the regional finals of a Betty Crocker cook-off with her "New-fangled Meatloaf."

At least young Kaylee was getting regular meals, as she prepared for September and her eighth school since kindergarten. Then came the fire at the Pierson's home, a smoky fire that had left the entire family homeless and dealt its greatest damage to Kaylee's newly decorated bedroom.

There was a picture with the article. Grief and shock altered everyone's appearance. The tear-streaked, gapemouthed girl leaning on the shoulder of a similarly afflicted older woman might have been the girl Emma had seen headed toward the master bedroom. Or she might have been the heavier, sullen girl she and Eleanor had seen on Saturday. Whichever, Kaylee Sharpe had endured the kind of life that attracted curses. The question stirring in Emma's mind was: Could Kaylee's misbegotten father have been the sort of man whose death spawned a curse?

Emma sent the article to her printer, and while that piece of hardware clunked and whirred and slowly laid lines of ink across a sheet of copier paper, she checked the Web site of the Bower dealer who'd had another S-series Integra on his lot. Assuming someone kept the on-line listings up to date, the car was still there. And would remain there until Monday; the dealership was closed until then. Em's printer beeped and fell silent. She removed the printed article and took it downstairs. The names, places, and especially the picture would become the starting points for a completely different kind of search once Eleanor made another reappearance.

Until then, Emma needed something more substantial than a jelly-coated English muffin in her stomach. She collected the sports section of the paper on her way to the kitchen. Em scanned the details while nuking her leftovers from the previous evening. The U's football team had won its game handily: three field goals, two touchdowns on offense, one on defense. They were having a typical season; an early West-coast loss had knocked them out of contention for the national championship, but now they were wreaking havoc in the conference portion of their schedule.

She returned the section to the living room chaos and pulled one of her three leather-bound curse-hunting books from the shelves beside her chair. There wasn't anything in the other two books that Harry hadn't added to his and in clearer handwriting than Emma or her mother possessed. None of the books, however, had anything remotely resembling an index or a table of contents. Em was reduced to flipping pages between swirls of pasta and vulcanized shrimp, hoping that "curses passed from one generation to the next" or similar words would catch her eye. Her bowl was empty well before she found one short note:

Norwalk family. Three curses in one household. Grandfather, son, and grandson. Watched to see what would happen but family went extinct before fourth generation born.

Emma could always call Harry and ask if he remembered making the note or if he had any other useful insights. She could call Redmond Longleigh, for that matter, with the same questions. Em was still sitting at the dining room table weighing her options when the door opened.

"I'm back! Did you think I fell in a hole?" Eleanor asked as she entered the living room from the hall.

Her arms were filled with a large box containing a set of stainless steel pots. Several plastic shopping sacks hung from her arms. Not one of them bore the logo of Bower's delicatessens.

"I tried not to think at all."

Em helped Eleanor unburden herself. Spin and Charm emerged from their hiding places to investigate the new arrivals as they landed on the sofa. The large box bored them quickly, but plastic bags offered a variety of amusements. Spin burrowed too deep into one of them and tumbled to the floor in a heap of dish towels. The noise and movement unstrung him. His feet didn't seem to touch the floor on his way to the basement.

Emma picked up the towels. "Why didn't you take these over to your house?"

"Forgot my keys."

Emma asked the obvious question with her eyes alone.

"I walked out without them. You were right: I should have them all on one key ring. I still had yours on the ring with my car keys, and I know you have a key to my house. You do, don't you? You have a master key, right?"

Em nodded and asked about the sandwiches.

Eleanor blanched. "Damn! I knew I'd forgotten something. Lunch just went completely out of my head when I drove by that kitchen store between downtown and campus and saw that it was having a going-out-of-business sale." She grimaced. "I'm sorry. You haven't been waiting all this time? You got something to eat? I did, I'm afraid—a big bowl of spicy noodles at this little Asian place next door to the kitchen store. Bower really does have some wonderful restaurants—more than you'd expect in a town this size."

"It's the university," Em explained.

There was no point in answering Eleanor's other questions or in chiding her for irresponsibility. Em might as well argue with the weather for all the satisfaction she'd likely get. Eleanor wasn't spiteful; she just had the attention span—and the ego—of a child.

"Students come here from all over the world," Em elaborated. "Sometimes they stay and open up a home-cooking restaurant. Sometimes the whole family comes over. Net result: great ethnic restaurants."

Eleanor's attention had moved onto the dining room table. "Oh, good—you did get something to eat. What's that? Harry's book? You're looking for something in Harry's book? What?" She picked it up and read the small number written in the upper corners of the facing pages. "Nineteen fifty-eight? Nineteen fifty-nine? You've found a connection to a curse Harry mooted back all those years ago?"

"No." Emma snatched the book from Eleanor's hands and closed it with a *snap*. "I was looking for a curse that recurred in successive generations in a single family."

Eleanor shook her head. "Never happens. That's not the way curses operate. None of that seventh son of a seventh son nonsense. You *can* have two curses in the same household at the same time. There was one like that in Paris. We managed to moot both of them. Not that it did any good. They got mixed up in the Resistance, and the Nazis got them anyway. When your number's up, it's up, and there's nothing mooting a curse can do about it. Were you thinking families because there are two curses operating in Union?"

Em nodded.

"A little town like that— Did you notice that nobody seemed happy? There're probably more curses in Union than in Bower. Well, no, maybe not, but Union has more than its share, probably, and Bower has fewer. Bower's crawling with optimists. You almost never find a curse attached to an optimist."

"Never thought about it, but I suppose that would make sense. Look, do you want help carrying this stuff up the street?"

Eleanor nodded eagerly. "Then I thought we could call out for a pizza and watch a movie. I bought a DVD—"

"I don't have a DVD player." Em didn't challenge the pizza. Pizza sounded pretty good, even pizza with Eleanor.

"I bought a player, too. We can hook it up to your TV until mine gets here. I broke down and called Harry on my cell. I asked him to ship me some things from the house in New York. He agreed that there was no sense in my buying *everything* new, so long as we were careful."

Cell phones and DVDs. It wasn't that Emma was a Luddite or couldn't afford the gadgets; they simply didn't appear on her radar until long after the early adopters had grown bored with them. She agreed to wire another electronic gadget to her television and wound up carrying the unopened box from her mother's living room to hers. Eleanor might be an early adopter, but she didn't have a clue how to wire her technologies together.

She was testing remotes when Eleanor came in, jangling her key ring in front of her.

"See, I've got them all on one ring now. No more getting locked out."

Emma let that assurance pass without comment. She opened Eleanor's new DVD disc and slipped it into its tray. The disc was Richard Lester's *Three Musketeers*; she couldn't claim to be surprised. Eleanor would win the friendship war; Em could see that coming. She didn't have the strength, much less the will, to resist the onslaught of consideration.

And the DVD picture was better than tape, too.

"What do you want on your pizza?" Em asked. "The usual?"

The usual, *chez Merrigan*, had always been pepperoni with extra cheese. Eleanor had gone along back in the spring, but she was a Graves now, not a Merrigan, and—who knew—her taste in pizza might have changed along with her appearance.

"The usual will be fine."

Em reached for the phone just as it began to ring, and, although her answering machine was always on to screen her calls, she picked up the receiver.

"Did you see that game yesterday?" Matt asked before Em could say hello.

"Missed it. Wish I hadn't, but I was out looking at leaves with my mother."

Matt was a bright young man. He'd extract several layers of meaning from that remark without breaking a mental sweat.

"You got a car?"

"No, still looking. I've seen a couple likely prospects on the Internet—"

"The Integra's gone?"

"Yeah, but there's another one—"

Eleanor got in front of Em. She moved her lips through the question: *Is that Harry?*

Em shook her head and mouthed the word *Matt* before finishing her answer to his question. "This one's right here in Bower. The mileage's a bit lower, and it's cheaper, but I think it's silver—"

Invite him over for pizza.

"Silver's not the end of the world, Em."

"But I'm not sure it's me. I've never owned a car that wasn't black—"

Invite him over.

"Eleanor's making faces at me and asking if you'd like to join us for pizza."

"And how do you feel about that, Auntie Em?"

"You haven't seen her since she came back to Bower."

"That's an 'okay, c'mon over'?"

What does he like on his pizza?

"Yeah, you could say that. I'm not really good at relaying conversation."

"Then, okay. When should I come over? Now?"

"Now would be good. How many slices of what kind of pizza should we put you down for?"

"Three of anything that doesn't have little fishies or peppers on it."

Emma ended the conversation and got another dial tone. She kept the pizzeria's number on her speed dialer. One touch of the number "4" button and she was in line to order a 'za.

Eleanor asked, "Has Matt changed any over the summer?" before Em had cradled the receiver.

"He bought a new shirt, I think, and enough spare parts to build two computers and a DVD recorder."

"Girlfriends?"

"He's in better shape than the average geek, but Matt Barto's still a geek, Eleanor. Until there's a programmable bikini, preferably one that runs Linux, women are not going to be his top priority—even when he says they are."

"No girlfriends, then?"

"None."

"Does he still help you research your curses?"

Em began gathering up the stray sections of the Sunday paper. Matt was a friend. The house didn't have to be spotless before he arrived, but it would be nice if there was a place for him to sit down. She answered Eleanor's question when she got to the comics.

"No—mostly because I haven't gone mooting after anything that required research since you took off. I don't

think I would have involved him, anyway. Harry's right—
Hell, *you* were right: It's not a good idea to involve outsiders."

"But Matt and Nancy were so much help—"

"It's not that they didn't help or that they wouldn't help.
It's just not a good idea," Em asserted and wondered when
she'd made up her mind. Yesterday, probably. Yesterday at
Meadow View when she'd realized that sooner or later she
was going to do some preventative youthening. Even if it
were as subtle as refusing to grow older, inside or out,
Emma would eventually have to follow Eleanor's lead and
become someone else. That would mean leaving Bower
behind, Bower and all her friends.

Emma recalled Sylvianne's word for people like themselves: *Adrêsteia*—the Inevitable. It was overblown by a
factor of ten, but maybe that was the right proportion when
the difference was between virtual immortality and inevitable death. She retreated to the kitchen to check on ice,
glasses, soda, and her sanity.

Things were just about under control when the phone
rang again. Thinking it was the pizzeria calling to check
the validity of the order—they did that sometimes, but not
usually for a single pizza to a regular customer in a well-
lit neighborhood—Em grabbed the receiver before the answering machine cut in.

"Em, is that you?"

Emma instantly recognized Nancy Amstel's voice. "It's
me. I thought you might be the pizza guy. I know, I
know—I should get Caller-ID. Are you back from Ohio?"

"About a half hour ago. I was going to ask you over for
dinner—for pizza, actually. I was going to make one for
John and me. Don't suppose you'd care to join us?"

Nancy's homemade pizzas, assembled from the best ingredients in the grocery store, were a treat to be treasured,
so long as Em didn't compare them to commercial ver-
sions with their specialty-oven crusts. She regretted turning the offer down, but—

"I've got Eleanor here with me, and Matt Barto's coming over."

"Oh." Nancy couldn't keep a tinge of disappointment from her voice. "Is something happening on that front?"

"No," Em lied.

There was a touch of jealousy, too, in Nancy's voice. Like Matt, she knew about Em's secret life, and, like him also, she made no bones about envying it no matter how many times Emma insisted that the two primary ingredients in a curse-hunter's life were boredom and terror.

"How did everything go in Ohio? Did you get the roommate situation straightened out?"

Nancy took a deep, sighing breath before answering. "We think so—hope so. It was a bigger mess than we thought, and Alyx was no help." Another deep breath. "I shouldn't start. You've got company. Eleanor, you say? How's that going? Is she living with you again? Listen to me! Your dinner's coming. Questions can wait."

"Sounds like we've got a lot of catching up to do." Em stated the obvious. "And I really want to know what's up with Alyx. I've been thinking about you guys all weekend. I hate to think of her getting into trouble." Truth was, Emma hadn't spared ten thoughts for Nancy's daughter all weekend, but she would have spared more, if she'd had the opportunity. "You've got to tell me what happened."

"But your pizza . . . your mother?"

"Can take care of herself for a few minutes—"

Eleanor nodded vigorously.

"The pizza won't be here for forty-five minutes, at the minimum. I'll just run upstairs and pick up the other phone. Unless this isn't a good time? I can call later, after everyone's filled up on pizza?"

"No. No, if you've got the time." Nance sounded suddenly on the verge of tears. "John's gone out for a walk. He's angry. We're both angry . . . at each other, at Alyx, at ourselves."

"What happened? No—wait, let me run upstairs."

Emma handed the receiver to Eleanor. "You're okay with this?"

"No problem. I'll keep Matt entertained when he gets here. You don't mind if I turn on the television?"

Em didn't mind anything. She jogged upstairs, blew the dust off her bedside phone, and resumed her conversation. A long weekend's worth of turmoil tumbled out of Nancy. She never lost her composure completely, but it was clear that the Amstel familial bonds had been stressed to their limits.

Alyx was unhappy with her roommate situation. She didn't like the parade of strangers, the arguments, the foul language, and the general disruption that came with a roommate who was majoring in substance abuse. But when her mother had shown up to fix the situation, Alyx had dug in her idealistic heels. The girl had convinced herself that she was the only island of stability in her roommate's life and that to walk out would send Roma, the roommate, over the edge.

And maybe Alyx was right; Nancy was willing to concede that the roommate had been puppy-dog polite the whole time. "Roma went to dinner with Alyx and me on Thursday. She grabbed the check before I got it and insisted that she could afford it because her father's given her not one, but *two* credit cards with twenty-thousand dollar limits. Em—John and I don't have that kind of credit! I wouldn't be surprised if there's more than a little envy from both sides. Alyx would love to have a snazzy new car and all the money she can spend; Roma would love to have parents who cared."

John and Nancy, though, hadn't been willing to become substitute parents. When Alyx wouldn't budge, Nancy went over her daughter's head to the college administration. The administration—citing a zero tolerance policy for illegal substances—had sent someone over to search the room for contraband. They'd found what they were looking for: a cache of prescription painkillers and another of

Ecstasy, but the kicker—the drug that got Roma tossed out of school—was a medicine used by veterinarians that Em had never heard of.

"John went to the library and looked it up. They put it in a girl's drink, and she's too woozy to say no or defend herself or even remember what happened while she was under the influence. And it was in Alyx's room—enough of it, the dean said, to knock out a whole sorority! You can't imagine the scene, Emma. Roma was in tears, hysterical, and Alyx was, too. She's blaming me for ruining her roommate's life. And I can't help but .think she's right—but what else was I supposed to do?"

Nancy paused to give Emma an opportunity to reassure her. Downstairs, the doorbell rang; Matt had arrived. Eleanor greeted him like a long-lost brother, then they went into the living room, and Em couldn't separate their voices from those coming from the television. Emma wasted a worry on the mischief the two of them might get into, then got back to Nancy.

"Nothing else. You've got to protect your kids. It's not as if that other girl—what's her name? Roma? There can't be a kid in any college in the country who doesn't know you're going to get tossed out if you get caught dealing drugs. You and John were only doing what any concerned parent would do—"

"Me," Nancy corrected. "John thinks I went overboard. God, he's the one who looked up the information. You'd think he'd be leading the charge, but, no, he thought I should have confronted Roma one-on-one on Thursday instead of going to the dean. He even asked me if I thought Alyx was in on the dealing, because the drugs were all over their room, not just with Roma's stuff."

The words, "You're kidding!?" slipped out of Em's mouth before she could stop them. "John's usually so rational about these things."

"There *was* a terrible scene Friday afternoon. Roma didn't want to leave—they practically had to drag her out of the room—they *did* call the police. School's too small to have its own cops like the U does. Funny, that's one of the things we liked about it, but they've got to call the town cops whenever anything starts to get out of hand. There's no leeway and maybe John's right. I should have looked for other options. He got there at just the wrong time. Yesterday's got to be one of the worst family days on record for the Amstel's. Today wasn't much better."

"They're kids, but it's not like they aren't making their own choices."

"Which one, Roma or Alyx? John and I will patch things up before we go to bed; we've had worse arguments. But I'm afraid my youngest daughter's not going to speak to me again."

"She'll come around. Just be nice to her. That's what Eleanor's doing with me, and, little as I like admitting it, the tactic's working. Not only am I likely to forgive her for walking out on me fifty years ago, I'm probably going to overlook the way she took my car and wrecked it—"

Nancy squawked, "What!?" and Emma remembered that they hadn't talked since Wednesday, when Em had still been expecting her mother to show up before bedtime.

They truly did have a lot of catching up to do. The pizza arrived while Em was explaining Redmond Longleigh and Sylvianne Skellings. Its aroma set Em's stomach churning; she made a sincere attempt to cut the conversation short, but John hadn't returned, and Nancy wasn't eager to be alone with her thoughts. Emma soldiered on, skating lightly over the misadventure she and Eleanor had shared in the wasteland and skipping her encounters with Blaise altogether. If Nancy got the idea that Blaise was moving through history—and recent history at that—she'd put her not inconsiderable cleverness to work figuring out a way to meet him.

Em finished with, "And now she's downstairs eating pizza with Matt. Somehow I feel this is not a good thing."

She was sure Nancy would take the hint, but they spent

another fifteen minutes talking about Alyx before saying their good-byes. She hurried down the stairs.

Eleanor said, "We left three slices for you. They're in the kitchen. You'll probably want to heat them up."

Nonsense. Em had been living on her own for the better part of a decade. She preferred hot pizza fresh from the oven, but she'd eat it cold, straight out of the refrigerator for breakfast, or lukewarm off the counter.

Between them, Matt and Eleanor had finished hooking up the DVD. They were well into the *Three Musketeers*. Emma hadn't lied when she'd called the film one of her favorites. She settled on the floor, not even asking Eleanor to vacate her chair, and tried to lose herself in the movie.

For the first time in some twenty viewings, the magic failed to work. Although the story took place in the first half of the seventeenth century, years before Blaise Raponde's birth, and had been written nearly two centuries after his death, Emma couldn't watch the derring-do without thinking of her lover. She stayed out of the commentaries Eleanor and Matt exchanged—except to observe that Eleanor was going out of her way to be friendly and agreeable.

Was Eleanor—octogenarian Eleanor—actually putting the make on Matt Barto?

Emma could think of a million reasons why that was the last romance she wanted to see flourishing and no reason to open her mouth with objections. By the time the credits rolled, Em had convinced herself she was imagining the whole interaction. She, not Eleanor, was the one who gave Matt a hug before he left with the last slice of pizza in hand and, God knew, her life had all the romance it needed without involving Matt Barto.

"Well, that was fun," Eleanor announced once the front door was closed and locked for the night. "Now, let's get to work."

"Pardon?"

"That girl's curse. You're ready, aren't you? You were

reading Harry's book when I got here, and there's this—"
Eleanor brandished the Web site printouts Em had made
earlier. "You were doing your homework, right? That's
quite an article. Lots of juicy bits. Well, there's no time like
the present to go after that girl's curse. Tomorrow night I'll
be sleeping in my own bed, so let's strike tonight, while the
iron's hot. Just let me change down into my pj's, and I'll
be your anchor."

"Right," Em agreed, collecting her printouts. She'd
been living alone for so long, the idea that someone else—
her mother—might poke into the business she left lying
around her house had never entered her mind. "Did you,
like, show this to Matt?"

"Of course." Eleanor paused with a sofa pillow in each
hand. "Why? Shouldn't I have? Isn't he still a part of your
team?"

"I don't have a 'team'."

"That's not what you were saying last spring. You and
Matt and your friend Nancy—and Harry, of course. You
told me. Matt and Nancy both told me."

"And Harry's been telling me I should be careful
about—" Emma hesitated, groping for the right words.
"—about involving *outsiders* in curse-hunter affairs. One
minute I think he's right, the next I don't, but I would have
preferred to make the decision myself, all right?"

"It's my curse, too. More mine than yours, really. We
agreed it's not the curse that woman told you about."

Em went from no headache to headache in a heartbeat.
"All right. I'm sorry I said anything. I'm sorry. I'll be more
careful in the future, but, you're right, we might as well see
what can be done." She looked at the VCR's time display.
"Nine-thirty. There's lots of time for curse hunting—" And
tomorrow she could tell Matt that there was no reason for
him to harness the power of the Internet to track down
Kaylee Sharpe, because the girl's curse was moot. "You
change, I'll change. You're still the guest. You get first dibs
on the bathroom."

"These places really could do with a second bathroom. Maybe I'll add one. Can I do that? How much will it cost?"

Emma knew the answers but didn't share them. She closed the heavy drapes and followed Eleanor up the stairs.

Twenty minutes later the two women were seated on the carpet. Emma's printout of the newspaper article lay on the floor between them. Before this, Em had used images, either clear memories or printed pictures, to focus her explorations of the past, but the printed word should work—*would* work, if she believed in it the way she believed in her spinning coin. She'd marked the sentence describing Andrew Sharpe's death and his daughter's miraculous survival with a chain of red circles around each word.

"Ready?" Eleanor asked.

Em nodded. She could feel the coin's weight somewhere between the palm of her hand and the middle of her mind. Closing her eyes, she felt the coin rise. In the here and now, she'd miss the coin more often than she caught it; and practice had not made perfect. In the wasteland—or on the way to the wasteland—her aim and her call were infallible.

"The ring, Emma! Remember the ring!"

Eleanor's last-moment warning ensured that Emma had thoughts of the ruby ring at the front of her mind as she called the imaginary coin. It was on the ring finger of her right hand when she became aware of the wasteland. The way-back stone was to her right, and the bolthole was on the far side of the rolling hill in front of her. Em didn't think Blaise was nearby and decided against looking for him. So far he seemed favorably impressed by the future; she didn't want his second impression to be a flaming car wreck.

With no pictures in her own mind, the bolthole window would be no help in getting to the root of Kaylee Sharpe's curse, but the chain of circles Em had drawn on the printout had made the transition to the wasteland with her. She had only to grasp one end and let it put her into the past.

Emma found herself on a blacktop road in the middle of night, the middle, she hoped, not of nowhere but of Sanilac County in Michigan's Thumb. In the west—probably a half mile away over cow pasture, not roads—a pair of porch lights broke darkness. A blinker light marked a right-angle intersection to the east. The land around the intersection was flat enough and the fields were cropped low enough that Em could see the headlights of a solitary vehicle headed north to south. It had its high beams on and was moving fast, maybe sixty or seventy, which was far faster than Em would have driven, but in line with how the locals drove the wide-open roads when no one else was around.

The vehicle wasn't signaling for a turn and wasn't slowing down, either. Emma expected it to zoom on past, but the driver stood on the brakes at the last moment. The vehicle squealed and skidded into the corner. Its back end broke loose. Em could tell, now, that the vehicle was a pickup truck. The driver steered against the skid, making it worse. Twin beams of light swept the road from shoulder to shoulder. They revealed a good-sized boulder on the far side of the road.

Michigan had been buried beneath glaciers during the ice age. Glacial rocks were still the state's most reliable crop. They emerged from the ground with the thaw each spring, heaved up by winter frosts. They could be found on the fringe of every farmer's field and on road shoulders throughout the state. Like icebergs, their bulk often lay below the surface, but even if the boulder across the road from Emma were absolutely flat on the bottom, it was still big enough to win any encounter with a pickup truck.

Though she was only an observer, Em put one foot behind the other, retreating a good ten feet into the grassy border before the inevitable occurred. She was grateful for the muting effect that accompanied her adventures in the past; she wouldn't have wanted to hear the full force of that crash of steel against granite, but the fireball she'd dreaded did not erupt. The truck's hood was sprung, and the entire front end had been canted upward by the impact. Both front wheels were off the ground, and the headlights pointed at the sky.

Had Emma not known that Kaylee survived, she would have assumed that father and daughter were both dead. Instead, after a minute or so, the passenger door popped open with a loud crack, and the teenage girl scrambled out. She ran across the road, coming close enough that Emma could see every detail of her face. The girl had cuts on her chin and across the bridge of her nose. She'd feel the hurt when her adrenaline stopped flowing, but she was moving every limb with unconscious confidence. She'd been luckier than she knew.

The same could not be said for the driver. By the glow of the truck's overhead light, Em could see a man slumped against the steering wheel. From the fact that she could see him, Em knew that the truck's electrical system continued to function. She guessed the key was still in the ignition and the throttle was open, an especially ominous thought, because the faintest odor of gasoline had reached the back of Emma's nostrils. If it was flowing onto the hot engine block, a fireball remained a distinct possibility.

Maybe—if Emma were half as lucky as Kaylee had just been—she could avert a curse by nudging the girl into taking the keys with her when she jumped out of the truck.

Beside her Kaylee balled her hands into fists and stamped her feet.

"Bastard! You bastard!"

Although those were the words Emma might have used to describe Andrew Sharpe, they were not the ones she expected to hear from his daughter. Nor did she expect Kaylee to run back across the road. By the time Emma had followed her across, the girl had a cheap cigarette lighter in her hand. There was a liquid pooling beneath the truck and, as Emma watched in disbelief, the girl tossed the flaming lighter into it. Kaylee had the sense—if *sense* were the right word—to race across the road before the fire exploded into an inferno.

"Bastard!"

Emma had dodged the flames as well, darting a good thirty feet in front of the truck. She might have flown, or teleported herself; she couldn't remember her feet touching the ground. The flames created a searing wind that reached into the shadows, where a delving curse-hunter observed the past.

Em braced herself for the whirlwind that heralded the creation of a brand-new curse—for surely the circumstances that drove a young girl to kill her father in such an opportune and horrific way were the same circumstances that would give rise to a curse. Her skin tingled, and her hair drifted on a static charge as a sense of impending doom bore down on the country road. Every instinct urged Emma to run away or at least avert her eyes, but she stood firm and kept her eyes open, for all the good her eyes could do her when a gritty wind swept along the path the truck had followed.

Then there was a flash of light. Em raised her hand to her eyes and watched through the cracks between her fingers. Even that stratagem didn't help much, at least as far as seeing the curse with her eyes open. But when she thought she'd sufficiently burnt the scene onto her retinas, Emma closed her eyes. There was bilious green throughout her blind vision, especially in an arc shooting across the road, from Andrew Sharpe to his daughter.

A fast-cycler, for certain, the curse couldn't have been in the wasteland for more than a second before finding its new host.

When Emma opened her eyes again the brilliant light was gone. Only the flames remained to reveal Kaylee crouched on the ground near where Emma had emerged from the wasteland.

Okay, Em thought to herself. *I've delved the moment; now I've got to figure out how to plunge and moot the curse.*

Emma had an idea how to do that. She couldn't get into the truck before it crashed—not unless she delved back to the moment when Kaylee or her father had last shut the door, so, instead, she would wait close beside the rock. Immediately after the truck hit the rock, she'd leap into the truck's open bed and take up a position leaning over the passenger door. When Kaylee shoved the door open— shoved it through Em's torso, which was bound to be an unpleasant experience—she'd drop down and wrap herself around the girl, plunging into the girl's psyche, urging her to take the keys before running to the far side of the road and *staying* there.

It might not be enough to save Andrew Sharpe, but saving Andrew Sharpe wasn't part of Emma's plan. With her coldest thoughts, she judged him worthy of whatever death fate could hand him. Em's only concern was protecting Kaylee from the curse her recklessness—and hate, surely there was hate and love inextricably mixed in the girl's heart—had engendered.

There was one flaw in Emma's plan: She didn't know how to roll back time without returning to her Bower living room and starting over. It wasn't a major flaw. She could always return to the wasteland or signal Eleanor that the moment had come to pull her out. But Em was so pleased with her plan—so confident that she could moot this curse—that she wanted to take a stab at rolling up the past right there on the lonely road.

Her first attempt, pure imagination, failed. It was not enough to *want* to move backwards through time. With her second attempt Emma added movement. Em faced the second of roadside where she'd emerged from the wasteland and as she imagined herself returning to that earlier moment, she walked toward it as well.

Walking against a hurricane-force wind couldn't have

been more difficult. She hunched down, lowering her profile and leading with her head. Each step sapped her strength in half, and she feared she might collapse before she saw grass beneath her feet, but, trembling from neck to toes, she made it. The wind ceased to blow against her the instant she stopped trying to move against it.

Raking her wind-tangled hair from her eyes, Emma saw that the crashed truck had disappeared. The road was dark and quiet again.

Did it! She rejoiced, then waited the better part of ten minutes for a pair of southbound headlights to heave into view.

History repeated itself as expected. Before the truck's front wheels had stopped spinning, Emma had her foot on the rear bumper. Climbing into the bed was a bit like threading a needle while wearing mittens—theoretically possible but fraught with difficulty. She was grateful that no one could hear her thumping, banging, and cursing her way to the corner of the bed nearest the passenger door.

Emma was ready when she heard the *click* of a seat belt being unbuckled. She was prepared for the worst as the door opened; and the worst was what she felt as layers of metal, plastic, and glass shoved through what she imagined was her body. She had a split second to squelch nausea before wrapping her intangible arms around Kaylee's shoulders like a shawl.

For a moment, Emma's world was darkness and pressure, as if she'd shoved herself into a space a size or two too small for comfort. There wasn't time for Em to get her bearings though; Kaylee had swung her legs out of the cab.

The keys! Em thought with all the stepparent authority she could muster. *Take the keys out of the ignition. Take the keys with you!*

She expected resistance, maybe even a brainstorm argument. Human beings weren't designed to take orders from somewhere near the back of their skulls; sane ones weren't, anyway. Kaylee Sharpe, though, obeyed without hesitation. The girl reached across the console and re-moved the keys before sliding to the ground.

Run across the road.

After she started influencing a person's behavior—rear-ranging history—a plunging curse-hunter couldn't be cer-tain that person would reclaim any initiative. Once again Kaylee proved biddable. She raced almost to the exact point where Emma had emerged from the wasteland and stood there, arms limp at her sides, mind empty of thought.

An utterly silent mind was a new experience for Emma, and not a pleasant one. There was nothing pleasant about Kaylee Sharpe's mind. It was small and cramped. When Em reached out to gather a few surface memories, the un-fathomable space around her began to quiver and mild pain radiated up her imaginary arm.

No remembering allowed? Em thought and was sur-prised when the mind around her relaxed. *Do your memo-ries hurt?*

Kaylee's mind quivered.

Emma had never conducted a conversation with her host before, but over the past year she had become accus-tomed to doing things for the first time and with little sense of what would happen next.

Removing the key from the pickup's ignition was only the first half of Em's battle. The second half would be thwarting the thoughts that sent her back across the road with a cigarette lighter in her hand. Emma imagined the control rods of a nuclear reactor and guided them forward, hoping to keep Kaylee calm and on this side of the road.

In Emma's current state, plunged into Kaylee Sharpe's mind, the girl's senses were awkward extensions of her own. Em could see what Kaylee saw, hear what she heard, and witness the slow progress of her thoughts. There wasn't a pale thought in the girl's head that didn't revolve around her father. She loved him, of course; chil-dren were hardwired to love their parents. She hated him, too, and Andrew Sharpe had given his daughter ample reasons to feed that hatred. The surface of the girl's mind was a veritable gallery of abuse—and that was only the surface. Emma shuddered to imagine what memories had been banished to the dark, painful corners of Kaylee's mind.

The scent of gasoline reached Emma through the girl's senses. The idea to set the gas afire followed it.

Go for help, Emma urged. *There's a light at a house. It can't be more than a half mile away.*

This time Kaylee hesitated. She had the raw hatred to kill her father on impulse, but walking away—leaving him unconscious in the truck—that was colder than she was prepared to go.

You can't help him. You need to find someone who can.

Em was reasonably certain that Andrew Sharpe was be-yond any help that his daughter could find for him. And, so long as his death didn't further harm Kaylee, that was fine with Em.

It's not your fault, Kaylee. None of this is your fault. He's been drinking. Em took a chance and drew a conclu-sion. *You know what he's like when he's been drinking.*

Kaylee drew her fingers into fists. The deadly idea bloomed in the forefront of her mind. Em rammed her con-trol rods forward to defeat it.

No good will come from that. Whether he lives or dies, you get to look at yourself tomorrow morning, and the face you want to see then—and for the rest of your life—is the face that did the right thing and tried to save him.

Suddenly there were faces everywhere. Most of them were a girl's face—Kaylee Sharpe's face—but a few were strangers, to Emma, not Kaylee. A wracking sob buffeted Emma's nowhere place in Kaylee's mind, and the girl's fists unclenched.

"I wanted him dead. I wanted him dead so much—"

It's not your fault whether he lives or dies. Go now and get help. See that light. That's a porch. Go knock on the door.

Hot tears were streaming down Kaylee's cheeks, stinging in her cuts and merging with her blood. She turned away from the wreck. Emma held her ground. They separated as the girl walked away.

Em watched and held her breath until Kaylee's silhouette had disappeared into the dark. "Did it!" she exalted. "Score one for the good guys!"

It was time to leave, time to revisit the burnt house on Union Street to confirm her success, time to return to Bower and treat herself to a celebratory glass of wine regardless of the hour. Em turned and stopped cold: There was a bilious green afterimage floating in her field of vision. She'd blinked as she'd watched Kaylee's retreat and blinked often enough that she'd effectively performed her eyes-closed trick for spotting curses.

How could Kaylee possibly have a curse? Nothing had happened. Emma had urged her away from doing the thing that had drawn the curse to her the first time around. She'd mooted the whirlwind of malice that heralded the curse's escape from Andrew Sharpe, its possession of his daughter!

Yet the truth was there, hovering before Emma's eyes. She blinked several times to clear the sensation and marched over to the wreck. Needless to say, the elder Sharpe hadn't been wearing his seat belt when his truck decelerated. It hadn't taken fire to kill Andrew Sharpe; the pickup's steering column and windshield had done that. He'd died with his eyes open. Blood had flowed heavily from his nose and mouth; his sleeve was drenched with it.

Em stared at him with her eyes open and with her eyes closed. There was no telltale afterimage. Andrew Sharpe was dead, and dead people didn't harbor curses.

"There couldn't have been a transfer!" Emma insisted, even though there was no one to hear her opinions.

Em climbed down from the truck and steeled herself for another go at the accident. She was exhausted by the time she crossed the road and wanted nothing more than to catch her breath, but she hadn't rolled up as many minutes as she had the first time. The pickup's headlights were already in sight and nearing the intersection. Em pulled herself together and ran to the rock.

She was in the truck bed as fast as possible, staring in through the rear window with her eyes closed.

"Damn!"

An elongated blob had grown in her mind's eye. It stretched from father to daughter, then, as Em watched, it shrank to encompass the daughter alone. She'd thought she'd understood the mechanics of curses, how they were created and how they moved from one host to the next, but none of the paragraphs Emma had read in her leather-bound books mentioned two hosts sharing a curse or curses moving from one host to the next like slugs or amoebas. And nothing even remotely suggested that a curse could be released to the wasteland by an *act*, rather than a death. Yet it seemed probable that the emergent curse Emma had watched before she began to rearrange the past had been released by an act alone; moreover, it had attached itself to a host that already had a curse.

While Emma pondered the mysteries of curse migration and creation, Kaylee unbuckled her seat belt. Kaylee put her heels to the passenger door and kicked it open. She hesitated on her way to safety, then reached back for the keys. Emma had successfully changed a very small chunk of human history, but the larger picture remained the same: Kaylee Sharpe had walked away from her father's death with a curse clinging to her.

Emma slid down to sit in the truck bed. She didn't have the strength to roll up the past again. Her legs were still jellied from her last attempt. She could come back tomorrow—one thing about the past: It was always there waiting to be changed. But what new change could she make? Should she be trying to keep Andrew Sharpe alive? Heaven knew, Em considered the world a better place without him. And if she wanted to keep him alive, how would she accomplish that? Short of nudging the bolthole window into opening into the cab of a speeding truck, Emma's only option was to roll up the past to the moment when the Sharpes had gotten into their truck. She imagined herself sitting in his lap, merging into his mind to keep him from turning east and losing control of his vehicle—

That might actually work—when Em had energy again. She studied the decals on the truck's back window, the mess of rusting tools, rags, and other trash strewn in the bed around her. The more details Em could remember, the better her chances of nudging the window toward a moving target tomorrow night. Until then, Emma was ready to get back to Bower.

She closed her eyes—

Eleanor? Wake me up. Pull me out.

The already muted past began to fade and break up. Emma could see her sofa, the outline of Eleanor's hand. She reached for it—

"Emma! Emma, can you hear me? Come to me, Madam Mouse. There is work to be done. . . ."

Em turned away from her mother's hand.

Eleven

"What happened?" *Emma* asked when she'd pulled herself together at Blaise Raponde's side.

"We had a visitor."

"Some visitor."

The hollow where their bolthole had hidden was shallower now and filling fast with chunks of dirt tumbling off the steep walls. The bolthole itself had vanished. Not a stick of wood, bit of metal, nor shard of pottery remained to say it had existed at all. Memory was Emma's sole certainty that she was standing in the right place.

"Must've been that *thing* Eleanor and I nearly got ourselves sucked into."

Blaise shook his head. "I have scoured the nearby area, and there's no sign of a curse or breech such as you described—" He held up a hand to stop Em's defense of her descriptive honesty. "*Tiens*, I do not say that you and your mother did not fall afoul of such a curse, only that it did not drift this way. I do not doubt that such a curse exists, only that you, yourself, said that you had walked far to encounter it."

Emma apologized for leaping to distrustful conclusions. "I taught myself something new tonight: how to roll up a few minutes of the past without leaving it. Maybe I'll do better with practice, but right now it's just about the most draining work I can imagine, and I've got two ex-husbands who'll swear I'm paranoid when I'm exhausted.

"What did happen? One of your rogues?"

Rogues had destroyed Blaise's previous bolthole and given him a nasty wound in the process. It was the need to provide shelter for an injured man that had spurred Em to create a bolthole for them to share.

"Perhaps." Blaise shrugged. "I have looked for roguish trails, too, and found none. The damage was done while I was *au-delà*, in Paris." Another shrug. "Had I been here—"

It occurred to Emma that the bolthole had probably been destroyed, or under attack, when she passed through the wasteland on her way to a dark summer night in the Thumb. "I should have come here. I could have helped you defend—"

Blaise raised his hand a second time. "*Pardieu*, I would not have risked anything to preserve a bolthole, nor should you. It was a lovely thing that you made out of your memories and imagination, but it was only memories and imagination. That is why I sought you just now. We shall make it again, shall we not? Together, yes? From hearth to magical garden?"

"Well, yes—" For Em, the bolthole with all its comforts was synonymous with the curse-hunting life. "But, right here again? Shouldn't we look for someplace new? Lightning does strike twice. In fact, it strikes repeatedly once it's found a good spot."

"Curses are not lightning," Blaise replied with the look that said he'd understood individual words but not their aggregate meaning. "We could walk, if you wish, but walking will not make us or our bolthole safer. It will make you more tired, and I see that you are very tired. We do not have to make our new bolthole at this moment. It can wait. *I* can wait until you are refreshed from your bed."

"No," Emma replied, susceptible as always to any suggestion of guilt. "It should be easier this time, right?" She sat down, cross-legged, in the dirt. "Let's see, last time I created a one-dimensional above-ground anomaly. This time I'll aim to put the bolthole underground where it belongs."

"Madame Mouse—"

Em grasped Blaise's hand and pulled downward. He knelt beside her.

"Close your eyes," she suggested, "while I remember that picture: *Marianne*, by Millais. That's the foundation. . . ."

Piece by piece Emma recalled her favorite painting, a copy of which had been part of her life since adolescence. There was Marianne in her dark blue dress with a red velvet upholstered footstool right behind her and her unfinished embroidery on a slate frame in front of her. Light for her embroidery came through a leaded glass window overlooking an autumnal disarray. The window was open— leaves were scattered atop the embroidery and across the tan flagstone floor. There was William Morris wallpaper on the wall behind Marianne and a private altar deeper in the background—

Emma imagined the altar without its triptych painting and ritual vessels. Beside her, Blaise inhaled deeply and held his breath.

Em moved beyond *Marianne* to the parts of the room Millais had omitted from his painting. Squeezing Blaise's hand tightly, she summoned images of his additions to her bolthole: the huge hearth with its cooking hooks and leonine andirons, the massive table, the roped-together bed with its buoyant feather mattress, a pair of sprawling chairs. . . .

Perhaps she could do a little judicious editing and replace the smaller chair with her living room recliner . . . ?

"*Pardieu*—"

Emma opened her eyes. The bolthole—the shapes that were in the process of becoming a comfortable wasteland refuge—hovered translucently and in miniature a scant arm's length in front of her. When Em allowed herself to marvel at her own inventiveness, the dollhouse-size room shimmered and began to dissolve.

"Quickly, Madam!" Blaise squeezed Em's hand.

She closed her eyes again and imagined the bolthole growing larger, heavier—sinking into the dark wasteland dirt—and becoming tangibly real. The task would have been difficult after a good night's sleep; coming on the heels of a plunging misadventure, it was a hair's breadth short of impossible. Finally, when Emma couldn't recall another detail nor support the weight of her imagination for another heartbeat, she let go.

"That's it," she explained and curled forward until her forehead rested on her ankles. "I've given it my best shot. Sorry if it's not all it should be."

"*Pardieu*, Madam, it is a masterpiece!"

Em opened her eyes, tilted her head. She'd restored the crescent-shaped hollow with its incongruous wooden door. Even the way-back stone had shifted to its accustomed place. Curiosity uncrossed Em's legs and got her up onto her knees, but it wasn't strong enough to raise her higher. Blaise offered his hand.

"Shall we?"

She agreed and they made their way down to the door, which, to the best of Emma's memory, was an exact duplicate of the old door.

"We did it," she said with a grin that threatened to become wrung-out laughter. "We did it!"

The door swung open. Blaise snapped his fingers, and a flame kindled on the wick of a lamp, which, like the door, was indistinguishable from its predecessor. The table, the stool, the embroidery frame were all in their appropriate places. There was even a rack of wood piled beside the hearth. Fresh white linen covered the pillows on the bed—an improvement over the drab cloth Blaise had thought up. His upholstered chair looked as uncomfortable as ever, but Em's chair, while still a far cry from a twentieth-century recliner, looked a bit better padded than it had in its prior incarnation.

Blaise's first move was toward the earthenware pitcher on the table. He poured a finger's breadth of wine into a goblet and sipped it cautiously. "Perfection!" He filled his glass and a second glass for Emma. "A toast to renewal."

Emma wasn't sure that wine was what she needed just then, but she wouldn't deny herself a glass—after she took a closer look at the garden window—

"Damn!" she muttered.

Blaise was beside her in an instant. "What's—?"

But he could see the problem for himself. Fog as thick as whipped cream swirled against the tiny, leaded diamond panes.

"I lost the garden!"

Blaise pushed the casement open. Tendrils of fog crept into the bolthole.

"It's been like this before," he said with something less than ringing confidence.

Em fetched a piece of wood from the hearth side. She tossed it through the open window. It arced downward and, by the silence, fell a good long way without hitting bottom.

"I didn't know how I'd made it in the first place. Beginner's luck—dumb luck. And now it's gone. And now I can't show you the future."

She was running on empty and couldn't keep herself from crying or shivering. Blaise wrapped her in a warm hug. He offered Em a sip of his wine. She drank several swallows more than a sip. Her tears dried up, but the shivering got worse.

"I've got to leave. I should stay and try to put things to rights, but I'm cold on the inside—"

"A certain sign that it's time to go back," Blaise agreed.

When a here-and-now anchor wanted to recall a wasteland-wandering curse-hunter, the standard operating procedure included pressing an ice cube against a hand or foot or the base of the hunter's neck.

"I'll come back as soon as I'm rested. I'll figure out a way to fix the window."

Blaise didn't argue. He gave Em a kiss and an embrace then stayed where he was, inside the new bolthole, while Em got down on her knees beside the way-back stone. She blinked and looked up into her mother's worried face.

"You've been shivering for the last fifteen minutes. I tried calling your name. When that didn't work, I resorted to the old ice-cube trick."

Emma was cold to the bone. She pulled the quilt off the sofa and wrapped it tight. "Tea. I need a cup of hot tea. Any chance—?"

"Stay right there." Eleanor hustled to the kitchen, ran the water, then punched buttons on the microwave. "How did it go? Did you find the curse?"

"Yes and no. I went back to the crash—the one where Kaylee's father died. I watched it play out and thought I knew where to intervene, but when I was done, Kaylee still had a curse. Make that she had a curse from the get-go; she'd been sharing it with her father—at least that's what it looked like. The curse that got loose after Kaylee set the truck on fire and turned it into a funeral pyre for her dad, *that* curse I managed to moot only to discover that it didn't matter. I thought I'd just made a mistake and intervened at the wrong time. So, I backtracked again.

"It was the strangest thing, Eleanor—I got a good look at the two of them in the seconds right after Andrew Sharpe died—I think he died on impact. He wasn't wearing a seat belt, the idiot. Anyway, I don't think Kaylee killed him. I think he was already dead. And I think he probably deserved what Kaylee had in mind for him, but that's not the point. I looked at the two of them together—looked with my eyes closed so I could see a curse, if there was a curse *before* Kaylee got out of the truck. And there was; there was green light everywhere. It was as though Kaylee and her father were under the same curse.

"The way it seemed to go—Andrew Sharpe had a curse and shared it with his daughter before he died. As he died, he gave it to his daughter. Then, *after* he died, a whole new curse sprang out of him; and it possessed Kaylee, too."

"That can't be," Eleanor interrupted from the kitchen where the microwave beeped. "People can't share curses. Curses can't share people. And nobody can have two curses. It's one to a customer, until death—or mooting— do them part." She poured water and returned to the living room with a steaming cup. "It's raspberry. Is that okay?"

"If it's warm, it's okay." Em took the cup. She inhaled the steam. The cold tension in her gut began to ease. "I'm telling you what happened. Andrew Sharpe and his daughter shared a curse, then he died, and she had it by herself. That's how it plays out now, after I plunged. If I hadn't plunged—" Emma took a mouth-burning sip. "If I hadn't changed anything, then the only way it makes sense is that Kaylee walked away from the accident that killed her father still under the influence of the curse they shared and after releasing a curse because of what she'd done—setting his corpse on fire and *believing* she'd killed—"

A bolt of insight struck Emma's mind.

"Wait a minute. Andrew Sharpe's death had nothing to do with the curse his daughter's act released, Eleanor. How can that be?"

"It can't. Curses are joined to death. You've got to be mistaken about what you witnessed."

"I know. I know I've got to have misread something. I'll have to go back. I've got to find some other point where I can intersect with the two of them. Maybe if I stop them from getting into the truck together. Or even if I can stop him from making the turn that led to the accident." Em drank more tea. "It shouldn't be hard. It's just that I can't shake the sense that there were two curses and every-thing's all tangled up."

"A good night's sleep, that's what you need."

Emma glanced at the VCR clock. "Good God—" It read 2:30AM. "I was out for hours. Worse, I've got to get up and walk to work in four hours."

"No, no walking. I'll get up and drive you to the library. It's the least I can do. You set your alarm for the last pos-sible moment."

Never mind that Eleanor had missed the boat more often than not, Emma wanted every precious moment of sleep she could wring out of what remained of the night. "I'll set my alarm for seven-thirty and I'll be ready to leave at seven forty-five. Please, don't get between me and the bathroom."

"I won't," Eleanor promised. "We can get together for lunch, too. I'll pick you up. We'll go out to that dealership that has the Integra. You can't be without a car another day longer."

Em didn't argue. Getting up at seven-thirty, she wouldn't have time to make her lunch, and she might as well look at the silver Integra.

Halfway up the stairs Emma realized that she hadn't said a word about the destruction and reconstruction of the bolthole, much less her failure to recreate the magic win-dow. She turned, took a downward step, then changed her mind and continued on to the comfort of her bed.

Remarkably, Em did remember to adjust her alarm clock, though she had no memory of doing so when it went off and it took her a few panicky moments to recall why she had changed it. More remarkably, Eleanor was already up, dressed, and staying clear of the bathroom as Emma raced through her morning routine.

They lost a few minutes scraping frost off the purple car's windshield, and Emma lost another being pleasant to the security guard in the library lobby. Still, she was leaving the elevator at eight—late for her, but strictly on time as far as library policy was concerned.

Betty was already in, looking sour and staring at Rahima's desk, which was unoccupied. Emma offered her cheeriest hello on her way past Betty's desk.

"She's late," Betty replied.

"Well, let me know when she calls."

"If she calls."

Emma kept going. She managed to get her coffee without making eye contact and was well into prioritizing her various messages when Betty loomed in her doorway.

"She's on line two."

Em picked up the line and got as far as "Hello," when Rahima broke down. In the midst of Rahima's soft speaking voice, her stifled sobs, and sudden problems with English syntax, Emma pieced together a picture of a disastrous weekend. Rahima's daughter—her name was Manal—who'd been so eager to live with her uncle's family the previous week had changed her mind on Saturday, but the uncle had taken a hard line and refused to let her leave his home.

Mother and daughter had communicated by cell phone until the batteries in Manal's unit went dead.

"Have you spoken to your brother-in-law?" Em asked when she had the opportunity.

That brought a fresh torrent of distress. Now that he had physical custody of one of his nieces, the brother-in-law had apparently disowned any relationship to his brother's wife. He'd apparently threatened with the INS and worse—not that Rahima seemed able to imagine anything worse than a meeting with officials from the Immigration and Naturalization Service. Desperate and panicky, Rahima had kept her youngest daughter home from school for fear that the girl would be kidnapped and, of course, she didn't dare leave the little girl alone.

"You need to come to work," Em said firmly. "Bring your daughter—" Betty would go ballistic, but they'd cope; somehow they'd cope. "This is America, not—" Em's mind went blank. For her life, she couldn't remember the countries from which Rahima or her brother-in-law had come. "—And in America no one's brother-in-law can hold his niece against her will, or her mother's will." At least no one in Emma Merrigan's America dwelt under that sort of harsh rule. But there was more than one America, and the one that involved green cards and the INS could be very punitive. Em hoped she wasn't giving Rahima false assurances. "Get yourself in here, and we'll figure something out."

"You don't know him," Rahima protested. "He is a very important man."

"Not around here he isn't."

If anyone should be worried about the INS, it was the brother-in-law. For all its talk about the sanctity of free speech, the U wasn't above intolerance and hypocrisy. Rahima's brother-in-law had been caught making sympathetic statements about suspected terrorist groups to his undergraduate students. Though he had his impassioned defenders, the man was effectively on a leash far shorter than Rahima's.

It took Em another five minutes to persuade Rahima to come to work, after which she spent the better part of an hour combing the combined resources of Bower and the university in search of cultural expertise. By the time Rahima and her daughter swept into the office, Em had finagled a noon appointment at the offices of a small activist outreach group dedicated to the rights of Arabic and Muslim women both in the United States and in their home countries.

"They say they've handled cases like yours before," Em explained to her assistant, and when Rahima balked at the prospect of discussing her problems with strangers, even sympathetic strangers with names a lot like hers, Emma made another spur-of-the-moment decision. "We'll go over together."

Of course, that meant calling Eleanor and canceling their lunch plans. Em called home and left a message on her own machine, then, before she'd stewed too long in her own juices, tried Eleanor's cell.

"Well, that's very noble of you," Eleanor decided when she'd heard Emma's reasons for rearranging her day. "But what about your car? The dealership closes at six. Can I pick you up after work?"

Em looked at the morning's work she hadn't done and the appointment calendar that showed two meetings this afternoon, the first at one-thirty, the second at four. The second was sure to run late. "The car will just have to wait until tomorrow. Or the next day. There's just too much on my plate right now to worry about what car I'm going to be driving for the next decade. I think I'll just call a rental company and rent one for a couple weeks."

"I'll pick you up at five-thirty. If we get there before the showroom closes, they won't kick us out—"

"No. I'm not getting anything done now, so I'm going to have to work late. And I don't have time to talk about it. I've got to get Rahima across campus."

"Call me when you need a ride home."

Em promised that she would then rounded up Rahima and her eerily silent younger daughter. She told Betty she'd be back in time for her one-thirty meeting and tried to overlook the ice-knives look she'd gotten in lieu of a reply. Any doubts that she'd done the right thing vanished once she herded Rahima into the outreach offices. The two women, one in traditional modest dress with a black head covering, the other in jeans and a bulky sweater, knew all the right words and knew them in the right language, too. Even the little girl smiled and whispered.

Emma was superfluous, but stayed discreetly in the background, taking mental notes, in case Rahima faltered along the path to the family reunion that the other women were plotting for her.

It wasn't until they were wrapping up that Emma stole

a lingering look at her assistant then turned away and closed her eyes. No greenish blob, no curse, and no accounting for who caught a curse and who didn't. Child of the sixties that she was, Em was uncomfortable comparing one person to another, but it seemed that she'd done more good in bringing Rahima and these women together than she'd done in all her nights plinking curses in the wasteland.

Armed with forms to file and numbers to call, Rahima and her daughter went directly to the downtown federal building to check on her status as the very legal widow of a duly naturalized citizen. Emma wandered across the campus by herself, deep in moral conundrums and uninterested in any lunch she could have picked up on the quick from the food court in the student union basement. She regretted that decision five minutes into her one-thirty meeting.

In the course of the annual budget chaos, Emma, as acquisitions director, met with liaisons from all the academic departments to help them set their library budget items. The meetings were formalities in the years when the U's funding was stable or expanding. In years when resources were contracting, Em fielded a predictable stream of complaints, ultimatums, and outright hostility. The U had been through bad years before—worse years than the one they were facing. Em had all the ego-armor she needed and the asbestos underwear, too, that allowed her to get through the liaison meetings without taking anything personally, but on an empty stomach, industrial-strength politeness left her light-headed and nauseated.

Emma stopped at the student union on her way back to her office and picked up a hard-roll sandwich the lunchtime mob of students had rejected. She had forty-five minutes before her second liaison meeting of the day and was in no mood for Betty's anti-Rahima campaign.

"She's my assistant, not a terrorist or a terrorist sympathizer, and if that's a problem for you, I hear they're looking for departmental secretaries over in English. I could always put in a good word for you."

Betty blanched. There were good and widely known reasons for the English Department's chronic inability to keep its staff positions filled. They started with the chairman and went downhill from there.

Em figured she'd have peace for the rest of the afternoon, maybe longer. Then she saw the message propped up in front of her computer monitor.

Come down to my office. I've got something you need to see.

Time was a note like that would have meant the network had emitted a perplexing error message and Matt hoped that Emma, who'd helped set up the library's portion of network back in the dark ages, might remember what it meant. But it had been a good six months since Matt had come to her for error message support. She picked up the phone, intending to tell her friend that she had no time for his discoveries, then put it down.

"Forty minutes," she muttered to herself, adding, "I'll be back for my next meeting," in a voice loud enough for Betty to hear.

Matt was bubbling when Emma arrived at his basement domain. He hurried to one of his three functioning monitors and brought up a page of text.

"Just look at this!"

Emma settled in a chair for a closer look. She'd forgotten her reading glasses—but she didn't need them as regularly anymore. All she had to do was squint and the type came into focus. Sometimes, like this time, she didn't even have to squint.

"What am I looking for?" she asked. The screen was filled with several dense columns of names and dates— some sort of genealogy page, she guessed, but she didn't see any familiar names.

"Look there—" Matt tapped the screen. "There's your Andrew Sharpe."

Sure enough, there was an Andrew Sharpe among the names: Andrew Sharpe Mayhew, son of Abigail Sharpe and Andrew Simon Mayhew. He'd been born in 1835 and died in 1871 in Sanilac, Michigan. Sanilac was one of the Thumb counties and, a few months ago, a different Andrew Sharpe, a plain Andrew Sharpe, had died on its back roads, but—"That can't be the Andrew Sharpe I'm looking for. He's really a Mayhew, in case you didn't notice. I don't need to go back a hundred and twenty-five years to find my Andrew Sharpe."

"I bet you do," Matt challenged. "You've got to get back to the guy who spit the curse out the first time, right? Well, look at this guy's wife and his kids."

Emma read the lines. The birth dates varied, but the date of death was the same for all six Mayhews—husband, wife, and four children between the ages of six and seventeen: October 8, 1871, in Sanilac. "Okay, it looks like they died together."

"Something like that could raise a curse couldn't it? A whole family wiped out in a single day? And there's more—" Matt reached over Em's shoulders to tap a few keys. "I found this searching for Andrew Sharpe, but once I'd found this, I started digging on October eighth. There was a fire—"

He brought up a page that told the story of a nineteenth-century firestorm that had ravaged the Thumb forests on the eighth of October 1871 and put an end to the lumbering industry there.

"Dollars to doughnuts, they burned to death," Matt said triumphantly.

"Dollars to doughnuts, they did," Emma agreed. "But they're Mayhews, not Sharpes, and even if they were Sharpes, it takes more than tragedy to create a curse. Think about the Twin Towers. If tragedy were sufficient, we'd have had three thousand new curses that day, but we didn't." She heard herself say: "This Andrew Sharpe who's really a Mayhew is just a coincidence."

"It's not, Em. This is a Sharp genealogy site. Sharp with an 'e,' without an 'e;' with an 's,' without an 's;' with an 'es.' There are thousands of them—hundreds, at least. I haven't found Andrew or Kaylee, but I will. I bet you I will. That curse you saw in Union on Saturday, it's stuck to the branches of the Sharp family tree. So, you can at least check out what I've already found, can't you? Set your dials for October eighth and see what really happened?"

"Watch a family burn to death?"

Matt blanched. "I hadn't thought of that. But the curse you're after is a fast-cycler, which means it has to have *cycled* a few times. What's fast for a curse? Ten years? Twenty years?"

"Beats me," Em admitted testily. "You should have asked Eleanor—" because she was certain Matt had picked up the fast-cycler label from her.

"All right, she said to look deeper in the past. World War One. She told me about this influenza epidemic after that war. It came to America with the soldiers coming back from Europe and killed more people than the war did." He hesitated. "I was only trying to help. Eleanor said you didn't have any luck last night."

"And just when did she say that?"

"Lunch. We had lunch. She was looking to buy a computer and wanted my input."

Emma fumed silently. Matt was a grown man, and he knew what Eleanor was, exactly what she was beneath that two-toned hair and flawless skin. Who was she to object to his choices, or to Eleanor's, for that matter? And though she could have built her mother a computer—she'd been putting her own together since Matt Barto was in high school—she couldn't blame Eleanor for seeking Matt's advice over hers.

"We're just friends, Auntie Em," Matt told her, a bit testy himself once he'd understood her silence. "Same as you and me."

"And it's no business of mine if you decide to become

more or less than that," Em insisted, mostly to convince herself. "You're right—it can't hurt to check this guy out. Can you print out those pages for me?"

Matt tapped more keys. An ancient ink-jet in the corner clattered to life.

"You'll let me know what you find?"

Em assured Matt with a quick nod as she retrieved the first printed sheet. "I'll check it out. Either you've dug up the solution to all my problems or I'm still looking. Lately, my motto's been 'No Coincidences,' so, little as I like the idea, you're probably on to something." She retrieved the second sheet with the reprinted newspaper article about the 1871 Thumb fire. "It's been a day, without curses. Saving the world from someone else's curse just hasn't been job one."

She told Matt, briefly, about Rahima's problems and the solution she had brokered. He was impressed that she'd found just the right outreach group in such a short time, and they parted without another word about curses or Eleanor Graves.

As she'd feared, Em's four o'clock meeting ran long. The office was deserted and dark when she returned at quarter of six. Her telephone message light was blinking angrily. It seemed everyone had tried to reach her before the end of work, Rahima and Eleanor included. Rahima was on her way to pick up her elder daughter, and Eleanor wanted to know when she'd be home for dinner.

Em called Eleanor's cell.

"Don't wait for me and dinner. I've got a half day's work staring at me. I'm not coming home until late. I'll call you for a ride, if that's not too much trouble."

"No trouble at all, and all the more reason I should fix your dinner. I'm standing in your kitchen anyway."

Emma's heart sank. "I thought you were getting your bed delivered today?"

"You were right: The stairway's too steep and the landing too tight for a king-sized bed. They had to take it back.

I've got a queen-sized due on Wednesday. It'll fit; they measured, but I've got to exchange all those sheets and pillowcases I bought."

"Wednesday," Em repeated without enthusiasm.

"Maybe Thursday. They've got to get the box spring from their Kalamazoo store. Listen, you've got work to do! Just give me a call when you're ready to come home. And don't worry about dinner. I'll have something ready for you."

Though Emma would never have admitted it aloud, the idea of a home-cooked meal on the table waiting for her sounded wonderful. She put her shoulder to the proverbial grindstone and, without the usual interruptions, had churned the pile of things that absolutely had to be done by eight-thirty.

Eleanor's cell was busy—touching base with Harry? Freeing up another wad of cash for a computer? Em dialed her own number and spoke to her answering machine.

"Eleanor? If you're there, pick up the phone, please?"

After a moment of silence, Eleanor's voice came on the line with a promise that she'd leave as quickly as she could button her coat. Em stared at her desk. There wasn't much sense in taking work home. She'd be back in less than twelve hours, and she could tell by the way her eyes were burning that she wasn't going to feel like doing much when she got home beyond eating, taking a steamy bath, and going to bed. So, Em didn't pack up any papers and since she hadn't brought either her coffee thermos or her nylon lunch sack with her in the morning, she left the office with nothing more than her purse hanging from her shoulder and a nagging sense that she'd forgotten something important.

The purple car pulled up to the library's back door pretty much when Em expected it to.

Eleanor greeted Em with, "You look exhausted!"

"I am exhausted, and starving. Whatever you've cooked, I can hardly wait to eat it."

Which was an honest enough statement, though Em had been expecting more than a can of tomato soup and tuna salad sandwich. Not that she didn't inhale both the soup and the sandwich, she'd simply hoped for something more.

"I forgot that you usually take your lunch to work," Eleanor said after Em had mustered up a halfhearted compliment. "We need to make your lunch for tomorrow right now and put a note by the door so you won't forget it."

Em nodded. Upstairs in the bathroom, an unopened bottle of aromatherapy, stress-reducing bath salts—Nancy's birthday present—was calling her name. In her mind, she was already sinking into the tub when Eleanor asked—

"Did you bring home those papers Matt printed out for you?"

The question brought Em back to the moment with an unpleasant jolt. "What papers?" she countered, then realized that Matt and Eleanor must have spoken to each other after she'd left his office. At least she knew now what had been bothering her when she left the library. The papers in question were sitting on her desk. "Damn, I wish you wouldn't do that, Eleanor."

"Do what?"

"Talk to Matt about curses and such. Nancy's one thing—she's got a life with kids; she won't get too close. But Matt gets caught up in what we're doing."

Eleanor stiffened. "Matt's a grown man. He can make his own choices, and, I'll have you know: *He called me.* He said he'd found the root of that curse you couldn't moot last night."

Before answering, Emma considered pouring herself a glass of wine to take upstairs, but wine wouldn't rest well on top of tomato soup and tuna salad.

"He found something interesting, that's all." Em was determined to minimize Matt's discovery. "A family named Mayhew—parents and four children. The father's name was Andrew Sharpe Mayhew. Matt thinks there has to be some sort of connection—like a family connection. If the Andrew Sharpe who died last summer were somehow related to Mr. Mayhew which he couldn't have been—not directly. The whole Mayhew family died together back—I don't remember quite when, sometime in the late eighteen hundreds."

"Eighteen eighty-one," Eleanor supplied. "Did you bring home the papers?"

"No. I forgot them. I walked out knowing I'd forgotten something. That's what it was."

"Well, we've got the name, the date, and a map of Michigan. That should be enough. You've been delving this curse for days. It's stuck to you. If there's a connection, you won't have any trouble finding it."

"Not tonight, Eleanor. I'm beat. I haven't recovered from last night—"

"All you have to do is poke your head out your window and see if there's a connection."

Now, Emma decided, was not the time to tell Eleanor that the bolthole had been wrecked by parties unknown and the garden window in the new bolthole wasn't working like the old one. "Did Matt tell you that he thinks the Mayhew family died in a forest fire? I tell you, I'm not up for sticking my nose into an inferno. There's nothing urgent about events that happened over a century ago."

"You don't know that. Time heals itself—that's why we call it 'mooting.' When we're done, it's moot whether a curse did or didn't exist. But you can't moot death, Emma. If you moot a curse after it kills someone, he doesn't come back to life."

"Thanks." Emma carried her dishes into the kitchen. "Nothing like a little guilt for dessert."

"I'm not saying you should moot the curse tonight, just take its measure. If it's the root you're looking for, you can take your time deciding how to moot it."

"That's not what you said a moment ago."

"Once you've witnessed it, I'm sure you'll know, straight off, how to moot it."

Em shrank from her mother's compliments. She left the dishes in the sink.

"All right. What was that date again?"

"Eighteen eighty-one. Sometime in the fall."

"*Sometime!?* I need specifics, Eleanor."

"Nonsense. All you need to do is follow your instincts."

"Then you follow yours."

"I would, Emma. I swear I would, but all my instincts are doing these days is pulling me back to the things I fear most. I nearly delved us into a pit of curses."

A few minutes, Em told herself, a few supremely unpleasant minutes and she could take her bath. She couldn't use the window, of course. She'd have to delve the old-fashioned way—by walking the wasteland until she felt the downward pull of congruence. Maybe—if Emma were lucky—she'd find herself too tired to delve properly. She could walk around, then come home, no worse for the wear.

"You'll pull me out the moment I start sweating or turning red?" Em asked as she settled herself on the living room floor.

"Absolutely," Eleanor promised, giving her glass of ice cubes a vigorous shake.

Emma wrote the words *Sharpe, Mayhew, fire, Sanilac, autumn*, and the date 1881 on the back page of the Bower newspaper. She imagined her spinning coin and emerged in the wasteland to the left of the way-back stone. The ruby ring accompanied her by habit, now. Its stone shone darkly in the magenta twilight.

Em had a welcome sense of the bolthole, and though a visit wasn't on her agenda, she made a beeline for the door. Blaise was absent and hadn't left any messages on the table. He'd reconstructed many of the details she'd neglected in her effort to bring the bolthole back into existence: tongs and pokers for the hearth, baskets for bread and fruit—Emma helped herself to a pear—an empty rack for his coat and hat.

Of greater significance, though, the fog was lifting from beyond the window. The garden walls were faintly visible through the mist and a tangle of old roses, trained along the walls. Emma opened the window and dared a lung-filling breath. The scent of fallen leaves had returned.

If she couldn't delve through the wasteland to Matt's fire, then there was a chance she could use the window, just not tonight. Emma wasn't in any hurry to test its delving properties. It could settle for another twenty-four hours.

As always, time and distance were difficult to judge. Em guessed she'd walked a mile at her regular four-miles-per-hour pace. She was starting to think she was on a fool's errand when her energy lagged and her feet grew too heavy for even a snail's pace—the telling sign that she'd come to her delving point. From her hands and knees and with her eyes closed, Emma focused her thoughts ever tighter on the words she'd written in the living room. Her entire body grew heavy. She felt herself sinking, gathering speed.

All in all, climbing through the bolthole window was a far less traumatic way to delve the past.

Emma's first impression was heat. Even with her wasteland-muted senses, she was aware of a stifling heat borne on a hot wind. She began to sweat almost at once. Her body's moisture mixed with grit from the air, and it clung to her skin like a thin sheet of plastic. The grit had an odor: soot and ash and meat that had been cooked until it charred.

At least I've come to the right place, she mused. Suddenly there was a blast of wintry air against her face. It felt wonderful, but, *No—not yet. Give me a few minutes to look around.*

Em rose from her delving crouch and for a heartbeat wondered if she'd left the wasteland at all. The sky overhead was a featureless dome of amber and gray. Half the horizon glowed with shades of red and orange, while the other half was twilight dark.

Matt had guessed that the Mayhew family had been wiped out by a forest fire and by the look of things, he'd guessed right.

Emma had delved herself to the side of an empty chicken coop. To her right stood a small barn, to her left, wide fields of unharvested wheat or hay, and straight ahead, a building that was smaller than the barn and was probably the family's home. Frantic shouts came faintly to Em's ears from the far side of the house. She walked toward the commotion.

There wasn't much doubt in Emma's mind about what she'd see once she cleared the corner. Andrew Sharpe Mayhew and his family weren't going to escape the fire. Her heart ached for the young man—he couldn't have been out of his twenties—as he struggled to harness a panicky horse to a wagon that was little more than a box on wheels.

Mayhew's wife appeared at the front door. Between the heat and the smoke, it was impossible to say if she was a pretty woman. She was certainly a young and frightened one. A toddler clung to her skirt. An infant nestled in the crook of her arm.

"Hurry!" the wife shouted, though her husband was doing all that he could.

A crown of flames had reached the woods on the far side of their plowed fields. Trees were exploding—literally exploding—as the fire touched them.

The family would be better off going to ground in their well, Em thought. Every homesteading family worth its hearth and plow had dug a twenty-foot deep, six-foot across well for both water and cool storage. If they huddled together and pressed damp rags against their faces, they might stand a chance. The racing fire might pass over them before they suffocated or burnt. One thing was certain, though—they weren't going to outrun the flames in a horse-drawn wagon. Curse or no curse, when Emma rolled up the past and got inside Andrew Mayhew's head, she was going to nudge him toward the well.

There wasn't any reason to wait.

Emma had read a newspaper article telling her how this story had ended, though she'd thought the children should be a bit older and that there'd be more of them. No matter. She lined herself up and plunged straight at Andrew Mayhew.

The same thoughts chased one another through the young man's mind: *Harness the horse ... Harness the horse ... Load up Lorna, Sarah, and Little Andy ... Get to the river ... Get to the river!*

Em needed every bit of her own strength just to get his attention.

"The well, Andrew. Take them to the well—"

Em expected resistance, but nothing like the surge of opposition that bore down on her from all directions. Though she'd never in her previous plunging adventures felt the conscious need to breathe, in Andrew Mayhew's mind breathing had become impossible. And he would not, under any circumstance, put his family in the well. He hadn't gone near the well since he'd dug it.

Phobia didn't begin to describe Andrew Mayhew's reaction to Emma's suggestion. She'd inadvertently triggered memories so dark that he would not—could not—do anything so long as that hateful idea was loose in his mind.

"Andrew!" the man's wife shouted. "Andrew Sharpe! Hurry, Andy!"

Perplexed beyond words and genuinely sorry that she'd crossed some invisible line in the man's mind, Emma retreated as quickly as she dared. She emerged into her own body—the shadow of her body that Em wore around herself when she delved into the past—a few strides behind the wagon. She faced the unharvested field and the fire beyond it.

The very air above the field seemed to shimmer. Em thought the shimmering was due to disorientation, then a wave of sheer heat crashed over her and there was fire everywhere. The house was on fire and the wagon. The horse burnt where it stood; it had died too quickly to fall. Andrew Mayhew—had his wife called him by a different name?—and his family became pillars of fire.

Emma was safe. The flames couldn't touch her, but she imagined air so hot it seared her lungs and stripped the flesh from her bones.

There wasn't a well this side of Antarctica that could preserve a family through this. Emma would have to come up with some other tactic—and not simply out of mercy. The fiery pillar that had been Andrew Mayhew was changing. Emma had missed the warning signs—the hot winds that heralded the creation of a curse. In this firestorm, they'd found the perfect camouflage.

Perhaps it was his failure to save his family from horrific deaths. Perhaps there was more to his rejection of the well than Em had been able to glean from his surface thoughts. Perhaps he'd carried some other dark and dreadful secret to his death agony. The precise truths didn't matter so much as the result, which was that Andrew Mayhew was giving rise to a curse.

Emma could scarcely tell where ordinary fire ended and a curse began. The homestead had become a forest of whirling flame, but the curse seemed darker, stronger. It bent the other flames—the flames born in flesh and wood—first inward to itself, then outward toward Emma Merrigan.

Her leather-bound books said it couldn't happen: A freshly decanted curse didn't have the strength to threaten a curse-hunter, especially not in the past, where the hunter was merely a visitor. But those leather-bound books were only as good as the curse-hunters who'd written them and contained as much myth and wish as fact. Better to remember what Blaise had said less than a week ago: Curses don't obey rules.

Emma made a fist and held it, chin high, in front of her.

She added ruby-red light to the mix of amber, orange, and crimson. The curse's flames retreated but did not shrink. A curse-hunter's weapons lost their potency away from the wasteland.

Now, Eleanor. Now before I burn up or worse!

Twelve

Emma came to her body with a gasp and a shudder. She was safe in her own living room with her mother kneeling beside her.

"Emma? Say something!"

"I'm cold," Em replied, which, though unexpected, was also the simple truth. After the torrid blasts of a forest fire and a curse, her living room seemed to have no heat at all. She began to shiver. "I'm freezing."

Eleanor grabbed the quilt from the sofa. "Does that help?"

Em wrapped the cloth around her shoulders and nodded. The spasms were still strong, but the quilt would warm her up soon enough, if she could just relax.

Eleanor patted her on the head. "You need a hot toddy. Sit tight. I'll make you one."

Before Emma could protest, Eleanor was headed toward the kitchen. She paused by the dining table and picked up a small, black object: her cell phone. "She's coming around. Cold as ice, though. I'm going to thaw her out with a toddy. Can I call you later?"

"Who was that? Harry?" Em asked when Eleanor had clapped the cover over her phone.

"No. Matt. I think I've decided to go with one of those flat monitors instead of a big, bulky CRT like you've got."

Emma succumbed to another round of head-to-toe shuddering. The memory of the newly emerged curse hovering wouldn't fade, and those of the Mayhew family burning like straw men had the power to give her a month's worth of nightmares. She had never been one to live on the edge and had come too close to disaster for comfort.

But there was a tainted element of resentment in her misery: Eleanor had offered to be her anchor; she should have been paying attention. Em concluded that she shouldn't have had to linger in the past until she could see the turbulent inside of a towering curse. She couldn't resist a jibe: "Maybe next time I'll ask Matt to be my anchor. At least he'd pay attention to what's happening."

Eleanor returned from the kitchen, empty-handed. "I was sure you were on top of the situation. It's not as if you were after a rogue, or something. What *did* happen to send you back at sixes and sevens?"

All the images her memory had collected from the Mayhew homestead gushed through Em's mind. It wasn't enough to be sitting on the floor. She needed to put a hand down on the carpet to steady herself. Significantly, there was a bilious green streak through many of the images she'd collected of Andrew Mayhew before fire engulfed him. The smears were like photographic double exposures or, in Em's case, the hallmark of a parasitic curse.

"Not a rogue," she agreed, "and not some fingerling either. Eleanor, I think we've got it all wrong about curses. I think I just watched a cursed man die and release not only the old curse he'd been carrying for God only knows how long, but release a brand-new curse as well. I don't know . . . maybe Matt is onto something. That second curse was the size of those flaming pillars you tangled with."

Eleanor had the grace to look concerned. "You must be

mistaken," she insisted. "The family died in a forest fire, didn't they? It would be hard to tell the difference between a curse and a flaming tree."

"Not that hard. I'm telling you: I watched two curses come out of one man. Actually, I missed the first one—my memory thing, again. I didn't see it until just now, when I remembered him, and saw his curse, and it escaping just as he died. After it was gone, while his body was still on fire—that's when the *second* curse began to gather. It was bigger than anything I've mooted. It was the size of those ones that got you, Eleanor, and it was aware of me. I could hold it off with the ring there in the past, but I couldn't moot it. Honestly, I'm beginning to think we're all wrong about how curses are hatched."

"The books all say—"

"I know what the books say, Eleanor, and they're copies of copies. Think about it: You have to be able to *delve* to witness a curse's birth. How many delvers are there, Eleanor? How many have there ever been? How much of those books on those shelves over there is the truth and how much is what someone wished were true? Don't forget, for thousands of years the best human minds thought the earth was flat and the sun revolved around it . . . pulled by a chariot of flaming white horses."

Eleanor didn't have answers to Emma's questions. She offered a different solution. "I'll get you that hot toddy."

"Thanks, but I don't need it now." Exasperation had gotten Em's blood flowing again. She was warm but bone tired. "I can go back there. I can try to do something different, but it's not going to be easy—the fire *explodes* around them. They're dead in an instant, and the one idea I had for saving them, I'm not sure it would work, period, but when I got into Andrew Mayhew's head and nudged him toward it, he froze up, like I was asking him to do the unthink—" Em stopped, mid-word. "My God," she whispered. "He was cursed. He was cursed, and when I told him to get his family into the well, I triggered something close to the curse he already had. Forget about how curses come into being. How does someone *catch* a curse?"

"Why ask me?" Eleanor groused. "Everything I know I learned from a book."

"Curses must delve, or do something very much like delving that puts them up close and personal with a human being on the brink of something awful . . . something that makes them susceptible. There's got to be something predisposing, maybe not all the time. Maybe not all curses are equal when they're hatched. Maybe some are stronger—if they spring up from a person who's already cursed. . . . Something's got to indicate to a free-floating curse that it's found a likely host. Then, when a curse has found what it's looking for—then they must plunge and never leave. They just stay there, festering parasites, trying to make sure that when their host dies, not only does the original curse get freed, but there's one more curse turned loose.

"I'm targeting intermediate points on a line. Kaylee's father, Andrew Sharpe, had a curse and made a curse. Tonight I went back to the nineteenth century, and Andrew Mayhew had a curse and made a curse. Think of it. Curses—at least two curses, maybe more—chasing each other down the time line, sort of like Slinkies tumbling down a flight of stairs."

Emma met Eleanor's eyes and waited for a reaction.

"It goes against everything we think we know."

"That's what they told Galileo, but the earth goes around the sun anyway."

Eleanor struggled with Emma's ideas; the effort showed on her face. Finally she said, "It could be true," and sighed with relief. "One time—when I was still quite young—I thought I could save a woman from being struck by a train. She was committing suicide, and I knew I could get inside her thoughts and make her walk in some other direction. This was when I was living with my father's people, before I understood my *wyrd*. Before I knew what a curse was. *Long* before I knew better than to plunge in the here and now. I put myself in her thoughts and said *Not now* and *Go home*. I'd done that before—nothing as dramatic as stopping a suicide, but I'd turned people away from where they'd been headed. It was very useful when I got caught stealing candy; I was a naughty child—an orphan on sufferance, you know.

"Anyway, the woman's mind wasn't like my aunt's mind. It was—after all these years, I still can't describe it, except to say that it was small and full of places where neither she nor I could go. And I couldn't make her stop. She walked me in front of that train. I damn near couldn't get out in time and, when I did—well, I witnessed my first curse and, Emma—I've never told anyone this—it came in two pieces. A small one—a tiddler that disappeared right away in the smoke from the train's engine; and a big one that came after.

"Years later, after I hooked up with the Europeans, I learned my lessons and assumed I must have been mistaken about what I'd witnessed on the railroad tracks. I couldn't have been more than eight or nine at the time, and I could have been mistaken. But it's stuck with me—that image of a big curse following a little one. And that woman's mind—her tiny mind with all its sharp corners and blind alleys. I suppose—if I listen to what you're saying, she could have been cursed—truly cursed—long before she stepped in front of that train. The first curse I saw, the tiddler, that could have been the new curse you're talking about, and the second curse, the big one, that one could have been inside her for a long time. It could have been inside a lot of people; it was that big."

"Are you saying that you believe me? Curses making curses? Curses emerging in pairs?"

"I'm saying I saw something once that could be similar to what you've described. But, Emma, no one will believe you."

"Harry will."

Eleanor laughed bitterly. "That doesn't mean anything.

Convincing Harry is worse than having no one believe you. You don't know half the wild ideas Harry's had over the years. If he weren't an absolute wizard with legalities and money, he'd have been laughed out of the Curia ages ago."

"Then I'll grab old Redmond Longleigh by the hand and take him back to Andrew Mayhew's farm to see for himself."

"He won't go. Red won't go anywhere that he can't lead, but you could trick him, Emma. If you told him about the window in your bolthole, he'd want to see that for himself. There's nothing like it in the bunker. Not a window anywhere, for that matter. It's all underground. He probably never thought of windows. But, you could make certain the window took him back to that farm, couldn't you?"

Emma squirmed. "Not at this exact moment."

"What do you mean?"

Em had trapped herself into making a full confession. By the time she finished, and finished answering Eleanor's question, her adrenaline had ebbed. When Eleanor said— "If something's attacked your bolthole, then we should go to the bunker. With or without the window. They need to know. Other hunters could be at risk."—Emma shook her head. "Tomorrow. The world can remain flat for another twenty-four hours. Whether it's wrecking the bolthole, the window, or Andrew Mayhew's double curse, I've got a bad feeling that meeting Redmond Longleigh for the first time is going to turn into a major scene, and I don't think I can handle another emotional scene." She covered her eyes and swore softly. "I've got to be at a lawyer's office at eight tomorrow morning. How could I forget?"

Eleanor, naturally, wanted to know what sudden business her daughter had with a lawyer. "You should have told me, Em. We have our own lawyers—"

"It's not for me, Emma. It's my assistant. She's having family troubles of the green-card variety, and we need to

be sure everything's kosher with her immigration status—
I don't believe I said that."

"Said what?"

"Rahima's Palestinian."

Eleanor understood the irony and agreed that Emma
was overtired. She thought a long bath was unnecessary,
but Em had her heart set on an up-to-the-shoulders immersion.

"If I'm not out in a half hour, you can come in and pull
the plug."

Emma made it out of the cooling water under her own
power with five minutes to spare. She left Eleanor to turn
out the lights and crawled into bed, where the cats were
waiting for her. If she fell asleep as soon as her head hit the
pillow—and she expected she would—Em would have
five hours of sleep under her pillow when the alarm went
off. She would have liked twice that, and would have considered taking personal time, were it not for Rahima's appointment with the lawyer. And if she were getting up for
a lawyer, she might as well put in a day at the library.

The clock radio wasn't playing morning music when
Emma next opened her eyes; that was her first clue that
something was wrong. The cats were both missing from
her bed; that was the second. The third, and by far the most
compelling was the absence of a little blue green dot alongside the numbers 6:45. With the blue dot, the numbers
meant morning. Without it, they meant she'd slept for
nearly eighteen hours.

Either way, the only light in her bedroom came up the
stairs, filtered and faded, from the living room. Emma
found her slippers by feel and staggered to the hall.

"Eleanor!"

There was movement in the living room—rustling papers and the *clink* of glass against a coaster. "You're
awake!"

"What happened? What day is it? You should have
woken me up!"

Eleanor appeared at the foot of the stairs. "You were tired. Tuesday. And, I did . . . twice and when I couldn't keep you awake for more than five minutes either time, I decided to let you sleep. I found your office number and called to say you wouldn't be in today—twenty-four hour virus."

That certainly covered the necessary bases, but—"What about Rahima? Good grief, I was supposed to go to that lawyer's office with her. She probably thinks I'm in league with her brother-in-law."

"Then she's a fool," replied Eleanor bluntly. "Anyone can catch a bug and not be worth the powder to blow them to hell for twenty-four hours. Now, is that as far as you're coming, or do you want some dinner?"

At the mention of food, Emma's stomach churned to life. She wanted dinner, possibly two dinners, and neither of them poured out of a can. "Dinner, definitely. Have you eaten? I could be talked into a trip out to Horatio's with less than two words."

The campus hang-out wasn't all-you-can-eat, but they served their pasta in fraternity-sized bowls.

"I'm game," Eleanor said, then added, "Wear something warm."

"What, has it snowed?"

Bower's first measurable snowfall usually hit over Thanksgiving, but mid-October wasn't unheard of.

"No, I've got something to show you."

"Your bed?"

"No, it's a surprise. Hurry up and get dressed."

Now that her stomach was up and prepping for a hearty Italian dinner, Em needed no urging to rush through her morning—make that evening—rituals. She was downstairs a few minutes after seven. Eleanor had her coat on and her keys in her hand.

Emma spotted the purple car—it was hard to miss, even by streetlight—but Eleanor took her arm and steered her the other way.

"What's—" Em began, then she saw it. "Oh, my God—"

Em wasn't the sort who internalized car shapes. Though she'd lived all her life in the Motor City's shadow, she could pick maybe five or six models out of a line-up, and three of those would have been classic cars, more than twenty years old. She couldn't have imagined an Integra's rear end if her life depended on it, yet she knew she was looking at one as soon as she saw the silver car parked directly under a streetlight.

"Eleanor!"

"Now, don't panic. If you really don't like how it drives and don't want anything to do with it, Matt says he's fallen in love, and I've told him that we can negotiate a loan, just like a bank—"

"Did you *buy* it?"

"Not exactly. It's your car, Emma. Your money paid for it."

Emma's internal temperature rose ten degrees between heartbeats. "You did *what!?*"

"After you were born— When I was back in New York and thinking you'd be showing up in a few years, I asked Harry to make some investments on your behalf; and he did. Then, when you didn't, he saw no reason to *unmake* them. I'm sure I don't know how he does it, but he's always got a couple dozen identities simmering, in case someone needs to make a quick change. I'm sure he's the real genius behind that government witness protection program. Fortunately, when you did surface, he hadn't given yours away. And, well, you know that money invested in the early fifties has appreciated quite nicely. There was plenty, and I didn't think we could count on another perfect car showing up."

"Perfect car," Em repeated.

Two bombshells had struck her life while she slept: Apparently she had a fancy new-used car and something like a trust fund of substantial proportions. By any capitalist measure, Em should sleep the clock around more often. But the feeling in her gut wasn't celebration.

Eleanor offered her a set of keys. "Think of it as a test drive."

Emma circled the car like a suspicious dog. It was sleek, but not too showy, and unmarked from its previous ownership. She put the key into the lock—

"Keyless entry. Just push the little button."

"Right."

She did as she was told and settled herself in front of an impressive dashboard of dials, gauges, and ergonomic buttons. At least the ignition and gearshift were in the customary places, but she needed help finding the headlights. If Em decided this was her new car—and, aside from stubborn pride, there was no reason she shouldn't—she was going to have a lot of reading to do in the owner's manual.

The vehicle, which was a giant step up in luxury and performance from any car Emma had owned, handled as befit its pedigree. Not that the in-town trip to Horatio's was a fair test of a high-performance car—except that it had handled well in undemanding situations.

"What do you think?" Eleanor asked eagerly.

Em had passed up the opportunity to parallel park the car on the street and nosed it into a slot behind the restaurant. There'd be time enough for parallel parking when they returned to the Maisonettes.

"It's real nice," Em admitted. "Very comfortable."

"Isn't it? Mind you, I like my little car—but if I'd known about cars like this. An Oldsmobile it's not."

Em played with a few more buttons before getting out of the car and locking it with a key chain button. Her mind was at war with itself, with one side wanting to embrace the Integra without reservation and the other side arguing principles, while the mother-voice sniffed, *But it's* SILVER.

The internal war raged throughout dinner. Eleanor was on her best behavior. From that perspective, so long as Em didn't mind that the waitress automatically handed her the

check, the dinner was a success with conversations that
never once strayed into tender areas.

Emma's first attempt with parallel parking was a success, too. The overall dimensions of the Integra were close
enough to her old car that the backup-and-cut maneuvers
were no more taxing than they would have been after a
week out of town without her car.

"Well?"

"It's nice and it's a surprise. I've got to get used to the
idea. Frankly, I've got to do some more research—like
how is it on snow and ice?"

"It's a *Honda*, Em. What do you expect?"

"And I've got to test it on the highway. I mean, I know
it's going to handle well, but what about blind spots? I
need a car that's built for a smallish driver."

"Too bad you can't take it to the Netherlands with you
and put it through its paces in front of the bunker. That
would get their attention . . . and their respect."

Em's suspicions could accelerate as fast as her new car.
"What about the bunker?" she demanded on the way to her
front door.

"Well, you're rested now, aren't you? You'll be headed
for the bunker to tell Longleigh and the others about your
bolthole problems and doubled-up curses in person. You're
not going to rely on a telephone, are you? You shouldn't."

"I really haven't given it much thought. Longleigh
made his business proposition over the phone, and, heaven
knows, I've talked to Harry often enough. If there was
some chance of the phones being tapped or overheard, I
can't imagine that Harry wouldn't have told me."

"It's not that. You need eye contact with Longleigh—to
see whether he's really listening or just playing along. And
there are always a few watchers at the bunker. If you can
convince the watchers to watch for your doubles, you've
won half your battle. All of it, if they find them."

Emma unlocked the door. The cats mugged her before
both feet were inside the door. They went wild for the

smells of garlic and tomato sauce, and she was carrying a box of Horatio's leftovers into the house. She'd learned the hard way that they wouldn't touch a crumbled-up meatball if she stooped to put one in their bowl, but that had never stopped them from making pests of themselves after she'd eaten Italian.

"I'd still have to call Longleigh, wouldn't I? It's not like he *lives* there, is it?"

"He'll be at the bunker tonight," Eleanor said with obvious confidence.

"You called him? You told him?"

"Called, yes; told, no. I thought I should let him know I'm back before the watchers catch on."

So, the watchers watched more than curses popping in and out of the wasteland. That was a piece of knowledge to store in an unforgettable place.

"He's expecting you, then, not me. Will Harry be there, too?"

"I hope not. I told you—Harry's not a good ally in this. You're better off going alone—"

"With you. I don't know the way, remember?"

"I won't interfere, I promise. I'll say my piece and be gone—unless you want me to stay. Another set of eyes and ears might not hurt."

Em decanted her leftovers into a sealable container and tucked it in the refrigerator. She noticed that the cats' bowls were empty; they'd missed their supper. She split a small can of food between them. Spin started eating immediately. Charm sat beside the bowl looking betrayed. Through a cat's eyes it had taken only two of Eleanor's more generous meals for her to assume the universe had expanded.

"Do you need anything to get ready?" Em asked her mother.

Eleanor grimaced and admitted she'd brought her flask of adulterated Scotch over earlier in the day, which prompted Emma to ask, "Did your bed arrive?"

"Tomorrow. They promised."

Emma watched with dismay as Eleanor swallowed the contents of her flask. It wasn't the size, so much, that disturbed her. She doubted it held more than a happy-hour double. But the grim determination with which she slugged it down.

"You're sure about this?" she asked. "I can always get on a plane and meet the Curia in the here and now."

Eleanor tightened the cap on the empty flask. "I'm ready. Let's go."

They assumed comfortable positions, facing each other on the carpet. Eleanor said the word, and Emma willed herself to have faith in her mother's abilities. The transition seemed long, but perhaps the Curia's bunker was a long way from Emma's bolthole. There was no way to tell in the wasteland. The sky never changed, and neither did the ground. It was familiarly dry and barren when Emma opened her eyes on what Eleanor said was the bunker's perimeter.

"We walk from here. No matter how well you visualize the doorways, you can't get closer. Don't ask me how Longleigh does it. I don't know, but it is a bunker, and it has defenses that keep the curses and rogues out. Us, too, unfortunately. Can you get a sense of where it is? When you come back, you'll aim for the bunker and it will put you down here; but once you're here, you need to know which way for walking."

Emma closed her eyes and concentrated. Quickly she had the sense of something heavy and seething to her left. "Over there?" she asked.

Eleanor nodded, and they began walking. The way-back stone followed for a little while. Then, to Emma's shock and surprise, it vanished. She felt naked, not knowing where it had gone, and refused to go further until Eleanor explained.

"Defenses—I told you. There's a doorway in the bunker itself. It's a little like your window, except it takes you back to where you started. There's nothing to be afraid of. Trust me, if there were, I wouldn't be here."

Grudgingly, Emma fell in step beside Eleanor again. She understood, now, what Blaise meant when he said he knew just enough about the bunker to avoid it.

Emma and Eleanor had gone what Southerners might call a "fair piece" when they came upon a woman seated lotus-style and slightly off center in a gridded circle about four feet in diameter and laid out on a table of dirt some eight to ten inches high. She wore a drab tunic over a darker leotard. Her eyes were closed, and her hands rested palms-up against her thighs. She held a tiny red stone—the purest bloom of red Em had yet seen under the color-distorting magenta sky—pinched between the thumb and index finger of her right hand. The hollow of her left ankle cradled a small heap of similar stones.

"Is she—"

Eleanor raised a finger to her lips for silence. She pulled Emma close and whispered: "A watcher? Yes. Rosemary. She's one of the best. Best not to disturb her. She's got something on her radar."

"How can you tell?" Em whispered back.

"The markers," Eleanor replied and drew Emma's attention to the watcher's grid, which had to contain at least a thousand squares, a handful of which contained a tiny red stone.

Em's engineering gene twitched mightily, but she overcame the temptation to ask questions.

The heavy, seething sensation Emma had felt upon emerging into the bunker's environs had grown steadily stronger as they walked. It had also spread out into discrete points, one of which remained more congested than the others. Em wasn't surprised that the congested point became the central point, the place toward which they walked.

Eleanor and Harry had both referred to the bunker as a small village. As villages went, the bunker was a charmless collection of low-slung hovels, each with a uniquely off-kilter doorway. By contrast Emma and Blaise's bolt-hole, with its stout, symmetric door, was a model of homi-ness.

"Is this the best the Curia can do?"

Eleanor shrugged. "It's better inside," and confidently led Emma to a hovel that looked no more dignified than the rest.

The hovel proved to be the cap over a steep stairway that went down some twenty steps—maybe fifteen feet below the surface—to a vestibule, which was, as Eleanor had promised, better. Flagstones not unlike those in her own bolthole covered the floor. The single door was wood and decorated with intricately carved scroll-work. A lamp that shone with an uncommonly steady flame hung by a brass chain from a ceiling that was about ten feet high.

The door, Em noticed on her second glance, did not appear to have a handle.

"Is there a bell or knocker someplace?"

The correct answer was password, and the password was simply *Atlantis*, and the room beyond the door reminded Emma of nothing so much as the library's reading room back in her student days when the carpets had been dark, the wood paneling darker, and all the chairs stuffed to the gills. Light came from overhead lamps.

Emma guessed the room was twenty feet wide and about forty feet long. They'd entered the room at one of its narrow ends. There were closed doors along the length of the room, all of them in the style of the door they'd just come through. A single, more massive door was centered on the opposite wall. Em supposed that her audience with Redmond Longleigh would take place on the far side of that door.

There were maybe a half dozen men and women that Em could see from the doorway. There might have been more. The chairs faced different directions and were mostly of the winged variety, within which just about anyone could hide.

They drew attention marching down the fringed Persian runner that ran the length of the room, but no one hailed Eleanor by name, and she allowed no one to catch her eye. Em followed. She kept her face forward and her vision peripheral. A man stood up when they were halfway home. Em would have loved to know who he was and why he'd seemed to smile as they passed.

The impressive door had both knocker and knob. Eleanor rapped once before turning the knob. The door opened easily, silently.

A man sat at a table, which was clearly the centerpiece of this much-smaller room. He looked up with only the mildest of curiosity apparent on his face. Em didn't need to wait for an introduction. She knew the man calmly looking her up and down was Redmond Longleigh as he chose to appear in the wasteland. His nickname, Red, was doubly apt, derived not only from his given name but from his fiery red-orange hair, which was worn full around his face but bound into a tail at the back.

From the neck up, Redmond Longleigh could have been kin to Thomas Jefferson. Longleigh's clothes, however, were more or less modern—did any real-world people actually wear silk smoking jackets over their slacks and ribbed sweaters?

After a moment of silence while the three of them took one another's measure, Red Longleigh rose gracefully from his chair and came around to the front of his writing table to greet his guests.

"Ah, Eleanor, my dear—"

Emma couldn't help but notice that Longleigh embraced her mother warmly, while Eleanor did not embrace him at all. Unfazed, Longleigh retreated and held Eleanor at arm's length.

"I see you've made a change," he continued. "I won't

say for the better, but you've lost nothing in the translation. Too bad Harry can't appreciate it."

The air had thickened; the emotional temperature had dropped like a stone. Em perceived the effects, but the causes were a mystery. If she trusted her instincts, there was history—intimate history—between her mother and Longleigh; and Harry had just been insulted in absentia. As usual, she was going to walk out of this room with more questions than she'd brought in.

Eleanor said nothing. She couldn't have looked unhappier if she'd been a wild animal caught in a trap. Longleigh held her arms a moment longer, then released her and turned his attention to Emma.

"And you must be the mysterious daughter, Merle—no, sorry, it's Emma, isn't it?"

She stuck out her hand, hoping to forestall an embrace. Emma Merrigan didn't hug strangers, and Redmond Longleigh was most definitely a stranger.

Longleigh's handshake was firm. His eyes were a dark, flinty gray that revealed nothing of his interior thoughts. He took Emma completely by surprise when he thwarted her handshake and wrapped her in an unwelcome embrace and gave her a dry-lipped kiss on the cheek.

Wasn't that the way *mafiosi* were supposed to say goodbye . . . forever?

"Welcome, Emma," Longleigh insisted, squeezing her again and not seeming to notice or care that her only response was a stiff spine. He released her with a cryptic, "It has been too long."

Emma, who was never at her best in power-based situations, took a step back and replied, "It's good to finally see this place. I've heard so much about it . . . and you."

There was another man in the room. Dark haired and standing in the shadows, Em hadn't noticed him at first— but, then, commanding attention in all respects came naturally to Redmond Longleigh.

"Ah, Pietro—" Longleigh said, acknowledging the second man.

Emma reminded herself she was in the wasteland, not a library and, who knew? Perhaps Pietro had materialized out of nowhere in the last ten seconds.

Pietro emerged into the light. He seemed to be a young man in his late teens or early twenties, but that meant nothing here. Broken-in blue jeans and a faded blue shirt completed Pietro's appearance. More than Eleanor, he had mastered the art of student camouflage. Pietro nodded, smiled shyly at Eleanor on his way to Emma.

"It is a pleasure to meet you at last," he said and lifted Emma's hand toward his lips.

Em was so surprised, she let him kiss her fingers without objection.

"You're the watcher?" she asked awkwardly when her arm was her own again.

He nodded—it was almost a bow. "At your service."

"I summoned Pietro when I knew you were coming."

Emma shelved that remark for future pondering. Though she already knew that hunters could announce themselves to one another over the shifty distances of the wasteland, it appeared that the Curia's master had refined the process.

Longleigh fastened his gray-eyed stare on Emma. "How are you doing with that fast-cycler? Mooted it yet?"

He had the same archly casual tone that Em found so annoying in her stepfather, but Longleigh added condescension to the mix, and that raised Emma's hackles.

"Funny you should ask," she replied, adopting for herself the manner she disliked in others. "That's one of the things I came all this way to talk to you about."

Longleigh blinked. He gestured toward the Chippendale-style chairs scattered around the room. "Pull one up and let's talk," he said and headed for his own, more ornate and imposing, chair behind the table.

Since she had, in fact, come to the bunker to talk about

the curse she hadn't come close to mooting—along with the destruction and recreation of her bolthole, which she quickly decided she wasn't going to mention—Emma meekly selected a chair. Eleanor chose one that put her on a collision course with her daughter.

She whispered, "Be careful, he's up to something," as they passed each other.

Emma had pretty much figured that out for herself. Any lingering doubts evaporated when, out of the corner of her eye, she watched one of the dark wood panels glisten unnaturally. When the glistening faded, Sylvianne Skellings, looking exactly as she had in Em's living room, had joined the gathering.

So, experienced hunters—hunters on good terms with the master of the house—did simply materialize.

The lean blond woman carried a silver mesh basket filled with fruit, which she set on Longleigh's table. Longleigh selected an apple. Its skin snapped loudly when he bit into it.

No one else, especially Emma, reached for the refreshments.

Sylvianne didn't bother adding a chair to the semicircle Emma, Eleanor, and Pietro had made in front of Longleigh's table. She simply perched on the edge of the table, literally positioning herself above everyone else, including Longleigh.

Longleigh rocked his chair onto its back legs and said, "So, Emma, tell us about the fast-cycler," over fingers he'd steepled in front of his nose.

Throwing caution to the winds, Emma opened with a bombshell. "It's not what Sylvianne said it was."

"And how is that?" Longleigh asked. He rocked his chair forward, planting his elbows on the table, continuing to hide his expression behind his hands.

"It's not one curse. It's two curses—at least two—twined together."

The corners of Longleigh's mouth twitched. Sylvianne

reached across the table for a cluster of grapes, momentarily blocking Emma's view of the Curia's fearless leader. Pietro, though, responded to Em's challenge first.

"That's impossible!"

"There you have it." Longleigh lowered his hands. He was frowning. "Pietro's been watching for quite a while. He knows whereof he speaks when it comes to curses."

"Watching from here. I delved that curse near the present, last summer, and back as far as I could reach, and every time there were two of them, traveling in tandem. One's pretty small but the other one, it's a full-blown fiery pillar. I'm not completely sure of the relationship between them—whether it's the same two curses or if the big one keeps sprouting and absorbing offspring. I've tried mooting one without the other, and so far I haven't had much luck—"

"You've plunged more than once?" Longleigh interrupted.

"Yes."

The red-haired man frowned. Em guessed she had given the wrong answer and grew cautious.

"Once earlier this very evening. I thought you should know there's something weird going on. What you're calling a fast-cycling curse is very likely a pair of curses—or maybe a succession of pairs—playing leapfrog down the time line."

"And how far back did you delve?"

There was no mistaking the condescension in Longleigh's voice now. The conversation was going down at the stern.

Emma meant to answer both honestly and precisely, but she had trouble recalling the exact date. Was it 1871 or 1881? She was sure of the eighteen and the one, but the decade was quicksilver in her mind. She didn't want to make another mistake, so she hedged in favor of honesty without precision. "Over a hundred years, back to Sanilac County and a forest fire that wiped out an entire family."

"And you say you found two curses?"

You're being set up, Em's mother-voice warned unnecessarily. *You've been set up from the beginning.*

"I watched a spindly little curse emerge from a man who was already cursed, then as he died, I watched the older parasite curse emerge as well. A pair of curses."

"Witnessed," Longleigh corrected. "We prefer to say witnessed. Watchers watch; delvers witness. You witnessed something you did not understand. I can't imagine what you did witness, but I do know that the curse I spoke to you about, that Sylvianne visited you about—"

Sylvianne met Emma's eyes directly for the first time since she'd come into the room. Her expression was so bland and benign that Em distrusted it completely.

Eleanor was right, the mother-voice concluded. *And either she's as outraged as you are, or they've got something on her bigger than you can imagine.*

"—Was a simple thing," Longleigh continued, unaware of Em's momentary concentration lapse. "Your challenge should have been more in terms of a moral dilemma. There is often more than one way to moot the curse. We wished to see which one you would choose."

"So, there never was a question of locating the curse." Em didn't try to hide her anger or her sense of betrayal. "You knew where and when it was all along. It was a test to—what? To see where I fit in? To see whether I was worthy of being part of your little club? What is it, the anointed adrêsteia?"

Longleigh cocked his head and gave a lopsided smile, as if to say, *Well, what do you think?* And it occurred to Em that she might have been very foolish to enter a place where her way-back stone couldn't accompany her.

"Are you going to tell me that I've failed your little test? That I'm not fit to moot curses?"

"A plunger who makes the wrong choice can be taught to make the right choices, but a plunger who cannot find the correct time and place and mind to plunge into is—I'm sorry to say this—as useless as a plunger who cannot make any choice at all."

From the corner of her eye, Em watched her mother cringe. If she'd needed proof that she was on her own, she had it now.

"I can make hard choices—when I'm good and ready. I'm not done yet," Em explained. "I'll get to the root of the problem, of the curse in question, but I thought what I'd found—curses sharing hosts, hosts sharing curses, and curses popping up when no one was dying—was important enough to bring to your attention. There's nothing like this in my black—"

Longleigh interrupted. "You're right there, Emma Merrigan. The things you're describing don't exist. We've been mooting curses since the beginning of time. Don't you think we'd have noticed if curses could be shared or if acts alone were enough to bring one into existence? There is only the beginning and the end when it comes to delving and plunging. The intermediate points serve no purpose but confusion, as you have discovered."

Emma couldn't ignore Longleigh's scorn. It had been more than seven years since she'd been subjected to such an acid-laced attack, but she'd survived her ex-husband, and she could stand against Redmond Longleigh, too.

"Just because you've got a theory that seems to work doesn't mean that you've got one that's right," Em retorted, quoting her father. "It's not as if you've got anything like a lab anywhere. Those books I've got sitting on my shelves at home are full of anecdotes, not experiments. And if I took their advice, I'd have turned myself into an opium addict—"

"That will be enough!" Longleigh snarled.

"Fine. I've got a curse to moot, maybe two. And a lot more to come."

"No. You'll leave the mooting of curses to hunters who know what they're doing!"

"Are you threatening me?" Em asked, though she knew,

no matter what Longleigh said next, that the answer was a resounding "Yes."

"I'm warning you to respect the wisdom arrayed against you, and I expect you to heed my warning. You've shown yourself to be both reckless and careless. You've changed the past without mooting a curse. There's no telling what other damage you've caused. There are *rules*, Emma Merrigan. Apparently you haven't read that portion of your mother's book. We cannot risk having them broken. Our entire existence is at stake—not just the Curia, but our very lives as hunters. You may continue your nightly walks along the absolute present. You may come to this place and, in time, you may be given another chance, but you *will* refrain from delving and plunging. Pietro has your measure now. He'll know, and *I* will know."

"You don't need to wait for Pietro. I can tell you right now—you can take your warning and forget it."

"You—" Longleigh spat the word. For an instant Em imagined that his gray eyes had gone fiery red, but that, surely, was only her imagination. "You will swear an oath—a binding oath, I warn you—that you will refrain from exercising your *wyrd*. You will not delve. You will not plunge—"

"Or what? You'll turn me over to rogues?"

Longleigh went pale when he heard Emma's suggestion. "You have gone too far, Emma Merrigan. This will not be tolerated."

With or without fire, there was no mistaking the outrage in Longleigh's eyes.

"They tell me you're an intelligent woman," he warned. "Don't let that be another lie. I will have your oath—"

A familiar-looking leather-bound black book materialized in the air between them. Emma willed herself to laugh, but the fear in her gut kept her silent. Her way-back stone hadn't followed her into the bunker complex. Suppose she couldn't find it? Suppose she couldn't leave this room? It was Longleigh's bolthole, not hers. He could bar the doors—

Stop that! Em chided herself with the mother-voice. *It's the wasteland. It's all subjective. If you think something's real—If you think that it could be true, then there's a damn good chance it* will *be true.*

The black book, so similar to a Bible drifted closer, and, as it did, Em experienced a sudden urge to do what she was told—to move her arm and make an oath. She'd bind herself with her oath. She was a fundamentally honest person who didn't make false oaths. And she'd honor the Curia; she would strive to regain the Curia's favor. The Curia was the glue that bound the adrêsteia together, that lifted them out of savagery—

Get out of my head!

Em conceived a violent spasm that purged her mind of alien thoughts and rocked Redmond Longleigh back an inch or two. Someone—Emma couldn't say for sure, because her eyes never left Longleigh's—gasped.

"How dare you!?" she demanded.

"You *will* swear an oath!"

The alien presence—Longleigh's presence—weighed down on Emma's psyche, and though it was undoubtedly instructional to know, from the receiving end, what plunging felt like, she wasn't interested in conducting scientific experiments. What she wanted to do was leave—and in the most dramatic way possible.

"You will not leave this room until you have sworn a binding oath!"

So Longleigh was monitoring her thoughts. Then let him have another taste of Merrigan outrage—

But Longleigh was wise to Emma's tricks. They were stalemated: She couldn't drive him out. He couldn't make her swear to anything—not yet, anyway. He would, though, eventually; there was no mistaking his strength and determination. She wouldn't be able to stand against him forever—not in his bolthole. He might well convince that her blood would boil if she reneged—

Fight it! You're making it easy for him. It's all subjective! Nothing's real unless you believe it is. Believe in yourself—

Emma imagined a coin, a common nickel with Jefferson's head on one side and Monticello on the other. She imagined it spinning a few feet above the leather-bound book and tried to contain her surprise when the coin became real—as real as anything else in the wasteland. When she was ready, she'd seize the coin and slap it down on the book. She would call "tails"—the opposite of her call when she was leaving her body—and she would return to her body, no harm done, no oath given.

But first—

"Eleanor—" Emma extended her hand toward her mother who hadn't moved—"Are you coming?"

Emma wouldn't have been surprised whichever direction Eleanor had jumped, but there was a certain satisfaction in watching Eleanor scowl at both Longleigh and Sylvianne.

"I'm with you," Eleanor said softly as she took Emma's hand.

"It's been a pleasure." Em smiled at Longleigh as she brought the spinning coin to a stop inches above her hand. She said, "Tails," and they were on their way to Bower.

Thirteen

"*You did it!*" Eleanor crowed.

She reached across the pillows to give her daughter a big, unexpected hug. They had returned to Emma's living room, no worse for their adventure.

"You got us both out of there!"

Emma stretched and flexed her legs. They felt as though she'd been immobile for hours. She glanced at the clock. Twelve-thirty. She *had* been sitting like a statue for almost two hours.

"Time matches up pretty close in the bunker," she observed. "Did you know that?"

Warily, Eleanor nodded. "I thought there was a chance he'd listen—a good chance—or I did until that woman showed up. She's against you, Emma. Dead-set against you."

"It wasn't Sylvianne trying to rearrange my thoughts," Em observed. "Is that something the Curia's fearless leader does often, or does he save it for special occasions?"

Emma realized before she'd finished that the question was unnecessary, even cruel. Still, she wasn't prepared for Eleanor's reaction—

"We've got to call Harry right now. He'll want to know what you've done. . . . He *needs* to know."

"You call him," Em countered. "On your cell. I think I've got to spend some time data-mining on the computer. Little as I like the idea, I think Mr. Longleigh might be right. There was something wrong about that man, Andrew Mayhew, that I found tonight—"

"He was cursed!"

"And he shouldn't have been. I can almost understand that Mayhew's death became a curse because he couldn't save his family from the fire, but he was cursed *before* he died, Eleanor. Just like Andrew Sharpe and his daughter, Kaylee. All these people I've been chasing—all these Andrews—it's as though they've all been predisposed to create a curse as they died because they'd been cursed while they lived.

"I'm missing something. Something basic. I need to go back to where I started—in the burnt house in Union. Something drew me there in the first place." Em sifted her memories. "If that girl I saw headed for the bedroom with her boyfriend *was* Kaylee Sharpe, and she probably was, then I've made some changes in her life. She walked away from that accident. She's still fighting the curse she walked away with, but at least she's not living with the memory of setting that truck on fire and the curse it brought down on her head."

Eleanor shook her head. "If you don't get to the bottom of things, it doesn't matter, really, how many little changes you make in the deep past. The woman who taught me, she always said the past preserves itself. That's why we use the word *moot*. We get rid of the curse, but we change very little. Sometimes we moot a centuries-old curse, and nothing changes at all for the people who carried that curse during their lives. They go on—their lives and deaths are exactly as they were before the mooting, and the only difference is that there's one less curse loose in the Netherlands.

"Now, if I understood what you were saying, this curse you're delving, it's one curse with many parts. Until you find the very first part and moot it, everybody who's carried that curse is still going to be carrying it when you delve to look at them."

"All the more reason to spend a little time digging around those sites Matt found, because I haven't found that very first part yet." Em recalled the sheets of paper Matt had given her as best she could. "Come to think of it, Andrew Mayhew should have had two more children. That genealogy chart showed six people dying on the same day—a man, his wife, and their four children; and I remember thinking that the oldest was sixteen. Tonight, all I saw were two children, one of them an infant, the other a toddler. And Mayhew himself didn't look old enough to have a sixteen-year-old kid. . . . Maybe I *did* delve myself to the wrong place."

"Red had no right to treat you the way he did. He knows you've got the *wyrd* and he also knows that you've had less than a year to learn how to use it. So you made a mistake. Red makes mistakes, too. He should be listening to what you learned from your mistakes."

Em couldn't help but notice that Eleanor continued to refer to Longleigh by his nickname. What had Harry said? *Longleigh's not a villain.* Could she believe that?

The Horace Johnson Library was rich in biographies of people who'd had a good idea, run with it awhile, and then run it into the ground. Business tycoons and political aristocrats were particularly prone to the pattern. And what was Redmond Longleigh but an aristocrat with a vision and an unnaturally long lifespan? The man who'd pressured her thoughts had burnt bright against his chosen enemies, all the curses of the world, but he'd been running his show for so long that he'd lost his tolerance for dissent.

If a person agreed with him—either by nature or pressure—Longleigh was the only man for the job of running the Atlantis Curia, but he wasn't the man for running Emma Merrigan's life.

"Call Harry, if you want." Emma retrieved the scrap of newspaper she'd used as her delving focus. "I'll be upstairs hammering away on the computer for a little while before I go to bed. If I wasn't watching Andrew Mayhew and his family burn to death, I've got to figure out who I was watching and why."

Em's concentration wasn't as sharp as it could have been. Her mind raced with competing ideas. Everything from Kaylee Sharpe and her boyfriend to the not-Andrew Mayhew she'd watched die to the six hours of sleep she wasn't getting and the piles of work undoubtedly waiting on her desk at the library. She couldn't type a word into a search engine without misspelling it once or twice, and even with corrections, she wasn't finding many matches.

Disgusted with herself, Em gave up on data-mining and checked her e-mail. Aside from the usual inundation of spam, there was a chatty message from Lori, which Em didn't read, and a spurt of e-mails from Matt telling her that he'd found something "interesting" and asking her to call him right away. They were all time stamped before ten o'clock.

There was no way Em was calling Matt Barto or anyone else at one o'clock in the morning.

Emma tapped the keys that would put the computer to bed and wished her own wasn't so far away. She'd gotten as far as pushing her chair from the desk and spinning it around when she noticed Eleanor in the doorway. There was no telling how long the woman had been standing there in silence. She had her cell phone pressed against her ear.

"Do you want to talk to Harry?"

"I want to go to bed."

"It won't take long," Eleanor said. "He just wants to congratulate you."

Short of shouldering her mother aside, there wasn't a way to get out of the room without putting the cell phone to her ear.

"Eleanor tells me that you lifted the two of you clean

out of the bunker and right under Longleigh's nose in the bargain."

"He was messing with my head as if I were some poor soul with a curse. *And* he was threatening me—trying to tell me I was stuck in his office until I swore him an oath that I wouldn't plunge and moot another curse."

"Not wise, on his part, I take it, though I would have warned you against going to the bunker. That's his home turf, far more than Atlantis. Strange things can happen there."

Stranger than floating books or spinning coins? Emma guessed the answer was a resounding yes, not that she planned on returning to the bunker any time soon.

"I've pretty much burnt my bridges where Longleigh and his precious Curia are concerned."

"I shouldn't think so."

"I defied him, Harry. Worse, I have every intention of finishing what I've started. I'm going to get to the bottom—the root—of this serial curse; and the next time I see a green blob around someone's head, I'm going to get to the root of that curse, too."

"Eleanor mentioned this curse-as-Hydra theory you've come up with—"

"It's not a theory. It's just the best way to describe what I seem to be up against with the Union thing. A couple generations' worth of a single family seem to be passing a curse around. Sometimes it oozes between two people, and sometimes it pops out like a regular curse and bolts for the wasteland. I've just about convinced myself that it's more than one curse, but they're interdependent."

"Interdependent," Harry mused. "A family member dies, a curse emerges. A family member gets born, a curse takes a new host. Fascinating."

That wasn't quite how Emma saw it, but she wasn't in the mood for heavy conversation. "Just don't mention it to Redmond Longleigh. He's not too keen on my notions right now."

"Oh, I shouldn't think you need to worry about Long-leigh, Emma. He'll nurse his pride for a little while. Any man—anyone at all—would do the same. It's been forty years since he's faced defiance in the ranks; and he's never lost a face-off that I'm aware of."

"All the more reason I'm on his shit list."

"Not at all, Emma. Not at all. Longleigh will do whatever it takes to strengthen his precious Curia, as you called it, in the war against curses. Even if he doesn't embrace your ideas publicly, you can be sure he's giving them careful thought right now. I never persuade Longleigh of anything—until a few years have passed and suddenly my ideas are his ideas. And you can be sure Longleigh's not going to let the talents of someone strong enough to defy him slip through his fingers. Mark my words: Redmond Longleigh will come a-courting with all the Southern charm he's got at his disposal."

"I've been divorced twice. I'm immune to that sort of thing, and I'm tired, Harry. I've got to get up for work in six hours."

"At least you have a car again."

"Good night, Harry."

Emma handed the phone to Eleanor. She didn't stop in the bathroom but went straight to her bedroom, where she considered closing the door behind her. The cats wouldn't stand for that, so she undressed by light from the hall and crawled between the sheets. Though Em could have fallen asleep on a ten-count, she forced herself to stay conscious. She spun her coin and slipped into the wasteland.

"Blaise?"

He wasn't in the bolthole or, apparently, within hearing range. She waited for what felt like five minutes then wrote a note:

You were right. I should have gone down the hall to the bedroom. Harry spelled it out for me. I've been concentrating on when the curses emerge. I should have been paying attention to when they go to ground. The window took me to the right place the first time. The right place to start, at least. No guessing where it's going to end, though I've got an idea that 1871 is still a good bet.

Em folded the paper and propped it against the wine ewer. She had a second thought and reopened it.

For reasons too lengthy to write down, I went to the Curia's bunker with Eleanor earlier this evening. Mr. Longleigh was not interested in anything I had to say. In fact, he wound up telling me to abide by his rules—which include no unauthorized curse-hunting—or else. I proved I wouldn't play by his rules by spiriting myself and Eleanor out of his bunker. Harry seems to think this is going to have Longleigh eating out of my hand, but I'm thinking otherwise. I intend to keep a weather eye out for my back and suggest you do likewise—guilt by association and all.

Sorry for dragging you into this—

The fog had lifted outside the bolthole window, though the view was dark as midnight. Em put Union, Michigan, Kaylee Sharpe, and a late summer evening in the forefront of her mind. Nothing appeared to change beyond the leaded glass. Then again, nothing should have changed. She was aiming for a closet in a fire-scarred bedroom.

A familiar soggy, acrid smell wafted through the casement when Emma opened it. She climbed through and made her way to the master bedroom, arriving well before the teenagers. The Piersons used their one bedroom chair as a throw-away zone for dirty clothes. Em sat in a corner, making mental lists of things known and unknown, until nervous laughter and a slammed door announced the arrival of her quarry.

Kaylee and her unknown boyfriend—the Mason Jar waiter? Em recalled her sense that he was somehow involved with the arsons—made their way through the house. They were barely on the stairs when Em began having second thoughts: There wasn't anything to be gained by spying on children. The engineering gene wasn't triggered by sex, vicarious or otherwise. She knew everything she needed to know about Kaylee Sharpe. She knew everything she needed to know about curses.

The curse was at it again. Amazing how similar a curse's urgings were to a plunger's.

Emma pushed herself upright, but resisted all urges to leave the room. It was too late, anyway. The kids were in the hall and there was an electric presence in the room—in the room *she* occupied, a little distance away from the world of the past. Em felt her skin tingle with a static charge and—yes—a faint wind had begun to blow straight down from the ceiling.

The teenagers burst into the room. Emma was close enough to see that the girl stretching her T-shirt over her head was the same girl who'd walked away from her father's truck, but—just to be absolutely certain—Em stared hard then closed her eyes. The greenish stain was there, smeared irregularly over Kaylee's features, as if she'd just toweled off after a swim.

When Emma reopened her eyes, she directed them at the ceiling, where the wind originated, and tried not to notice that the boyfriend was a little too old and Kaylee a little too knowing. They wasted little time with romance or foreplay, but bounced to the center of the bed, directly under the wind that blew harder now in the shadows where Em lingered without touching anything, anyone else.

Em could have left right then. The urge was there in her mind and strong enough that she planted her hands on the back of the chair to resist it. She clenched her fingers so deeply into the upholstery, she could feel the twill texture of the fabric on her fingertips. Then, because she truly did not want to watch, Em closed her eyes.

Besides, she could see the curses better that way.

If curses leapt out of men and women as tongues of fire, they approached a prospective host as jade droplets seeping down the vanes of a three-dimensional cobweb that reached through the bedroom walls as though they weren't there. Em opened her eyes to confirm the web's focus. The boyfriend was clean; he was merely a catalyst, and luckier than he knew. He'd likely walk out of this room with nothing worse than a guilty conscience, if that. The incoming curse flowed exclusively toward Kaylee Sharpe.

"How stupid," Emma sighed. "Intercourse . . . conception. What better way to find a suitable host than to hitch a ride alongside several thousand agitated sperm? Kaylee had been carrying both curses with her the first time I stood outside this room. She brought them down from the Thumb after the accident. I changed that—but not by much. Her father's second curse is still getting its new host on schedule."

And getting it from where—?

The engineering gene always had a question or two. The obvious answer was everywhere. There were pale jade droplets rising from the floor, inching toward Kaylee neither faster nor slower than their downward flowing counterparts. The accurate answer, though, was everywhere except where Emma stood.

It wasn't merely that she blocked curse droplets from reaching Kaylee. By looking over her shoulder, Em could see that there were no droplets streaming toward her. As fascinating as that discovery was, its practical consequence was that Emma was trapped behind the Piersons' dirty-laundry chair.

Fortunately, and before Em could work up any anxiety about her confinement, the curtain came down on Kaylee Sharpe and her boyfriend's peep show. Hundreds of droplets vanished instantly, and Emma was free to move. It would have been a simple thing to roll up a few minutes of history and give Kaylee's boyfriend a dose of sex education that would douse his ardor, for what? A few hours?

Em had no illusions that she could keep the teenagers apart for long and, whether it was in the Piersons' bedroom or the backseat of a car, Kaylee was going to catch a curse. She was going to get pregnant, too, and no matter how successful Emma was in mooting the curse, there wasn't much Emma could do to prevent that.

The limits of a curse-hunter's influence were weighing heavily in Em's mind when she climbed through the bolt-hole's casement window. Blaise hadn't returned, and that was fine with Emma. She wasn't in the mood for her lover. The way-back stone sent her back to Bower where the bed-side clock glowed 2:45.

She had to disturb the cats and turn on a light to reset the alarm. Tomorrow Emma would be driving her new car to work. Unfortunately, her staff-parking sticker had gone the way of her old car, and she'd have to park with ordinary citizens in the fringe lots. It would almost be easier to leave the car home and walk to work.

But she didn't. Emma wasn't ready to admit it yet, but she'd fallen in love with her new car, and there was no way that she was leaving it on the Maisonettes streets. She would have to get over to campus security sometime during the day to get the car registered and permitted for staff parking.

Betty was running late and not in the office when Em arrived—thank heaven for small miracles. Rahima broke into a cheek-splitting smile when she spotted Emma. It had been hard, the timid woman admitted, to visit the outreach lawyer's office by herself, but she'd managed to keep the appointment, and it had gone better than she'd dared hope. With a single phone call to her brother-in-law, and a few discreetly worded threats, the lawyer had solved all Rahima's problems. Manal was home, and the brother-in-law had sworn he'd have nothing more to do with them, ever.

"He thinks he has made it harder for me," Rahima explained. "But, in fact, he is making it easier. Even with my job here—it's *my* job now, not the job he got for me."

On impulse, Emma gave Rahima a hug. "You've got that right. From here on out, I'm the only person you've got to worry about."

Em's office was a disaster area. A whole day's mail and memos crowded the seat of her chair. She added it to the layers on her desk and fired up the computer to check her e-mail. Without e-mail, the paper in her chair would have spilled onto the floor. She'd barely gotten it sorted between emergencies and nonemergencies when someone knocked on her open door.

Matt chided Em from the doorway. "You didn't call last night. I was getting worried. Did you—? Have you—?"

"I didn't get your messages until late . . . after one. I didn't see much point in calling then."

"I was thinking about your car."

Em nodded. "Eleanor told me you're next in line, if I decide I can't hack having my mother bribe me with a fancy new car."

"What did the Greeks say to the Trojans—Don't go looking gift horses in the mouth. It's a great car, Em. So, Eleanor arranged things with that bank Harry works for. She got you a good deal. That's not a crime, and she means well, Em; she's just clumsy showing it sometimes."

Something was definitely brewing between her mother and the library's system administrator. Em told herself she neither wanted nor needed to know any more than she already did and, to change the subject, pointed at the roll of papers Matt had tucked under his arm. "Been data-mining the Internet?"

Matt nodded eagerly. "I've got it *all* figured out, Em. I even know where curses come from!"

There were moments when Emma would have pawned her soul for the ability to raise one eyebrow. Failing that, she raised them both and said nothing.

"Comets, Em. *Comets!* And meteorites."

"And meteorites," Em repeated. "You know, I've got my problems with the amount of myth and wishful thinking that's gone into this curse-hunting business, but, so far, they've resisted putting the blame on outer space."

"No. No kidding, Em. It's all here." Matt added another

layer of white paper to Em's desk. "First—there *were* two fires in the Thumb. That was the first big thing I discovered. When you went looking for cursed people the first time, you hit the wrong one. The printouts I gave you Monday—the ones you left here?—they were about the Mayhews who died in the 1871 fire. But Eleanor, she gave you the wrong date. She said 1881 and—wouldn't you know it—there was an 1881 fire, even bigger and more destructive than the 1871 fire. Mostly because there was all that half-burned, ten-year-old wood lying around from 1871. I don't know who you mixed with in 1881—"

"I've got an idea," Em interrupted, "but, do tell me about the comets. Where do they come in?"

"Well, that's the 1871 fire. It wasn't just one fire. You know the Great Chicago Fire—the one with the cow—"

"They've pretty much cleared Mrs. O'Leary."

"Yeah, like *one* cow and *one* lantern could have done that much damage. The Chicago Fire, the fire in Michigan's Thumb, and an even bigger fire in Wisconsin all started on the same day—"

"The comets, Matt."

"There was only one comet, a Comet Biela, or the remains of Comet Biela. There was a meteor storm the night of October 8, 1871. Not a shower, but a storm! Thousands of meteors, all that remained of this Comet Biela, and the Earth plowed into them that night. Sure, thousands of them burnt up in the atmosphere, but some of the meteors were big enough to make it to the ground. It wouldn't have been so bad, except there'd been a bad drought and everything was tinder dry throughout the upper Midwest. I found a map—"

Matt switched papers. Em found herself looking at a blurry black-and-white map of the western Great Lakes region with a dozen or so white dots of varying sizes marking a rough V-shape from Wisconsin to Illinois to Michigan.

"Those are the fires . . . and the places where meteorites

were found afterward. It's the exact ballistic pattern you'd expect if the Earth had plowed into a cloud of meteoroids before midnight, local time, on October eighth."

"And 1881?" Em asked.

"Ten years later, the Earth plows into the *same* meteoroid cloud. And keeps plowing into it. You know that big mystery in Russia, the Tunguska Event that flattened miles and miles of trees without leaving a big crater? Well, that was Biela meteorites, too—they're chemically the same as the ones that've been found on the shores of Lake Huron and Michigan."

"This relates to curses *how*?"

Matt blinked. "Isn't it obvious? Comets are the oldest stuff in the solar system—the oldest stuff in the whole galaxy, maybe, and they're loaded with organic chemicals. That's how life gets started here . . . *all* kinds of life, Em, including curses. I mean, they've got to be something like viruses, right? Maybe prions—protein molecules too small to be viruses but big enough to replicate themselves."

"In my head, Matt, I'm with you all the way." Em got out of her chair and went to the farthest corner of her office, the better to distance herself from Matt's handiwork. "There's got to be some hard, tangible, *scientific* explanation for all that's going on. In my gut, though—comets with prions? I just can't buy it. And you know it's not just curses. Me . . . people like me, we do more than fight prions. There's the whole wasteland, not to mention walking through the past."

"And we're still looking for proof that you really do walk through the past. Lots and lots of circumstantial evidence, but no smoking gun. You could be doing it all in your heads . . . some sort of collective subconsciousness trick. Now, if you could get a sample of curse stuff—"

Em thought of the pale jade droplets flowing toward Kaylee Sharpe, but kept her thoughts to herself.

"If we could find someone to analyze it. Maybe we'd

find something alien. Maybe there's something alien about *you*."

"Gee, thanks."

"No, seriously. You got it from Eleanor. She got it from your grandmother, and so on. Something's getting inherited, so something's got to show up somewhere. It's just a matter of knowing where to look. It even makes sense that what sets you and Eleanor apart is related to what makes curses spread in the first place. The system has to be closed, Em. It has to close."

"Maybe," was as far as Emma would go. "But you're sure about there having been two fires up in the Thumb?"

"That's absolute," Matt said without enthusiasm. "In 1871, the Wisconsin fire was the terror and the one in Michigan was just a bad fire. Pretty bad for everyone who lived through it—and not everyone did. The Mayhews got wiped out. But it wasn't a firestorm like the one in Wisconsin. They call that one the Peshtigo Fire. Then, in 1881, Michigan got its firestorm. The 1871 fire had wiped out the timber industry—pulp industry, really. The pulp operators just pulled out. Ten years later, the Thumb was filled with homesteaders cutting farms out of the Great North Woods."

"Okay, that family I watched, assuming I watched them in 1881—I'd be willing to guess they were homesteaders." Em stared across the office at her desk. "Don't suppose you brought up another copy of that genealogy listing you showed me on Monday?"

"No, but I can get it fast enough." Matt slid into Em's chair. He tapped two-fingered across her keyboard. Her screen changed over to an Internet view. "Yeah, here it is. Andrew Sharpe Mayhew, died 1871. What did you want to look at?"

"His kids. Does it give their names?"

"They're sort of just footnotes. Genealogical dead ends. But, yeah—starting with the eldest: Andrew, Mary, Robert, and Sarah. What about the kids? They all died."

"No middle or family names?"

"Nope."

"And Sharpe, that was Mayhew's mother's maiden name that was being kept alive as a family name?"

"Yeah, but there are lots of Sharpes. The whole site is dedicated to Sharpeses. The Mayhews are footnotes. Evolutionary adventures that went nowhere."

"But if Sharpe was important for Andrew senior, maybe he passed it along to his eldest son?"

Matt connected the dots. "Oh, I get it now—Andrew Sharpe Mayhew Junior, son of Andrew Sharpe Mayhew Senior, and maybe he didn't die with the rest of his family in 1871. Maybe ten years later the 1881 fire got him, and that's what you watched happen."

"You got it. The man I delved was young—mid- to late twenties, I'd say—and his family was young, too. I swear I heard his wife call him Andrew Sharpe, not Mayhew. I plunged into his thoughts—I thought it was pretty clear what had to be done. I tried to get him to take the family into the well. It wouldn't have kept them alive. I don't think anything could have kept them alive. But I didn't know that, and he didn't know that, so it wasn't that I'd put a bad idea into his head. There just wasn't any way he was going to hide his family in a well, not after what happened in 1871.

"I didn't get it at the time—I'm still building my database, as it were. But my Andrew Sharpe had secrets *and* he had a curse. Now, suppose he survived the fire that killed the rest of his family—"

"Suppose it wasn't the fire that killed them," Matt suggested. "He—or his father—could have committed the perfect crime. That could get him cursed, couldn't it?"

"That and a meteorite."

"Seriously."

"Seriously, I don't know. The main thing I'm getting out of all this is that assumptions have gotten me into trouble. I've got the real date now. I'll plunk it into my equations and hie myself back to the right year next time. I want to see what happened in 1871— Well, I don't really *want* to see it. I can't get the pictures of the 1881 fire out of my head. It's like the Twin Towers. I don't have to remember what we all saw that day; I just have to think about remembering and I feel like flinching."

"Post-traumatic stress. I guess you've got to be real careful."

"Careful, or take up drinking the way Eleanor does."

It was Matt's turn to flinch. He was ready to let the conversation die. "You'll let me know, won't you, when you're going to do something about the curse?"

"If I have my way, nothing's going to happen until the weekend. Doing this stuff in the middle of the week wrecks my schedule. I hardly know what day or time it is."

"I'm going to be home this weekend," Matt assured Emma, and she assured him that she'd keep him informed. Matt, of course, hoped he'd hear before excitement happened; Em hoped it would be after.

Betty had shown up while Matt was in Em's office. The two women exchanged glances, nothing more, after he left and Emma put herself in low gear for plowing through the paper piled up on her desk. She ate a quiet lunch at her desk, paid a quick visit to campus security for a new staff parking sticker, and, courtesy of a rare afternoon without any meetings, was able to power down before six.

She approached the silver Integra slowly. This was her last chance to deny that the car was hers. Once she peeled the staff parking sticker off its backing and stuck it on the windshield, the die would have been cast.

Live a little, the mother-voice advised.

Em pushed the little button on the remote entry device. Locks retracted, exterior lights blinked, interior lights shone warmly, invitingly. She opened the door.

It's not a bribe if there's no quid pro quo.

The sticker backing came off easily. Em pressed the

dark blue square into its assigned place in the driver's side corner of the windshield.

"I'll call Harry when I get home. I'll get to the bottom of this 'investment fund' business. Hell, maybe I'm well enough off to take an early retirement—"

Emma wasn't ready to give up her life at the Horace Johnson Library, but she'd claimed the car. If Matt wanted a new car to replace the Escort, he was on his own.

A right turn at the parking structure entrance would have pointed Em toward home. A left put her in the stream of traffic headed for the Interstate. She turned left and enjoyed a half-hour of highway driving on the ring of roads encircling the city. The passenger-side blind spot in the rearview mirror was a bit larger than she would have liked, but the electric-controlled exterior mirrors soon made up the deficit. Emma would have to adjust her viewing habits—

That took about a half-mile.

She returned to the Maisonettes from the opposite direction and found her overnight parking spot on the opposite side of the street. Her own home was properly dark; Eleanor's was bright with the purple car parked at the end of its front walk. Em figured she'd be looking at brand-new furniture before the evening was over, but first she wanted to be alone in her own home for a little while.

The mail was uninteresting and there were no messages blinking for her attention from the answering machine. Eleanor had left a note beside the coffeemaker asking for a call after dinner. Emma shed a layer of worry and tension she hadn't realized she'd been carrying. Eleanor wanted to be alone, too. Maybe they could survive as neighbors.

After getting reacquainted with her cats and spooning food into their bowls, Emma threw her own dinner together—leftover Horatio's pasta and a heaping cup of steamed broccoli, both prepared in the microwave and ready to eat before she'd finished changing down into comfortable jeans and wildlife-printed sweatshirt. She ate without tasting a single bite, topped off the wine glass, and took it to the table beside her favorite chair.

The university's public radio station hadn't finished with its extensive daily news coverage. Em picked the first CD on the pile next to the stereo. Intricate choral music in a language she couldn't identify softly filled the living room. She sank into the chair and raised its footrest.

"All right," Em said to herself as Spin claimed her lap. She scratched the eternally itchy places around his ears and stroked the thick fur on his flanks. He looked into her eyes as if he'd understand anything she might share with him.

"So, where do I go from here? Back to Longleigh? I've witnessed a curse laying claim to an unborn child. That's something that I haven't read about in any of my black books. Something every curse-hunter ought to be aware of. Every plunger, anyway. It only makes sense. Curses come to the wasteland when death sets them loose, but they don't *stay* in the wasteland. We've got tactics to deal with them when they emerge. We ought to have tactics at the other end, too. They can't all be piggybacking on unborn children and their cursed mothers. Kaylee got her curse from her dad. And Andrew Mayhew—? Andrew Mayhew Junior whose wife called him Andrew Sharpe, the same name as Kaylee's father? Could they be using the same names over and over if they *weren't* somehow related? Think of what Harry does . . . Eleanor Merrigan, Eleanor Graves. The net result of genealogy is confusion, not clarity."

Emma stared across her living room, listening to her music and trying to get her mind to settle down.

"Longleigh was right," she conceded. "Wrong dates. Wrong fire. Wrong Andrew Mayhew. I missed the boat, missed it by ten years. I let Matt do my research and listened to Eleanor—of all people!—when I'd forgotten to bring home what Matt had found for me. If the damn Curia had wanted Matt or Eleanor to check out their fast-cycling—"

Em's thoughts took a turn away from self-flagellation.

"I *know* what a fast-cycler is. I can see it—like those big fiery loops on the sun. Speed is only half the story. Sure, Andrew Sharpe's July curse didn't have to waste time looking for a new host—it already had a foothold in Kaylee. I wouldn't be sure it even needed to breech in the wasteland. What Pietro spotted probably was the curse that breeched when Kaylee turned the truck into a funeral pyre. The first time around—before I started plunging and nudging—Kaylee carried that curse away from the truck. She carried it, along with her own curse, to the Piersons' bedroom, and she's going to carry it around, two curses on her shoulders, until her baby's born. And she'll probably name him Andrew. The second time around, when I'd plunged and nudged her, she didn't carry it down to Union, but it was waiting for her in the Piersons' bedroom—"

Em picked Spin up and held him so their noses were nearly touching. "Curses communicate with each other. Some of them do, anyway. Those curses of Kaylee Sharpe's—the one that she's got *and* the one that's after her baby—they're the latest incarnation of a curse that's been splitting itself into pieces and communicating with itself since 1871. 1871, up in the Thumb—that's the one time and place I haven't visited yet.

"What do you think, Spin? Should I take a look at what happened back in 1871? Should I see if I can get ahead of Kaylee Sharpe's curse?"

The cat writhed in Em's hands. She had to put him down and, when she did, he took off for the basement without a backward glance.

"Okay, it's not the greatest idea, but it's the best I've got right now."

Eleanor would have anchored her daughter, but once again, Emma convinced herself that she could dispense with precautions. She didn't plan to nudge anything in

1871, merely see how it played out with Blaise Raponde, she hoped, at her side. Em called her lover's name as soon as she was aware of the wasteland dirt beneath her hands and feet.

He came out of the bolthole to meet her. "I am here. Is something wrong?"

"I need your help tracking down a curse." Em lost her footing. She skidded down the steep slope, fighting for her balance and grateful for Blaise's hand when it came into reach. "A complicated curse. How's the window doing?"

"I have tested it for Paris, and it is working properly. Why? What manner of complicated curse? I have read your note many times. That girl's curse did not seem so complicated to me."

"It's a history thing. It's one curse, spawning new ones and then—I think—absorbing them again a generation later. The main branch is always getting stronger. I've got to get to the root of the main branch."

Em had hoped Blaise would be content with a shorthand version of events, but he wanted to know everything, especially about Redmond Longleigh and the Curia's bolthole. The way he got up and began pacing when she described the Curia's head honcho, Emma could almost have believed Blaise was jealous.

"He threatened your mind!" Blaise countered after insisting that he would never waste his time by being jealous of another man. "That is what rogues do. Does it not concern you that the man who claims to have united the hunters has, himself, the manners of a rogue?"

"I'd stopped trusting him before he messed with my head. Harry said it best—we're on a thousand-mile journey against curses and rogues. Redmond Longleigh's good for nine hundred of those miles, and since we're not near the nine hundred mark, we're all still traveling together, whether we trust one another or not.

"Look, I think I'm onto something here. I think the window makes it easier to catch up with curses as they're slipping in and out of hosts and not just at their inception points. That's kind of worked against me with this assignment I got from Longleigh—I haven't been back to delve the root yet, but I've seen things that are making me rethink what I know about curses. If you and I had gone behind that bedroom door, we'd have seen a curse positioning itself to sink its hooks into a baby as soon as it's born."

"And today, what do you expect to see in this year, 1871?"

"If I'm lucky, I'm going to see why surviving the fire that killed the rest of his family set one young man up for a curse that's been passed down through at least two separate branches of his family for generations."

"*Pardieu*, let's go." Raponde strode to the window. "Time is wasting. Show me this Great North Woods."

Em kept her mouth shut. They could have left a half hour earlier, if Blaise hadn't had so many questions. The truth was, though, that time never went to waste in the wasteland. It flowed in fits and starts and, with the window functioning again, the past was always waiting for them.

The fog beyond the bolthole window didn't so much clear as it changed, becoming wispy and reddish, as though the light of either a sunrise or sunset were passing through it. A tree at least a yard in diameter rose an arm's length in front of the window, blocking their view of anything the fog didn't conceal.

"Do you want me to go through first?" Em asked. "Like last time?"

"I didn't want you to go first last time."

Blaise opened the casement. One whiff and Em was confident that she'd finally summoned the right moment in time for getting to the root of Kaylee Sharpe's curse. The warm air wafting into the bolthole smelled of smoke and pine resins. She waited for Blaise to get his feet on the forest ground then climbed up on the windowsill. Blaise held

Em's arm, steadying her as she dropped some four feet onto a layer of dry leaves and other forest debris.

There were no signs of fire until Emma looked up. Starting about twenty feet above the ground, every tree in sight had been burnt black. Not one branch held on to a leaf or pine needle, and most of the smaller branches were gone as well. That squared with Matt's research—the Thumb fire of 1871 differed from the 1881 fire in that it had spread primarily through the forest canopy, not along the ground.

As Em spun slowly, getting her bearings, charred branches crashed to the forest floor where they raised small clouds of dust and smoke. About two hundred yards to the east, if she was right and the sun was rising, not setting, a clump of bushy trees were burning. There was no wind, and the fire didn't seem to be spreading, but it was a bright reminder that the forest could rekindle at any time.

Blaise tapped Emma on the shoulder. He pointed at something rising halfway out of a streambed. Em needed a moment or two to realize the irregular shape was human.

The two curse-hunters moved silently across the tinder-dry forest floor. Blaise jumped down into the streambed— A drought must have preceded the fire: The banks were carved a yard deep, and at its deepest, the stream itself barely came up to Blaise's knees when he carried Em across.

"Some other time you can experience water flowing through your bones," he said as he set her down on the opposite bank.

Ten feet away, Emma could see that the body was a boy in his late teens. She assumed he was alive because she assumed the bolthole window had opened to this time, this place for a purpose. He seemed whole—soot-stained, ragged, and nursing a good-sized gouge in his right leg, but fundamentally whole. Circling around, Em got a look at his face and hands. Beneath the grime, his skin was red, as though he'd been out in the sun too long. His eyes were swollen and leaking tears as he slept.

"And now you use your talent for stealing a man's thoughts?"

"I don't steal them. I don't even borrow them. I just observe—unless there's something I can do to thwart a curse."

"I'll keep watch, then, in case you attract attention."

"We're not on the streets of Paris. A fire's just ripped through here. I doubt anyone's going to come walking by."

Blaise replied by drawing his sword and sitting cross-legged on a nearby rock.

Em knelt beside the boy. She'd never plunged a dreamer before, and she touched him gingerly, not knowing what to expect. Dreamers, as it turned out, were easy to plunge, but hard to understand. Their thoughts moved—danced, really—in intricate patterns made from images, sounds, textures, and—for this dreamer—the taste and smell of smoke. What Em didn't sense—assuming she could have sensed it—were a curse's cramps and corners. Andy—the name echoed through the patterns—had lived through a terrible fire. He'd seen and done things that were likely to haunt him the rest of his life.

Emma almost lost her place within the boy, when she realized that she knew exactly how long Andy Mayhew would live, but as he lay in the life-saving shelter of the streambed, he wasn't cursed. He was, however, leaving his dreams behind. Em retreated to her own consciousness.

"He's starting to wake up," Em told Blaise. "I think—"

Blaise leaped down from his rock. He put his arms around Em and helped her stand. "What's wrong? What did you see in there?"

"Not *in* there. Out here. Eleanor says I'm contrary; I've always got to be different. Away from the wasteland I can't see a curse with my eyes open, but I can see it with them closed. This boy—Andy Mayhew—he's not cursed inside, not yet, but he's surrounded by one. It's swirling around him like a swarm of bees—same as the curse gathered around Kaylee when she was with her boyfriend in the Piersons' bedroom."

"If he carried a curse, I would know it—"

"He's not carrying it. Not yet."

The boy groaned as he awakened and splashed water against his eyes before opening them. He favored his injured leg when he stood. Em guessed he'd sprained the ankle in the fall that had carved up his calf. She wished she could have done something to ease his pain, which was bound to get worse walking home.

She and Blaise fell in behind the boy.

"What did you learn inside his skull?" Blaise asked.

"It was a dream. Where I come from there are scientists who say dreams are your brain's way of organizing a day's memories. Memories are opinions of reality. They don't have to be true—I hope they're not. But if they are, then the sun didn't rise around here yesterday. It was dark as night overhead and red orange along the horizon. All along the horizon. His father came to him and said, 'We have been given dominion over the animals' and 'We mustn't let them suffer.' The words are burnt into Andy's memory like the Ten Commandments.

"They went around the farm slaughtering the stock. They took turns. Sometimes Andy held the animals' heads while his father slit their throats; sometimes the father did. I've got to tell you, Blaise—that alone would be enough to get me primed for a curse. But when they were chasing the chickens, Mrs. Mayhew comes out of the house, followed by the youngest sister. The little girl takes one look at her father and brother—

"They were covered with blood. Those stains on his clothes, they're not just soot and grime from the fire—

"So, Mrs. Mayhew, she starts screaming at Mr. Mayhew. 'What have you done!' Like it wasn't terribly obvious what they'd been doing. And Mr. Mayhew's shouting back that he's doing the Lord's work, and why aren't she and the children in the well—"

Em cast a sidelong glance Raponde's way, expecting that he had an opinion about what was and what was not the Lord's work in any situation, however extreme. Blaise just looked grim and had nothing to say.

"That was my mistake in 1881—trying to get this boy, Andy, to lead his family into the well for safety. You have to bear in mind that all the while they've been slaughtering the animals, the fire has been closing in on them. The air is hot as a furnace and driven by a steady wind. There's hot ash in the air, and it's only a miracle that nothing's fallen on the roof to set it alight. Getting the family down into the well is really the best chance they've got.

"Andy stops chasing chickens and helps his mother climb down the side of the well. It's not that difficult; they use the well for storage. It's lined with stones, and the water's only a few feet deep. He's handing down the little girl, the last sibling, when he turns around and sees that his father's exchanged his slaughtering knife for his government-issue rifle—

"A rifle," Emma explained, in case the word didn't translate. "It's the size of a musket with the wallop of a cannon. And Mr. Mayhew's going to use it on his family, because the Good Lord gave him dominion over them, too, and he can't let them suffer. We've got an expression— shooting fish in a barrel—for when a fight's so uneven that the other side doesn't even have the chance to hide, much less fight back. Well, that's what Mayhew had, literally, him with his rifle and his family crowded together at the bottom of the well.

"Except for Andy. He hadn't gone down yet. And he didn't go. He ran for his life, and, obviously, he survived, but he's feeling guilty about it. Real guilty. Odds are, we're following him back to the farmhouse, and that's where he's going to pick up his curse."

Emma fell silent. The boy wasn't walking fast. Wherever they were going, they weren't nearly there yet. She could wait for Blaise's reaction, which wasn't that long in coming.

"Burning is a terrible death, not at all quick. If this rifle gives a quick death, then it could be counted a mercy. The Church lets the executioners strangle a heretic after they're bound to the stake, but before the pyre's lit—if they've properly confessed their sins."

Em couldn't have been more shocked, more repulsed than if Raponde had made a speech in support of slavery. It was all she could do to keep a civil tongue in her head as she asked, "So, you think the father was right to kill everything in sight?"

"Not at all. The livestock, perhaps, if he could not turn them loose. But not his family. A man should know that a fast-moving fire burns up, not down. When Paris burns, people run to the river, they hide in their cellars and in wells and the sewers, anyplace that's low and wet."

"You agree this was a fast-moving fire?"

"The tops of the trees are burnt far worse than the ground. A house might burn, or it might not, but underground should have been safe." He kicked a tussock of dried, but unburnt, grass to prove his point. "And it is the gravest sin for one man to claim to know the hour of another's death. This boy's father was surely not doing God's work."

Emma relaxed, but not for long. A farmhouse silhouette had appeared in the smoky haze ahead of the boy. The simple fact that it was still standing did not bode well for anyone who'd been doing the Lord's work with a government-issue rifle. A similar thought seemed to have occurred to the boy. He gimped along at a faster pace and began shouting the names of his family.

They drew close enough to see that the house was untouched and that there was a man sitting on the porch.

"Pa," the boy shouted, doing his best to break into a run. "Are they alive, Pa?"

The elder Andrew Mayhew answered by raising his rifle to his shoulder and firing one shot at his eldest boy. The shot went wide. The boy didn't slow down, not until the man shifted his grip on the rifle. Without pause or hesitation, he tucked the muzzle under his chin and pulled the trigger.

The boy screamed; Emma did, too. Her life would never be long enough to forget what she'd seen. She felt the gathering wind of an emergent curse, but couldn't force her eyes open to witness it.

"It's over," Blaise said when the wind had died. "The boy has his curse."

Em couldn't talk. She could barely breathe. Her skin had gone clammy, and the ground seemed to be unstable beneath her feet. Looping her arm around Blaise's arm, she followed him closer to the porch, hanging back just a little so his shoulders blocked her view of the worst of the gore.

The boy had collapsed on the porch. "Why?" he cried repeatedly as he alternately hugged his father and beat the man's chest with his fists.

"How am I supposed to fix this?" Emma asked rhetorically. "I don't think I reach in and talk Mr. Mayhew out of shooting everybody. History manages to record that the whole family died. The boy's going to run away. He's going to drop the name Mayhew altogether and go by his middle name, his mother's name, Sharpe—for all the good it's going to do him."

"You could let him kill the boy—"

"That," a stranger said from within the house, "would be a serious mistake."

Fourteen

The owner of the strange voice proved to be none other than Redmond Longleigh himself. With his red hair loose around his shoulders, he walked out of the unburnt house in country-gentleman clothes sliding a stick of pale wood between the fingers of his left hand. To Emma's eyes, the stick had begun its existence as an orchestra conductor's baton, but she had no doubt that in this time and place it was a curse-mooting weapon. And possibly a weapon against curse-hunters, too.

"You were warned," Longleigh said calmly, almost friend-to-friend. "No delving. No plunging. No mooting of any curse thicker than your little finger." He waggled the digit in question and managed to make the gesture into an insult.

Blaise had released Emma's hand, but they were still close enough that she could feel his muscles tighten. She was sure that he was ready to draw his amber-pommeled sword. When it came to weapons, Em imagined the sword was mightier than the baton, but had no desire for proof. Without breaking Longleigh's stare, Emma laid her hand on Blaise's forearm.

This was her battle, and, little as Emma liked battles of any sort, she didn't want anyone fighting it for her.

"I thought you might have noticed—I wasn't impressed by your threats. My *wyrd* is my own. I don't need a watchdog telling me what I can or can't do."

"You might have plunged for the boy's death."

The boy in question remained hunched over his father's corpse. It was disconcerting in the extreme to be sparring with another curse-hunter while Andy Mayhew was grappling with his grief and rage. Emma's instincts were to kneel beside him and, at the very least, numb his pain.

"You're wrong there, absolutely wrong." Em squeezed Blaise's arm as she spoke and hoped he wouldn't open another battlefront. "There's no way I'd moot a curse by raising the body count. One of the first lessons I learned from Eleanor: The power of time can heal the wound caused by letting someone live past the moment of their historic death, but there's no bringing someone back from the dead."

"Then you realize there's nothing you can do here. This—" Longleigh spread his hands to encompass both Andrew Mayhews and their homestead—"is a curse that cannot be mooted by delving and plunging. There is nothing even the strongest *wyrd* can accomplish. The family dies; the boy walks off with his father's curse."

Emma wasn't prepared to concede complete defeat, but the circumstances were daunting. She couldn't readily think of a plunging intervention that would moot the Mayhew curse without saving lives. Over a century of history had played out since the elder Andrew Mayhew had destroyed his family, and it held no provisions for survivors.

"There's got to be a way," Em insisted, more stubborn than persuasive. "I've got to study all the angles and think things through."

"Not here," Longleigh countered. "You've been warned. This curse is off-limits. Oh, maybe someday it will finish cycling and join a pack in the Netherlands, and the trackers might run it down, but you missed your chance, Emma Merrigan. There's no place in the past for a careless plunger. Leave now, before I have to send you away."

Longleigh was fussing with his baton again. An itchy trigger finger? And Harry had been so certain Longleigh wouldn't hold a grudge. Staring into his eyes, Em couldn't tell what the Curia's founder was thinking.

"No problem. Like I said, I've got some thinking to do before I moot—"

"Don't even think about it," Longleigh snarled. "Long before you were born, I brought curse-hunters out of the dark ages. There are limits to what the hunters do. We moot more curses in a year than our ancestors mooted in a lifetime, and we moot them according to *rules*. Ask your roguish friend what life was like when hunters did as they pleased."

Em wouldn't have bothered, but before she could come up with a suitable retort, Longleigh was on another tear—

"If you had come to Atlantis and asked for advice ... *instruction*. But, no—I am not an unreasonable man, Emma Merrigan. I would gladly have taught you the ropes, shown you the way we live. You have a great *wyrd*. There's much you could have done for the good of us all. But you choose to live as a rogue—"

"That is enough," Blaise interrupted.

The testosterone levels on the front porch rose to dangerous heights, and it was that, or sheer coincidence, that put young Andy Mayhew on his feet. The boy was shaking and weeping as he stepped away from his father's corpse. Em thought he was going to run back into the smouldering woods, but he headed for the well. It had to be the curse driving him, adding to his burden of misery and horror. Once again, Emma wished with all her heart that there was something she could do to lessen his pain.

"In my day," Blaise continued, "we knew a rogue by his works, and you, sir—"

Emma squeezed his arm. "No."

Blaise put his opposite hand over hers, and with no

other warning, Emma's subjective reality was knocked for a loop. She had the sense that her entire being had become a bungee cord stretched to its maximum length and released. The recoil took her breath away. Then, as unexpectedly as it had begun, it was over. She and Blaise had returned to the wasteland. They stood on the bluff of an orange-wedge depression. Looking down, Em could see her way-back stone in its customary waiting place beside the bolthole door.

"That man is more dangerous than any rogue," Blaise complained.

Emma could almost forget Redmond Longleigh. She had other questions. "How did you do that?" she wanted to know. "One moment we're back in the shadows of 1871. The next we're here *outside* the bolthole. No window. No anchor. I thought that was impossible."

"I forgot about the window," Blaise admitted. "It is still very new to me, you know. It doesn't leap into my mind. And as for anchors—" He shrugged and began the hike to the wedge's shallow slope. "I had no luck with them when I could have made use of them."

"But *how* did you do it? Do you have some ritual? A gesture? A mnemonic? And do you always come back to the same place regardless, or do you have to steer yourself across the great wide-open?"

Blaise wouldn't answer any of Em's questions until they were settled inside the bolthole.

"It would not be wise to share this with any of your friends in the Atlantis Curia, but you know that curses drill holes *au-delà* all the time while they're questing for a new host, and rogues come and go in a heartbeat?"

Em nodded. She had learned about the speed with which rogues could exit the here and now, but she'd never put much thought into curse mechanics, other than believing that most curses wore themselves out looking for a suitable host, and that fast-cyclers, like the Mayhew-Sharpe curse, were supposed to be rare.

"Do you pretend you're a curse?" she asked.

Blaise confessed—"A rogue. It bothered me greatly, once I'd found myself trapped au-delà, that rogues could come and go so easily while I was bound to one place . . . this place. So I studied them. They taught me how to make my first bolthole and how to go where I wished."

"And how is that?"

"How is anything au-delà? It's a matter of expectation. Most of existence is au-delà, Madame Mouse. The here and now is only a tiny bit of existence. Very important, *pardieu*, but very tiny. All the rest is au-delà, and all au-delà is the same, whether its shaped like the past or scarcely shaped at all. I *expect* to be here, and here I am. I expect to be *there*—"

Blaise raised his hand. He pointed at the hearth, but before Em's eyes refocused, her lover had vanished and reappeared beside the fire.

"—And I am here. There is a little rogue in all of us, I think."

Emma closed her mouth before her tongue fell completely to the floor. "Just like that? And you can be anywhere?"

Blaise heaved another shrug and walked across the room. "Anywhere is very large. It is easier to find one place and return to it again and again—a bolthole. Curses are simpler. When they're questing for a host, I think of them as a blind man reaching into a stream, looking for something he's lost. He reaches many times from the same place before he shifts his body upstream or down. Rogues range more widely when they're questing for a new host— or perhaps they build a treasure trove of expectations. I can expect to find myself on many different streets of Paris, depending on my mood. Or I could expect to be in a smoky forest, or standing on a black street beneath lamplight that does not flicker."

"Just snap your fingers—figuratively speaking—and you'd be there."

"In Paris, yes. Or on the bluff above our bolthole door. I have been careful to return to exactly the same place. Sometimes there isn't enough time to snap my fingers."

Em poured a glass of wine. "Then this hasn't been a complete waste of time."

"You have seen the face of a man you cannot trust."

"That was yesterday's discovery—or the day before. I start to lose track after a while. No, today I found a curse I can't moot. Just when I was starting to get used to the whole idea of mooting curses, my wings got clipped."

Blaise got wine and sprawled across his chair. "It's not as if we're ever going to run out of curses."

"That boy's got ten years to live—until he dies in a fire more destructive than the 1871 fire—and he's got to live them with a curse tainting his every thought. I mean, I know this is all fraught with Einsteinean paradoxes, but I *believe* that if I could have seen a way to moot his damn curse, then those ten years would be better years, even though, either way, they were all lived a hundred-plus years ago. And there's Kaylee, the girl in the bedroom. Bad enough that she's going to have a kid before she gets out of high school, but right now she and the kid are going to wind up carrying curses. I would have liked to change that."

"You believe that red-haired man?" Blaise asked in a tone that dripped skepticism.

"I believe I can't undo death."

"So, you believe him."

"Not *him*," Em insisted. "Whatever hold Redmond Longleigh manages to exert over my mother and Harry, it sure doesn't extend to me. The man is a little tin god badly in need of melting. But—nobody's perfect, and I think he's right. From a twenty-first-century perspective—and that's the only working perspective—that curse has managed to spawn in an inaccessible spot."

Blaise leaned forward. He caught Em by surprise and

caught her arm as well. He drew her back to the chair, which had enough room for them both.

"And I think you will prove him wrong . . . or, perhaps, I will prove you both wrong."

Em laughed, and they set their glasses aside.

It was nearly midnight when Emma reopened her here-and-now eyes. She'd slumped sideways in her chair and given herself a stiff neck. Out-of-body adventures were best begun from the floor or her bed, where the chances of self-injury were minimal. She thought about calling Eleanor and dismissed the thought immediately. Even if Eleanor were still awake and interested in showing off her new furniture, it was too late for family visits.

Em put herself to bed and, to her disgust, lay there wide awake until well after two, thinking of all the things she could have said to Redmond Longleigh. In those cracks and moments when Emma wasn't thinking of Longleigh, she was back in 1871 trying to find the magic formula that would free the Mayhews and the Sharpes from their curse. Somewhere before two-thirty, Em stopped watching the clock.

By any external measure, Thursday got off to a good start. For the first time in a week, Emma drove her own car into the staff parking structure. She found one of the prime new-car slots sheltered between a cement wall and a support pillar. The world's largest SUV could park next to her, and its doors wouldn't endanger the silver shine on the Integra's side panels. Rahima was already at her desk, working hard and smiling at her boss; even Betty seemed to be in a good mood. Em's computer woke up without a glitch, and there were no surprises in any of her mailboxes.

A good start, by any external measure, and for that reason alone, Em found her thoughts drifting to small towns and prior centuries. The engineering gene worked overtime in search of a solution, but it wasn't until Em was fighting to stay awake at Gene Shaunekker's mahogany table that the pieces began to fit together in a useful way. Cooperation was the key, or so said the woman from cataloging, who was in the middle of a sales pitch for yet another upgrade to the on-line cataloging system. Cooperation and multipoint access.

What curse could possibly be more arcane or intractable than their modified Library of Congress cataloging system? What curse could not be mooted by cooperation among curse-hunters and a little multipoint access? Em could think of at least two likely access points along the Mayhew-Sharpe curse's time line: Kaylee Sharpe's indiscretion and the young Andy Mayhew's decision to revisit the family homestead rather than get a head start on his life as an orphan.

It was harder to account for the turn of thought that took Emma back to the bolthole and replayed the conversation she'd had with Blaise for the umpteenth time. She laid Blaise's description of curses fishing for a new host over her memory of the Piersons' bedroom and the pale jade droplets marching toward a no-longer virgin womb. The Mayhew-Sharpe curse had staked its claim to Kaylee's newly conceived child, but it could hardly have set up housekeeping in a collection of undifferentiated cells.

The engineering gene simply wouldn't accept that notion, which left Emma imagining a curse stretched out the way she'd been stretched when Blaise snapped her between 1871 and the wasteland bolthole and remaining that way for nine and a half months. If there was any justice in a subjective reality, such a stretched-out curse had to be vulnerable to mooting. All a curse-hunter needed to know was where in the wasteland a curse's nether end made its home.

For almost a year Emma had been mooting little curses as they emerged into the wasteland from the here and now. She had no idea where a night's curses came from. Proximity in the wasteland didn't imply proximity in the real world. Her daily quota of curses could have come from

Michigan one night and Outer Mongolia the next, or—
more likely—from a handful of widely scattered points on
the map every night.

There was a correspondence between points in the
wasteland and points on a map, or an infinite series of
maps. That was the operative principle behind the grids
Harry had designed for the watchers and behind delving,
too. Em could delve to a point in the past by walking until
the wasteland stuck to her feet, then sinking through to the
past. The question that Emma answered as she stifled a
yawn was, could she pinpoint where in the wasteland the
Mayhew-Sharpe curse was waiting out Kaylee Sharpe's
pregnancy? And the answer was that she couldn't, but her
mother could.

Eleanor had walked them right into the Mayhew-
Sharpe curse's parlor when she'd tried to delve Kaylee's
curse. The shifting landscape, the sense that they were
being sucked into a hole—all those sensations corresponded nicely to the bungee cord analogy and Em's new-
found conviction that the curse couldn't fully victimize an
unborn child.

The cataloging meeting ground on for another half
hour, and when it finally disgorged, Emma made a beeline
for Matt's office in the library basement. His lights were
on, but the door was shut, locked, and bearing a handwritten notice that he was in the main reference room, working
on a computer that wouldn't respond to anything less than
human intervention.

Em could have chased him down, but she flipped to a
blank page in the notebook Matt kept thumbtacked to his
door and left a cryptic message asking if he'd be free
around 8:30.

After that, nothing could keep a firm hold on Emma's
attention. She looked up at every sound and talked herself
out of calling Eleanor and Harry more times than she cared
to count. At five o'clock Em made a break for freedom
worthy of any student, any grade. Her tires squealed as she

swung out of the parking space—which caused her to let go of the steering wheel in embarrassment and swear silently that she'd be lighter on the gas in the future.

Rolling into the Maisonettes, Emma had her choice of parking spots and chose the one closest to the little purple car. She went directly to her mother's door.

Eleanor greeted her with a surprised and wary, "You're home early."

"I've got a plan for mooting my curses—and I need your help."

She'd finally said the four words her mother had been longing to hear. With an uncontrolled smile, Eleanor welcomed Emma into her almost-furnished home.

Emma had to comment on the chairs, sofa, and tables that had manifested themselves in the downstairs rooms and follow Eleanor upstairs to view the queen-sized bed in the midst of its suite of two dressers and a mirrored dressing table. If nothing else, wandering from room to room gave her the chance to bring Eleanor up to speed before they settled at the pristine dining table.

"I feel like I've sunk a little into the darker waters of quantum mechanics and cosmology," Em began, "but I think we can moot curses because they exist like a stray thread woven through the fabric of time. We pull one end, and the whole thing disappears. Or we can attack the middle. That's harder, but if we work together we'll be strong enough to pull up both ends. And if we attack several places at once—if we're careful about where and in what sequence—we might be able to pull it out even if it's tangled. Even if we can't, we can force it to defend itself and whittle it down—"

Eleanor held up both hands, palms out. "Whoa. I'm not big on theory. I don't need to know why. Just tell me what you want me to do."

Emma had been spewing theory by the bucket because she was nervous. She took a deep breath and said, "I want you to go back to that place where the curse nearly swallowed us . . . if you're willing . . . if you can."

"You want me to attract another curse?" Eleanor's face was more eloquent than her words; she'd sooner have eaten ground glass.

"I don't think you attracted it. I do think it attracted you. More to the point, I think you found the point in the wasteland where Kaylee Sharpe's curse is when it isn't somewhere else, specifically where it's hanging out waiting for Kaylee to have her baby."

Eleanor's expression hadn't changed. "You'll be with me?"

They'd come to the tricky part. "I'm going to go after one of the other ends. A young man—boy, really—who gets the curse from his father. I can't do anything with the father. He does way too much damage for a little plunging to fix, but I think, maybe, I can keep the boy away from his father at the critical moment and—if I'm right about the timeless nature—"

"You won't walk with me?"

"You won't be alone. Blaise will go with you."

Em hoped. She hadn't asked him. She couldn't be certain he was even available. On the other hand, they didn't have to test her theories in the next four hours. They had time, at least until Kaylee gave birth. After that, Em would need another theory.

"What about Harry?" Em asked her still-dubious mother. "I've been thinking about asking him. Succeed or fail, it's thumbing my nose at Redmond Longleigh and his precious Curia. I figure you burnt your bridge when you let me pull you out of the bunker, but . . . I don't know about Harry."

"He's not much of a hunter," Eleanor sniffed, "but if I know Harry Graves, he wouldn't miss an opportunity to twit Redmond Longleigh—if he's home. You never know with him. He always leaves a number, but you're asking him to travel—"

"Would you be comfortable—feel safe with Blaise and Harry on either side of you? And me, too, as soon as I can get there. Once I've done what I can with Andy Mayhew."

The wide-eyed panic look hadn't completely faded from Eleanor's face. "Anchors," she decided. "I want Matt here."

"I left a message for him at work. He didn't get back to me before I left the library, but unless the whole system's crashed around his ears, he should have gotten it by now. I told him eight-thirty. He's probably called my house already and sent me a dozen e-mails."

"He'd have called here," Eleanor said.

Em conceded the point without discussion. "He can keep us both under observation."

"No. Sharing's no good. If something happens, I don't want him to have to make a choice or be distracted. You'll have to call Nancy or someone else."

There was only Nancy who, when called, was willing to come, but not without her husband.

"John wants to see some of the excitement."

"You told him that your end of all this is about as exciting as watching ice melt?" Em asked, then, remembering that the Amstels had been hissing at each other as recently as Sunday night, relented and invited John to join them at her house at eight-thirty.

While Emma had been on her cell phone talking to Nancy, Eleanor had been talking to Matt.

"He wants to know if you saw the comet?" Eleanor asked after Emma had shut down her phone.

Em shook her head. "No comets. No meteors. That's one theory we're leaving untouched for the moment. Can he come over?"

"Eight o'clock," Eleanor confirmed and ended her cellular conversation.

"Eight-thirty," Em quibbled.

"He said he's been running late. Do you want me to call Harry?"

"No, that's my job—"

"You really are assembling your team."

Emma made a sour face. Team building, like personnel management, had never risen to the top of her career-goals list.

"You've put together your own Curia."

"Never."

"Then something else. We've got to have a name—"

Em's scowl put a stop to that line of discussion. She punched in the number of Harry's house in Westchester, and while it was ringing, she asked Eleanor if she had any plans for dinner. Before Eleanor could answer, the heavily sighing James picked up the line. With a notable lack of enthusiasm, he conveyed Emma's call to her stepfather.

Like Eleanor, Harry delighted in hearing those four little words, "I need your help" coming from Emma's lips and he was even happier to thwart Longleigh.

"Did he actually threaten you?" Harry demanded for the second time.

"Veiled threats. He didn't come out and say he was going to lock me up someplace, but he got his message across loud and clear. I'm afraid you predicted wrong when you said he'd come around. The only thing he wants to give me is my head on a platter."

"You're jumping to conclusions, Emma. If you can pull this off—mooting a curse right under his nose—he's going to have to make elaborate peace with you, no matter what Pietro, Sylvianne, and his other chums think, or he risks a schism. Word will spread, Emma."

"So long as you're not the one spreading it," Em bantered while stowing a sentence that mentioned Longleigh, Sylvianne, and Pietro together in the *to be examined at leisure* corner of her memory.

"You know me, I'm the soul of discretion, but you're bound to make a bit of noise, you know. If we do nothing more than moot a larger-than-average curse or pull, as you say, an odd string out of time's weave, we're going to be heard."

"If they can hear so damn well, why don't they do more for the people whose lives get scrambled by curses? Wasn't the Curia functioning back in 1871 when this mess got started?"

Harry couldn't answer Em's questions. He promised to be at the bolthole a few minutes past eight-thirty with his walking stick *and* his onyx ring.

Em steamed rice and broiled a pair of rapidly thawed chicken breasts—lighter fare than the multi-item pizza Eleanor had suggested. While the rice steamed, she whipped together a cheese spread and chip dip.

"And you say you haven't built a team," Eleanor chided from the kitchen doorway.

Emma let the comment ride. She dished out supper and had the dishes washed and draining in the sink before Matt arrived at eight. He wanted to talk comets and the extraterrestrial origin of curses. Em passed and watched Eleanor pick up the slack. Beyond a doubt, there was some serious pair-bonding going on in that quarter.

John and Nancy arrived at eight-thirty and brought with them an awkwardness that not even the best cheese spread known to man could completely cover—though John was willing to listen to Matt's comet theory. He curled up within arm's reach of the crackers to read the binder of Internet downloads Matt had brought with him. Nancy and Eleanor eyed each other nervously. They put the maximum possible distance between themselves when Em sat down on the living room carpet and announced that it was time for the great experiment to begin.

She took Eleanor's hands. They were cold as ice and trembling, perhaps because Eleanor had left her flask and vial behind and was determined—for Matt's sake—to make the wasteland transition without chemical assistance.

"Ready?"

Eleanor nodded, and Em envisioned her spinning coin.

She called "heads" and felt the real world slip away. Emma offered her hand to Eleanor, who needed steadying as she stood.

"You're sure about this?"

"The hard part's going to be seeing Harry again. Get me through that, and I'm good to go." Eleanor ran her fingers through hair that was no longer two-toned. "I could kill for a cigarette."

"Try not to," Em advised and led the way toward the bolthole.

To Eleanor's palpable dismay, they met Harry on the rim. He was, as always, impeccably attired, leaving Em to wonder what new changes Blaise would make to his appearance, because Blaise was relaxing in the bolthole when the three of them arrived. Tactically, Em would have done better had she slipped into the wasteland alone and brought her lover on board with her plans for the evening in private. He was not happy about walking off with two curse-hunters he trusted only because Emma asked him to, but in the end she persuaded him. She watched the three of them—Eleanor in the lead—climb the shallow slope, then returned to the bolthole and the window.

Em summoned the smoky forest of 1871 with no difficulty. She climbed over the window sill and made her way to the stream where young Andy Mayhew had ridden out the fire. Her time was a bit off. Not critically, but the boy was beginning to stir as Emma knelt beside him and plunged easily into his dreams.

The boy's need to return to the Mayhew homestead was strong. Emma confronted it from several perspectives: He already knew what had happened to his mother and siblings—Em made up the sound of a rifle being fired. The gunshots—four of them—resonated so completely through Andy's mind that Emma wondered if she had made anything up at all or merely awakened a repressed memory.

She found a stream of worry and waded into it. Andy thought he needed to see the bodies. Emma assured him that he did not. At best, they would have been overtaken by the fire and burnt beyond recognition. At worst, he would see the horror his father had wrought. The images Emma swirled into the stream were cruel, but effective, and the flow of worry began to shift. Emma encouraged the shift by adding the notion of Andy walking away from the stream without a backward glance. She suggested that he start calling himself Andy Sharpe—knowing that when the boy's date with death came in 1881 he would be using his grandmother's surname.

Andy Sharpe wiped his eyes with stream water before he opened them. He got to his feet slowly. His legs were numb from hours in the running water—except for the cut he'd gotten the previous day. No matter where he went, he was looking at a painful walk.

Now that the boy was awake, Emma was more cautious about stirring his thoughts. She limited herself to a quiet voice whispering, *Start over . . . Start a new life . . .*

He clutched the shirt over his heart, and Em feared she'd gone too far, then he climbed the bank on the opposite side of the stream. He walked away from the Mayhew homestead and away from Emma Merrigan. She closed her eyes and watched him with her curse-sensitive vision. Greenish particles still swarmed around the boy.

In the grip of the engineering gene at its worse, Emma strode out on the path the boy avoided. She told herself that she needed to see if her experiment had worked—if increasing the physical distance between the boy and his father would prevent the transfer of the father's curse to his son or at least delay it until Eleanor, Harry, and Blaise had begun their assault on what Em fervently hoped was the curse's wasteland bolthole.

But confirmation was cover for the real reason she jogged along the trail. Emma wanted to see if Redmond Longleigh would magically reappear on the homestead porch now that she'd plunged the boy and changed his path. She hoped Longleigh would reappear. She very much wanted to see his expression when no one—not the boy nor a pair of troublesome curse-hunters—emerged from the smoke-shrouded woods.

Crouched amid yellow-leafed scrub at the edge of the homestead clearing, Emma kept watch on the front porch. Her time-stream change had begat other changes already. The smoke was thicker this time around, as if the boy's movement in the woods had cleared the air. Without the boy, Em could barely see the rifle in the elder Andrew Mayhew's lap.

One thing that hadn't changed was Andrew Mayhew's curse. The green stain was clearly visible from his head to his heart.

Emma lurked in the scrub long enough for twin senses of guilt and shame to rear their heads in her mind. Though she did not doubt that the elder Andrew Mayhew would end his life, without his son to spur the act there was no way to predict when he would pull the trigger. And while Em waited, sating the worst sort of curiosity, her companions—her handpicked *team*—were facing down a wasteland curse.

She resolved to give history another ten minutes, to watch its progress past the point where, in the original version, the limping boy had appeared before his father. If the elder Andrew Mayhew did not commit his messy suicide on schedule, Em promised herself that she would pull herself back to the wasteland.

There was, of course, no precise way of measuring ten minutes. Em thought her time was nearly up when Andrew Mayhew got to his feet. Rifle in hand, he left the porch and wandered the yard, calling his son's name.

Though movement and sound attracted attention, Emma concentrated on the front door and was rewarded when Redmond Longleigh once again appeared in the front doorway. He was immediately joined by a slender figure with a striking mane of blond hair: Sylvianne

Skellings. Their agitated conversation was marked by gestures toward Andrew Mayhew and the incriminating well.

Then Andrew Mayhew, still calling his son's name, began walking toward the scrub where Emma had hidden herself. She told herself his change in direction had nothing to do with her and everything to do with the trail. She should have moved farther from the trail before hunkering down. It was too late to move. Andrew Mayhew wouldn't notice, but the two curse-hunters on the front porch surely would.

Mayhew wasn't more than ten feet from the scrub when he dropped to his knees. The rifle went off by accident—corresponding to the shot that missed the boy. Tears streaked Mayhew's grimy face. He didn't have the look of an evil man, merely one who'd gone too far down the path of good intentions. A hot wind had blown up. It whipped through Emma's hair, but didn't touch the dry, yellow leaves. After shouting his son's name one more time, Andrew Mayhew ratcheted the rifle and tucked the muzzle under his chin.

Emma closed her eyes, but she couldn't close her ears. Mayhew was still calling for his son when he ended his life. Em felt her own heart skip a beat. If she could have located her stomach, she would have vomited.

Em? Cold pressure touched her wrist.

No. It's all right. It's all according to plan.

Emma regained control and opened her eyes. Wasteland flames were rising from the wreckage of Andrew Mayhew. Em decided to risk a short-cut. She imagined a bungee cord and followed the fire.

She landed hard on the wasteland dirt. Howling flames surrounded her. The ground tilted, forcing her backward, downward. She made a ruby-ringed fist and imagined freedom.

"Emma! Emma! This way, Emma!"

On her hands and knees, Em burnt a path to her mother.

"You've brought the rest of it—"

Em nodded. She didn't waste time or strength trying to stand but added her will, focused by her great-grandmother's ring, to the mooting power already battering the curse. With four curse-hunters—three and a half—it didn't last long. The ground was dark and level when the men joined the two women.

"You might have warned us you'd be bringing guests," Harry said with what Em hoped was good humor. It was always hard to tell with Harry, doubly so when her ears were still ringing.

"I wasn't sure what would happen when I broke the connection in eighteen seventy-one, or even if I could break it. Did we get the whole thing? Listen to me—did *we* get! Did *you* get it?"

Eleanor offered Em a hand up. "I hope so!" she said as she pulled.

"There's only one way to be certain—" Blaise said from a half-step behind Harry's shoulder. He didn't look happy. There'd be a reckoning—at the very least a lecture about risk and safety—from that front before the storm clouds faded—"Go back to the points you know and see what remains."

Emma had churned a lot of energy chasing Mayhew's curse from one subjective reality to the next. And there were the memories she'd collected of his suicide—from two perspectives now. Even for good news she didn't have the stamina to delve the past.

"Tomorrow," she said, looking at Harry. "Our time. Nothing's likely to happen before then?"

"Phone calls." Harry exchanged a look with Blaise. "I wouldn't be surprised if you got one from Longleigh. He's bound to find out sooner or later."

Sooner, Em thought, much sooner, and began to giggle.

"We've got to leave," Eleanor decided. She grasped Em's wrist. "Phone calls will be sufficient—"

Em? Are you ready?

Yes.

The magenta sky faded and became a wall with pictures. Emma found herself sitting on the floor with her fists clenched and a pillow crumpled in her lap. Though her stomach was leaden, she hadn't vomited. Eleanor was already chattering about the "huge" curse they'd "plastered" and driven out of existence.

"Would you like tea?" Nancy asked. "The water should be boiling by now."

Em looked at the clock. It was five after nine.

"Yeah, tea sounds great."

"We're a real team now!" Eleanor exalted. "All of us. Nobody's done anything like we just did. I led us to the exact place where that curse was lurking. No guessing about which curse was responsible for what. I *knew* as soon as I got there: We'd found what we were looking for. Then Emma—she *herded* the missing pieces back to us so we could fry them.

"Hunters and anchors, that's what we are—hunters and anchors born under the sign of Orion." Eleanor nudged Emma's forearm. "All of us. To hell with Red Longleigh and his Atlantis Curia, his overblown adrêsteia. We're your team—Orion's Children. Aren't we?"

Em managed a smile. "Yes, that's us . . . Orion's Children."

She had a feeling, come whatever, the name was going to stick.

LYNN ABBEY

The spellbinding novel from the author of
Jerlayne and co-editor of *Thieves' World* is a
fantasy fan favorite.

BEHIND TIME

0-441-00831-3

The novels of Lynn Abbey are:

"Brilliantly conceived."
—C.J. Cherryh

"All the things that make
fantasy worth reading."
—*Booklist*

Powers unused are useless powers—

Out of Time
by
Lynn Abbey

From the fantasy world of Lynn Abbey,
co-creator of *Thieves' World*™, comes a novel
of modern witchcraft and one woman's
newfound powers.

0-441-00751-1

THE NOVELS OF LYNN ABBEY ARE:

"BRILLIANTLY CONCEIVED."
—C.J. CHERRYH

**"ALL THE THINGS THAT MAKE
FANTASY WORTH READING."**
—*BOOKLIST*

Available wherever books are sold or
to order call 1-800-788-6262

National Bestselling Author of
THE LOST YEARS OF MERLIN

T. A. BARRON

"A superbly
likable book."
—Brian Jacques,
New York
Times best-
selling author
of Redwall

heartlight

0-441-01036-9